EX LIBRIS

_____

_____

_____

Romance Treasury

THE ROMANCE TREASURY ASSOCIATION

TORONTO · NEW YORK · LONDON
AMSTERDAM · PARIS · SYDNEY · HAMBURG
STOCKHOLM · ATHENS · TOKYO · MILAN

These stories were originally published as follows:

BACHELOR TERRITORY
Copyright © 1977 by Gloria Bevan
First published by Mills & Boon Limited in 1977

THE LAND OF THE LOTUS-EATERS
Copyright © 1966 by Isobel Chace
First published by Mills & Boon Limited in 1966

A CURE WITH KINDNESS
Copyright © 1970 by Ruth Clemence
First published by Mills & Boon Limited in 1970

ROMANCE TREASURY is published by
The Romance Treasury Association, Stratford, Ontario, Canada.

Story Illustrations by Emile LaLiberté
Book Design by Charles Kadin
Printed and bound by Kingsport Press Inc.

ISBN 0-373-04118-7

CONTENTS

Bachelor Territory

Gloria Bevan

Craig Carter was all wrong for Alison. In fact, he was the one man in all Australia with whom Alison could least afford to become emotionally involved.

He was a constant reminder of the past she was trying to forget and of the home she felt she'd lost forever.

And unless Fate started dealing with Alison a little more kindly, Craig would also be an inescapable, heart-wrenching reminder of the chance she'd wish she'd taken on love.

CHAPTER ONE

ALISON SWUNG her blue Mini off the main northern
New Zealand highway, turning into a long straight
broken by clumps of tall cabbage trees that looked as
though it would go on for ever. At the turn-off she had
left behind the busy city-bound traffic and now there
was only the empty road with green farmlands on
either side and beyond the hazy blue of distant hills.
Presently she was following the course of a swiftly flowing river, discoloured with soil washed down from the
hills of the hinterland and bordered with raupo and
blowing flax. At intervals along the route corrugated
iron sheds with notices of kumeras for sale flashed into
view. Then she was driving over a long bridge spanning
the river, pulling into a bay to allow a great stock transporter with its double row of tightly packed sheep to
thunder past. Ahead she glimpsed the scattered buildings of a small town. So this was Dargaville, the northern river town with its history of gum-digging and its
Yugoslav settlers. She moved slowly along the quiet
street, taking in the white stone buildings of an earlier
era, the rambling Colonial-style timber hotel with its
red iron roof and shady verandahs under which was
parked a line of dust-smeared Land Rovers. No doubt,
she mused, the Yugoslav names on the stores were a
legacy from early settlers who a century ago had made
their long journey by sailing ship to a new and unknown land to wrest a living digging gum from the giant kauri trees covering steep bush-clad hillsides. There
was, however, nothing out of date about the stock in
the stores, for the tastefully arranged show windows
displayed a variety of late model goods ranging from

farming equipment and fishing gear to fashion garments and exquisitely crafted furniture.

A brief pause at a small clean shop for coffee and sandwiches, then she headed the Mini towards a petrol station on a corner of a side street. As she waited for the attendant to appear from inside the building her gaze lifted idly to a painted sign swinging overhead: HAERI MAI. KAKASE. Everyone knew that the Maori word meant "welcome," but the Yugoslav word was unfamiliar. All at once she became aware of the attendant, a thin youth with unruly fair hair and a shy grin who was eyeing her with frank interest. Alison, however, was accustomed to meeting that particular expression in masculine eyes and took little notice. It was a reactionary thing—her hair, that bright mop of coppery-red curling strands that sunlight turned to living flame and no amount of vigorous brushing could subdue.

"Will you fill the tank, please?"

"Sure, sure." But he continued to stand motionless, gazing in her direction. At last he moved towards the pump and picked up the hose. "Staying long in Dargaville?"

"No, I'm just touring around the north, having a look around."

His face fell. It would have been too much to hope for, a girl like this staying right here in town. A girl with that open eager look about her face and crisp copper-coloured curls that made you want to run your fingers through them.

In an effort to divert his attention she indicated the sign above her head. "Kakase—that's a new word to me. It's Yugoslav, isn't it?"

"That's right." It was a feminine voice who answered and Alison swung around in surprise to meet the smiling gaze of a tall well-built girl in T-shirt and jeans who had paused beside the car. Dark eyes, long black hair caught severely back from her forehead, a sleepy-eyed smile. Alison liked her from the start.

"I know a little of the language," the stranger was saying, "enough to know that the word means 'welcome.'" She had a low pleasant voice with a smile in it. "It's the first two words that get me puzzled."

"That's easy," Alison told her. "*Haeri Mai* means 'welcome' too, in Maori."

"So that's it! I guessed it must be Dargaville's way of saying 'Hi.' I've only just arrived here myself—going far?"

Alison was watching the needle flickering on the dial of the petrol pump. "I don't know yet. I'm heading out towards the coast, having a look-see."

"Me too."

For the first time Alison noticed the canvas hiker's pack lying at the other girl's feet.

"I'm touring the district too," the stranger was saying.

"Could I give you a lift between here and there?"

"Oh, would you!" She smiled with warm friendliness. "I was hoping you'd ask me. I may as well come clean and tell you that's the reason I followed you in here. You don't mind, do you?" The slow smile broke across her face once again. "I only arrived in Auckland from London a few days ago by air and I'm hitch-hiking my way north. So if you've got a seat to spare—"

"Hop in!" Alison leaned across to throw open the passenger door, then made to shift the bags to the back seat.

"Don't bother, I'm used to travelling steerage."

"Not this time," Alison said firmly, and tossed her bags to the rear of the car. She paid the attendant and slipped the car into gear. "Right, we're on our way!" She guided the blue Mini out towards the main street and soon they were running through the town.

"I'm Mary, Mary Vasanovich—"

"Alison."

In no time at all it seemed they were through the shopping area and making their way into suburban areas where the wide streets were lined with homes of an earlier era, each one surrounded by lush green lawns and bright with flower borders.

"Mmm, smell those roses!" The dark-haired girl sniffed appreciatively as they swept past an archway festooned with great blooms of Shot Silk. They were entering a newer part of the town where modern timber bungalows painted in rainbow shades of pastel blue, salmon pink, lilac and lemon shone in the sunlight. Each house was set well back from the roadway and spreading lawns swept down to the street. A wealth of blossom was everywhere, carnations, stock, petunias. "Hey, look up there!"

Alison's glance swept up the green slopes at the roadside where the white timbers of an old mission house glimmered amongst clustered native trees. Evidently the building was now the local museum, for on the hillside lay a long open boat all of sixty feet in length.

"It's a carved Maori canoe," Alison explained. "The early Maoris usually used to build them of totara timber, carve the prow with their primitive stone adzes, then hide the canoes from enemy tribes in swamps and rivers. This one was probably dug up from one of the lakes around the district. The canoes still turn up occasionally from some swamp or river bank, even these days—tell me, how did you get on hitch-hiking up from Auckland?"

A smile tugged at the corners of the other girl's wide mouth. "I didn't set out to hitch-hike. I got forced into it. Actually," she confided laughingly, "it turned out to be more of a pick-up."

"How come?"

"Well, you see, I started off from the city on a motor scooter. I'm used to travelling that way at home and I thought it would be fun to pick up a cheap used scooter while I was in the city and then make my way north that way. Fun! I must have been out of my cotton-pickin' mind!"

"It wasn't?" Alison's eyes were on the road ahead.

"Not for long, not really. English roads are a whole lot different from these winding highways, for one thing. I hadn't allowed for the northern route being one sharp bend after another, up steep hills and down again, and it's just too bad if the big trucks almost shave you off as they pass. I could have coped with that, though, but half way up the steepest slope of all, bang, the motor scooter gave up the struggle. I tried and tried to get it started again—no way! Then just when I was wondering what on earth I could do with the thing myself, along came this knight of the road—"

"Don't tell me, let me guess!" Alison guided the car past stockyards at the roadside, swept on between long lines of macrocarpa pines. "He was driving a big American car with oodles of power—"

Mary's dark eyes were twinkling. "Better than that!"

"Big English car, then, driven by a guy with nice manners, English tailored clothes?"

"Guess again! The American limousines and the English luxury jobs were the ones that passed me by and left me standing there on the road with that great useless lump of metal. I was just about giving up, wondering how long it would take me to push that flipping thing up the mountainous slope, when along came my rescuer, a huge Maori man with a big smile driving a brewery delivery van."

Alison laughed. "Did he put you and the scooter in the back of the truck?"

"Did he ever! He had a couple of his mates in the front with him and he told me if I didn't mind going in the back of the truck with the casks he could take me and the scooter. I jumped at the offer! He was wearing a black work singlet and you should have seen his shoulder muscles! He picked up that scooter as though it was a kid's toy and tossed it into the back of the truck, then he heaved me in after it. He even dropped that heap of metal at the local garage here in Dargaville for repair." Mary's low voice held a chuckle. "It was

worth putting up with the remarks hurled at me whenever we stopped at one of those funny little settlements
along the road.''

"I can imagine. Cheers, calls, miming, shouts of
'Have one on me!'''

"How did you guess?''

They were out in the country now. Mile after mile
whizzed by with the green sheep-dotted hills on either
side, and a fragment of road stretched ahead as they
climbed towards a cloud-filled sky.

A few miles further and they had left even the scattered farmhouses behind. Now they were sweeping up
clay banks where there was nothing in sight but the vast
sheep-dotted hills with their long boundaries of macrocarpa pines, the black steers grazing in valleys far below. All at once the smooth surface of the highway
gave way to rough metal, and loose stones thudded
against the undercarriage of the car.

Mary broke the silence. "Actually," she confided,
"Grandfather Vasanovich gave me this trip out to New
Zealand as a birthday gift. He insisted on providing me
with spending money too. Wasn't that good of him? I
mean, a trip isn't much fun without something to
spend.''

"An overseas trip half way around the world," Alison marvelled. "How lucky can you get?''

"Oh, it has a few strings to it.''

Alison taking a hairpin bend swerved sharply to
avoid a pile of red clay that had broken away from the
cliff above and subsided over the greater part of the
roadway. "Such as?''

"I'm supposed to be on a sort of mission. There's
something I'm supposed to look up or come across or
ferret out somewhere in this part of the world and take
back home with me when I go. Not that I think there's
a chance of it turning up. Out this way, on the road to
the coast and the sandhills, happens to be my starting
point to begin operations—Help!'' Mary drew in her
breath sharply as a small one-way timber bridge loomed

ahead and a silver milk tanker bore down on them. Alison, however, had braked to a stop and the next moment the driver, with a friendly salute, swept past, leaving a cloud of dust in his wake.

Alison asked curiously, "But whatever could you find up here? Not even fossilised gum that the place was famous for once. That's all been worked out years and years ago."

"Aha, you'd be surprised! How about a husband? Preferably one with a Yugoslav name! Oh, Grandfather didn't spell it out, but I've got a sneaky suspicion that was his whole idea in sending me out here. In a way I don't blame him for trying. Failing the husband it seems he's depending on me to bring him back some news of his long-lost relatives who he thinks might still be living somewhere about these parts. That part of the plan he's quite open about. Guess you'll know that Vasanovich is a Yugoslav name," she went on, "but I'm really three-quarters English. Grandfather emigrated to England when he was a young man. He married an English girl and he's stayed there ever since. His only son was my father who died when I was a baby, so I never knew him, or my mother either, come to that. Anyway it seems that Grandfather had a brother who left the family home at about the same time, but he went even further afield, out to the wilds of New Zealand, and from what I can gather it was wild in those days. From what Grandfather told me all you needed then to make a living in the country was a tent and a pick axe so you could collect the fossilised gum from the huge trees that grew all over the hills. Kauris, they called them, didn't they?"

Alison, changing gear to take the steep slope rising above, nodded. "There are still a few trees left down in the gullies. See, down there—" She gestured with her hand. "The tall leafy trees with the straight trunks heading for the sky non-stop. In those days, so they tell me, kauri gum was worth real money. Those shops in the main street of Dargaville with their Yugoslav names—I expect they would be the descendants of the pioneering stock." She slanted Mary a teasing glance. "You're one of them yourself, almost."

"Could be. Grandfather's really keen on the ancestor-bit, though I've got a feeling he'd be even more interested in the idea of a modern guy with a Yugoslav background as husband material for his only grandchild. What a hope! As to those long-lost relatives, heaven only knows if I'll have any success when it comes to tracing them. It would be a different story if there had been any correspondence to refer to, but there's been nothing to go on except an old letter. Not much to go on, is it? And Grandfather hasn't even got the letter. He just has this vague idea there was one that came years and years ago from a place in the north of New Zealand called Dargaville, but it was all so long ago. It would be awfully lucky if anyone of that name happened to be living up this way."

"Oh, I don't know," Alison flashed Mary a smile. "Who knows? This trip might be lucky for you! Might even bring you a Yugoslav husband, maybe, with the name of Babich or Simich—something like that."

"Now you're talking like Grandfather—am I boring you to tears with all the family history, or rather, the lack of it?"

"No, no, go on. So you're out in New Zealand with the idea of looking up your family connections?"

"You could put it that way. Oh, there was one other thing, what really sparked off the whole enquiry, I expect—a report by an old crony of Grandfather's who had been out in this country on a tour. He happened to mention that somewhere on his travels through the north of this island he'd noticed the name Vasanovich on a gatepost. He couldn't remember which gatepost, which town, only that it was somewhere out towards the coast after the tour bus had left Dargaville. But all that was five years ago. Not much to work on, is it? All the same, it's nice having a tour around the district and," Mary smiled her slow smile, "it's fun looking."

After a moment she went on, "Grandfather knows

I've always been crazy about foreign travel and evidently he decided to kill two birds with the one projectile, bless his scheming old heart! So here I am!" She gave a low chuckle. "The old boy doesn't dream that I'm on to what his real idea is behind all this overseas trip he's given me, or that I happen to know what this locality is famous for. Can't you guess?"

"Kumeras," said Alison promptly. "It's kumera country and that's for sure. All the way along the road today I've been passing big storage sheds with notices, kumeras for sale. You must have noticed them."

"Kumeras?" Mary stared across at her. "What on earth are they?"

"A sort of sweet potato. The early Maoris were the first ones to grow them. Guess they hadn't much else to live on except birds they managed to snare, fish and seafoods and the odd fern-root. The district must have the perfect soil conditions for growing them, because now it seems like the whole population is busy producing them for the city markets."

Mary burst out laughing. "Well, anyway, you're wrong! It's bachelors!"

"Bachelors!" Alison echoed blankly.

"It's true! Seems the district around here is full of them. They're working on farms, living in huts on their own or else they're partners in homesteads and holdings and farms with other single guys. They're living on their own, coping with cooking and cleaning and household chores, at least I hope they are, just waiting for the right girl to walk in." Mary gave her crinkly-eyed smile, "or drive in at the front gate. Grandfather's old crony was a bit hazy about the Vasanovich bit, but he was downright certain of the bachelor part of his story. Said he'd run into them all over the place. The way he put it was that the district around here was lousy with them, all wanting wives."

"You mean," Alison slanted her a teasing glance, "they're desperately wanting a cleaning woman or live-in cook."

"Don't be so unromantic! Don't you believe in... love?"

"Love?" Alison laughed her clear young laugh with the catch in the throat. "What's that? From all I gather after listening to my friends it's something that's highly overrated, especially after you've been married for a year or two."

"Married friends? You?" Mary looked astonished. "But you're only about seventeen."

Alison pulled a face. "Twenty," she corrected promptly, "all but. I just look this way. It's maddening, but there's nothing I can do about it. It comes of having a young face and a mop of silly babyish curls."

"Twenty," Mary marvelled, "and you've never been in love? The real thing, I mean, sweep-you-off-your-feet, don't-care-about-a-thing-else-in-the-world variety. I just don't believe it! Hasn't there been *anyone*?"

Alison laughed. She changed gear and they swept up between high hills where arum lilies grew wild on cleared green slopes. "Oh, I've had one or two near misses, guys I liked for a while or they liked me, but it didn't last. Maybe I expected too much, maybe they got tired of me. Who knows?"

"Are you telling me you've never met anyone special?" Mary persisted incredulously. "Any man who stirred you?" Her sideways glance swept over Alison's mobile young face, the short nose and sweetly curved mouth, coppery-coloured curls blowing back from a tanned forehead in the breeze.

"Not really."

Mary's tone was thoughtful. "You've always lived at home with your parents, in a small town?"

Back where she came from there hadn't been a town, but Alison let it go. "That's right, in the waybacks, actually. This is my first venture on my own. How did you guess?"

Then why, Mary wondered, the wistful note in Alison's voice, the shadow in the clear hazel eyes? Aloud she said, "I thought so. There's something about you...not like a city girl...more open, somehow—"

"Outspoken, you mean. I'm always getting into trouble because of not stopping to think before I say something awful."

It seemed, however, that Mary was not to be diverted from her subject. "Living in the country all your life you must have met young sheep farmers, lots of them?"

Alison's gaze was on the tea-tree shaded bend ahead. "Practically nothing else but."

A rural delivery van sped past and when the dust had settled Mary pursued her enquiries. "And you didn't fall for any of them?"

"Why should I? What's so special about the breed?"

"What's so special? I'll tell you something. Back in England where I come from there's a sort of romantic legend grown up around your young New Zealand sheep farmer."

"You're having me on!"

"No, no, it's true! He's lean and tough and bronzed and strong as they come. A hard worker too. A colourful character who can ride hell for leather over the hills all day and dance all night. And as a lover—a girl only has to look at him once and pow, she's head over heels, overboard fathoms deep!"

Alison laughed. Somehow it was easy to laugh with this companionable girl who in some odd way she felt as though she had known for ages. "I wouldn't know. I've met swags of sheep farmers, young and old and in between, but never one like that except..." She broke off in some confusion—for unbidden, there he was right there in her mind, the dark stranger whose face stayed with her. Young and vital, lean and bronzed with an impression of whipcord strength about him and the look in his eyes of a man accustomed to gazing into far distances. To her chagrin she could feel the pink creeping up her cheeks. "Well, only once," she confessed as the silence grew, "and then I only saw him for a minute."

"Must have been some man, some minute," so Mary had caught that betraying tide of colour, "to make you remember him so clearly."

Now when it was too late Alison tried for careless-ness. "Just like you said, only more so, I guess." She attempted to shrug away the masculine picture in her mind, said with studied nonchalance, "but I never got to know him."

"Too bad."

"Not really." Alison bit back the confidences that trembled on her lips. She *must* remember to heed the warning red light that had clicked on in her mind. And only just in time. From now on she had to check her naturally impulsive outspoken nature and keep her thoughts to herself. "He was just a man I saw once." In spite of her resolution not to give anything away regret tinged her tone. "I didn't even know his name."

But you have a pretty good idea! Craig Carter, a name, a man you couldn't ever forget.

Mary was saying incredulously, "You didn't try to see him again?"

"No." She wondered what her companion would say were she to tell her that she was at the moment running away from that very possibility. See him again... un-expectedly something deep inside her said quite clearly and without the slightest quiver of doubt. If only I could!

To change the subject she switched back to their ear-lier conversation. "How did you come to know that this was bachelor territory? The beer truck driver?"

"No, not him. It was Grandfather's old crony, the travelling one, who passed on that bit of interesting information. I happened to be there at the time he mentioned it. All those unmarried young farmers and a Yugoslav settlement too in the north of New Zealand was enough to give Grandfather ideas." The smile was back in Mary's voice. "Quite a way to go to find a made-to-measure husband, wouldn't you say, but a little thing like distance wouldn't put Grandfather off, not once he'd set his mind on anything. And believe me, he's really set his heart on his one and only grandchild keeping up the family traditions and changing her name to something like Vasanovich, even if it does cost him a couple of thousand dollars to pull it off. I guess," she said wryly, "he thinks it's my last chance and for that it's worth taking a risk. Luckily he can afford to please himself. I could have told him, I did actually, that he's throwing his money away, because frankly as a husband-catcher I'm a dead loss, seeing I couldn't come up with one even in England. I mean, you can scarcely count two broken engagements. Anyway, what odds if I am still on my own and haven't met anyone I really care about! When you're pushing thirty it doesn't do to hang on to all those romantic notions. You have to toss them overboard and settle for a life of your own. I've got a good job in a law office, promotion coming up, a cosy little flat—I'd be a fool to throw it all away. I think Grandfather's got an idea I'm a bit lonely, with no husband or children, no relatives except him. What he doesn't seem to be able to get into his dear old head is that there are worse things than loneliness, like getting hitched in marriage to the wrong man. He's too old, I guess, to remember about love. Or could be he's right. Maybe love is just a trap, a delusion that can complicate your life, who knows? After all," Alison caught a wistful note in the quiet tones, "you can't have everything."

"Those two broken engagements," Alison asked curiously. "What happened? Or would you rather not talk about it?"

"Oh, I don't mind. It's ages ago now. Funny, things that happened to me when I was nineteen or twenty seem part of another life. It's just me, really. I have this failing, character flaw, whatever, this sickening sentimental trait. I always fall for men who in one way or another manage to get my sympathy. Maybe it's something to do with always having wanted to be a nurse and having been sidetracked into office work. Colin was in a wheelchair when I first met him. He'd been in a terrible car smash that had left him crippled for life. I guess I was sorry for him and that was all, because when the crunch came and the wedding date was only three weeks away I changed my mind about marriage. Everyone thought I was cruel and mean to let him down at the last moment. I suppose I was in a way, but he had no problems financially. He could afford to have someone around to take care of him. It was only at that last minute that I came to my senses and realised our relationship wasn't exactly a love thing, not on my side anyway. Pity, sympathy, yes—but that's not quite the same, is it?''

"I guess not."

"In those days I thought a lot about love, all that madness you read about in novels. It just never happens to me. I don't know why I'm going on and on about my love life, if you could call it that—"

"You said there was another engagement that didn't work out?"

"Oh yes, Mervyn. Another disaster, actually. I was sorry for him too. You wouldn't think you could make the same mistake all over again, would you! Don't you believe it. I was taken in all over again. I was sorry for Mervyn too, but for different reasons. He'd had a financial crash, lost all his property and assets, his life savings really, and had finished up with having a go at taking his own life as a way out of his difficulties. I suppose I comforted him, bolstered up his flattened ego, and after a while he came to rely on me for everything. It was quite a time," Mary observed wryly, "before it hit me that all he wanted was a mother figure. I did him a service when I finished everything between us and gave him the ring back. After that he learned to stand on his own feet again. The last I heard of him he had started up in business again, modestly, but at least it was a new beginning—not wildly exciting romances, are they?''

CHAPTER TWO

THE NEXT MOMENT Mary was cheerful again. "I'll tell you something. For me this trip out to the other side of the world is the fulfilment of a dream, something I've always longed to do. Guess I've been brought up on tales of that gum-digging ancestor of mine. So when the chance came to make the trip out here I said to myself, why not? Mary Vasanovich, this is your chance to see something of another country. New Zealand, here I come! I was so lucky! The firm where I work gave me three months' leave of absence and their blessing. I do seem to have been going on and on about myself—now tell me about you. You're Alison—?"

"Car—Wynyard." Swiftly she caught herself up, hoping Mary hadn't noticed the slip. She would have to do better than this in future when it came to remembering her unfamiliar name.

"Live at home, you said?"

"I—used to, until three weeks ago. There's nothing much to tell really." In spite of the resolute brightness of her tone, her voice faltered. "I—lost my parents a while ago...in an accident."

"Oh." For a moment Mary was silent. "I'm sorry. Tough on you."

For a moment the sheep-flecked hills merged into a mist of green and Alison blinked the moisture from her eyes. "I'm all right, most of the time. It was just...so sudden." Swiftly she ran on, "My mother wasn't very strong and Dad ran the farm on his own. I used to help him with the outside work and somehow it was awfully hard to get away for holidays. Now I'm taking a break.

I'll have to find myself a job sooner or later, but right now I'm just touring around."

"All by yourself?"

"I don't mind. There wasn't anyone else I could ask to come along with me."

"Here's one girl who'd be glad of the chance!" grinned Mary. "I could go equal shares with you for expenses, petrol and all that. It's up to you—but I just thought I'd ask."

"Love to have you along."

"Done!" When Mary smiled her eyes crinkled up and she had a low infectious laugh. Somehow the other girl seemed to Alison to be a good friend to have around. For all Mary's gaiety Alison sensed the other girl's easily-pierced armour, an insecurity Mary tried in vain to cover. *She's alone in the world as I am, but she's brave and resourceful and she won't let circumstances get her down.*

It was merely an offer from a stranger, yet a little of the chill unfamiliar feeling of isolation and being utterly alone in the world was falling away. It was almost as though something deep inside, a hard frozen lump, had begun to melt, as if she were coming alive again. For the first time since the start of the journey she was swept by a feeling of freedom and adventure.

"That's settled, then," Mary was saying happily. Her gaze lifted from the sombre mass of pine plantations on a hillside they were sweeping past to the road ahead, curving upwards towards a fleecy white cloud on the horizon. "Where did you say we were heading for?"

"I didn't. I just had this crazy idea I'd like to take a look at the coast. I've never seen this part of the country before, though it's not a great distance from where I come from. Somehow it's always fascinated me, just hearing about it—the great harbour and wild coast with its strong rip and dangerous currents. It seems so remote, way off the tourist route, nothing but sea and farming land and sandhills." She added laughingly, "And the wind! No wonder all the homesteads around here have those high shelterbelts of trees around them. This is my second week on the trip. I spent the first one in Auckland, staying in a motel and lazing on the beaches. It was quite an effort to tear myself away."

"Where will we put up tonight, do you think?" asked Mary.

"Oh, that's no problem. There's a little tent packed away in the boot of the car. We can put that up if we have to, but if we decide to stay around here for a few days we'd only have to knock at the door of a farmhouse for shelter. They're probably quite used to strangers turning up for a bed away up here in the hills."

Mary quirked an expressive eyebrow. "You mean, the bachelor establishments?"

Alison laughed. "I'd forgotten about them. Failing that we could always go back to a hotel in Dargaville. Let's play it by ear, shall we?"

"Suits me. You didn't plan the trip, then?"

"Plan it? Heavens, no! This time last month I would never have believed I'd be here on the road. It was just—" her voice broke and she blinked the moisture gathering at the back of her eyes. She said huskily, "—the way things happened."

The way things happened. In the silence the miles fell away. Alison's gaze was fixed on the road winding ahead but her thoughts wandered. Could it be only three weeks since they had brought her the message? Even now she hadn't fully recovered from the shock and horror that had overcome her on learning that both her parents had been killed outright in a head-on collision on the road while returning from a visit to friends a few miles distant.

Not that they were actually her parents, but as good as, far better than. The matter of birth made not the slightest difference to her feelings towards them. How could it? For no flesh-and-blood parents could have been more loving than Jim and Dot Carter.

Indeed, as the years had slipped by she had all but

forgotten that although everyone called her Alison Carter her name was actually Alison Wynyard. Funny how she remembered the name of Wynyard, although she had heard it mentioned only on one occasion. That was when, as a child of eight, she had been told by her foster-mother the circumstances of her birth. How Dot Carter had a lifelong friend who had always been closer to her than a sister. The friend had married and gone to live in Sydney, then on learning she was suffering from a terminal illness and having no close relatives of her own, she had written begging Dot to take the baby girl and bring her up as her own child. "My husband Victor travels all over Australia in his work," the sick woman had explained, "so it would be impossible for him to care for her. He agrees with me that you are the one we would like to entrust her to." So a month before the brave mother passed away the Carters had made a trip to Australia and brought the baby girl home with them to New Zealand. "And I'm so *glad* we did," Alison's foster-mother had told her with a close warm hug. It was the best thing that ever happened to Jim and me, having you with us," Perhaps it was, for the years passed and to their regret no children were ever born to the couple.

Jim Carter, quiet and kindly, was an indulgent father. He adored Alison from the first moment he saw her. He had always intended to arrange a legal adoption for the daughter he loved so dearly, but the years had slipped by without the matter having been attended to, and anyway, what did it matter?

It was the same with the property, the lush green hill paddocks he had broken in from rough scrub country over half a lifetime of hard physical toil. "It'll all be yours when we go, lass," he had told Alison often enough. Poor Dad, how horrified he would be were he to be aware that things hadn't turned out that way. It wasn't his fault that fate had taken a hand in events. Such a simple thing to shatter two lives, a truck approaching at speed on the wrong side of the road, a collision on a sharp bend. In a matter of seconds the shining new car of which Dot and Jim had been so proud was a mass of crumpled metal in the dusk. *It wasn't fair.*

It was only later after the funeral that the impact of shock had given way to a chill sense of loss, a feeling of emptiness in the house that was far removed from ordinary periods of absence. This was for ever.

A week later the family lawyer had come out from town to express his sympathy and to explain to Alison her legal position in regard to house and property.

At first she couldn't take in the information the lawyer was trying to get through to her. It was strange how his clipped tones seemed to be coming from a distance even though he was seated right there at the table opposite to her in the shadowy lounge room.

In the absence of a will, he informed her, the estate would pass to the Carters' nearest relative, a nephew living in the South Island, a man of whom Alison had heard of only vaguely and never met. The lawyer, a small neat-looking man of middle age with shrewd grey eyes, allowed himself a moment of compassion for the stricken-looking girl who seemed so alone in the big empty house. The next moment he pulled himself together. "Your position would of course have been entirely different had there been any legal adoption. I'm afraid your guardian made a big mistake there. I tried to get him to see to it on quite a few occasions over the years, but he always put it off in the same way as he never got around to making a will. I haven't a doubt but that he and his wife fully intended the property to be left entirely to you, but their sudden deaths... and as the law stands... a combination of unfortunate circumstances... I'm afraid—"

"It's all right, I understand. I'm not blaming them." Alison's voice broke. "They were wonderful to me. I owe them everything."

"Not quite everything," he said with irony. Through the open window his gaze moved over lush green hill

paddocks neatly fenced, black steers grazing on the
flats below. Hillsides were dotted as thickly as daisies
with newly-shorn sheep and in addition to all this there
were many hundreds of acres of green productive land,
farm machinery and vehicles, not to mention this well-
built old homestead. It was too bad. If only Jim Carter
had followed legal advice and made a will years ago—
but he had always put it off, with the result that his
neglect had dealt an irrevocable blow to the girl he had
always regarded as a dearly-loved daughter. "However," the lawyer cleared his throat and sought to offer
what comfort he could, "I have no doubt that matters
can be satisfactorily arranged to your benefit. It is to be
hoped that the nephew," he consulted his papers,
"Craig Carter, will arrange as suitable monetary com-
pensation once he becomes aware of the circumstances.
No doubt we could come to some arrangement—"

"No! Please—" Alison's soft lips were set firmly. All
at once the thought of haggling over the place that had
always been her home was unbearable. This cold calcu-
lating discussion concerning the affairs of the two she
had loved best in all the world was something she
couldn't take. "I don't want anything from him! I
wouldn't dream of accepting it!" She leaned forward,
urgency and appeal in her voice. "You'll tell him, won't
you? You'll make it quite clear to him that it's okay, I
can look after myself. I don't need to take charity from
anyone!"

"Charity!" Mr. Black was shocked. "My dear girl, I
don't imagine you fully understand the position your
parents' unexpected death has put you in. You'll have
nothing. Look at it this way," he went on in a milder
tone, "isn't it only what Jim and Dot would have
wished?"

"*Please* tell him!" It was no use. He could see that
her mind was already made up. "It's time I learned to
stand on my own feet," she summoned up a shaky
smile, "and the sooner the better. Promise you'll tell
him exactly what I said."

He looked at her oddly. "If you prefer," he murmured soothingly. Alison thought he was speaking to her as one would to a fractious child.

Shock, he was thinking, she's still in a state of shock. Give her a week or two, then when she gets back to normal she'll see things in a different light. Good Lord, she would be a fool to refuse to accept a little financial help after losing what amounted to a sizeable inheritance. Something about this girl touched him. She was so alone, and so damnably independent! It was a combination that didn't augur well for a girl left to her own resources—but then, his trained legal mind flicked back into action, it wasn't likely that she would be on her own for long, not with those looks and that glorious copper-coloured hair. Even now when she was so pale with dark shadows around her eyes she was quite lovely. There was something unconsciously appealing about her. Jim Carter and his wife should have had more forethought, leaving their ward penniless as well as alone!

He jerked his thoughts aside. He couldn't imagine what had come over him, letting himself get involved personally with his client. He must be getting soft. Aloud he said, "I understand the nephew is the owner of an extensive sheep station in the South Island. It is possible that he may decide to sell out here, in which case—"

"Sell Te-o-nui?" Alison's eyes were distraught. The next moment she pulled herself together. What difference would it make? She wouldn't be there. But Banner would! Her heart gave a stab as she remembered the graceful white mare she had raised from a long-legged foal. No doubt at this moment, she thought forlornly, Banner was no more than an item on one of the long lists of items set down amongst the papers on the table. Just part of the estate along with the stock ponies and the goats who ran wild on the far hills. "On second thoughts," anxiety sharpened her tone, "there is something you could arrange for me with the new owner—"

"Good, good." Mr. Black was endeavouring to hide the note of triumph in his voice, "I knew you'd come around to seeing things my way." Picking up a pen, he drew a sheet of paper towards him. "Now, about the amount involved. I would suggest that under the circumstances you settle for no less than—"

"No, no, not money! I told you, I thought I'd made it clear. It's my horse—"

"Your—horse?" Plainly the lawyer was taken aback.

"Not just a horse," protested Alison indignantly, "she's a wonderful mare, a show-jumper! It would tear me apart if Banner went to someone else, some stranger. Do you know I raised her from a tiny foal." All at once the shadows fled from her face, her voice was animated, eager. "She's got such a big heart! You wouldn't believe the trophies and ribbons she's won at shows and gymkhanas. I've hunted her for the last three seasons. Oh, I've lots of offers to sell Banner, she's quite well known in riding circles, but I could never part with her. I didn't think," she said very low, "I'd ever have to. You'll tell this Craig Carter man—"

"Of course, of course." Rarely were the lawyer's feelings stirred by professional visits, but there was something about this girl, a fierce independence, a desperate courage, that touched his heart. "If it would help," he spoke briskly to hide his unexpected rush of emotion, "I could make it clear to Carter that the mare means a lot to you and if he's willing to let you have her—"

"Let me have Banner!" Indignation sparked her tone.

"I'm sure there'll be no difficulty about it," Mr. Black said smoothly. "I'll pass on to him your special request that the animal is not to be sold and that you will come and collect your mount as soon as you have a permanent address."

"Oh, would you?" Alison's face shone with relief. That was another thing about this girl, the expressions that chased one another across her face. You could tell her feelings at a glance, though she would probably be horrified were she to know that her emotions were there for anyone to read, plain as day. Extraordinary girl...she had appeared quite unmoved at the loss of an inheritance that should have been hers in the ordinary course of events. Yet here she was blinking away tears over the chance of losing her mare. Just as well he had remained a bachelor. He would never understand women, not in a hundred years.

"But supposing," her hand flew to her mouth, "the property is put on the market right away and Banner—"

"Don't worry, my dear." Could that be himself speaking in that sickeningly father-like tone? "There's plenty of room on my property to graze your mare. She'll be looked after there if the estate is sold in a hurry and you can come and collect her at your convenience."

"Thank you, thank you. It wouldn't be for long, a month or so. Only..." bewilderment and worry struggled in her expression. She had no intention of letting either the lawyer or the Carter man have her address. The last thing she wanted was to be pestered with his charity-cheques. Meantime, the man was a sheep farmer, he must know how to care for animals. All at once the solution was plain. She would arrange for a horse transporter to call at Te-o-nui and collect Banner. She wouldn't need to have any contract with Craig Carter. She decided to use her own name from now on. That way he would never find her.

"You'll tell him, won't you, that Banner's a show-jumper, a very special one? He mustn't let anyone else ride her. I'll take her away," the eager tone faded into indecision, "one of these days...before long."

The lawyer nodded. "I'll pass on your instructions, don't worry." He thought again, if only Jim Carter hadn't been such an impractical, obstinate fool. Now this lovely girl found herself out on her ear. No office training either, he suspected, to help her get on her feet. He wouldn't mind betting she had never been away from Te-o-nui in her life. She'd been too busy helping Jim run the place—and what had she got out of it all? Exactly nothing! That nephew had fallen in for an estate worth more money than most folk would get their hands on in a lifetime. It wouldn't hurt him any to make over a lump sum to the girl. *If she would accept it.* Without warning the shaft of pity pierced him once more and silently he cursed the Carters for their happy-go-lucky attitude towards all legal commitments. The girl seated opposite him at the big table seemed so defenceless. It was her eyes that got you, they were so clear and trusting, like a child's. Aloud he said, "Pity you couldn't have had a word with the man yourself—"

"Oh no!" she cried in alarm, "I don't want to do that!"

"But he won't be here until next week. I had a word with him on the phone and he's coming up to have a look around and decide what he's going to do. He mentioned something about putting this property and the South Island one on the market and taking up land in the north, but of course he hasn't even seen Te-o-nui yet and he may well change his mind when he gets here. You've made some plans for the future?"

"When I leave here, you mean?" If he were carefully skirting the painful truth she seemed determined to face up to it. "Oh yes." That was another lie, and this time she suspected Mr. Black was not taken in, although he gave no outward sign.

"You'll be able to cope, then?"

"Oh yes!" Unconsciously she lifted her rounded chin. "I have a little money of my own, enough to carry me along for a time." The moment of bravado faded and a shadow darkened her clear-eyed gaze. "I thought I'd take a holiday and tour around the country for a while. I've never been further north than here. The Mini's my own," she added hastily. "Dad gave it to me on my last birthday. Everything else..."

"That makes sense," Mr. Black agreed as her voice faded away on a sigh. He gazed around the comfortably furnished room with its deep wing-chairs and long picture windows. "The place does seem a trifle large for one small young woman."

The next minute Alison had recovered herself. "That's what I thought too. I've only got to pack my things," the bright voice faltered, "and say goodbye to Banner." Swiftly she ran on, "The nearest neighbours, the Gilberts, have been ever so good. They've offered to look after the stock and keep an eye on things until," she took a deep breath, "the new owner arrives to take over. They're going to store a few boxes of things I won't need right away, riding gear and all that."

"And after your holiday? Had you anything in mind, Miss Carter?" So he hadn't believed her after all. "I understand there's a typist's job coming up in my office shortly, one of the girls is leaving the district. If you've had some business training you might be interested?"

Alison shook her head. "No, I haven't." The only training she had was in farm work, helping to dock the lambs, riding and mustering, drafting cattle, ordinary things like that. Looking at Mr. Black's impeccable city suit, his cold grey eyes, she decided it would be useless trying to explain.

For Dot, always delicate and easily tired, had taken no part in the outdoor activities that formed part of the life of the average New Zealand sheep farmer's wife. She preferred listening to the radio, working on her tapestry pictures, reading and knitting. So Alison helped her father with the endless tasks of the seasons and she had loved it all.

"Alison's a home girl," Dot had often observed contentedly, and she supposed she was in a way. Or could it be merely that she had never had a chance of being anything else? Certainly she enjoyed baking a cake, watching the dough rise for home-made bread, whipping up a batch of feather-light scones to take to the hungry shearing gang down in the shed. But that didn't mean she wouldn't enjoy another type of life, something quite different. She didn't know what exactly, but something.

"I understand that country folk are always on the lookout for domestic help," Mr. Black's unemotional voice cut into her thoughts. "You would have no problems there. You could even find work in the district if you preferred to stay around here."

Stay here, to be patronised and pitied by Mr. Craig Carter! Mr. Black, you've got to be joking! She bit back the angry words, took a deep breath and said quietly, "No, not here."

"I understand, and maybe you're right. Personal feelings might get in the way. But there are other places." He was gathering up papers and placing them neatly in his leather satchel. "You will be sure to leave me a forwarding address as soon as you've finished your holiday?"

"Oh yes, of course." But she had not the slightest intention of keeping the promise. Leave an address where the Craig Carter man could send her his charity cheques and handouts, all at the lawyer's suggestion? She could imagine Mr. Black's smooth tones. "Perhaps in view of the circumstances a certain sum set aside for the foster-daughter would be in order? Merely a suggestion, of course, there is no legal obligation."

Never! She couldn't bear the thought of wrangling over a home that had always stood for love and security. Charity from a strange man was something she didn't have to take. "I'll let you know." She wasn't used to lying and was afraid it would show, but apparently Mr. Black had his mind on other matters.

"Good. I think that about wraps it up." The lawyer rose to his feet. "Perhaps things will work out right after all."

Privately she reflected that if by working out all right he was referring to her accepting money from a man she had never met she didn't give much for her chances.

"Goodbye, Miss Carter! And good luck!" Even his handshake, Alison thought, was dry and lifeless. She summoned up a smile and accompanied him to the door, watching as he climbed into his dust-smeared car and moved down the long drive towards the road.

She supposed it was a stupid impractical way of looking at things. There was no doubt Mr. Black had thought her quite out of her mind to refuse the financial assistance he had offered, but when you came right down to it, it was a handout, made out of pity to a girl who had missed out on her inheritance. Her foster-parents had done more than enough for her, she was quite agreeable for their property to be passed on to one of their own flesh and blood. What she was concerned about was the thought of accepting money from *him*. Nothing would induce her to consider such a thing. She fancied the lawyer had got the message as to her feelings on that subject, but if by some unhappy chance the nephew contrived to communicate with her directly, despite her change of name, she would make the matter plain in no uncertain terms.

Unconsciously she sighed. It didn't help any to stand here at the doorway just looking, not with the grass blowing in the wind, sheep dogs barking, cats frisking around her legs. She only hoped the new owner would look after the animals properly. Oh, what was the use of thinking? Better start to pack. Tomorrow she would leave here for ever. There was nothing to stay for—now.

In the evening she drove down to the Gilberts' farm taking with her a large carton of clothing and personal possessions which Mrs. Gilbert, kind and motherly, had offered to store for her in a spare room. They were so kind, the Gilberts, asking no hurtful questions as to why she was leaving without waiting to greet the new owner. Perhaps they already knew. "Don't worry about anything back here," Mrs. Gilbert told her. "Boy"—Alison knew she was referring to the single middle-aged son who lived at home, "will move up to Te-o-nui

tomorrow and stay until the new man comes to take
over." It was nothing, they were only too pleased to be
able to do something to help. The unspoken sympathy
was comforting and eased some of the sense of loss and
emptiness she couldn't seem to shake off.

Next morning she fed the farm animals as usual,
then carried her luggage out to the Mini. Her zipped
travel bag held summer clothing, shorts, sun-frocks,
swim-suits, and in the big cardboard carton she had
packed her most precious possession, the Topanti
saddle for which she had saved for so long and had sent
out from a firm away over in London.

Now there was only one thing left to see to, and that
was something that wrenched her heart.

As she moved up the slope Banner caught sight of
her and nickered gently, moving towards Alison with
her prancing gait, long white tail blowing in the wind.
The foolish tears pricked Alison's eyes as she stroked
the mare's head. "You'll be all right," she whispered
against the thick white coat. "The Gilberts will look
after you until *he* comes." She brushed away the tears
with the back of her hand and fled. To look back would
only make the parting harder to bear.

Back in the silent house she went through the
rooms, satisfying herself that she had left nothing of
her own behind, closing the long lounge room picture
windows against the threat of fleecy gunmetal clouds
hanging low on the horizon. The windows—all at once
she froze, looking down a vista of green paddocks to
the road below where a long red car was approaching
and somehow she just knew it was about to turn in at
this entrance. The next moment it did. She watched as
a tall masculine figure sprang out of the vehicle to open
the gate, drove through the opening and closed the gate
behind him. What if he were the new owner arriving
earlier than expected to look over his inheritance? He
would be bound to be impatient to see over the property he now owned—but he wasn't going to see her,

that was for sure! She mustn't let herself be trapped here, forced to meet him, accept his hateful sympathy and worst of all, become involved in sickening arguments concerning the place she had always thought of as home. She couldn't bear it, she wouldn't! She went on peering through the venetian blinds. Thank heaven for slats that permitted her to look out and remain unseen. Now he was driving through the second gateway. Flight for her was out of the question, but maybe she could still avoid a meeting. She would wait in here and hope his inspection would be concentrated on the land and the stock. A sheep farmer himself, he would naturally be interested in the lush paddocks, the newly-shorn sheep and the black beef cattle roaming the slopes. One thing, he was alone, and that meant he hadn't brought his wife along with him to see the property. A woman would be far more inclined to linger in the house and garden. With a little luck plus the help of the floor-length yellow velvet drapes at her side Alison might yet avoid coming into contact with Craig Carter.

She held her breath as the stranger closed the last gate behind him and sped up the winding drive towards the house. Now he had braked to a stop in the driveway and was getting out of the car. She could see him clearly, a tall man, broad-shouldered and younger than she would have expected him to be. My, but he was good-looking in a tough, sun-bronzed sort of way. A typical sheep farmer, slim-hipped with a deceptive leanness. She wouldn't mind betting he could toss a fully grown sheep over a fence and think nothing of it. He was taking his time, glancing around sheep-studded slopes around him, a tall man in beige slacks and navy blue shirt, soft suede shoes, thumbs hooked in the leather belt encircling his hips. Presently he took from the pocket of his shirt "the makings" and leisurely proceeded to roll himself a cigarette, running the flimsy paper along his lips.

Somehow she couldn't tear her gaze away. Dark hair

blowing back from a strong rugged face, a goodhu-moured mouth—she could even glimpse the deep cleft in his chin. Now he was gazing towards the house and it seemed impossible he could remain unaware of her scrutiny, but of course venetian slatted blinds took care of that.

She went on looking, she couldn't help herself. There was something about him that held you, an impression of authority in his stance, a feeling that he was a man to be reckoned with. The sort of man you could be drawn to—she pulled herself together—in other circumstances.

At last, just when she felt she couldn't bear the suspense another minute, he came striding up the concrete path and she heard the small garden gate shut behind him. Swiftly she slid behind the shelter of the curtains. It seemed to her fevered imagination that even his footsteps were firm and decisive. The next moment she heard the door open into the back porch and presently she could hear him moving through the kitchen, going into the passage, opening bedroom doors on either side, then closing them again. Clearly he was giving the house a brief inspection, no more. With luck she'd get away with it! Scarcely daring to breathe, she heard footsteps approaching the lounge room and knew he was in the room. Help! He was approaching the window where she was hidden from view. The footsteps stopped and the silence seemed to last for ever. Then the quick decisive steps moved on and Alison let out her breath on a long sigh of relief. It must only have been the view from the picture windows that had attracted him. She was overcome with a wild desire to giggle. What if he had attempted to draw the curtains? Or supposing he had brought a wife with him? She would probably have made a close inspection of the newly-hung gold velvet drapes that had been Dot's pride. At least that was something to be thankful for. Odd that he hadn't brought his wife. Odder still were he to be unmarried, a man like that—she pulled up her thoughts with a jerk.

When she ventured another glance outside he was striding towards the garages and a few moments later he took out the Land Rover. So he intended having a run over the back paddocks? Well, that suited her fine. Once over the brow of the high hill at the back and he would be out of sight of the house. She could slip into the Mini and make her escape long before he had returned from his tour of inspection. Thank heaven he hadn't entered the garage where her car was parked. It would have been awkward had he noticed its absence on his return. Somehow he hadn't looked like the sort of man to overlook anything.

It seemed an age until she saw him taking the rise. She took a chance then and slipping out the back door, hurried across the yard. She was almost at the garage when she saw the Land Rover stop. What if he were returning right away? In a panic she rushed into a nearby shed and in the shadowy rear of the small building, rubbed away the cobwebs from a forgotten window and peered through, For goodness' sake! She stared in amazement, for it was Banner who had captured his attention.

He was standing at the gateway patting the mare's white neck and Banner, traitor that she was, appeared to be enjoying his attention. The next minute he had vaulted the fence and taking an old bridle hanging on the wires, slipped the bit into Banner's mouth. So that was the idea—he was going to take her over the jumps in the paddock and try her out. How dared he ride Banner. Who did he think he was?

Alison watched breathlessly as he set the white mare to the painted rails, each one set a little higher than the last, that Alison had put up herself. Of course Banner took them without a fault. Anger melted away in pride as the mare gathered herself up spread out and sailed effortlessly over the bars. At least he would see what a fantastic show-jumper Banner was. He could ride, she admitted grudgingly, and he wouldn't do the mare any harm. He might even keep her in training. He took the mount back over the jumps and again she performed brilliantly. At last, with a parting pat, he let her go free. Surely now, Alison reflected, he would get on with his journey over the hills.

She waited for a few minutes, then ventured to push open the door and peer around it. Goody, goody, he was back in the Land Rover, and even as she watched the vehicle vanished over a grassy rise. Now was her chance! In a flash she had run into the garage and was flinging open the door of the small blue car. Luckily she had a brand new battery and the motor started at a touch. Better close the door behind her so he would notice nothing different. She sped down the winding drive, opening the closing gates with fumbling fingers that shook with haste. Then at last she was out on the quiet road.

Wow-ee! She had made her escape—but only just in time!

Out on the open road her taut nerves relaxed and she slackened speed. There was no point in hurrying away now that the danger was past, "danger" being one Craig Carter.

All the way to Auckland she couldn't seem to stop thinking of him. No wonder, for unwittingly or not, he had turned her life upside down. Travelling along the northern motorway she reached the city in late afternoon and booked into a clean and quiet hotel within walking distance of the city.

Auckland fascinated her, this essentially outdoor city set between two harbours with its volcanic cones and bushland and seascapes. It's the start of summer, she thought, strolling down Queen Street where the men wore light shirts and walk shorts, the girls summery frocks, and the gay lava-lava of the Pacific islanders from Samoa, Tonga, Cook and Nieu Island, brought gaiety and colour to the main street.

The days slipped by as she explored the city where there were so many places to visit, so many things to see. It would all have been so different had she had someone to see it all with, a companion, someone like—Unbidden a masculine face, sun-bronzed, with lips that lifted at the corners, invaded her mind. Funny how she couldn't get him out of her thoughts. For the hundredth time during the past few days she thrust the picture aside and endeavoured to concentrate on the present. Tomorrow she would drive around the winding waterfront road that curved close to the sun-sparkled harbour where small bays were clustered with yachts and craft of all description. Or maybe she would take a climb up the mountain that had once been an active volcano, or settle for a ferry trip over the harbour to explore the high volcanic mountain with its ever changing colours. Tomorrow... lazing on the beach, strolling through green native bush or motoring along suburban streets, the lazy sunsoaked days drifted by. Gradually with them went some of the shock and tension of the past weeks and in its place came a sense of restlessness. Fascinating though she found this colourful city, she had planned to visit other parts of the country, especially the northern areas with their historical landmarks and flawless bays.

"There it is!" Mary's excited tone jerked her from her musing. "At last, the coast!"

Alison followed her gaze towards the sea of tea-tree at the roadside and beyond to the misty blue of the Tasman. "Civilisation too!" She was looking up towards a farmhouse set high on the brow of a hill above cleared green slopes. The white-timbered home sprawled against a shelterbelt of tall trees.

"Wait! Stop!" Mary jerked her arm so violently that the car swerved to the side, then Alison braked to a sudden stop. "What on earth—?"

"Didn't you see? The name on the gatepost of that house up on the hill? It was Vasanovich! I didn't think I could be so lucky! I've just got to go up there and find out if it really is that family name of mine. Do you mind?"

"Mind?" Alison turned towards her with a smile. "I'll come with you."

CHAPTER THREE

"IT'S WORTH enquiring about anyway," Mary said as Alison swung into the driveway. "If it does happen to be one of my long-lost cousins won't Grandfather be pleased!"

"Don't forget," warned Alison as she slowed to a stop, "that in the country it's the custom for the passenger to get out and open the gates."

"It's worth it." Mary was already opening the car door and running forward. When the Mini was through the opening Mary closed the gate behind them and Alison, putting the vehicle into a low gear, went slowly over the paddock, cutting a trail through the black steers who ambled from approaching wheels as the last moment. They rattled over a cattle stop, then followed the winding track up the grassy slopes. Above, the low ranch-style house lay bathed in afternoon sunshine, orange-tiled roof bright against a backdrop of dark macrocarpa pines. Around the dwelling sloping lawns studded with flowering shrubs fell sharply away to paddocks below. They passed through a second gate, then a third, and soon were skirting a mellow red shearing shed, passing implement sheds, stables and garages.

Alison pulled up at the small gateway leading to the back of the house. "At least there's someone at home. The door's open and there are children's clothes on the line...more or less." She reached up to untangle small garments that were whipped around the line in the prevailing wind. Mary, however, was hurrying ahead up the white-concreted path and knocking on the door leading to a back porch.

There was no answer to the summons and as Alison

came to join her Mary knocked again, louder this time.
"If they don't hear that thunderous noise they must be
deaf—or miles away." Still there was no response.

"They must all be outside." Mary turned away.
"Let's take a look around, shall we?"

Together they climbed a grassy slope behind the
house, scanning the vast sheep-threaded hills rising
around them. The intense stillness of the country was
broken only by the lowing of cattle. Or was there
another sound, Alison wondered, a faint echo borne
towards them on the wind?

"No luck," Mary was saying. "They must have
taken off over the hills somewhere."

"Listen!" Once again Alison caught the faint sound,
almost like someone calling for help. There it was
again, a feminine voice, calling for help. "Do you hear
what I hear?"

Mary nodded. "Someone's in trouble. It's coming
from just over the hill, but I can't see anyone."

"Come on!" Alison was hurrying down the slope
and Mary ran along beside her. It wasn't until they
reached another rise that they caught sight of a tousled
grey head apparently protruding from the grassy hillside. There was no doubt about the voice now. "Help,
somebody! Help!"

Alison was the first to reach the middle-aged woman
whose grey locks were visible from the opening in the
ground in which she was apparently trapped. A farm
motorbike lay upturned at her side and the face looking
up at them was scarlet with frustration and anger.
"Thank heaven you've come! I've been here for
hours, seems like hours anyway! Get me out, will
you?"

Obligingly Alison knelt down, extending her hand,
but the tall heavy woman released her grip almost immediately, the colour draining away from sun-weathered
cheeks.

"You're hurt?" Alison asked gently.

"It's my knee, curse that motorbike! I've put my

knee out and it won't take my weight. Even without that, though, I couldn't get out, I'm stuck in this darned hole. I don't suppose either of you can drive a tractor?"

"I can!" With a call to Mary, "Stay with her till I get back!" Alison hurried away towards the shed. "I won't be long."

Presently she came bumping over the grass in the tractor and soon she was backing the vehicle towards the trapped figure. "I'm going to winch you out," she told her. "Do you think you can hold on to the rope while I winch you up to the tractor?"

"I'll do it," vowed the angry voice, "I'll do it if it's the last thing I ever do!"

"Here we go, then! Catch!" Alison tossed the rope down the hole and very slowly winched the woman upwards. Grimly the stranger clung to the rope, her face a deep crimson now with exertion.

"You're going to make it," encouraged Mary, and at last the woman was free. Mary helped her into the tray of the tractor and steadied her as the tray lifted and they went slowly over the humps and hollows of the grassy paddock.

Both girls assisted the stranger up the path and into the house, then with a sigh of relief the woman collapsed into an easy chair in the dining room. "What a relief!"

"Is your knee very painful?" Mary asked.

"It's not too bad," but she had tightened her lips. "I can stand it."

Mary said, "What about pain-killer tablets? Have you any in the house?"

"In the bathroom cabinet—"

"I'll get them." In a flash Mary had left the room.

"As things turned out I'm jolly glad you two girls happened along today." Alison met the big woman's rakish grin. She was tall and raw-boned, Alison saw now, with a weather-roughened tanned skin, a beaky nose and bright brown eyes.

Aloud Alison said, "If you'll tell me where you keep the brandy—"

Again the rakish grin. "I'd rather have a cuppa!"

"And so you shall." Already Alison was plugging in the cord of the electric jug and reaching to a shelf above her head for the pottery teapot. Funny how in farm homes the teapot was invariably kept on a shelf above the sink-bench, together with the tea-caddy.

When the injured woman had swallowed the tablets Mary brought her, and had drunk the hot tea, a little colour returned to the weather-roughened, deeply tanned face. "You'll feel better after that," Alison comforted her. "We'll help you into your room and you can rest up for a while while we ring the doctor. Have you his telephone number handy?"

"It's okay, love, I don't need a doctor. This is something that's happened before, worse luck. It's a weak knee—I hurt it in a fall from a horse last year and it goes out of action at the drop of a hat. It's the remedy I'm worried about. No need to ring the doctor, because I know exactly what he'd say—complete rest for at least two weeks. That's where I'm really in trouble. Thing is," she went on in a worried tone, "this darned ulcerated leg of mine," she indicated the elastic bandage wound tightly around her plump leg. "The doctor's ordered me to put my foot up, it's the only way, he says, it will ever heal. Now I've opened it up again and with this other trouble on top of it... I just can't do it!" She put down her teacup with a clatter.

"But you said yourself," Alison pointed out, "that nothing else will heal the ulcer—"

"I know, I know, but it's not so easy."

"It never is in the country," Alison agreed gently, "don't I know it!"

"It's a lot worse than you know. This couldn't have happened at a worse time! That darned motorbike—I always said horses were a lot better than bikes on any farm. I never dreamed there was a hole in the ground. The grass had grown over it and the first I knew was finding myself down there with a sharp pain in my knee. That's the trouble when you've taken over a new place, you don't know the ground. If it had been my old home I knew every inch of the land. Now I just don't know what to do." She seemed thankful to unburden the frantic worry that possessed her. "They're depending on me, my son and the children—"

"But surely his wife—" Alison murmured.

"No, no, you don't understand. He's not married. The twins are my niece's children. She's my favourite niece too and if I'm stuck in bed for weeks and weeks who's going to look after the family?"

Mary said in a puzzled tone, "Couldn't the children's mother come and get them? If they're just here on holiday, the twins—"

"No, she and her husband are not even in the country." Again the note of desperation in her tones. "I may as well tell you that Karen and her husband," she drew a shaky breath, "haven't been getting on well lately. Their marriage is in a pretty precarious state one way and another. All this talk of marriage counsellors... I was really worried about them. Then out of the blue came an offer from Switzerland, a chance for them to stay overseas for two months. Ben's a skiing instructor, you see, and the experience would mean a lot to him. It was just too good an opportunity to miss, what with the fares paid for both Ben and Karen. The only catch was it would entail a lot of travelling, so of course I offered to look after the twins. I was only too glad to have them, the darlings, and then—" her voice dropped to an exasperated frustrated note, "this had to happen!"

Sensitive always to another's pain and problems, Alison cried impulsively. "But that's no problem! I could stay and look after things here until you get on your feet again! My friend Mary and I, we're just touring around the countryside having a look around. I wouldn't mind a bit."

"Would you really? It just seems too good to be

true, your dropping in like this just at the right time."
The eager light in the brown eyes was dashed. "But
what about your own plans?"

"I haven't any!" Alison said cheerfully. "Nothing
that can't be postponed for a few weeks, anyway."

"I can't believe it! You really will? You won't change
your mind?"

"I never go back on a promise," said Alison gaily.

With the nagging worry removed from her mind the
patient brightened. "Couldn't you stay here too?" She
glanced towards Mary. "There's swags of room and
you two could be company for each other. *Please?*"

"I don't see why not." Mary had a way of talking
with her hands, Alison noticed. White hands that unlike her own tanned paws looked as though they had
never engaged in any hard physical toil. "So long as
you let me help with things. Who knows?" she smiled
her slow sweet smile, "it might just happen to work in
with my own plans."

"Don't worry," the older woman appeared delighted
with Mary's decision, "there's plenty to do here both
inside and outside the place. I won't mind taking it easy
for a while now, not now you two girls are being so
good to me, spoiling me and taking over all the chores,
and the twins. They're good kids, though, Sue and Patrick, they won't cause you too much worry."

"We could start," Mary suggested, "by making you
a bit more comfortable. How about letting us take you
to your room and pop you into bed? Then I can bring
you along a bowl of warm water and clean up some of
those cuts and bruises."

The older woman gazed down at her bare arms,
covered with scratches, at the trickle of blood running
down below the elastic bandage on her leg. "I must
look a mess."

"You'll look as good as new once I've done with
you," Mary promised laughingly. The big woman laid
an arm around the shoulder of each girl and they proceeded up the long hall and into an end bedroom.

While Alison helped her to undress Mary searched in a bureau for a nightdress and before long the patient, freshly washed and cool and comfortable, was settled in her bed.

"Now let me get this right," she glanced towards Alison, "you're—?"

"I'm Alison."

"And your friend is Mary. I'm Frances, by the way. I was so unlucky today falling into that hole—well, not exactly a hole. It's an ancient tunnel the Maoris must have made years and years ago to bring their water from the fresh water lake up to their *pa* at the top of the hill."

Alison looked surprised. "How did you know?"

"Oh, I've studied Maori customs quite a lot. As soon as I came across that hill I knew it was the site of an old Maori *pa*. It had all the signs of occupation even if it was a hundred years ago—cooking pits with the grass growing over them, banks of pipi shells. I was so excited about my find then bang, that farm bike tipped me off on a mound of earth and down I went into that hidden tunnel with the grass growing over it."

For something to say Alison murmured, "You're interested in Maori archaeology?"

"Oh, more than interested! I'm really keen about finding out all I can about how the Maoris lived before the pakehas arrived here. I've taken a course in Maori language and now I'm doing my best to find out the old Maori proverbs. My aim is to make them into a book when I've discovered enough. Such a pity the race had no written language, just legends and tribal lore passed down by word of mouth or chants or dances. Still, I'm getting quite a few proverbs. Fascinating it is too. They're such a poetical race, the Maoris, with a gift for words, lyrical really, and they can pack a punch when it comes to making up proverbs. You wouldn't believe it," the excited tones ran on, "but from what I've been able to find out they had a proverb for almost every possibility."

Mary tucked an extra pillow beneath the grey hair and taking a hairbrush from the top of the dressing table, ran the brush down the short wiry strands. "How about your troubles today? Did they have one to cover anything like that?"

"Don't stop brushing, love. It's so soothing to have someone attending to your hair. Oh yes, there's one for what happened to me just awhile ago. I'm putting it in my book under the heading 'difficulties overcome.' *'He manga wai koia kia kore a whitikia'*—'It's a big river indeed that cannot be crossed.'" All at once her voice was dreamy. "I can relax now. The twins will be home soon, and my son won't be long after them. He's gone to a stock sale at Dargaville. You'll tell the children, Patrick and Sue, about me? They'll be so upset if they don't see me about when they get back from school." Fear sharpened her tone. "You will be here, won't you?" She gazed anxiously from one girl to the other.

"Don't worry, Mrs. Vasanovich," Mary murmured, laying down the hairbrush, for the older woman's eyes were closed and she appeared to be on the verge of sleep. "We'll take care of everything for you."

There was no answer and it was clear that the pain-killing tablets were fulfilling their purpose. Presently, when the even breathing assured her the patient was asleep, Alison crept from the room. In the hall Mary was coming towards her, a travel bag in one hand and the cardboard carton in the other. She grinned, her sleepy eyes crinkling with amusement, "Seeing we're going to move in I thought I'd better get started. I travel light myself—what on earth's in this monstrous carton?"

"Only my saddle."

"Your *saddle*? Well, one thing, you'll be able to make yourself useful around the place. But of course, you're a country girl, you told me yourself. I was forgetting."

"Do you think we should call the doctor? Evidently this trouble is something that's happened before, so he'll know how to treat her."

"Let's leave it until the son comes home, shall we?"

"It might be an idea." They were moving along the passage together, peering into a bedroom with two single beds covered in cotton spreads, a painted chest of drawers and empty wardrobe.

"This one looks like a guest room." Mary tossed the luggage on one of the beds. "We'll share?"

"Yes, of course." Alison's lips twitched at the corners.

"What's so funny?"

"Oh, nothing really. It was just that something struck me. That Maori proverb Mrs. Vasanovich quoted, something about 'It's a big river indeed that cannot be crossed.' I keep thinking about the big river we crossed today. Seems funny somehow."

Mary was taking toilet accessories from her canvas pack. "Not so funny as it's going to be soon when the son comes home and finds two strange girls all nicely settled in his home!"

"You'll have to look after him," Alison teased. "He's your second cousin, or something. Me, I'll settle for the twins."

As if in answer to her words at that moment the murmur of childish voices floated past the open window. Presently there were sounds of the kitchen door being flung open, followed by loud calls of "Gran! Where are you—can we have a cookie?"

"I'd better go and put them in the picture before they wake her!" Alison hurried on ahead into the kitchen where the five-year-old twins were seated on the floor, busily snapping open the catches of their incandescent pink lunch cases and strewing papers all over the floor.

Cropped dark heads jerked upward as Alison came into the room and two pairs of blue eyes glanced curiously towards her.

"Hi!" She dropped down beside them. "You're Sue, aren't you, and you're Patrick? I'm Alison and this is my friend Mary. What have you got there?"

"Look, I drew this picture." Sue was thrusting a crayoned sketch towards her. "I got a star today."

"Look at mine," cried Patrick, "look at mine first!" He got to his feet, clutching his drawing paper to a small chest. "Where's Gran? I want to show her my picture."

"You can't," Alison told him. "She's in bed. You mustn't worry her, because she's sick. She's hurt her leg in a fall from her motorbike out in the paddocks. We found her there and brought her inside. Now she has to stay quiet and rest until she's better."

Anxious-eyed, the children stared up at her. Then with total lack of sympathy, they wailed in unison, "But who's going to look after us?"

"We are," said Mary promptly, "and that means you'll both have to do as you're told. For a start how about picking up all that mess from the floor and coming to sit at the table while I get you some cool drinks?" She muttered in an aside to Alison, "I only hope there is something in that line." She moved towards the large refrigerator in a corner of the room and soon she was pouring chilled orange drinks into plastic beakers and reaching up to a shelf to take down a tin of home-made cookies.

Slightly subdued by two strangers, the twins picked up their sketches and laid them on the table beside them. Gravely Alison inspected the crayoned pictures. "Very good." She was gazing down at a coloured sketch of an elongated skinny figure with flyaway hair, bared teeth and staring purple eyes. "Who's this?"

"Can't you see?" Sue's note was one of exasperation. "It's Uncle Craig, of course."

"Is it now?" In the babel of childish voices Alison hadn't heard anyone approach. Now at the deep and amused masculine tone she swung around.

"Uncle Craig!" The children ran to him, both talking at once, as they endeavoured to show him their sketches. Over their heads Alison's distraught gaze met that of the man standing in the doorway. She was unaware that her lips were parted in horrified amazement. It couldn't be, things like this didn't really happen, there must be some ghastly mistake. But deep down where it counted she knew there was no mistaking the man who was entering the room. She would recognise his step anywhere. Here was Craig Carter himself, as coolly confident and—admit it—as disturbingly attractive as ever. The frantic thoughts went whirling through her mind. Then she did a double take. Don't panic. Remember *he doesn't know you. He's never set eyes on you before.* All you have to do is to remember to play your part and he'll never suspect a thing. He mustn't! For the implications of his finding out her true identity just didn't bear thinking about.

"That's enough for now kids. Quiet!" he thundered, and immediately the children's voices subsided.

"I'd better explain." Alison tried to gather her senses together. If only he wouldn't look at her! There was something in his glance that scattered her thoughts and put everything out of her mind, everything sensible, that is. She took a deep breath. "My friend—Mary—and I, we happened to come up to the house—" Heavens, but she was making a complete mess of all this, the explanation was becoming so involved—

"That's right," Mary's quiet voice cut in. Thank heaven the other girl had taken up the narrative. It was different for Mary when it came to explaining their presence here. There were no hang-ups for her concerning one Craig Carter. Alison wrenched her thoughts back to Mary's voice. "I was hoping to look up some distant relatives of mine and when we noticed the name on the gate I couldn't resist coming up to the house to enquire. You see, my name happens to be Vasanovich too."

"Now I get it!" His puzzled expression changed to one of enlightenment. "Sorry to have to tell you, but the family have moved away from here. They're still in the district, but they've invested in a big block of land a bit further north. I took over from them a week ago."

It all ties in, Alison was thinking. He's bought this

place. Probably he's put in managers on the other two properties, but he's living right here. He's the boss and I've promised his mother I'll stay here and look after the family until she's well again. *What have I done?*

"That explains a lot," Mary was saying in her reflective way. "When we got to the house we couldn't find anyone at home, though it looked as though the occupants weren't far away. So we went looking up in the back paddocks, heard someone calling and found your mother—"

The smile fled from his lean bronzed face. He said tersely, "Mum? An accident? That damned motorbike she's so crazy about. Is she all right?"

Mary nodded. "She's not badly hurt. Seems she took a fall from the bike and landed herself in an overgrown old tunnel on the hillside. She hurt her leg a bit—"

"Put her knee out again, I bet! It happens to her every now and again. She'll be hopping mad if she's forced to rest up for weeks. I'll go and have a word with her."

"She's asleep," Mary told him. "We gave her a couple of codeine to ease the pain. We thought we'd wait until you came home to see about calling a doctor."

"Good thinking. I sure do appreciate—" He broke off as a strong feminine accent reached them from the direction of the bedroom up the hall. "Craig, is that you?"

"Be back soon." Turning on his heel, he hurried from the room.

In the silence the small girl said in a hushed tone, "Poor Gran, will her leg get better?"

Patrick answered her. "Course it will. But she won't be able to ride her motorbike." His tone was tinged with wistfulness. "I wish I could ride her bike. I bet I could ride a farm bike if I tried—"

"You could not so," his sister argued repressively, "'cause Uncle Craig wouldn't let you—now look what you've done!" For in the argument a beaker of orange drink had spilled to the floor and Alison went in search of a cloth to mop up the sticky liquid.

When she had cleaned the floor the children ran out to play. She became aware of Mary's thoughtful look. "What were you looking at me in that odd way for a while back? Didn't you want to stay here?"

Alison looked away. "I can't stay."

"But you were the one who was all for it. You can't back out now. Why have you changed your mind all of a sudden?"

"Just something I've remembered...something..." If only she could explain the truth—but clearly that was out of the question. "But you can—"

"Well, I'm not staying without you," Mary declared flatly. "You're the one who knows all about farm work, meals and all that, it's all Greek to me. Besides, you promised. You can't leave that poor woman in the lurch like that—" She broke off as Craig came back to the room.

Alison decided to throw it over to fate. What else could she do?

"She's doing it hard, having to be laid up." There was a frown on the bronzed face. "Says she won't have the doctor—guess she knows what he'll say to her when he sees her! I gave him a buzz from the office and he'll be along to check her over as soon as he can fit it in. Says to keep the patient in bed meantime. I've just been hearing about that offer of yours—" From his height he glanced down at Alison and she wondered if he could sense her nervousness. Why did he seek her out instead of Mary? Mary who was so much older and more capable looking than herself, with her mop of coppery curls and small slim figure? "She's been letting me in on how you two rescued her today, and better still, that you've offered to stay on in the house keeping things running along until she gets well enough to cope." His glance towards Alison was deep and intent and somehow very difficult to sustain. He perched his long length on the table and taking the makings from the pocket of his drill shorts, began leisurely to roll himself a cigarette. As she watched him Alison was reminded of the last occasion on which she had observed him doing just that. He ran his lips along the tissue paper. "You two dropping in here like this at just the right time seems too good to be true."

It is. But she said the words silently.

He held a light to his cigarette and blew out the flame. At last, Alison thought, his glance had shifted to Mary. "It's a terrific stroke of luck, your staying on so far as we are concerned—but," he was eyeing her narrowly, "how about you? For all I know it might put finish to some schemes of your own for the next few weeks."

"Not to worry," Mary assured him smilingly. "Honestly, it will be quite an experience for me, staying on a New Zealand sheep farm. I've only been in the country a short while."

From out of nowhere Alison was assailed by a stab of—could it be jealousy? Ridiculous to feel this way, merely because Mary had confided to her those romantic notions about the Kiwi sheep farmer breed. Craig Carter meant nothing to her...on the contrary. Indeed, at this moment she wished him far enough.

"It's a deal, then?"

Frantically Alison strove to catch Mary's eye. Her lips mouthed a soundless NO! and she shook her head vehemently, but Mary merely stared back at her in bewilderment. She had a suspicion that Craig had caught her out and intercepted her silent signal, so she didn't dare repeat the effort, not with those oh-so-perceptive blue eyes once again fixed on her downcast face.

"We couldn't do anything else," Mary assured him laughingly. "Your mother was so terribly worried, not about herself, but about the household, and especially the twins. We just had to offer to stay, and it wasn't any sacrifice really. Seeing we're both just touring around the country it seemed a good idea."

"It's a fantastic idea!"

A good idea! Alison thought desperately. Surely he must have caught on by this time that no matter how happy Mary is about the arrangement, I'm not keen to stay. He must guess by my silence that I'm not feeling the same way at all, not with him right here in the house, *his* house! But what excuse can I give to get out of staying on? I can't get out of it.

She brought her mind back to Craig's deep tones. "I can tell you this much. Mum would be more than upset if you two hadn't come to her rescue today. It's about all she seems to be thinking of at the moment—apart from keeping the doctor at bay, that is. Those girls, those two nice girls, they'll stay, both of them...you see, they *promised*."

Alison felt slightly sick at the thought that she was the one who had done all the promising. How simple the matter had seemed half an hour ago, and how devastating the position in which she now found herself.

"Great! If you two can stick around until Mum gets mobile again that will suit us fine. She'll put you in the picture about the household chores, the time to get the kids ready for the school bus at the corner of the road down there, all that stuff. Meals shouldn't be too much of a problem. I take off for work fairly early in the day and get back for a late breakfast around eight. I take lunch with me and usually get home about dark. But there's no need for the rest of you to wait dinner for me." Bushy dark eyebrows lifted enquiringly. "You've sorted out a room for yourselves?"

"Oh yes." It was Mary who answered. Alison reflected that he must surely regard her as the most uncommunicative girl he had ever come across. It was as well that Mary was taking all this in her stride, considering the chaotic state of her own feelings. To the other girl all this was merely an interlude, an amusing episode to relate to her friends back home in England when she returned.

"Terrific! I'll make it worth your while financially of course. Good of you both to help us out. The usual

wages doubled in this case—no problem. It isn't everyone who'd take on an invalid up in the bedroom at the
end of the hall as well as five-year-old twins, and all at a
moment's notice!''

Not to mention the one man in the world you're trying to avoid? She realised he was regarding her with his
intent look. ''You're very quiet, Miss—'' He broke off.
''I didn't get your name.'' Even in the tumult of her
emotions she found herself thinking that his smile was
really something.

She hesitated for a split second. *Careful, Alison,* you
don't want to give the game away right at the outset by
some stupid blunder. Very clearly she said, ''It's Wynyard,'' and could scarcely believe that the name made
no particular impact on him.

''Well, Alison Wynyard, what do you think about
the arrangement?'' Belatedly she realised he was awaiting an answer to his question, *the* question. She found
her voice at last and said thickly. ''There's just one
thing—''

''Anything you say. Just say the word—''

She told him. She had intended to say something
like, ''I hope you understand, but I may have to leave
quite soon. I'm expecting word from home and may
have to go unexpectedly?'' Under his mesmeric dancing gaze, however, the words that came from her lips
were quite different. ''Where do you keep the potatoes?''

Suddenly he was light-hearted and friendly. ''Come
along and I'll show you around.'' He waited while both
girls preceded him out of a side door and they entered a
spacious porch. As he flung open the door of a side
cupboard they caught sight of bags of potatoes, onions,
pumpkins, butternuts and the inevitable kumeras with
their lumpy shapes and dark crimson skins. ''In here
is the storeroom.'' He flung open yet another door and
they were looking into a room containing a huge upright freezer and high cupboards stacked with an endless variety of tinned foods. Mary gazed down at the

variety of packaged and labelled meats stacked in the long white cabinet. "What a monstrous deep freeze!"

"Not too big for the Vasanovichs, with four grown sons in the family, all living at home."

Mary's lips were twitching at the corners. "No! Not *four* of them, all bachelors?"

"That's right." He grinned. "Interesting, isn't it? I'll take you along to meet them one day soon, then it will be over to you."

"Kissing cousins?"

"Something like that. It's up to you. They tell me," he added meaningfully, "that the district here is a bit short on girl-power."

"Is that why you came?"

Watching the other two laughing together, Alison was once again pierced by that curious pang. Only it couldn't be jealousy, for how could your feelings be stirred by a man you scarcely knew and didn't like anyway?

When they had inspected the pantry with its long shelves of packaged foods and jars of home preserves ("Mum brought those jars of apricots up from the South Island," he told them) they went up the passage and into the bedroom where Frances lay on the bed, her cheeks slightly flushed, her eyes excited.

"Well, old lady, how are you feeling now?"

Frances apparently saw nothing untoward in her son's form of endearment. She grinned cheerfully. "Never mind about me! I was right, wasn't I?" she queried triumphantly. "The girls are staying, both of them?"

"That's right," he assured her. "We've got it all jacked up. Not that you deserve treatment like that, careering along on that farm bike over hills when you're supposed to be taking care of an ulcerated leg. You don't need to take a course in Maori, what you should be studying is survival training! I told you to watch it—"

Frances looked unrepentant. "I might have known!"

She appealed to the girls standing near the bed. "You see how it is—no feeling from him, no sympathy." But the brown eyes softened as they rested on the tall man gazing down at her. "I just don't know what I would have done without your kind offer, girls."

The answer came promptly in deep masculine tones. "You'd have got Karen and Ben back from their cruise ship and sent the kids packing, that's what!"

"Oh, I couldn't do that, Craig!"

"Why not?"

"You know why I couldn't bring your cousin and her husband back right at the start of their holiday. It would spoil everything. One of my Maori proverbs puts it beautifully."

"I knew it!" groaned Craig. "The Maoris had one to cover every eventuality and a few more besides, according to Mum! Okay," he grinned goodhumouredly, "we're listening, old lady. You've got yourself a captive audience. Fire ahead!"

Taking no notice of his raillery, Frances reached towards a bulky folder lying on the bedside table. "It's one about marriage," she murmured, riffling through the loose handwritten pages. "Got it!" she announced triumphantly, and slowly voiced the soft Maori syllables. *"'He hono tangata e kore e motu kapa te taura waka e motu.'"*

"Don't look at me," laughed Mary, glancing up into Craig's dark face, "I'm fresh out from London."

At Alison he didn't look, and all at once piqued, she heard her own voice saying quickly, "A human bond cannot be severed unlike the mooring rope of a canoe which can easily be broken."

In the startled silence she was aware of Craig's dark blue eyes, a flicker of amusement in their depths.

"Oh, it was easy for me to pick up some of the Maori language. I was brought up in—" a warning red light flashed in her mind and she broke off, to go on in some confusion, "in the depths of the country. At the school a lot of the children were Maori, families of the timber workers in the bush. I couldn't help picking up some of the Maori words and a few of their sayings too."

"Did you hear that?" Craig grinned down at his mother. "Man, are you on to a good thing. I'd say this was your lucky day, accident and all!"

A little later as the two girls were preparing the evening meal, Alison paused in her task of slicing bread, her eyes thoughtful. She had told no one of her change of name, it had all come about so suddenly—and anyway, it was her secret. The fewer people in whom she confided the less chance of Craig Carter discovering her identity, just supposing he did have any ideas in the matter of easing his conscience in that direction. Probably she was worrying needlessly, but supposing he put the matter in the hands of a private enquiry agent? The thought made her say diffidently to Mary, "If you don't mind there's something I'd like to ask you—a favour. Look, don't say anything to anyone here about the accident—my parents, you know?"

"Oh, I won't! I do understand how you feel. Having folks talk about it must bring it all back. You can depend on me to keep quiet."

With a lighter heart Alison knew that she could trust her new friend to keep her word.

A few minutes later the doctor arrived at the house. A small man with a lined face and tired smile, he said to the girls, "Dr. Anderson's my name. My patient will be up the hall, I expect," and went striding up the passage.

From somewhere in the paddocks behind the house Craig must have caught sight of the unfamiliar car in the drive, for shortly afterwards he came strolling into the room just as the doctor returned. Craig introduced himself and the two men shook hands.

"What's the verdict, doctor?"

"Just as I thought. The knee's out of action for a week or two, an old injury it seems. The ulcer will take time to heal. Your mother's put up a good fight, but I managed to convince her that a month's complete rest for her is a must, feet up and no running around after the kids. She had no excuse for not obeying orders after she'd let on about the minor miracle that happened along here today with two helpers strolling along to rescue her and offering to stay on to give her a hand with the chores for a few weeks. Wish my wife could be as lucky. Domestic helpers these days are like gold-dust." He smiled his jaded smile. "Even unattractive ones! Well, that's about it. Keep her quiet and make her rest." He was writing on a pad. "I'll prescribe something to hurry up the healing and you can pick it up tomorrow in town. "I'll call back in a couple of weeks to check up on her progress. Meanwhile," his glance included both girls, "I know I'm leaving her in good hands."

When Alison took the tastefully arranged tea-tray into the bedroom Frances was sitting up in bed, a cheerful grin lighting her lined face.

"I hear," Alison put down the tray on the bed, "that the doctor argued you into staying put for a few weeks."

Frances chuckled. "Hadn't a leg to stand on! Oh well, I don't mind so much now. One thing, I've got plenty to keep me occupied." She sent a distasteful glance towards the knitting wool, needle and pattern on the low table beside her. "Plenty I *should* be doing, I should say."

"You like knitting?"

"Hate it," Frances answered cheerfully. "It's so slow, and the wretched things never turn out anything like they look in the books. I know I should be knitting for the twins," her face brightened, "but it's such a marvellous chance to get on with my book. I'm putting all the proverbs together, or trying to. After all, it's time someone collected them all. That's one reason I was so glad when Craig decided to take over this place. There are so many Maori people in the North and I might find a few new proverbs, though I've already got swags of them. Now I'm working on the translations, and that's where I'll be calling on you for help. Sometimes there just doesn't seem the right word in our language to match the meaning." Launched on her hobby, Frances' character-lined face was alive with interest. "Would you believe that I haven't been able to come across any Maori word meaning 'the day after tomorrow' or 'day before yesterday'?"

"There isn't one, as far as I know. I guess it was because they thought those times didn't really matter...only today. Maybe they had something there. May I see your list?"

"I'll show them all to you tomorrow. I'm keeping you from your meal, child. Now you go right back to the others."

Alison, who was feeling decidedly uneasy at the prospect of sitting down at table to this first meal with *him*, made a further effort at postponing her arrival back in the kitchen. She dropped down on the bed. "I don't mind."

But Frances, who in some respects appeared to be as forceful as her son, waved the offer away. "Now you're not to worry about me, I'm quite all right. The pain's a lot better now and I'm going to enjoy this meal I haven't prepared myself—children behaving themselves?"

"Oh yes. Mary's got them bathed and in their pyjamas ready for bed."

"Good for her! Now I can really relax. Now off you go, love!"

At the table she found the others waiting for her. The children were chattering and Mary was trying in vain to restore order. Craig's quiet, "That's enough for now, kids!" brought a silence that lasted for exactly two minutes, then broke out the childish voices again. "I found a kingfisher's nest in the bank today!"

"Yea, and there were babies in it. You could hear them, squeak! squeak! squeak!"

"Another squeak out of either of you two," Craig thundered, "and you'll have tea on your own!"

This time silence prevailed, a silence that Alison found disconcerting. She was thankful when Mary queried Craig about farming methods in the north and before long he was drawing her out as to her life in England and her recent air trip out to New Zealand. Inevitably the subject of travel led to the Vasanovich family. Alison found herself hoping that with a bit of luck the Vasanovichs would last them until the end of the meal. Anything was preferable to answering questions concerning who she was and where she came from, questions for which she had no answers. She must take no chances on Craig Carter putting two and two together and coming up with the truth.

That evening she sat up in bed in her green shortie-pyjamas of sprigged cotton. Her hands were clasped around tanned knees and tendrils of hair still damp from the shower curled around her forehead. "He's autocratic and domineering," she was scarcely aware that the dreamy tones were voicing her thoughts, "just like I thought he would be."

Mary spun around from the bureau mirror, a hairbrush suspended in her hand and long black hair streaming over her shoulders. "You thought? How could you know anything about him?"

"Oh, I don't! I don't!" Swiftly Alison gathered her wits together. "It was just something his mother said," she added hurriedly.

"Did she? I didn't notice." Mary pulled her hair over one shoulder and resumed her brushing. "I thought he was rather nice... terribly attractive."

"Yes, you would, the Kiwi sheep farmer image." Alison couldn't understand why she was feeling so suddenly out of sorts, as though her skin didn't quite fit and everyone hated her. Aiming a punch at the pillow, she flung herself down and turning her face to the wall made a pretence of going to sleep.

CHAPTER FOUR

WHEN ALISON AWOKE the next morning a glance towards the other bed told her Mary was still asleep. She dressed quickly and went into the opposite room where she could hear the twins chattering together. "Hello, you two! How about getting yourselves dressed?" She was sorting small clean garments from a drawer in the bureau and laying them on the bed. Then with a final reminder to wash their faces and to brush their hair she went into the kitchen.

Craig would have left the house and started his work hours earlier, probably at daybreak. She could relax for a while free of his disturbing presence. She set the table, found cornflakes, butter, milk and marmalade, and soon the twins were eating breakfast. The children's endless chatter left her free to pursue her own troubled thoughts, for how ever was she going to get through a month of living here in enemy territory, *knowing what she did* ...

Patrick's excited voice broke into her musing. "Can I wake Mary up?"

"Let me! Let me!" clamoured his sister.

"Okay. You can both go in when you've finished your breakfast."

A few minutes later, a piercing scream came from the direction of Mary's bedroom. "What on earth—?" Alison hurried away to find a terrified Mary standing at the foot of the bed. Of the twins there was no sign.

"What is it? What is it?" Mary cried. "I'm terrified of insects, I always have been!" She shuddered. "Ugh, isn't it horrible—is it poisonous, do you think? I might have died—" She was gazing in horror at the big dark insect with its long feelers moving over her pillow.

"It's only a weta—"

"Only! It could kill you, I know it could! It looks evil! Those little monsters, they crept in here, then they let that thing out of a box and put it down on the pillow! They said you told them to wake me up."

"It does look horrible," Alison admitted. "It could give you quite a nip with those long feelers too, but it wouldn't kill you. Get dressed in the kids' room and I'll get Craig to deal with it when he comes in."

With a last shuddering glance towards the insect Mary snatched up her garments and hurried away. In the confusion Alison heard Frances' forceful tones echoing down the hall. "Have those kids been up to their tricks on you girls? I heard a scream and saw them both running outside. They're hiding in the shed. Don't stand any nonsense now. Get Craig to deal with them when he comes. He'll soon settle all that!"

"I'll do that," Alison told Frances as she reached the bedroom. Privately she reflected that Craig was in for a busy morning. When he arrived back, however, a rather subdued pair of twins had already left the house to wait on the main road below for the arrival of the school bus. Alison could hear Craig in the washroom off the porch and a little later he was in the room, facing her with his warm disturbing smile. "You're on duty, I see. How's the old lady feeling this morning?"

It was easier, she found, if she didn't look directly into his eyes. "She's had a good night." A smile tugged at her lips. "She's been waiting for you to get back—"

"That's mother love for you!"

"To administer justice—will two eggs suit you with bacon and tomatoes?"

"Please—Don't tell me, let me guess. It's the twins again, up to their usual tricks. I'll kill that Patrick if he's been putting insects in your bed! Scared the wits out of you, did he?"

"Not me." Alison turned the sizzling bacon on the

stove, switched on the coffee percolator and cut bread for toast all in quick succession. "It was Mary who got the treatment."

"They *said* they were waking me up." Mary stood in the doorway, relaxed now and smiling, pushing the dark hair back behind her ears. "Alison said it was a—a weta." She shuddered in spite of herself. "It's still there, in the bedroom. I shut the door and left it. Alison said you would know what to do."

"No problem. I'll just have a word with Mum."

When he came back to the kitchen Alison had the eggs cooked to a turn and the appetising aroma of percolating coffee stole through the sunshiny room.

"She's not in any pain," he said with satisfaction, seating himself at the table. "Sit down and have coffee with me?"

"I've just finished breakfast," Alison said quickly. "I was thinking I could take a run into town this morning and pick up the prescription from the chemist."

"Not to worry. I've got to shoot through today to pick up a tractor part and get some machinery replacements. When you move into a new place there's a heck of a lot of sorting out to be done. Actually I had quite a decision to make over the past few weeks. I'd made up my mind last year to get rid of the station I was running in the South Island and to come north. Then something came up out of the blue—a property that I inherited down country, a good productive place it is too. Good grassland, ample rainfall with none of the summer droughts that make life such a problem up here. Trouble was the place that was left to me wasn't big enough by half for me. I tried to buy land near to it, but there was none offering, so in the end I bought this place and sold the other."

Alison was very still. "You—sold it?" Dismay and shock got the better of her and even to her own ears the words were fraught with emotion. She couldn't help it. Banner—what had become of Banner? Had Mr. Black kept his word about caring for her white show-jumper? The terrible part of it all was that she couldn't even ask about the mare. Thank heaven he hadn't appeared to notice the untoward emotion in her voice.

"That's right." He was rolling a cigarette, spilling tobacco along with flimsy paper.

"I mean," wildly Alison jabbered on in an attempt to cover the slip, "it seems a pity, if the place down country was in such wonderful order."

"You reckon?" He looked up at her, eyeing her with his brilliant gaze, but now she had herself well in hand. "You haven't seen this place yet. It's quite something. High hills, fresh-water lakes to take care of the droughts that seem to be the main disadvantage around the place—know anything about sheep farming, Miss Wynyard?"

"Alison." She began gathering up plates from the table. "A bit. I used to live in the country." For a long moment she feared he was about to enquire the whereabouts of her home, but then she realised with relief that she need not have concerned herself on that score. "I'll tell you something, this place is worth having. Peringales are a new breed to me, they're different from the Romneys I was running down south. They look different and they don't act like the others."

"Oh, I know! I know! They're so much more alert and intelligent. Look at them now—" She moved to the window looking across at the high grassy hill close by where sheep flowed over the tracks on the hillside like a white river.

He followed her gaze. "At first I thought the dogs were moving them, but it seems they're just playing. They do that most mornings about this time. After a while they're puffing like hell, but they don't stop. There they go!" The white mass spread over the hillside, then as if at a given signal, turned and pelted back the way they had come.

"I'll take you out for a look around when I get back from Dargaville." There was no doubt who gave the orders around here, Alison mused. "Bring Mary too if she'd like a run out. Mum will be all right on her own for an hour or so."

At that moment Mary came into the room. "I've been up with Frances," she smiled. "She says she's feeling as comfortable as can be and she can't wait to get on with her notes. She was telling me there's a type-writer in the office, so I'll be able to type the pages out for her when she's got them ready."

"Help yourself!" Craig gestured towards a small room off the passage. "Come to that, I could do with some help myself with the paper-work. How lucky can a guy get? Alison here to cope with the domestic chores and a private nurse-cum-secretary as well!"

For no reason at all Alison felt hurt and angry. It was always the same where she was concerned. She remembered the lawyer's dampening advice to her concerning job-seeking. "Plenty of domestic work available on the farms." For Mary, the interesting task of keeping his books, helping him compile tax returns, profit-and-loss accounts, stock sheets, important things like that, while for her—she clattered the dishes in the sink.

Over the clink of crockery she caught Craig's lazy tones. "Care to look around the place, Mary? I'm tak-ing off soon with Alison on a sight-seeing tour, so—"

Mary picked up a tea-towel. "Thanks, but could I come another time?" Alison couldn't understand her secret pleasure at the words, especially as she liked Mary. "Your mother might just need something and I'd rather be handy."

"Good of you."

"It's not really." She smiled her slow sweet smile. "I was telling Alison I've always been sorry I didn't take up nursing, I got shuffled off into office work at the beginning and afterwards it seemed a bit late to change jobs. You're really doing me a favour, if you could call helping Frances to get on with her Maori proverb book nursing! Anyway, there's someone I want to get in touch with, and I thought I'd give them a ring. You did say the Vasanovich's still live in the district?"

"Sure they do. I got it from Papa Vasanovich himself—the address. The phone number's on the pad by the telephone. Two of the sons were running sheep and steers on land a bit further away, then they decided they'd team up with the parents and get a family farm. So if you ring through to that number you'd be in touch with the family all in one go. Did you tell me you were a relation?"

Mary laughed. "A distant connection, more like it. The name's the same, so that's a start. I've got a grandfather back in England who's very anxious for me to look up any of the family I can find. Rumour has it they settled here in the old gum-digging days, so...It's all pretty vague really, but I'll get in touch with this family now that I'm here."

"Why not?"

Craig left the house shortly afterwards. Allison could see his dust-spattered car moving down the main road. To her, sweeping and vacuuming, washing out children's garments, whipping up a batch of fluffy scones for morning cuppa, it seemed no time at all until he was back. Strong and vital, he seemed to bring a breath of the outdoors with him, or was it some masculine magnetism, Alison wondered, that made her so acutely *aware* of him? She could catch his deep tones as he spoke with his mother, then he came back to the kitchen where she had cups laid out on the table.

"Hmm, smells good." He had lifted the cloth covering a plate of warm scones.

"I'll just take some tea up to your mother."

"Thanks, love." Frances made room for the tray amidst the handwritten pages that entirely covered the bed. "Now you go right back with the others. I'll be fine."

Alison found Craig explaining to Mary various aspects of sheep farming in New Zealand. "You'll see what I mean when you get around the paddocks. Ever been on the back of a tractor? Or out in a Land Rover? Some spots up here in the hills are pretty inaccessible."

Mary shook her head.

"There's always a first time."

"But not just now," Mary protested. "I'm waiting for a call back from the Vasanovichs. I rang through and someone, it must have been the father, said he'd get his wife to ring me the moment she came in from outside. She was feeding the calves or something."

"Sounds like a farmer's wife. I got the idea when I met the family that Papa Vasanovich leaves all the big decisions to Mama." Craig swung around to face Alison. "How about you? Feel like coming out with me for a look around the place?"

There was no escape, no real reason why she shouldn't go with him. It was an ordinary enough request, she knew. Being alone with the boss was just one of the problems she must cope with here. She would be fine so long as she kept a constant watch on her impulsive tongue and didn't spoil everything with some stupid remark. She nodded carelessly. "If you like. I'll just fix the dishes."

"You won't, you know," Mary told her, "you'll leave them to me. Off you go, and have fun!"

Fun! Reluctantly Alison rose from the table and accompanied Craig out into the sunshine. Yet seated beside him on the high seat of the Land Rover, unexpectedly she was swept by a surge of wild sweet happiness. It must be something to do with the warmth and sunshine, the translucent blue sky against which the pine plantations were cut so sharp and clear.

They swept past the implement sheds and garages and took a track up a rise, two sheepdogs running alongside. All at once Craig braked to a stop and Alison wondered why. Then she realized the reason, for there in a grassy paddock sheltered by tall leafy trees she saw her own graceful white mare. He was out of the vehicle and strolling towards the paddock, but Alison was quicker still, hurrying ahead and flinging open the gate. In that moment she forgot everything but Banner, who was nickering softly as she came trotting towards her.

The mare reached her and Alison, gently stroking the white muzzle, was scarcely aware of the masculine tones. "She's not mine. Actually she belongs to a girl down country on the other property. I'm just taking care of the mare until the owner comes to collect her."

"Oh." Alison bent her head to hide her scarlet cheeks and went on stroking the white muzzle. For something to say she murmured in a muffled tone, "When?"

He shrugged. "Your guess is as good as mine. She's going to get in touch when she's found a place of her own, somewhere to keep the mare. Meanwhile," his gaze was disturbing and difficult to sustain, especially with those pink cheeks, "why don't you try her out?"

"Me?" Now she had no need to feign astonishment. "How do you know I can ride?"

He laughed. "Anyone ever told you you've got a very expressive face? The way you were drooling over that mare when I caught up to you just now...you can't tell me you're not a horse-lover."

She nodded, feeling her way carefully. "I've always loved horses. I can ride—a little." No need to let on about being a show-jumper. The thoughts chased one another through her mind. How difficullt it was to dissemble and pretend...and how hard to make herself remember.

"Well then, here's a job for you if you'll take it on. How about your keeping the mare in trim? Feeding, exercising, grooming—you know what to do. Interested?"

"Oh, that would be fabulous!" Pure happiness made her forget to be careful. She reached out a hand and affectionately patted the mare's thick white chest. "You'd like that, wouldn't you, Banner?"

She realised her blunder the moment the words were out.

He was quick to pick her up. "How come you know her name?"

She turned her face aside to hide her confusion. She

seemed to be always turning her face away this morning. "Just a guess," she mumbled, "a lucky guess." The words came quickly, jerkily. "I mean, at shows—" another blunder. She prayed he wouldn't notice the slip—"you often come across white horses called Banner... or Blue... or Misty." She heard herself babbling wildly on. "Haven't you noticed?"

"I've noticed."

She didn't quite trust the thoughtful glance he was sending her. Could he possibly suspect the truth? But no, that was ridiculous. It was only her own guilt that prompted her to read a special significance in his tone.

"Why don't you try her out?" he suggested once again.

"I will...sometime." His look was hard to meet.

Back in the Land Rover they lurched and bumped over the grassy paddocks with the dogs leaping alongside the wheels and sheep scattering in panic at their approach. They swept past a mellow red timber building that was the shearing shed, climbed up a steep slope. Now the wind was stronger, tearing at Alison's hair, sending the short curls blowing around her face. Around them drifted an elusive perfume, sweet as frangipani, but how could that be, she wondered, away up here miles from anywhere?

He seemed to read her thoughts. "Can't you guess what it is? The cabbage tree perfume drifts for miles on the wind."

She gazed towards the clumps of palm-like trees dotting the slopes around them. High at the top amidst the tangled green banners fluttering in the wind, she caught sight of a shower of creamy-pink blossoms.

They were sweeping up a steep grassy hillside and soon he was bringing the Land Rover to a stop just below the summit. As they got out to climb the last few feet of the rise Craig took her hand in his and once again for no reason at all Alison felt ridiculously happy, evasions and all.

They stood on the narrow point in the shadow of a

concrete reservoir, evidently erected on the highest point of land. The wind was stronger than ever here, whipping Alison's jeans around her legs and fluttering her cotton blouse against her slim figure. Beyond was the misty blue of the Tasman and near at hand rose high sandhills, the sand endlessly moving in the restless wind.

"They had to plant the marram grass and put in pine plantation to save the land around here," Craig was saying, and she followed his gaze to the marram grass creeping up the slopes. "Survival tactics, otherwise the drifts of sand would have covered the lakes in the prevailing wind, and the paddocks too, just as they have over there—" Gently he put a hand to her tanned cheek, turning her head away and for a dizzy moment Alison's emotions soared, quivering like the shimmering sun on the sandhills. The next moment she recovered herself, becoming aware of the tops of tall tea-tree protruding through the sand.

"Goodness, it must have taken quite a time for the trees to be covered like that," she murmured breathlessly.

"Not so long as you'd think. Without the pines and the marram grass the whole of the property would be lost over a period of years—come on, I'll show you Swan Lake, just over the next rise."

Once again he took her hand. Was it his touch or her own clumsiness that made her stumble on the dry broken ground as she jumped down? Luckily he arrested her fall and before she could tumble headlong down the slope he had caught her in strong arms, arms that held her a minute longer than need be, a minute while she could feel the beating of his heart through the thin cotton of his shirt. He released her with a quizzical glance that told her that he too had been conscious of the brief physical contact. He said nothing, however, and the next moment he was holding open the heavy door of the vehicle against the prevailing wind.

On and on, climbing slopes so steep that nearing the

summit they could see nothing beyond a green peak and a patch of blue sky. Then plunging down over winding sheep tracks while the curious black steers eyed them from adjoining hills. At length they lurched up to the summit of yet another rise and Craig braked to a stop. "There it is, down there—Swan Lake—see what I mean?"

Alison drew in a sharp breath of wonder. "I would never have believed it! It's exactly the shape of a swan, even to the long curve of the neck and spread wings." For far below glimmered a lake in a giant swan shape, the rippled blue waters surrounded by densely growing tea-tree with its filmy mist of white blossom.

"I got a shock when I saw it first too, and that was only last week. When Papa Vasanovich told me about it I took it he meant a lake with swans on it, and that was right too."

"I see what you mean." Alison's fascinated gaze was fixed on blue waters, ruffled by the wind, where black swans sailed close to the banks or sought for food amongst raupo and flax growing at the lake edge. As they plunged on down the slope she said with a smile, "Mary should have come with us. She'd have liked all this. It would have been an experience for her." Even as she spoke, however, a traitorous thought intruded. She was glad Mary hadn't come with them today, and that was odd, because she liked Mary a lot and Craig Carter she didn't like one little bit...at least...

She realised they were nearing the foot of the hill and presently Craig was bringing the vehicle to a stop. He pushed a way through tall tea-tree and soon they had reached the water's edge. Already black swans were swimming away from the shore, gliding out into the centre of wind-stirred waters.

"Lovely," she murmured, as they moved away.

"There's another lake yet," he told her as they made their way back to the Land Rover, "one without all the bush around it where we can swim."

Soon she realised they were ascending yet another

rise and in a few minutes they came in sight of a lake, larger than the other two they had seen, where grass grew down to the water's edge. As they strolled towards the water Craig said, "According to the locals I've talked to, they've had drought after drought up here for the past five summers. Luckily these lakes never run dry." He turned towards her and she caught the warmth in the dark blue eyes. "I'll take you swimming here next week. It's a date."

"Love to." Her pulses leaped at the thought of swimming in the clear lake water *with him*. She made an effort to curb her emotions which seemed to be getting out of hand. He was altogether too disturbingly attractive. But that was no reason for her to lose her wits over him. She said, trying for lightness, "It would be a great place to bring the twins for a picnic. They'd like that."

"We'll do that too some time." His tone was careless. You simply couldn't win with him.

All at once she realised that the elusive perfume was becoming stronger, wafted towards them in drifts of sweetness. Although she couldn't see them there must surely be cabbage trees growing nearby.

They strolled on over the cleared ground towards a patch of thickly-growing native bush. They were so close to the sandhills now that at the far part of the bush, tall trees were all but covered in drifting sand. Soon they were climbing over a gate and all at once they were in the cool fragrance of leafy undergrowth where the ground was mossy and damp underfoot and the air spiced with the pungent odour of the bush.

"This happens to be a bird sanctuary." Craig told her as the silvery notes of a tui cascaded in a flood of melody around them, "and I'm going to see that it stays that way! Even in this remote area there aren't many stands of native bush left. They were burnt out early-on, more's the pity."

They emerged at last into sunlight near the lake edge. A timber fence ran out into the water. "Just to keep the stock out," Craig explained.

But Alison's attention had been caught by a cabbage tree that had fallen across the fence. Above the floating green banners just clear of the lake water she glimpsed the drifts of the gossamer pink and white blossom. No wonder the cabbage tree flowers had perfumed the air for miles around.

She was kicking off her rubber "jandals," running ahead of him, throwing over her shoulder, "I'm going to get some of that cabbage-tree flower to take back to the house—"

"Don't be a fool, Alison, come back—"

She only laughed and sped on. Quick as a wink she leaped up on to the narrow timber railing of the fence and poised on the top rail, made her way, one foot over another, towards the fallen tree.

"You'll be sorry," he warned. "Those timbers are rotten—" She took no notice. "I don't care." But she was mighty careful all the same, picking her way like a tightrope walker along the narrow rail. She would hate to prove him right after all. A warning crack alerted her to danger and a piece of rotting timber fell into the water below, scaring away a black swan swimming nearby.

"It's not worth it!"

She didn't dare turn around.

"It is to me!"

She reached the fallen tree at last and taking care not to overbalance, managed to reach down and pluck an armful of the clustered pink and white blossoms. Now she had only to make her way back along the rail. Another portion of rotting fence broke away as she turned, but she was safely past the danger spot. Only another few feet...She allowed herself to hurry and then she felt the railing sag beneath her. Another moment and she would have been in the water giving a disgraceful exhibition of herself as a wet rat, but Craig had moved fast. No doubt he had been expecting this to happen all along, for he had splashed through the water towards her and caught her in his arms. He waded towards the bank and up on to the grass. Once again he was in no hurry to release her and Alison was caught in a moment of heady excitement that was somehow all mixed up with the sweetness of the cloud of blossom crushed between them. It seemed an age until she came back to reality and he dropped her lightly to the springy grass below.

"You did warn me," she said unsteadily. Then looking down at his dripping shorts and wet legs. "You're soaked—!"

He grinned. "All in the day's work! Last week it was a stray steer that went into the drink and had to be rescued. One thing's for sure, I'll have to repair that fence before I lose any of the stock."

So—he placed her in the same category as the wayward steer, Alison thought resentfully. The wild excitement of the moment fled, blown like a puff of thistledown in the strong wind from the ocean. And just as well too, she told herself, a man like that. There was something about him, a masculine magnetism there was no denying. This was something she hadn't bargained for. She would have to be on her guard against her own feelings from now on.

Presently they were back in the Land Rover and lurching over the hills once again. Alison didn't know whether she was glad or sorry that they were moving back in the direction of the house.

She brought her mind back to what he was saying. "You haven't told me much about yourself—"

The red light flashed on in her mind. "Nothing much to tell." Quickly she ran on. "I'm up in this part of the country on a holiday, happened to run into Mary in Dargaville and we decided to join forces. She was free-wheeling round too, so—"

"A holiday from what? Office, shop? Somehow you don't strike me as an office girl. Let me guess—"

His sideways glance took in the clear tanned skin innocent of make-up, the bright mass of curly coppery-red curls tossing around her forehead. "You worked in the country, right?"

"In a way." He was getting uncannily near the truth.

"Land girl? Or how about a supervisor of correspondence lessons for kids on a back-country farm?"

"Land girl's near enough," she said cautiously. There was no need to explain the exact locality of her duties.

"Brought up in the country, I bet?"

He had caught her off guard. "Does it show so much?"

He flashed her a sideways grin. "Does it ever! The way you handle meal times up at the house. No need to tell you about a sheep farmer's hours—and other things. So don't think you can put anything over me," he was making fun of her of course, nothing more, "because I'm warning you I'll catch you out every time! Your face is a dead giveaway, for one thing!"

Golly, he was on about her expression again, and how could she do anything about that? It wasn't going to be easy to keep her identity a secret from him that was for sure, yet somehow she had lost all desire to escape. What if he did imagine he could see through her deceptions with ease, even guess at her thoughts from the way she looked, she could outwit him. It was a challenge she was beginning to enjoy.

"And you ride to shows and gymkhanas?" His tone was deceptively careless, but now she had her wits about her.

"Oh, that was ages ago, when I was young."

"Young?" His quizzical gaze swept the sensitive young face with its soft lips and downcast eyes. "I thought maybe I could rope you in for the local hunt, you and Banner?"

The temptation to agree was overwhelming, almost, but she forced herself to resist, said on a sigh, "Oh no, I couldn't!"

"I'll change your mind about that one of these days." He seemed quite confident in the matter.

They swept past the swan-shaped lake in its setting of thickly-growing tea-tree and moved on over the hills.

After a time they approached the paddock where Banner was grazing, but alerted to danger, Alison averted her gaze, even though it was an effort to do so.

"You still haven't told me about yourself," he reminded her as they approached the house.

She sent him a glance of mock-exasperation. "What was it you wanted to know?"

"Well, you could fill me in on the important bits like—" his tone softened and she found she was holding her breath, "boy-friends? Any special guy who might be missing you, inclined to follow you up here?"

"Oh, *that*!" She laughed, relieved that the question had not been the one she dreaded—Where exactly did you live before you turned up here, Alison? What place? Which farm? "That's the least of my worries!" and thought how true were the words.

He said quietly, "That's all I wanted to know." Suddenly he frowned angrily. "Hell! Look at those steers! They've broken through from the hill paddocks. The Vasanovichs weren't too particular about their fences. I'll have my work cut out for weeks replacing them."

Alison thought, bless the Vasanovichs and their unreliable ageing fences. At least it had served to change the subject.

"This is quite a big place. What other staff have you?"

There was a glint in his eyes as he raised bronzed well-shaped hands. "Just these."

Alison laughed in spite of herself.

CHAPTER FIVE

SHE PUT PROBLEMS from her mind as they lurched and bumped their way over the rough grassy slopes. He went on to talk of farming matters, of the differences in climate and soil conditions between North and South Islands as affecting sheep-farming, and Alison was content to listen. She didn't really care what he spoke about (so long as it wasn't anything concerning her own affairs) in that rich deep voice that was almost caressing.

When they got back to the house she found two big jars and filled them with puffs of fragile pink and white blossom. The perfume drifted through the house.

Mary had already sliced cold lamb and prepared a green salad for lunch. Alison made a mental note that she and Mary must organise some sort of work programme between them. The thought, however, brought with it a depressing reminder that she was good only for the domestic side of things, or so Craig imagined.

As they sat down to the meal Alison asked Mary, "Did you come to any arrangement with the Vasanovichs?"

Mary smiled her sleepy-eyed smile. "I thought you'd never ask! They're coming to collect me this evening and take me to their place. That is," she threw Craig an enquiring glance, "if it's okay with you?"

"Good as gold."

"So far as I can work out, they're not actually related to me, just connections by marriage, but at least it's something, and won't Grandfather be pleased when he hears about it? They're a distance away, about an

hour's drive, but they didn't seem to worry about it.
They were thrilled to hear from me—nice too."

"Better watch it," Craig warned with his teasing
grin, "four bachelors in one family! You could take
your pick, you wouldn't even need to change your
name!"

Mary laughed. "That's what Frances has been telling
me. I've been helping her to sort out her notes and she
found a Maori proverb to suit the occasion. Something
about the attraction of women. I wasn't very flattered,
actually."

"What was it?" Alison enquired.

Mary helped herself to salad. "I can't remember the
Maori words, but it all boiled down to 'A handsome
man will not be sought after, but even a plain woman
will be run after eagerly.'"

"You never know your luck," Alison said demurely.
"After all, it's bachelor territory up here."

Immediately she regretted the words. Who wouldn't,
with Craig throwing her that quizzical make-of-it-what-
you-like look?

"Frances is determined to come down to the dining
room tomorrow," Mary reported. "She says she can
keep her leg up on a stool. She seems to think she's
missing out on things, being stuck up there in the bedroom."

"That's an idea," Alison said. "She could rest up
here just as well."

"And keep her finger on things," put in Craig. "It
might be an idea at that, save a devil a lot of hawking
trays around all day."

He's thoughtful too, Alison told herself, then brought
her thoughts up with a jerk. Too! What was she thinking? Merely because he chanced to be attractive in a
rugged, take-it-or-leave-it sort of way that was no reason
for her to keep thinking about him. She took herself
firmly in hand. He's not for you. Remember, Craig
Carter is the one man in the world with whom you can't
afford to be friendly.

That afternoon Craig went down to the stockyards to draft cattle. From the window Alison caught glimpses of him as he rode amongst the black mass of steers. She could see the dust rising, hear the crack of a stockwhip above the barking of dogs and lowing of cattle. Nothing would have pleased her more than to slip a saddle and bridle on Banner and gallop down to the stockyards to help, but she knew there were duties here at the house. The children would be coming in from school. There was a pile of ironing waiting in the big Ali Baba basket in the laundry, empty cake tins in the cupboard.

Mary had moved Mrs. Carter down to the living room and settled her in a low wing chair. "Now this is much better," Mrs. Carter observed with satisfaction. "I hate being shut away in the bedroom and I can keep the old leg up on a cushion just as well out here. It will save you girls running after me all the time too. Craig will tell you I'm just moving down because I can't bear to miss anything that's going on. He might be right at that, but it isn't every day I have two nice girls to talk to—or Craig either. If only it wasn't for—" She broke off on a sigh. "Oh well, there's no sense in worrying about things you can't do anything about." Reluctantly she picked up a shapeless piece of knitting. "Suppose I'll have to do a bit of this, but it's so frustrating. I'm sure the folk who invent knitting patterns deliberately make them difficult to follow. Look at this, Mary," she regarded the work distastefully, "did you ever see such a mess?" She jerked angrily at a gaping hole that promptly ran down the rows of stitches.

Mary took it from her. "If you don't mind my helping—"

"Take the darned thing and fix it for me, will you?"

"I'll have to undo it from the beginning."

"I don't mind."

Mary's tone was puzzled. "What exactly is it supposed to be?"

"A suit for a toddler. These are the pants, believe it or not."

Mary was carefully unravelling the shapeless piece of knitting. "If you could start over again using smaller needles? I could help you if you'd let me?"

"Let you? My dear girl, I'd be delighted. I wouldn't have started the wretched thing except that I promised my niece I'd do it. It will never turn out looking like it's supposed to, they never do. I just keep on hoping and trying." An expression of delight crossed Frances Carter's face. "But if you did it? I mean, who's to know?"

Mary smiled her slow smile. "It's a thought. Then you'd be free to concentrate on your Maori proverbs."

"Now," said Mrs. Carter happily, "you're talking. Pass me my pad, will you?"

Alison, coming into the room with a cup of tea, made to place it on a low table when a photo album fell to the floor. "Sorry." She picked up a coloured picture and found herself looking into Craig's smiling face. How strange to see him in evening dress and how tall and attractive he looked. Her gaze moved to the girl at his side...strong features, a flashing smile.

"That's Craig and Jo," Frances was saying.

"Jo?" Something stronger than herself prompted Alison to say quickly. "Is he—are they—"

"Oh no, they're not serious about each other, not any longer." She broke off. "At least, I hope not. It's all over as far as I know—but then," she grinned rakishly, "mothers are always the last to hear of anything in the romantic line from their sons. Oh, they'll run on for hours about some deadly dull thing like top-dressing paddocks or the price of mutton, but ask them anything about girl-friends and they'll clam up immediately. I've given up trying long ago."

Mary came to Alison's side to peer over her shoulder. "Looks as though it was taken on board ship."

"It was," Frances told her, "the *Oriana*. Craig had gone over to England on a study course, brushing up on wool markets, buyers in all parts of the world, all sorts of business I never can get the hang of. Then on the way back from London he met Jo. She's nice enough in her own way when things are going along just as she wants them, but she'd never make a sheep farmer's wife, not in a hundred years. She stayed with us for quite a while just after she and Craig arrived back in this country. Almost a year ago now, it was.

"Not a great success, actually. It turned out she was much more at home on board ship with all the parties and dancing and fun than she was on a way-back sheep station. She was a city girl and she hated everything about the country from the start, especially the isolation. But she liked Craig a lot, so she set about trying to make him give up the land and put his capital into a tourist motel in a fashionable beach resort up the coast. Can you imagine Craig in that setting? I could have told her at the beginning she hadn't a hope, that you can't push Craig into things, it only makes him go the other way. Anyway, she didn't have a chance of changing his ideas. He's a born man of the land, a *tangata whenua* as the Maoris say. But she gave it a good try, I'll give her that. Three months she stayed with us and she never let up for a moment."

She chuckled. "She never got any forrarder either! She even asked me to put in a word on her side about making Craig give up the station property. I told her straight that I haven't been able to make Craig do anything he didn't want to since he left boarding school, and that's quite a few years ago. Not that she didn't try other methods too. She could wheedle anything she wished for out of her parents and she can be quite charming when it pleases her, but even that didn't work. All that charm didn't make a scrap of difference to Craig. Sometimes," Frances mused, "I wondered if he really cared enough to make sacrifices. Anyway, one night they had a blazing row and the next morning Jo left the house saying she was never coming back. It was shortly after that that Craig decided to sell out and move up to the north, and the last I heard of Jo was that she had got herself a position as hostess on a cruise ship and had gone away on a world cruise lasting about six months. Shove the picture back in the album, will you, love? It doesn't matter where, it's out of date now anyway. At least, I hope it is. I did hear a rumour that she'd met someone on the cruise ship, an Australian, and they were expected to team up together. Perhaps they're married by now.''

Alison, pushing the picture out of sight between the pages, found herself echoing Mrs. Carter's wish.

That night at dinner the two children were subdued and clearly on their best behaviour. Both left their plates clean.

Mrs. Carter, the tea-tray balanced on her ample thigh, was delighted. "They never eat their vegies without a fuss as a rule," she told Alison. "It must be the way you cook them, so green and appetising. They're good kids really.''

"Good!'' exploded Craig. "Can't you see they're putting on a show, hoping they won't cop it for what they did to Mary this morning?''

Mary said, repressing a shudder, "It wasn't all that bad.''

"Just a weta crawling around on your pillow,'' Craig's tone was grim. "If ever I catch you kids at that trick again I'll dock your pocket money for a month and cancel the order for those two ponies that are due to come along around Christmas time. Bad enough if it had been Alison, but to pick on Mary—''

Alison felt a stab of resentment. What was so special about Mary? The other girl was looking mystified.

"Why me?''

"Ask yourself! Alison's a country girl, it sticks out a mile. It would take more than a couple of wetas to throw her.''

Her heart lifted on a wave of relief and her bright smile flashed. "I'm not all that fond of them, especially walking around on my pillow. Yuck!''

"What sort of things are you scared of Alison?'' queried Patrick with his deceptively innocent gaze.

"Spiders? I know where there's a—" The childish tones died away beneath Craig's warning look.

Presently as the two girls were clearing away the dinner dishes a loud knock sounded on the door, and a few moments later Craig came back into the room accompanied by two men. Tall and powerfully built with dark eyes, the two men were obviously brothers, although one appeared much younger than the other.

"Mate Vasanovich," the older man introduced himself, "and this is my young brother Nick." Soon everyone was talking at once. Alison mused that the one named Nick had a pleasant face and a warm smile, but she wished he would lift his gaze from her face. His obvious interest in herself was becoming a trifle embarrassing. It was a relief to hear Mate say, "If you're ready, Mary, we'll get cracking right away. Mama's pretty impatient waiting at home. She's in a hurry to catch up with all the family news."

Mary said with a smile, "If we are family."

"Either way we'll have fun sorting things out," said Mate with his booming laugh. "You coming, Nick?"

Reluctantly his brother moved with him towards the door. "Be seeing you... Alison." The lingering backward glanced he tossed over his shoulder lent meaning to the commonplace phrase.

It was late when Mary returned to the house. As she tiptoed into the bedroom Alison switched on the bedside lamp. "Had a good time?" she asked sleepily. Then, becoming aware of Mary's air of subdued excitement, "You did, I can see by your face." She sat up in bed blinking a little, hands clasped around her knees. "How did you get on? Were they really your own people?"

Dropping to the end of the bed, Mary pulled a comb from her hair and the long black strands tumbled around her shoulders. "In a way."

"How do you mean, in a way?"

"Oh, they were relatives, but only by marriage. Someone's aunt married an uncle of mine." She seemed abstracted. "Connections, they call it, don't they?"

Alison was fully awake now. "All the better! Won't your grandfather be pleased at that news! Now you can get married any time you like. You can take your pick! Or didn't you like the Vasanovich men?"

"Oh, I liked them all right, especially Tony."

"Tony?" Alison queried.

"He's one of the older brothers. Trained for years to be a lawyer and got all his qualifications. Now he's given it all up to come back to the land with the others. Tony's really something, I could like him a lot, but marriage is out, even if it did happen by some wild chance that things worked out that way. It just wouldn't be possible, not for me."

Alison looked puzzled. "Why ever not? Don't they like you, the family? I suppose they made you feel an outsider, a stranger who's trying to burst in on the clan?"

Mary stared at her. "They were just the opposite. They just couldn't have made more of a fuss of me! You've no idea. Talk about a family gathering! There were relations from Dargaville and all over the district. So many people in the room you could scarcely move. Anyone would have thought I was visiting royalty, the way they treated me. And the supper—I've never seen so much food laid on for a social gathering. The wine was flowing too, heady stuff. Papa Vasanovich makes it himself. He told me he adds extra sugar to make it more potent, and I can well believe it. By the way, the young one, Nick, kept asking me about you—where you came from, how long you're staying here. He's going to ring you, he said. I think he got extra interested after I told him that you do all the cooking around here. The parents were nice, awfully kind; they kept asking me to move over there and stay as long as I liked."

"What did you say?"

Mary laughed. "Told them to ask me again in a

month when Craig's mother is on her feet again, if they still want me around by then."

"Thank heaven for that!" Alison breathed a sigh of relief. She had all at once realised how much she would miss Mary were the other girl to move away.

"They told me," Mary was saying, "that they'll move away to a small house in Dargaville once the boys are married—"

"Oh, they've got hopes, then?"

"Hopes! I got the feeling they had me lined up for the altar already! Especially the old grandmother—"

"Grandmother!" Alison burst into a peal of laughter. "What has she got to do with it, even if she has ideas of matchmaking?"

"Matchmaking is a mild way of putting it." Mary was slipping out of her garments and donning cool cotton pyjamas. "I guess you can't blame her altogether. She told me that she came out to New Zealand as a mail-order bride herself. The marriage was arranged long before she ever set foot in the country. Marriageable girls were scarce up here in the gumlands in those days."

"They still are," Alison remarked smilingly.

"Unfortunately."

"Unfortunately?" Alison settled back against the pillows. "You've got to be joking. I still can't see why you're so upset about the grandmother and her marriage-making plans, if it's true."

"It's true all right. You didn't see the way she was looking at me all evening, sizing me up. I could just about feel her mind ticking over, imagine her saying to herself, 'Now here's a nice marriageable girl for one of our men. Yugoslav too, or near enough.' I could tell exactly what she was thinking. Would this girl make a good wife? Can she cook a man-sized meal? And those slim hips, not the best for child-bearing. You should have heard the questions she asked me! Why wasn't I married by now? Had I any special man in view? All that stuff. Oh, Grandmother Vasanovich doesn't dodge around a subject, she asks you things straight out!" Her eyes twinkled. "And she got some straight answers!"

A glimmer of mischief lighted the sleepy eyes. "Maybe I should have invented a conveniently absent fiancé just for self-protection. I'll need something in that line if I'm going there again. I got the feeling all the time I was there that they're determined to make me one of the family, one way or another. I'm sure they're longing for an excuse to put on a big party with me as the star, and invite their relatives. It wouldn't surprise me," Mary added wryly, "if they hadn't arranged for their own band to play at the wedding already. It would be a chance for them all to wear their national costumes and dance all night. Never mind about the bride. Any nice girl would do."

Alison burst into laughter. "You're dreaming it all up! Anyway, supposing the grandmother did happen to be looking you over as prospective wife material for one of her grandsons, what does it matter?"

"Matter? You haven't met her! In that family there's only one head of the tribe, and guess who it is? What she says goes. You can tell that just by meeting them."

"Oh well," Alison offered mildly, "it couldn't make any difference to you, how could it?"

"You'd be surprised at the difference it could make!" Mary's voice was low and tense. "Even if, I'm just saying *if*, I got to like one of those Vasanovich men and he wanted to marry me, how could I be sure that he really wanted me for myself? That he wasn't just doing what suited the family?"

Alison's lips twitched. "I guess you'd just know, you'd feel—"

"Perhaps." Mary's tense look faded and she slipped between the sheets. "What on earth are we arguing about?" She slanted Alison a crinkly-eyed smile. "The trouble with this place is there are too many bachelors, and girls are like gold-dust."

"I know," Alison agreed happily. "Fun, isn't it?"

THE THOUGHT DRIFTED with her into sleep. She was glad she'd come here in spite of Craig Carter and his annoying habit of delving into her personal life.

She was awakened at some time through the night, alerted by an unfamiliar sound—a scraping from somewhere in the house. Could one of the twins have woken up and decided to explore the house in the early hours? As she fled along the passage she glimpsed a light still burning in the small room Craig called his office, but the slight noise seemed to emanate from somewhere at the opposite end of the house. A swift peep into the children's room showed two dark heads on the pillows. Then the noise came again and she decided it must be in the lounge. Flinging open the door, she pressed the switch and light streamed into the room, pinpointing a woodbox beside the open fireplace, a box that was apparently moving along the floor of its own accord. Even as she approached it, however, a furry animal leaped out, making for the fireplace, and a moment later a bushy tail disappeared up the chimney.

It was the sound of footsteps that made her swing around, coppery curls tumbling around her forehead. Craig too was eyeing the soot falling from the chimney.

"A possum. It must have come down the chimney from the big apricot tree outside. I'll get a gun." Already he had turned away. "You go outside and keep an eye on him. This is one year the possums aren't going to get away with stripping that tree. The Vasanovichs warned me about that."

All at once Alison was conscious of shortie-pyjamas and tousled hair. Oh well, he didn't seem to *see* her as a person, his mind was on the possum. He was always giving orders—"Don't walk on the fence," "Go outside and keep an eye on him," do this, do that. Nevertheless she went to the front door and wrenched it open. Outside moonlight silvered sloping lawns and flowering shrubs. She stood still gazing up at the spreading tree close by. Surely that darker patch of shadow high above was moving.

"Is he still up there?" Craig hurried towards her, rifle in his hand, and she wrenched her mind back to the marauding possum. Had the dark patch melted away under her eyes? Now she could see no specially dark shadow amongst the high branches with their hanging fruit. Or was it that she was finding it hard to concentrate, something to do with the disturbing nearness of the man at her side? There was something about him that threw her into a tizzy. She would have to take herself in hand and do something about it, *if she could*.

"Too late!" He was still scanning the big tree. "He's got away."

Alison felt sneaky sympathy for the possum. "If you like I'll get a ladder in the morning and pick all the ripe fruit, beat the birds and...the...possums." Her voice died away and something seemed to be happening to her pulses. It was the silence. She could feel him looking down at her and even in the moonglow she could swear that his mouth had that quizzical twist. His mouth...his lips...He bent and kissed her full on the mouth. She had never known a kiss could be like this. The star-ridden sky seemed to explode in sudden radiance and it was quite a time before she could concentrate on his deep tone. "That's for helping."

His voice wasn't dictatorial any more, but husky and sort of...loving. Was it the moonshine that made his eyes so dark and brilliant? She murmured unsteadily, "I didn't do anything."

"You did, you know." Abruptly he released her. He said in an odd tone she couldn't interpret, "Better go inside, Alison."

It was only later, on the verge of sleep, that she wondered what it was Craig had been referring to. Did he mean her helping out with Frances? Or the possum? What odds, the wild sweet excitement stayed with her. All that mattered was that he did like her after all.

CHAPTER SIX

IN THE MORNING Alison was up and about early, but Craig had already left the house. She caught a glimpse of him mounted on one of the station hacks, riding over a ridge. Now she was free to ride Banner. What bliss to take saddle and bridle from the harness shed and be off over the paddocks! She wouldn't use her own saddle, it might pinpoint her as a show-jumper. A few minutes later she was carrying the riding gear from the stables and climbing the rise towards the paddock at the back of the house.

The mare saw her coming and nickered softly as she came trotting up to the gate. "Here's your carrot!" Soon Alison was slipping the bit into Banner's mouth and throwing a fluffy white sheepskin over the broad back. A swift glance towards the hills told her that the boss was out of sight. She put Banner to the gate and the mare gathered herself up and rose effortlessly. Then they were away, racing up sheep-nibbled slopes, clearing seven-barred fences and dropping down on the other side while sheep scattered before them in panic and steers pelted away from the flying hooves, with the wind surging in her ears and the early morning sun gilding the tops of the sandhills.

Exhilarated and for some reason extraordinarily happy, at last she took Banner back to her paddock, brushed her down and with a parting pat, left to attend to more mundane duties in the house like seeing the twins off to school and taking Mrs. Carter her breakfast. It was all becoming so routine. Strolling down the tree-shaded path, a bridle jingling from her arm, she mused that it was almost as if she belonged here she felt so much at home. She simply couldn't understand it.

Once back in the house, however, she had little time to dwell on anything but the matter in hand. For the children had no sooner waved her goodbye and gone down to the road below to wait for the school bus than Craig arrived back. She could hear him in his office making telephone calls.

She was alone in the kitchen when he came in, a different Craig this from last night. Now he was wrapped up in his work, involved in timetables for the coming week.

"Hi, Alison, how's breakfast?"

From the sink bench she glanced up to meet his smile—but she need not have concerned herself, she thought wryly. Clearly he wasn't thinking of her or of last night, only of the day's programme. What was a kiss anyway? Aloud she murmured, "Bacon and tomatoes coming up in a few minutes."

"Not quite ready? No matter—I'll get back on the blower. I've just got word over the grapevine that the shearers are due over the road today, but there's been a cancellation, so I'll book them up here for tomorrow."

He was back in a few minutes, helping himself from a big pot of tea and peering into the pan Alison was stirring on the electric range. "Hmm, smells good—I've jacked up things for an early start in the morning. With a full gang the boys bring their own cook with them, but when it's only a matter of a few stragglers to be shorn, the gang can meal at the house. The old lady'll fill you in about all that." He was eyeing her hopefully, expectantly. "Can do?"

"Oh dear, Craig," Mrs. Carter must have excellent hearing, Alison thought, to have caught the words from the dining room, "It's an awful lot to ask of her, all that extra work. I'm afraid she hasn't an idea of what it means. Working against time as they do, the men drink gallons of tea—and eat! If only I wasn't stuck here out of action."

"Not to worry." Just in time Alison remembered that she hadn't let on to Craig how experienced she happened to be when it came to cooking for a shearing gang. Evidently there were only two shearers due to arrive at the shed tomorrow and not the full gang. Sternly she repressed the smile that twitched the corners of her mouth. "I'll try," she murmured demurely.

"Sweet corn fritters," boomed Mrs. Carter from the adjoining room. "That's what I always fall back on for the shearers. I make piles of them and put them in the deep freeze until they're needed. And are they appreciated by a Maori shearing gang!"

"It's an idea." Already Alison was switching on the oven elements on the electric range.

"The pressure's on," she told Mary later in the day. "A couple of shearers are due to start work in the shed first thing in the morning and that means they'll need gallons of tea and lashings of scones or fritters or sandwiches or what have you for smokos."

"Smokos?" queried Mary.

"Tea breaks to you. They really work, those men. Wait until you take a look at them in action tomorrow."

"You're the one who's working," Mary pointed out as she helped Alison to beat up yet another basin of batter. "All those mountains of corn fritters! The shearers couldn't possibly eat them all."

Alison wiped a hand across her hot forehead, leaving a long smear of flour. "You'd be surprised. We'd better whip up another batch just to make sure."

Indeed, when at smoko the next morning Mary carried down to the shearing shed a tray laden with a massive teapot, cups, scones and fritters, she realised the need for food to working men in the ceaseless activity of the shed. The strong Maori men with smiling pleasant faces and bulging muscles under black work singlets were working at pressure in the heat of the shed. Sweating shoulders bent, each man grappled with a hefty sheep, slicing steadily through an oily fleece, then the sheep was sent down a chute and another one brought in from the holding paddock outside. Another dark-skinned New Zealander was busy sewing up the great filled bales, marking them with the black stencil indicating the farm from which the wool had come. Even while Mary watched, the noise of the machines stopped and in the sudden quiet the shearers straightened their backs and smilingly greeted Mary.

"How did you get on?" Alison asked her when she returned to the house.

She was wide-eyed. "It looks so exhausting, working at pressure like that. And the heat! I can see what you mean now about the shearers needing lots of food to replace the energy they're using up in that job—" She broke off. "There was one thing I couldn't understand, though. Just as I came in the door someone yelled at the top of his voice, 'Sixty-nine!' but there weren't that many sheep shorn, so it couldn't have been a tally."

Alison couldn't suppress the laughter. "They've got a language all their own," she explained when she could talk again, "and 'sixty-nine' referred to you."

"Me?"

"It's the traditional shearers' signal when a woman comes in to the shed. Means something like 'watch your language, mate.'"

Now it was Mary's turn to laugh. "So that was it! Gentlemen of the shearing shed! What next?"

On the second day, as suddenly as it had begun, shearing was finished. The big shed, slippery underfoot with the oil of the fleeces, was empty and the two cheerful shearers were paid their wages, then piled their gear on the back of their battered truck and drove away to their next assignment.

Craig came into the house in the afternoon, flipped his sunhat across the room, where it landed on the dresser. "You need a break, Alison." He studied her thoughtfully. "You did say you could ride?"

For once she remembered to school her eager voice, "A bit."

"Good. That's good enough for me! I'm driving some cattle over the sandhills today. There's a place over the dunes where I can put them to graze for a while. Care to come along and give me a hand?"

Would she care to do just that? Her heart gave a crazy upsurge and she didn't dare glance towards him for fear he would catch the excitement in her face. Aloud she murmured, "If you think I can help?"

He nodded. "That's settled, then." She might just as well have been a farm hand employed around the place for all he thought about her personally. "I've got the steers all ready to shift." He added carelessly, "Better bring along your swim-suit and we'll take a dip on the way back along the beach."

Alison was half way to the door already. "I'll go and get Banner saddled up."

"That's my girl!"

Was it the matter-of-fact words that warmed her heart or something in his tone?

She sped past Pedro, Craig's station hack tied to the railings, and soon with the ease of long practice she had saddled her white mare. She was riding down to the house when Mary came hurrying into the yard. "Alison, wait! A message for you! It came over the phone just now. It's from Nick—you met him the other night with Mate. He's going to a barbecue tonight at a friend's place and wants to take you with him. He's holding the line. Shall I say—"

"You can tell him to forget it!" It was Craig at his most authoritative. Lightly he mounted his horse. "Alison can't talk to him now. She's giving me a hand with the steers, taking them over the sandhills to the other side. We could be quite a time, mightn't be back until late. You can tell him that too. Got it, Mary?"

"Yes, I guess so, but—"

"Right! We're on our way! See you!" He turned on the rein and wheeled away.

He might have asked me, Alison thought as she fell in beside him, but she didn't really mind. For who

could waste time on thoughts of young Nick when one
was with Craig? Just being with him put a sparkle into
the day.

Presently they were driving the long line of cattle up
the slopes. The steers seemed bent on wandering off in
all direcions, but the dogs were well trained and strays
were swiftly brought into line with the heaving black
mass. In the clear atmosphere the flack of Craig's
stockwhip sang in the air above the lowing of cattle. He
hadn't merely been talking, Alison realised, when he
had told her he needed help in shifting the steers. Forgetting she was supposed to be an indifferent rider, she
was soon galloping off in pursuit of a fleeing black beast
or wheeling suddenly to head off a recalcitrant steer.
Seated on Banner, she opened one gate after another,
and all the while the vast dunes, their drifting sand
borne towards them on the prevailing wind, were becoming nearer. After a time they passed by the swan-
shaped lake in its tea-tree setting, but today she had no
time to pause to admire the black swans fleeing majesti-
cally towards deeper water, nor to seek the source of
the perfume of cabbage tree blossom—sweet, pervad-
ing, elusive—that filled the air around them.

"Head them off this way!" Craig called, and she
urged Banner up a precipitous slope and down the
other side while steers hurried ahead and the dogs ran
around cutting out stragglers. They were approaching
long symmetrical lines of pines, moving on to the sand
dunes where marram grass clung to the slopes and the
wind was endlessly blowing. The drifts of sand were
deeper now, slowing down the pace of horses and
steers as they plodded over hot sand. Already Alison's
eyes were stinging and her hair felt gritty from the
blowing sand, but she didn't mind one bit, not when
she was with Craig, helping him with work she knew
and loved. She became aware that he was eyeing her
with his engaging grin. "Thought you told me you
weren't an experienced rider?"

"Did I?" She floundered in search of some excuse,

came up with, "It's Banner really. She corners so well, responds to every pull of the reins."

"Don't be so modest—" At that moment a steer broke away from the milling throng and he sent the dogs to cut it off and bring it back to the moving mass of black beasts. Plodding along in fine sand, they were making slow progress, but somehow Alison was enjoying the ride, sand in her hair and all. At length they reached a ridge and there below was the misty blue of the Tasman, with its wild coastline and endless expanse of sand. Below on the flats she glimpsed an expanse of lush green grass. Even the steers seemed to take fresh heart at the tempting picture below and rushed headlong down the windswept dunes. At last the cattle were herded through gates and penned in grassy paddocks with their long boundaries of tall macrocarpa pines.

Craig had reined in his mount and was busy with the makings. But the task did not prevent him from gazing towards Alison. It was a look she was finding increasingly difficult to sustain. Was it because she was a girl with a secret, or could it be something more personal, an acute *awareness* of him against which she had no defence? She wrenched her mind back to his deep tones. "We'll take the horses back along the beach. You haven't seen the coast yet, have you?"

She pulled up at his side. "Not yet. Isn't it supposed to be awfully dangerous?"

He finished running tobacco into the flimsy paper and moistened the cigarette with his lips. "You can say that again! There's a terrific current running through the main channel. You can see the rip from here." She followed his gaze to the swiftly-flowing tide. "Not exactly the sort of sea you venture out on in a small boat—come on, let's go!"

They urged their mounts towards the long line of breaking surf and soon they were moving along the shore, the horses' hooves leaving deep imprints in wet and shining sand.

"The blue penguins nest up there," Craig told her,

gesturing towards high sandstone cliffs at their side.
There was nothing to be seen but the tossing sea, and
endless expanse of grey-white sand marked with the
footprints of innumerable seabirds. The wind was
stronger now, salty with the sea tang, and the surf spray
blowing towards them was cool and fresh on her face.
Funny how she felt so content riding along this lonely
shore. They passed by a great bleached log lying sub-
merged in the sand, a sting-ray washed up by the tide,
then skirted a crumpled tangle of rusted iron. "It's an
old wreck," Craig tossed back over his shoulder,
"you'll see them along the coast."

Indeed as they went on Alison realised that the long
expanse of coastline was strewn with bleached timbers
thrown up by the sea. A name-plate that had once belonged to a foundered launch, a splintered mast, a
rusted anchor protruding from the sand which fortunately Banner caught sight of in time to avert an accident. It was the loneliest place she had ever seen,
nothing but sea and sky and sand, yet still the sense of
utter content, the deep inexplicable happiness, persisted.

They had ridden some distance along the wet sand
when a pile of rocks loomed ahead and Craig urged his
mount over the tide-swept boulders. Alison followed
on Banner, then pulled rein to look down in surprise at
the small sheltered bay. Out of the main current the
wind-rippled waters were shining in hot sunshine.

"I thought this would surprise you," Craig said.
"Look up there." She followed his gaze upwards to the
towering trees that lined the bank, their twisting roots
snaking down through the sand. Amongst the leafy
branches was a dazzle of fluffy scarlet blossom. "Pohu-
tukawa's out in flower already. Even for this part of the
country, it's early. Let's hope the Maoris aren't right
with their saying about early flowering."

"You mean that we can expect a long hot summer?"

"Meaning one more drought where we happen to
live."

"Maybe it isn't true," smiled Alison. "We can always ask your mother about it. She's such an authority on Maori proverbs. She's probably well up in legends and sayings as well."

He bent on her his warm grin. "Where do you think I got the story from in the first place? I promised you a swim, remember?"

"I know, I know. I'm so hot and dusty I can scarcely wait to get into that cool water. I brought my swim-suit. I only wish," she added ruefully, "I could wash the sand out of my hair."

"Your hair—" Before she realized his intention Craig reached out his hand. She could feel his touch on the back of her neck, then he was ruffling and blowing copper-red strands. "Has anyone ever told you—"

Suddenly she was confused. "Well then, what are we waiting for?" They tethered the horses on a patch of grass and Alison hurried towards the sheltering bushes growing above the bank. It took only a matter of minutes to change into her brief black bikini, but when she ran down to the sheltered lagoon he was already there, clad in swimming shorts. She hadn't realised his splendid physique. He was like a man carved from bronze, slim yet whipcord-strong. Then he was taking her hand in his and they plunged into the salt water that was deep and crystal clear and, after the first breathless instant, delightfully invigorating.

They swam for quite a time, then floated on their backs. It was very still. Relaxed, Alison gazed up into the shining blue dome above.

"Had enough?"

"Okay."

They splashed through the shallows, then threw themselves down on the warm sand while the sun beat down on them.

Craig's head was dropped on to his crossed arms. Alison stole a glance towards him. The sun was striking lights in his dark hair. He could almost be asleep.

"How come you're so cagey about yourself, Alison?"

She jumped with surprise, then playing for time, she picked up a handful of sand and watched it trickle through her fingers.

"How do you mean?"

"Come on, you know what I mean."

Such a lazy tone, almost uninterested...or was it? "What—do you want me to tell you?"

He rolled over on his stomach and she caught the quizzical gleam in the dark blue eyes. "Whatever you want. Anything, everything! Oh, I know," as she made to speak, "you've been in the country before and you can ride a bit. A bit! And kindly mind your own business, Craig! Is that it?" Even without looking up she was disconcertingly aware of his intent glance. "Anyone would think you had something to hide! Something like a husband?"

"A husband!" The suggestion was so unexpected that she burst out laughing. Or was the laughter born of a sense of relief? "For heaven's sake, whatever gave you that idea?" Wildly she ran on, "You'll be saying next that I'm in hiding from the police. What do you think I've done—robbed a bank, or something? I don't know why you've got all these funny ideas about me."

It seemed he was not to be so easily diverted, "Just a hunch." He challenged her with alive, penetrating eyes. "Your own fault for not being honest with me at the start! Why not come right out with it and admit you've lived on a sheep station before? You didn't turn a hair at laying on meals and all that for the shearers. You know as well as I do that a city girl would have thrown a wobbly at the mere thought of all that."

She said very low, "I didn't say I was a city girl."

"You didn't say anything, remember? But I'll forgive you," he stretched out his hand and drew a gentle line along her cheek. His touch sent a quiver of excitement darting down her spine. "I guess you had your reasons." His voice softened, deepened. "If there's anything that's worrying you, anything at all, you can trust me."

"Oh, I know. I know!" She couldn't think clearly for the dizzy happiness surging through her. The next moment the nagging worry began to crowd in on her once again. "It's nothing," she mumbled in distress, "at least—"

Unexpectedly he laid a bronze finger against her chin, raising her face until she was forced to meet his gaze. "Forget it. No need to spell it out if it worries you all that much." His smile was warm as a caress. "I just want you to know that I'm here if you need me."

She fought the urge to come right out and tell him all she was hiding. And spoil everything? All the brittle happiness she had stumbled on? She forced a smile and said unsteadily, "You mean, a shoulder to cry on?"

"If you like."

Why did it hurt so much to keep a still tongue in her head? He must think she was acting very strangely. Yet to confide in him was unthinkable—him of all men! Because she had to say something to break the silence she murmured very low, "I was brought up in the country. I've been used to housekeeping on a sheep farm, cooking for shearers and all the rest of it."

"I get it," he said, and waited. A question lingered in his eyes. "Isn't there a bit more to it than that?"

"How could there be?"

"Okay, if that's the way you want it!" Did she imagine the frustration in his tone? Impatiently he sprang to his feet and putting out his hand pulled her up beside him. "We'd better get cracking."

All at once she felt helpless, obscurely annoyed with him and angry with herself for being trapped in this impossible situation. She said, "We won't be back late, then? Maybe I could have made the barbecue after all."

He threw her an odd unreadable look, said coolly, "I got the idea we'd had all that out hours ago, decided it was no go."

She met his eyes defiantly. "*You* decided."

He stared at her incredulously. "Are you telling me you wanted to go out with that Nick character?"

Suddenly her throat was tight with defiance and anger. "I wouldn't have minded," she said, and slipped away up the bank to the spot where she had left her garments.

They completed the remainder of the journey back to the house in frustrated silence, the horses splashing through the edge of the breakers and the dogs frisking over flecks of sand blowing on the sand while around them along the empty shoreline, sky, water and land seemed to merge together in a pale no-colour blur.

When they had brushed down their mounts and put away the gear Alison preceded Craig into the house. She was still seething with annoyance towards him and in some obscure way, with herself. It had been such a heavenly outing, just the two of them away in the still hot world of the sandhills and then she had to spoil it all. That was the worst of deception, she reflected on a sigh, it got you into all manner of unpleasant situations you hadn't counted on when you started off under another name, even if it did happen to be your own. Was it possible that Craig had a suspicion of the truth? She was such a hopeless nit when it came to lies and evasions. Could it be he really suspected her of running away from all manner of unpleasant things, ranging from theft and a possible prison sentence to an unwanted husband? At the thought she couldn't help giggling to herself. Oh, Craig, if you only knew! But thank heaven you don't! That would really ruin everything between us. Everything? There was nothing between her and Craig, nothing at all. He was hateful, hateful... questioning her... trying to make her betray herself... probing into her personal affairs. By the time she entered the house she had worked herself into an even deeper sense of resentment.

In the kitchen Mary was peeling potatoes. "Hi, I thought you mightn't be in until late, so I thought I'd get dinner on the way—" She broke off. "What's the matter? Did all that sand get too much for you?"

Alison pulled herself together and forced a smile. "No, no, it was wonderful to see. We even had a dip in the sea. It was super..." Until Craig began his enquiries. Did he really suspect her? He seemed to know she had something to hide.

She wrenched her mind back to Mary's careless tone. "Remember young Nick? He came over here with Mate to collect me when I called at their home the other night."

"Vaguely."

"Well, he remembers you. He couldn't stop talking about you the night I was there with the family. He's really fascinated by you. He's phoned three times today, hoping you'd get back early by some chance."

"I told him I couldn't go to the barbecue with him—"

"Don't tell me, tell him! He just wouldn't take no for an answer, said he'd push his luck and call for you around eight anyway, just hoping. I told him I'd pass on the message, but I didn't give much for his chances."

"You're wrong, you know." Alison could have laughed at the expression of surprise on Mary's face. "I can change my mind, can't I—"

"But Craig—"

"Has nothing to do with my affairs." She rather spoiled the bravado of the statement by adding, "Anyway, he won't be here. He found a fault in the pump this morning and he's going out down to the gully soon to fix it. He said he wouldn't be back until dark." And a good thing too. She just knew that given half a chance Craig would prevent her from going out with Nick. He would invent some urgent task, contrive somehow to stop her going out tonight, heaven only knew why, unless... But he couldn't be jealous of young Nick on her account. It didn't make sense. Unconsciously she sighed.

When she went into the living room she found Craig there with his mother. Frances was telling him how Mary had typed out some pages of the long lists of Maori proverbs she was working on.

"You're lucky, you know," Craig told her. "Without the old leg out of action you'd never have found the time to get on with your bits and pieces."

"Look who's talking!" retorted Frances. "Without the old leg laid up you would never have had Alison to help you take the cattle over the sandhills today."

"That's a point."

But glancing towards his dark inscrutable face Alison got the impression that at this moment the boss wouldn't care where she was so long as she didn't happen to be living right here in his home. And all because she wouldn't, couldn't answer his persistent questioning. For there surely couldn't be any other explanation for his forbidding expression.

Frances' bright brown eyes darted a glance from Craig to Alison. "So that's how it is, you didn't enjoy your ride over the sandhills today?"

"Oh, but I did!" It was the truth. She had been enjoying it—oh, so much, until... All at once she became aware of Craig's enigmatic look and tried to infuse some enthusiasm into her tones. "It was fantasic."

Craig was silent and she heard her own voice running nervously on. "We rode miles and miles over the sand and when we got over the dunes there was this lush green grass with the sea beyond. The view from the top was worth the ride and the sea-breeze blowing on your face was a joy. Just wait until you go there!"

"I will, one of these days," Frances said. "What did you do then?"

It was Craig who answered. "Came back along the beach and had a swim in the bay."

Mrs. Carter's glance rested on her son's face. "You don't seem very excited over your first swim of the season." She grinned her rakish grin. "Maybe it's just a case of *'ma roto hoki kia ora ka paite korero.'*"

"Goodness, whatever's that?" Alison spoke absently. She was still acutely conscious of Craig's firmly-set mouth.

"What she's trying to get through to you," came his sardonic tones, "is 'put the kettle on.'"

"I get it." Alison moved towards the electric jug. "Even if I never ever learn another Maori proverb, I'll have to remember that one."

"That's only Craig's interpretation," his mother told her. "What it really says is, 'if the inner man is refreshed the conversation will be agreeable.'" She was looking at Craig, who had moved to the window and was staring out towards the sheep-threaded hills.

He said grim-lipped, "I wouldn't bet on it."

When dinner was over and the children safely tucked up in their beds, Alison hurried away to get ready for the evening ahead. A quick shower, a light dusting of powder on cheeks still slightly warm from the effects of the hours spent on the sandhills during her afternoon ride with Craig. For a moment she stood motionless facing the mirror. Craig...why couldn't she get him out of her mind?

CHAPTER SEVEN

PRESENTLY SHE WAS READY for the outing, cool and fresh in an embroidered muslin dress that swirled around her ankles, white sandals on her feet. The coppery curls she had tamed into waves with only a few rebellious tendrils escaping around her forehead.

At that moment the doorbell rang and Mary went up the hall to answer it. As Alison came out of her bedroom she caught the eager boyish tones. "Evening, Mary! Tell me, is Alison back yet?"

Alison went along the hall to meet him. "Right here! How are you, Nick?"

"Fine—now." There was a warm glow in the dark eyes, and glancing up at him Alison realised that Nick had taken infinite pains with his appearance. The thick black hair was brushed and shining and around him she caught the perfume of after-shave lotion. "You're coming!" There was no doubting his expression of incredulous delight at sight of her. Indeed it seemed he couldn't take his eyes from her face. "Gee, it's my lucky night!"

"Think so?" She turned away with a smile. "I'll just go and say goodnight to Mrs. Carter." When she returned Mary was chatting with Nick. "You should come along with us," Alison suggested to the other girl, and was aware from a corner of her eye of Nick's transparent expression of dismay.

Mary waved the invitation away with a lift of her hand. "Some other time, maybe. I'm busy here tonight, and besides—" Alison saw Nick's boyish face relax. "Run along you two." And to Nick, "Take care of her." A serious note threaded the light tones. "I'm giving you fair warning. If anything happens to Alison you'll have to answer to the boss."

Nick flung himself around. "What's it to him?" he asked sharply.

"Nothing, nothing," Alison said quickly. "What Mary's getting at is that Craig's all on his own on the place and I can lend him a hand outside. You know? Mustering, boundary riding, all that stuff. I was brought up on a sheep farm." Careful, Alison, don't let yourself get too carried away. "I guess," she said with an odd little pang, "he's just got used to having me around."

Nick looked relieved. "If that's all there is to it. Don't worry," he grinned towards Mary, "I'll take good care of her. Have to," he added with boyish candour. "I've borrowed my brother's new car for the night."

"Borrowed?" Mary flashed him a glimmering secret smile.

"Sort of. He just doesn't know about it yet," Nick admitted. "I thought it was safer to do it this way. Tony's a bit particular about who he lends his car to. He's away somewhere tonight, catching up with someone he knew in town. I'll let him know tomorrow, if he happens to ask. That's what comes of being the eldest of the family," he explained to Alison with a grin. "Tony gets the best of everything. He was the one who was sent to town for a college education. He went through university and came out of it with a degree in law. He was in practice in the city for ages, that's how he came to afford a car like the one I've got tonight, then what does he do but throw it all up and come back to join the rest of us on the farm! Not that he isn't a heck of a help when it comes to keeping the books and records, and we could do with an extra hand around the place—guess he's told you the story, Mary? You two seemed to have a lot to talk about the other night?"

"That's right." For the first time Alison saw Mary uneasy and clearly at a loss for words. Why, she was actually colouring, Mary who had always seemed so coolly in command of her emotions. Could she and Tony possibly—She shook the thought away.

"You say Tony's away seeing someone?" Mary was speaking diffidently, as though the words were being dragged from her lips. "I didn't know," she said very low, "that Tony had a special girl-friend."

"Old Tony—a girl-friend!" Nick broke into a chuckle. "If he has he keeps her pretty well hidden away. No, you're way off beam there. A guy from town called him up and they took off for a day's shooting further up country."

"Oh, I see." Could this be Mary, marvelled Alison, with this swift change of mood? For now her eyes were shining and even her voice was different, light and happy. "I just wondered." The next moment she was back to the placid-natured girl Alison had come to know. "I'll see you off." Opening the front door, she peered outside, taking in the long red car illuminated in the light from the passage. "So that's Tony's car. It's awfully opulent-looking, isn't it?"

"It's a beaut!" Enthusiasm rang in his tones. "I took her out for a burn the other night, got away with it while Tony was out. On the open road you can really put your foot down. You wouldn't believe the speed I hit—" Catching Mary's glance, he broke off. "It's okay, I told you I'd take good care of Alison."

"You'd better," warned Mary. "I don't envy you facing up to Craig if any harm came to her."

"Goodness, what is all this?" Alison broke in with a teasing smile. "We're only going to a barbecue, not a speedway meeting. Come on, let's go!"

Outside an amethyst haze lay over the hills. There was no sound but the melancholy lowing of the steers. As they strolled down the drive Nick sent her a warm sideways glance. "Gee, you look great!"

"Thanks." But she wasn't really listening. She was scanning the shadowed scene in search of Craig. She should be relieved that he hadn't yet returned to the house, yet somehow she wasn't. For what satisfaction was there in gaining a victory over one's opponent when the enemy wasn't at hand to be made aware of his defeat?

Soon they were seated in the shining vehicle, lurching down the winding path from the house. She slipped out of the car to open gates and close them again and presently they were on the curving grey metal road where raw cuttings slashed the darkened hillsides. As they sped on shadows lengthened in the blue dusk and tops of cabbage trees were black spears cut sharply against the lemon afterglow of sunset. She suspected that Nick was engrossed in the powerful car he was driving, enjoying the sensation of speed.

"Where are we going?" she asked.

"Turner, the name is. It won't take long to get there. It's not far."

She threw him a laughing sideways glance. "Like ten miles?"

"Eleven, actually."

Dust rose behind them as they sped on, car lights sweeping in an arc over the road ahead and playing over dustcoated bush. She caught a swift glimpse of lake waters at the side of the road, then they were moving on at speed, sweeping between banks of tall tea-tree sombre in the shadows.

Presently they fell into a companionable silence. She suspected that to Nick having her here with him was sufficient to make the evening a success. As for herself, the adoring sideways glance he sent her every now and then was comforting to her battered ego. Now had it been Craig who had been her companion tonight probably by now, in that disturing way of his, he would be shooting questions at her. Questions to which she had no answers, or at least none that she could confide to him. Why was she thinking of him all this time anyway? To divert her mind she said to Nick, "How come you haven't got a car of your own?"

For a moment he was silent. "I—well...thing is I had a prang a couple of weeks ago, put the car out of action. It was a bit of a write-off."

She was only half listening. "You weren't hurt in the crash?"

"Good grief, no! I'm used to them, I guess. It was the old jalopy that let me down, but," his tone lightened, "I'm picking up another one next week, an English job." She knew by his animated tone that she had sparked off a subject that promised to keep him happily engrossed for some time, leaving her free to pursue her own thoughts.

Darkness had fallen when at last they rounded a curve and came in sight of a ranch-style house set high on a rise. Lights streamed from wide-open doors and windows and wisps of smoke were rising from a flare-lighted enclosure in the shelter of tall trees. Nick sped up the winding driveway and soon they were being warmly welcomed by a group of young people who came hurrying towards them. "You're just in time, Nick!" In the chatter and laughter she failed to catch the various names, but there was no doubting the warmth of the welcome extended towards her. Clearly in numbers the men far outnumbered girls, and she wondered if that could be the reason why she was suddenly in such demand, everyone pressing her to glasses of wine or dips or tiny savouries.

Presently they all moved to a grassy spot sheltered by high native trees, tea-tree and ferns. Smoke was rising from a barbecue area where benches and long wooden tables were set out on the grass. The girls had brought bowls of rice, salad and garlic bread and the men were soon busy cooking lamb chops, sausages and potatoes in foil. Later someone plucked at a banjo and voices rose in the songs of the day. All at once in a silence a guitar sobbed out a haunting Maori melody that brought a mist to her eyes. Was it because it made her think of Craig...always Craig?

"What's wrong?" Nick, his young face flushed from

the heat of the glowing coals, came hurrying towards her.

She put on her brightest smile. "It's the guitar music. It always does things to me."

Nick nodded. "I know what you mean. He's not bad, Kevin. Never had any lessons either." His gaze went to a young man whose fair head was bent over the guitar. "He's a natural—hey, what would you like to eat? Chops? Steak? Sausages? Just say the word. Don't be put off by the look of the bananas. They may look repulsive, but with a dab of ice cream and brandy poured over them you'd be surprised how good they are!"

"It doesn't matter. Just bring me something—anything, I don't mind." Alison knew it would be difficult to force herself to eat the food. Somehow for her the evening wasn't going at all well and it was all her own fault. She stood in the shadows, only half aware of the chatter and laughter echoing around her. It wasn't Nick's fault that right from the start she had been conscious of a heaviness of spirit she couldn't understand. Why couldn't she enjoy herself here like the others? She was away from household chores with Mary well able to see to Frances, and the twins if need be. She should be feeling as free as the air—yet perversely her mind kept reverting to the house on the hill. Craig would be back there now. What would be his reaction to her taking off to enjoy herself, defying his orders and doing what she pleased instead of meekly agreeing to his demands? Enjoying herself? Of course she was, in a way. *You're not and you know it. Without Craig everything seems deadly flat, to have no real meaning.* Even when he's being overbearing and demanding he still makes life...interesting. Nothing seems to register without him. I wish I were there to see his face when he finds out that I've gone out with Nick. Anyone would think he was violently jealous of young Nick. I wish he were. I wish he cared enough for me to be jealous. Where were her thoughts leading her? She couldn't love him—or could she? The truth came with devastating impact. To think she had really imagined that she could make her own way, plan her life the way she wanted it. *The way she wanted it!* Now she had fallen in love, deeply, irrevocably, hopelessly with man who regarded her as no more than a help on the farm. Worse, with a certain degree of suspicion. The stern lines of his face came back to her. Oh, she should have known, that first kiss should have told her what was happening. A kiss that he had no doubt already forgotten.

I wish I could forget. No, I don't. I wish he would care for me, love me, so that when I confessed to him who I really am, he'd trust me, believe me when I explained to him that coming to his home was a sheer accident, that I had no idea it was his property that day I walked in with Mary.

"Don't you like it here?" Nick's anxious tones jerked her from her reflections. His soft dark eyes regarded her with concern. "They're a good crowd really. They won't mind if you're a bit shy."

Shy! If only that were the reason for her lack of animation. Evidently she wasn't very skilful at disguising her feelings for some time later, though the gathering showed no sign of breaking up for hours yet, Nick whispered: "Had enough? Shall I take you home?"

She nodded agreement and with a murmured farewell to their hostess they slipped away to the car. It was funny, Alison mused as they shot down the winding drive and lurched into the dark deserted road, that she didn't much care how fast they travelled so long as she was going back to Craig, besotted idiot that she was! Lost in aching longing, she was scarcely aware of the fragment of road unfolding ahead in the glare of the headlamps as they sped up dark slopes and hurtled down again on the other side. After travelling along a flat road for some distance they approached a cone shaped hill. They were nearing the top of the rise when she became aware of a continuous blaring from a car horn from somewhere in the darkness ahead.

"Nick, stop!" A premonition of danger sharpened

her tone. "Slow down, *please!*" But it was too late. They swept over the top of the hill straight into the midst of cattle milling over the roadway. The crashing metal echoed above the frantic lowing of steers as the car was jolted to a violent stop and Alison felt herself flung forward. The safety belts saved them, she realised a moment later, from being flung out on to the road.

She could feel the trembling of Nick's arm against her own, hear his distressed cry, "Alison! Alison! Are you all right?"

"Yes, yes!"

Still he kept repeating the words, seemingly not able to take in her answer. Dazedly she realised that another car was approaching, pushing its way forward between the groups of terrified cattle moving over the roadway. A few moments later the vehicle was pulling up beside them and Craig was leaping out, wrenching open the door of the crumpled car. "Alison!" His tones were hoarse with feeling. "You're not hurt?"

"No—"

"If you only knew what it means to me to hear that, my darling—"

"She's okay, we both are." Nick appeared to have recovered his wits. "It's the car—"

"To hell with the car!" She had never heard Craig's voice so harsh and forbidding. "Didn't you hear my warning?"

Nick said uneasily, "There was something—"

"Only you were going too fast to pull up in time *with Alison in the car with you!*" Roughly he jerked him forward. "Get out!"

"TAKE MY CAR," he rasped. "Stop at the first house you come to and rustle up a couple of men. Tell them to bring dogs with them and torches and to get up here *fast!*"

"Can do. I'll come back and give you a hand with the stock."

"You!" Craig's scathing tone implied a cold contempt for the younger man. He bent to take a flashlight from his car. "I'll patrol the road until the others get here. Now *get going* before there's another smash-up!"

Nick said, shamefaced, "I'm on my way. Coming, Alison?"

"No!" Craig's tone brooked no argument. "Alison stays here with me! I'm letting you have my car, but I'm not trusting you with Alison. Not now—or ever. Get it?"

Without another word Nick stumbled towards the car and got behind the wheel. Headlamps of the turning vehicle pinpointed two badly injured cattle lying nearby, then lighted the shattered glass on the road and the other car slewed around at an angle, its bonnet crumpled. As Nick slowly moved amongst the panicky cattle she had a moment's apprehension. What if he were more affected by the accident than he realised? "Do you think he'll make it?"

"He'd better." Craig's tone was grim.

"He didn't know you were trying to warn him."

"He should have—I made it plain enough. Anyone else would have pulled up long before that after I gave the alert instead of trying to prove to you how fast his car would go."

"I'm sure it wasn't that."

He ignored that. "Here's hoping," he said grimly, "the next guy who shoots over the hill has a bit more sense."

"Nick didn't *know*—"

"Your friend," he pointed out, "is lucky to be alive. Taking risks with you right there in the car with him! Don't ask me to feel any sympathy for him. He deserves all he gets, and more!" All at once his voice was gentle. "Don't worry, I'll get someone to run you home."

"You won't, you know."

He was talking to her as though she were a child with no mind of her own. Maybe the full effects of the crash would hit her later, but meantime she had no intention of allowing herself to be meekly ordered back to the house. For she knew, who better, that Craig would need all the help he could get in rounding up the steers now moving towards the dark bush at the side of the road.

"I'm staying here to help," she told him firmly.

"Good for you!" A reluctant appreciation tinged his voice. He added with a sigh, "If only I could be certain you're fit enough to do the job."

"Try me!"

For once she had an advantage over him. She knew he had little time to argue, for another vehicle might come over the rise at any moment. Before he could make any further comment she had moved to Nick's car and running her hand along the dashboard, found what she sought, a powerful flashlight. All at once she remembered the other guests at the house she had left. With luck they might not yet have left the barbecue and might not be on the road until the danger was past.

"Stay where you are, Alison." He was bending over an injured steer and the next moment a rifle shot echoed above the lowing of cattle. Another shot followed as Craig put the badly injured beasts out of their misery.

When she came back to his side she said, "If you like I'll keep watch at the top of the hill."

"You'll stay right here with me until we get some help. I'm not risking anything happening to you—not again." As if to emphasise his words he threw an arm around her shoulders, imprisoning her at his side. Alison didn't know whether it was the effect of his nearness or the results of the recent collision that caused her to tremble so violently. How could he help but notice? He did. All at once his voice was low and concerned, "You're shaking."

"It's nothing," she lied. It just went to show the odd way in which shock could effect one, giving rise to ridiculous urges like this longing to fling herself against his hard muscular chest and find safety and protection in his arms.

It seemed an age waiting, each moment filled with dread. Supposing the batteries of the torch failed? Or what if a vehicle moving too fast to brake in time at sight of the warning light caused a second accident?

At last, however, they caught the gleam of approaching car lights as a car moved slowly and carefully up the rise, and taking a zig-zag course through the moving cattle, pulled in beside Craig. In a few terse sentences he arranged for the two shepherds with their dogs to help him and Alison to round up the straying steers. The other two men in the car he posted with flashlights on the road to warn approaching traffic of possible danger.

"That is," his voice was suddenly gentle as he turned towards her, "if you still feel up to lending a hand?"

"Let's go!" she said, and soon she was running through the bush with the others as they rounded up the cattle and guided them back through the opening from which they had strayed.

There was a pre-dawn lightening on the horizon and the others had returned to their home when the last black steer had been returned to the paddock. Craig secured the gate. "Come on, Alison, I'll take you home." Did she imagine the tenderness in his tone, just as she must have imagined that "my darling" at the moment he had arrived on the scene of the accident?

He saw her into the car and soon they were moving along the shadowy road. The pale glow in the eastern sky changed and deepened to the shining gold of sunrise. A delightful feeling of relaxation stole over her. She was suddenly sleepy and awfully content. Her head drooped to his shoulder and his arm was around her, warm and tender and infinitely satisfying. She murmured drowsily, "I thought you'd be angry with me."

"Angry? With *you*, Alison?"

"You know, about my taking off tonight with Nick. You didn't seem to like the idea."

His arm tightened around her. "Not your fault. You weren't to know the reputation he's got for crazy driving." The hard angry note was back in his voice and she knew that once again she had spoilt the happiness of the moment with her stupid remark. "He's smashed up car after car and so far he's managed to bale out in time or had the incredible luck to walk out of a crash unhurt—but to hit those speeds is asking for trouble. Not that it isn't what he deserves. But to take risks with *you* in the car. I won't forgive him for that in a hurry!"

Her heart swelled on a wave of elation. He'd been concerned for her safety. That was the reason he had offered resistance to Nick taking her to the barbecue tonight. He'd thought enough of her, been sufficiently concerned to come searching for her. At least, so it would seem. "How did you come to be there at just the right time?" she asked, and held her breath for the answer.

Craig's eyes were on the road ahead. "Had a ring from a guy heading for Dargaville, a neighbour a few miles away. He almost collided with a steer along the road himself, knew I leased some land up here and thought they might have belonged to me."

So—Alison jerked herself up the seat—his concern had been for his stock. Typical! She wrenched her mind back to the deep vibrant tones. "I can tell you I couldn't get here fast enough. You were on my mind all the way, but I was too late." He pulled her back close beside him and blissfully she relaxed once again. "You are feeling okay?" he asked with solicitude. "No aches and pains, no headaches?"

"Not a thing. I'm fine, honestly!" She hoped he wouldn't guess at the reason for the radiance in her tone.

They drove on in silence and as they reached the entrance gates on the roadway gently he released his arm from around her shoulders. "You stay put, Alison,

I'll do it." Feeling deliciously cherished and all at once *cared for*, she waited while he opened and closed the wide gates one after another. It was almost worth having been involved in one of Nick's accidents, she mused dreamily, to be treated so tenderly by the boss instead of being merely his Girl Friday.

The eastern horizon was slashed with bars of gold against tumbled crimson clouds as they drove in at the last gate. Craig shut off the engine and came around to her side of the car. "You've had a rough time tonight." She was unaware of a cut across her forehead where the blood had congealed, of grazed arms and dust-smeared face. She only knew that he was looking at her with an expression she had never seen in his eyes before. Maybe she hadn't imagined that "darling" after all.

"Me? I'm all right..." Her voice slurred and she seemed to be drifting away on a dark sea of ineffable content. "Are you taking me home, Craig?...Back to...Te-o-nui..." Her voice trailed away into black folds of oblivion. Then the mists cleared and she was aware of Craig gathering her up in his arms.

"All right now?" He bent his head and she could feel his breath on her face. For a heart-stoppng moment she thought he was about to kiss her, then he went striding up the path. At the door he set her gently down. "I wouldn't have had you hurt for anything."

Shakily she replied, "You did try to stop me going out tonight."

His voice hardened. "Next time I'll make sure."

She smiled up into the dark closed face. "What had you in mind? Locking me up in my room? Keeping me here for ever?"

"I wish I could." The words were so low she barely caught them.

A moment later he pushed open the door and a girl who had been seated on the window seat jumped to her feet. "Craig! I thought you were still asleep!" Running across the room, she threw her arms around his neck and kissed him on the lips. "Pleased to see me?"

He didn't appear to hear her. "What are you doing here?"

"Waiting for you. Aren't you surprised?"

He disengaged the clinging arms. "Never mind that now. Alison's been in an accident," he explained briefly. "We've been quite a time clearing up afterwards."

"Oh!" The stranger's cool glance raked Alison's dishevelled figure. "She looks okay to me." The next minute she was laughing up into Craig's unresponsive face, chattering on without pausing for breath.

So this, thought Alison with sickening certainty, is Jo. She had an impression of a round-faced girl with cropped dark hair, pouting red mouth, a full voluptuous body. Alison wrenched her mind back to the strong assertive tones. "I came the moment I got to hear about your mother being laid up. I knew she'd be needing me to help out and I wasn't going to let her down. I'd just got home when I heard the news and I made arrangements to come north right away. What do you know? I happened to run into a friend who was motoring up this way to her aunt's place for a holiday. We arrived there late last night, so I decided I'd come over here as soon as I could." A gay ripple of laughter. "The farmer went out at daybreak on his way to work somewhere miles from here, so I got him to drop me off on the way. I wanted to surprise you only it was me who got the surprise! I thought you'd be coming out to get breakfast and—"

"Pack it up, Jo—" The deep peremptory tones cut across the stream of chatter. Over Jo's head Craig's gaze went to Alison. "You've done a great job tonight, but you need some sleep now. I'll get you a brandy first, though, something to settle you down. Right?"

She nodded, raising her heavy glance to his face. I'm doing exactly what he tells me to do and all at once it doesn't seem to matter. Now that Jo is back in his life he won't be caring whether or not his Girl Friday goes against his wishes. The curious floating sensation surged over her once again. Somehow the impression of being ignored by Jo was more humiliating than if she had been insulted. Just a nothing person, not even worth a thought. Angrily she lifted her chin, gulped down the drink Craig had handed her, and made her way to the door. She was only vaguely aware of Jo's sweetly provocative tones. "You're making me curious. What's so world-shattering about what she did tonight, whoever she is?"

Craig's tone was abrupt. "Tell you some time." But of course he would have matters to discuss with the girl he might still care for, things of far greater import to him than herself. At the bathroom door she paused, staring incredulously at the mirrored reflection. Small wonder that Jo had dismissed her as someone beneath her notice. What a mess! Blood smeared across her forehead, the fine muslin of her dress torn and bedraggled. She shook her head and a shower of earth and leaves fell to the floor.

Forcing back the tears that threatened to overflow, she washed away the dried blood from her face as best she could and, thankful that Mary was fast asleep, stumbled into bed.

CHAPTER EIGHT

THE BRANDY Craig had insisted on her drinking must have made her sleep soundly, because it was hours later when she awoke. Hazily she lay listening to voices echoing from the dining room, then all at once realisation came rushing back. A dull throbbing started over her eyes and a sense of bitter anguish threatened to overwhelm her. Clearly Jo had come here with the intention of making up old differences between herself and Craig, and somehow—Alison swallowed over the lump in her throat—she would have to force herself to get used to the situation. How could she bear to be here, seeing the other two making up their quarrel? Yet she couldn't leave Mrs. Carter and the twins to the indifferent care of a girl who was obviously using them as a means to be with Craig. Besides, hadn't she promised Frances she would be here for as long as she was needed, and she sensed that Mary would be leaving the homestead now that Jo had taken up residence here.

And Craig...how was she to hide her feelings for him beneath his deep perceptive gaze? But of course he would have no eyes for her, not now. He would have Jo, experienced, travelled, probably an expert in all manner of accomplishments with the single exception of the outside work that came so naturally to herself. And where had it got her? Being his Girl Friday was about as unromantic as being employed as a general hand on the property. Even Frances regarded her first and foremost as Craig's outdoor helper. Only a crazy idiot like herself would ever have allowed herself to dream up a lasting relationship with Craig.

Honestly now, what did she have to go on? A few

brief moments of tenderness, light kisses to which—
her cheeks burned—she had been all too responsive, a
whispered promise in the treacherous moonlight. Add
to that a certain male jealousy over young Nick, who
meant nothing to her, nothing. When you came right
down to it it wasn't much to build a dream on, not half
enough.

You've been in love with him ever since that first
sight of him, back in your old home, only you wouldn't
admit it even to yourself. How could you have been so
stupid? You might have known that a man like Craig
would have someone else in his life, someone who was
older, more experienced in the ways of love. Oh, no
doubt he'd meant what he had said to her, *at the time*.
An older girl, someone like Mary, would never have
allowed herself to be taken in by such trivial incidents.
Nor would she be, ever again. She made an effort to be
stern with herself. Put it down to experience, forget all
about him. But how forget when just to be in the same
room with Craig sent her senses spinning wildly, and
why did experience hurt so much?

"Coming, ready or not!" Mary thrust her head
around the door, then carried a laden tray towards the
bed. "Don't get up! You're supposed to stay in bed all
day, boss's orders! My, you were lucky," she ran on,
putting down the tray and crossing the room to draw
the curtains, "not to be really laid up today—" She
broke off, taking in Alison's strained pale face. "You
are all right aren't you? You look awful!"

"I'm okay." Alison forced a smile. "Such luxury,
breakfast in bed! Or is it lunch? After this I'm getting
up."

Mary eyed her ruefully. "The boss won't like it."

"Too bad." To change the subject Alison said,
"Have you heard how Nick is today? He rushed off in a
hurry last night. Craig made it fairly clear that he didn't
want him back on the scene."

"I can imagine. I could have let you in to what Craig
had against him—driving like a maniac, I mean—but I

didn't like to mention it, and then later I wished I had. Not that it would have made any difference to your going with him last night. You're a stubborn thing when once you make up your mind."

"I know. But is he all right?"

"Nick? No real damage, according to his mother. I was speaking to her over the phone and she's hoping that maybe, just maybe, this time he's learned his lesson. Seems he's terribly upset over you being in the smash-up with him. He keeps ringing through to us with messages for you. I told him you were asleep and that's kept him quiet for a while. I don't envy him if Craig happens to answer the call next time."

Mary dropped down to the end of the bed. "You're well out of it this morning. If I were you I'd stay right here for the day. Jo's arrived. You know? The girl who Craig nearly married and thought better about. You can understand why when you meet her—"

"Don't tell me. I did meet her last night, just for a minute."

"Bet she made the most of that minute!"

"She did, rather."

"Boy, does she order everyone around to suit herself! But she didn't get far, just managed to upset the whole house. The twins have gone off to school in tears, Frances is hot and bothered and thinks she's running a temperature, and Craig's going around looking as though he hates the whole world. I can tell you I'm keeping well out of his way while he's in that mood."

"Do you think," Alison schooled her voice to deceptive casualness, "she'll be staying long?"

"It all depends on Craig, I take it. If she thinks she has a chance—" Why did putting the truth into words make it hurt so much more? Alison wondered. She wrenched her thoughts back to Mary's voice. "Craig doesn't strike me as a guy who's crazy about being reunited with his lost love. On the contrary."

That's only because of my being at the house to complicate matters. Mary's cryptic tones cut across her an-

guished thoughts. "Something tells me Jo isn't going
to like either of us being here. She hasn't got down to
getting everything out in the open yet, but when she
does—" She threw up her hands in a gesture of resignation. "I've washed out my one and only presentable
pair of jeans and they're drying on the line, just in case
I have to take off from here in a hurry."

Alison pulled herself out of painful imaginings.
"You don't have to rush away just because of her, unless you want to."

A smile tugged at the corners of Mary's wide mouth.
"I mightn't have much choice, going by what Frances
has been telling me about Jo. Seems she isn't one for
other women. Frances doesn't imagine Jo's ever had a
real girl-friend all her life. I gather she just can't stand
competition. Not that that means a thing as far as I'm
concerned. Craig's a great guy and I like him a lot, but
there's another one living not too far from here who
rates pretty high with me, not that Jo would know anything about him!" Her teasing glance rested on Alison's pale face. "But with you it's different."

Competition, Alison thought hollowly, was scarcely
the word for her and Craig's relationship. Girl Friday,
dogsbody, general hand, perhaps. Aloud she murmured, "How do you mean?"

"Can't you guess? I might be way off the beam, but
the way he looks at you sometimes, the tone in his
voice when he's talking to you—"

Alison felt her pulses leap, then settle again. "You're
imagining all that."

"Am I? You don't imagine that special sort of feeling between a man and a girl. It's something in the air,
you can't mistake it."

If only it were the truth! When Mary had taken away
the almost untouched meal Alison went to the bathroom and turned on the shower taps. It took her quite a
time to remove traces of earth stains. Then she washed
the dust from her hair and towelled it dry, combing the
waves into order. When she was dressed in a cool

sprigged cotton shirt and blue jeans the bruises on her legs were hidden and even the long cut on her forehead didn't show when she pulled over it a lock of springy hair. If only heartache were as easily put aside!

She was going down the hall when Craig emerged from the doorway of his office and for a fraction of a second their glances met. Her heavy gaze fell away and to her mortification she could feel the hot colour creeping up her cheeks.

"Alison!" He was at her side in a couple of strides. "Don't look like that! It's not like you think. I can explain—"

"Don't bother." The words cost her an effort, but she got them out in a choked voice. She shrugged away his detaining hand on her arm. "I know about Jo—"

"You don't, you know!" Roughly he swung her around to face him. "Now look at me, Alison! Will you listen—"

"No, I won't!" Hurt and pain made her fling the words at him. "Don't tell me, tell Jo—" She wrenched herself free and hurried away, then, aware of his ominous silence, glanced back over her shoulder. He was standing motionless, his brilliant eyes pale and bleak— some trick of the dim light, surely. Why hadn't she noticed before the deep lines etched down each side of his mouth? "What's the matter?" she asked unsteadily. "Did you want something?"

"Yes—you!"

She ignored that and went on, knowing that to stay a moment longer would be to undermine all her defences, for the sight of his sombre shadowed face was almost more than she could bear. And why not? She reminded herself; hadn't he good reason to feel ill at ease with herself and Jo right here beneath his roof?

When she entered the dining room she saw at once that Frances was upset. Two bright spots of colour burned through the leathery-brown of her cheeks and she glanced up at Alison with a tense expression. "Thank heaven you're all right, dear! You're looking awfully pale today, but that's only to be expected after last night. Craig said you met Jo at some unearthly hour this morning?"

"Yes," she schooled her voice to a noncommittal note. "She was waiting for us when we got back."

"She tells me," groaned Frances, "that she's come here to take care of me! Heaven forbid! Not that she hasn't got her good points, but patience isn't one of them. I pity any invalid who gets 'taken care of' by her. I can't stop her, of course. And the twins can't stand her at any price. They came to stay for a couple of weeks while Jo was with us last year—and talk about fireworks! Jo just doesn't understand children one little bit!"

"If you'd like me to go?" Alison heard her own voice, curiously expressionless.

"And abandon me to Jo's tender care? Not to mention the twins! No, no, better wait and see. I don't want to lose my helper," her smile for Alison was warm, "or Craig his Girl Friday either, if I can help it."

A shaft pierced Alison's heart. That was all she was, his farm helper. Another girl would ride with him over the sheep-dotted hills, *if she loved him enough*. It was Jo who would share his name. And to think, she mused with bitter irony, that I already share that name, did he but know. She wrenched her mind back to Frances' worried tones.

"Jo must have heard about my mishap on the bike right after she got back to New Zealand and she's come haring up here on the chance. It's not me that she's worrying about, I'm just the excuse." Under the stress of emotion Frances seemed to be giving voice to her thoughts. "It's a good excuse, the old leg. It's been responsible for quite a lot, one way and another. One thing I know, and that is that Jo's set her heart on being Mrs. Craig Carter, otherwise she wouldn't be here. And she's the sort of girl who gets her own way, or else."

"I shouldn't imagine," Alison heard herself saying

in a low distressed tone, "that Craig could be made to do anything he didn't want to."

"That's true," agreed Frances. "But don't you see, that's just the point. Does he want to? He never let on to me how he felt about Jo. To tell you the truth, I wasn't sorry when they broke up. Two strong-natured people like Jo and Craig aren't likely to get on well together for long. Jo must have seen that for herself by now. All those quarrels and making up don't make for a happy married life, I wouldn't think. Of course I don't know how much feeling there was between them. I was hoping that in these past six months he would have forgotten all about her. Perhaps he has. He doesn't look overjoyed at the big reunion—but then with Craig you never can tell."

Alison hoped she could hide the sense of anguish that was flooding her once again. Why hadn't Craig made mention to her of Jo? Because he had put her out of his mind or because to speak of the girl with whom he had been deeply involved, still gave him pain? About Jo's feelings there seemed no doubt. How delighted she must have been to learn of Frances' accident, giving her an opportunity to make things up with Craig. Perhaps even—a cold hand seemed to close around her heart—absence had wrought a change in Jo's attitudes and she was now willing to accept marriage on Craig's terms. For how could any girl who was loved by him do otherwise?

"Come in, Jo!" Alison forced her mind back to the present. Frances was sweeping aside a pile of papers from a nearby chair. "I want you two girls to get to know each other, Jo, this is—"

"We've met." Jo didn't even give Alison a glance. *It wasn't fair*, she thought hotly. She knew she looked years younger than her age. Blame it on those irresponsible reddish-brown curls that *would* cluster all over her head. But that didn't give Jo the right to treat her as a slightly tiresome child. There was no doubt that in the other girl's estimation she rated about on par with the pet sheep grazing near the hedge outside. "Craig told me he had someone here to see to the housework. I've met Mary too. She's just travelling around the country, I take it, stopping off here for a night or so on the way north."

"A night or so? Goodness no!" Mary had entered the room. Now she perched herself on the edge of the table, swinging long jean-clad legs. The sleepy eyes glimmered with mischief. "I'm employed to look after Mrs. Carter while she's laid up. Didn't Craig tell you?"

"No, he didn't!" snapped Jo crossly. "I've scarcely seen him to speak to." Swiftly she covered the slip. "I mean, with the accident and everything. Then he had to go out ear-tagging steers right after he got home. If I'd known—" she broke off in confusion.

"You'd have come up here just the same," put in Frances with her rakish grin. "I can see I'll have to put you in the picture about what's been happening around here." She went on to explain the details of her recent fall from the motorbike followed by the timely arrival of the two strange girls at the empty house. "It was fate, that's what I say," she concluded happily. "Without Alison and Mary I would have had to go to hospital, and as to the twins—I can't imagine what would have happened to them."

"Oh yes," Jo murmured carelessly. "I heard that Karen and Ben had taken off to Switzerland on a skiing trip. If only I'd been available at the time you were hurt it would have saved everyone so much trouble."

"No trouble," murmured Mary with her mocking smile.

Jo, ignoring the interruption, swept on. "But there's no need for you to worry any more, Frances. Now I'm here I can take over. It's what I want to do more than anything." Even to her own ears the statement must have had a slightly false ring, for she added hurriedly, "For you, Frances, I mean. I'd do anything for you. I think it's a great idea, suits you fine, and me too. I mean," the excited expression in the wide blue eyes lent significance to the words, "I've got to get my hand in."

Alison was conscious of an almost physical blow. Oh, she should have known! She had really, but all the time she'd kept hoping. Jo might have circled the world, but she wouldn't have found a man to compete with Craig, as she had no doubt come to realise. *I'll always love him, even knowing about him and Jo. I wish I didn't, but there's nothing I can do about it.* As from a distance she became aware of Jo's dictatorial accents. "This place could do with a face-lift. I couldn't live in a house with these low ceilings, and the bathroom's archaic. A mauve door with silver fittings and crystal taps, I think. But of course," she added, "the main thing is to do what *you* want—"

"Well then," suggested Frances promptly, "why not stay on here for a holiday? No need for you to worry about anything else. I know how you've always felt about housework."

Jo's round blue eyes widened innocently. "Oh, but I couldn't! I'd feel such a nuisance. No, I've made up my mind." She turned to Mary. "There's no need for you to stay any longer. I'm sure Craig will fix up your wages. Probably," she added carelessly, "he'll throw in an extra week's pay in lieu of notice. You must be anxious to get on with your travels—"

Alison intercepted Mary's amused glance. "Not really."

Jo looked nonplussed for a moment, then she rallied. "These relatives of yours you told me about, the ones who live in the district—"

"Not relatives, connections," Mary pointed out, still in a tone of quiet amusement.

"Connections, then. What does it matter?" A faint flush stained Jo's clear satiny cheeks. "You could go and stay with them."

Frances laid a hand on Jo's arm. "Jo, *please*—"

Jo shook herself free. "It's all right, Frances, I can handle this. I'm sure," she went on with a visible effort at self-control, "that once she understands the position Mary will come to see things my way. It's not as if she's indispensable here, and now that I'm here to take over—"

At last Frances got her say. "But I can't do without her," she wailed. "She's my secretary, or just about. She's been helping me to compile my notes. She types them all out for me and between us we've got my book of Maori proverbs well on the way. Besides," she announced triumphantly, "she promised to help Craig with his accounts. He spends hours in the office working on the books, and Mary happens to be a trained secretary—"

"It's all right, Frances," Mary's composed tones cut across the older woman's apprehensive accents, "I'll come back and see you whenever you need me and we'll sort out those last few chapters together. Craig can give me his account books if he wants to and I'll work on them while I'm over at the Vasanovichs'."

"Oh, Mary, *would* you? I feel so awful about your leaving like this. As if we were throwing you out." Genuine distress tinged Frances' low tones.

"You don't need to," the mocking smile still played around Mary's lips, "I was going anyway." Her eyes signalled a message to Alison. "I'll be glad to leave here—now."

Good for you! Alison's silent nod beamed the message back. The next minute came the thought, Now it will be my turn to get my notice of dismissal. I wouldn't mind going, the way things are. *Liar, you can't bear the thought of being away from Craig, even now.* She thrust away the inner voice. But someone has to be here to attend to the housework and take care of the kids. *She* will be too busy running after Craig to even think of ordinary things like washing clothes and changing beds and keeping the cookie jars filled.

"You too, Alison," came the imperious tones. "There's no need for you to stay either."

"No! Alison stays!" Craig was standing in the open doorway. "Get it?" His tone, very quiet, very definite, brooked no argument. "Alison's pretty important around here! She came to our rescue when Mum copped the fall off her farm bike. With the kids and all we couldn't have coped. We can't get along without her."

Heartsick and miserable, Alison looked from Craig to Jo.

"Oh!" Jo stared blankly back at him. Her eyes narrowed as her gaze moved to Alison. "You're the housekeeper here, then?" she asked uncertainly. Plainly, Alison thought wryly, she had been promoted in status. Could it be something in Craig's tone that was making Jo suddenly aware of the copper-haired girl in shabby jeans?

"Sort of." Hurt and anger mingled in the glance she sent Craig. "Girl Friday, dogsbody, land girl, whatever—"

"Don't listen to her," Craig cut in, "she's my right-hand man."

But not your woman.

She wrenched her mind back to Frances' incredulous tones. "Do without Alison? I couldn't possibly. I always think of her as my little piece of greenstone. It's one of my Maori proverbs," she went on to explain. "I put it under the heading of Quality, not Quantity. *'He iti ra, he iti mapihi pounamu.'* I may be small, but I am an ornament of greenstone. Frankly, I just don't know how I'm going to get along without her when she goes." At the expression of unguarded delight that crossed Jo's face Frances added hastily, "But that won't be for quite a while yet. It will be another month at least before I'll be able to manage on my own."

"But I'm here," persisted Jo.

"It's Alison I want," Frances said stubbornly. "She's used to me and my funny ways." Alison realised that the older woman was kindly avoiding the truth, that as a help in the house looking after children and a semi-invalid Jo wouldn't register. "You will stay on, won't you, Alison?"

"Of course." Fool! You know you're grasping the opportunity that allows you to remain here in Craig's home, even knowing that he belongs to another girl. She despised herself, yet seemed powerless to tear herself away. She knew that even had Frances not been incapacitated her feelings would have been the same.

She brought her mind back to Craig's decisive tones. "You too, Mary, you're welcome to stay for as long as you want to."

Mary shook her head, the long dark hair falling around her face. "Thanks a lot, Craig, but I've promised the Vasanovichs I'd move over there for a visit just as soon as I wasn't needed here any longer. So if it's all the same to you—?"

His gaze was deep and intent. "If that's the way you want it?"

"It is, truly. But I'll keep in touch, and I can still give you a hand with the books."

"Thanks, Mary, but it's okay, I can manage."

"Well then," she leaped lightly to the floor, "I'll go and pack my gear." To Alison Mary didn't appear in the least put out. It was almost as if she welcomed an excuse to leave the homestead. Who could blame her now that Jo was taking over everything in her imperious manner?

"No need to take off in a hurry," Craig told her. Then taking in her smiling gesture of denial, "But if you insist on going I'll run you over there. We can throw your bike in the back of the Land Rover."

Jo sent him a dazzling smile. "I'll come with you, just for the ride."

"There's not much room in the front." His face still wore a bleak closed expression—but then, the gleam of hope faded as swiftly as it had come, what was a ride of a few miles to lovers who in all probability had the rest of their lives to be together?

Alison found Mary in the bedroom stuffing jeans and a denim jacket into her canvas haversack. "It takes more than Jo to throw you," Alison observed. "You don't look too worried at being tossed out of here at a moment's notice."

Mary's long eyes glimmered with secret amusement. "Shall I tell you something? I was just wondering what excuse I could think up to get away. I've been looking forward to moving over to the Vasanovichs', but I wouldn't have gone, not while you and Frances needed me. Now it's different."

"Different's an understatement," Alison agreed on a sigh.

"I hate having to leave you here with her." Mary buckled the canvas strap of her pack. "Why don't you get going and 'shoot through,' as Craig would put it? Jo's always raving on about how much help she's going to be around the place, why not let her get on with it?"

Alison shook her head, the coppery curls bobbing around her face. "I couldn't do that."

"Why not? With Jo here—"

"Do you really think she'll do anything but please herself?"

"I guess you're right, but I'll tell you something she will do, and that is do her best to get Craig into her clutches again."

The words brought back the ache of longing. Alison fought against it in vain. It was an effort for her to say, "Well, I'm not risking it, not with Frances so nearly better. I'll stay as long as she wants me." *If only it were Craig who wanted me!*

Mary's shrewd glance was altogether too perceptive. "Are you sure you can take it?"

"Don't worry, I'll be a match for her," but she knew that wasn't what Mary had meant.

"Well, if you're determined to stay." Mary slipped the canvas straps over her shoulders. "Me, I can't get away from here fast enough! But I'll come back and see you. We'll keep in touch."

Jo strolled into the room as they were leaving. "You're all ready now? Have you got everything?" Clearly now that she had gained her objective she could afford to be affable. "You've got friends to go to, you said?"

"Oh yes," Mary sent her a sleepy-eyed stare, "I was leaving anyway."

Alison Jo ignored. Somehow the fact of being ignored was even more humiliating than being insulted. Just a nothing person, not worth a thought. Angrily she tilted her chin once again and went out of the room while Mary went to make her farewells to Frances.

In the kitchen the twins, arriving back from school on the school bus, regarded them for a moment, then turned away to fling off sandals and cardigans.

"Say goodbye to Mary," Alison told the children.

Two pairs of eyes gazed towards Mary in astonishment and small lips drooped. "Are you going away?"

Mary bent to kiss each small face. "'Bye now, and don't worry. I'm not going far and I'll come back and see you both. You'll have Jo to look after you—"

Both children shrieked in dismay. "Is she going to *stay* here?"

"I'm not going to do what she tells me!" yelled Patrick. "She wouldn't let us stay up even one little minute—"

"She said only babies played with teddies!" shouted Sue in enranged tones. "She threw away my Toby!"

"She tipped my tadpoles out of their jar," howled Patrick. "She said they were dirty, and they weren't! They weren't!"

"Once she hit us, *hard*—"

"Just 'cause we took a cookie from the tin without asking, and she said we could, she did, she did!"

Roused to indignation, the twins seemed bent on raking up old scores against the girl who had evidently treated them with scant regard for their helplessness.

In the uproar Mary, with a parting wave to Alison, went to seat herself in the Land Rover and Alison hustled the children away to their room. Patrick was still protesting in loud tones, "She's not the boss of me!"

"I heard that," Frances called, and Alison went to join the older woman in the dining room. A frown lined Frances' weathered brown forehead. "I'm afraid they've got something to complain about with Jo. I was hoping they'd forgotten about being left in her care before, but evidently they haven't." Her gaze moved to the window. "There they go now. Jo's not going to enjoy her ride very much, squeezed in between the other two in the Land Rover, but I don't suppose she'll mind, so long as she's managed to get her own way. Oh dear, I do wish she'd stayed away a little longer, just until I'd got on my feet again."

Alison, watching at the window as the vehicle swept down the winding drive, found herself wishing that Jo could have stayed away for ever. All at once anguish caught her by the throat and she stumbled blindly from the room. Fool, pull yourself together before someone guesses how you feel about him. Mary knows already, or at least suspects the truth, but she'll never tell.

"You feel things too much," her foster-mother had often told her when Alison had been brokenhearted over the death of a loved horse or a faithful farm dog, or bitterly hurt over the perfidy of a supposed friend at school. "You take things too much to heart. You'll have to get over it, but maybe you won't. You're really just like your mother. She took things hard too." For a moment Dot's face had softened. "Just as long as you fall in love with the right man and he with you. Otherwise," she shook her head, "I don't know what you'll do."

"Find someone else, I guess," Alison had remarked cheerfully. She was thirteen at the time and falling in love seemed as far away as the stars of the Southern Cross pricking a kite-shape in the night sky. How simple it had all seemed then!

All at once, conscious of the heavy sweet perfume of cabbage-tree blossoms, she ran to the pottery bowl and gathering up the showers of creamy-pink flowers, flung them out of the window on to the grass below. How could she ever have imagined she liked the cloying sickly-sweet smell?

Because you couldn't run away, not when Frances had need of you—for a time. You went on with life, somehow, forcing yourself to follow the familiar pattern of household chores, trying to appear as usual, heartache and all, hoping the anguish didn't show. She hadn't expected Jo to be of any real assistance in the house and indeed her help was so negligible that it scarcely counted. Not that Alison minded the extra work. In a way it kept her from thinking, most of the time.

Jo didn't get out of bed until late and by the time she had showered and made up her face lunchtime was almost on them. She insisted on sharing her midday meal with Frances, one problem solved there. The remainder of the day Jo spent either driving into the township from which she would return laden with fruit, magazines and chocolates for Frances, or flooding the older woman with needless attention. She would continue to fill flower vases and tidy up Frances' precious notes until at last Alison heard her cry in exasperation, "I know you mean well, Jo, but for heaven's sake, will you just *leave me alone*!"

"Very well, then," Jo had said huffily, "if that's the way you want it. I was only trying to help."

"I know, I know, that's just the trouble—"

The violent slamming of a door cut off the words.

So far as the twins were concerned Jo had them in a state of continual uproar. It was a different matter when Craig happened to be present, because on these occasions Jo's laughing approach and friendly attitude towards the children was in direct contrast to her usual antagonism, a fact which the children were quick to seize on and use to their own advantage.

After a stormy few days Jo gladly abandoned the twins to Alison's care. "I can't stand kids," she excused herself, "especially little horrors like those two who won't do a thing they're told! Of course if I'd been in the house from the beginning it would have been a different story. As it is, you may as well keep an eye on them." As an afterthought she added carelessly, "It will be something for you to do!"

Something for her to do! Alison's quick temper got the better of her. "Have you any idea," she flared, "of what there is to do around here?"

"Not really." Jo's voice was bland, "and quite frankly I don't care. I loathe farming work and everything that goes with it. I prefer to leave all those messy details to the folk who are paid to do it."

Alison, who had been on her way to the laundry at the back of the house when Jo intercepted her, left the room before she really lost control of herself and hurled one of the "messy details," in this case a work-stained shirt of Craig's she held in her hands, in the direction of that oh-so-superior face.

It wouldn't be for long, she reminded herself, striving for calmness. Only a few days previously the doctor, calling in to see Frances on a routine check-up, had pronounced her well on the road to recovery. "Perhaps," he had murmured, "another three weeks." One could endure anything for three weeks. Beyond that she didn't allow herself to dwell. She only knew that the mere sound of Craig's step in the porch, or the sight of his bronzed face, could stir her unbearably. Watching him ride away on a muster, she mused forlornly that only a week ago he would have been glad of her help. Now his hard impersonal gaze cut her to the heart.

One morning she was giving Banner a brush-down near the fence when she realised that Jo had intercepted Craig on his way out of the back door. The wind, blowing a gale as always up here in the hills, tossed Jo's words clearly in her direction. "I got up specially early to see you. Seems I scarcely ever have a word in private with you these days. You're away over the hills all day and stuck in the office all night. You know something? You're a hard man to catch, and there's something I specially want to see you about. When are you going to teach me to ride? I've asked you about it so many times."

She couldn't help overhearing both voices. Craig sounded surprised, even disbelieving. "First I've heard of it."

"But don't you remember all the letters I wrote you from the ship? Oh, I know you couldn't reply with me moving around all the time from port to port."

And that's an excuse, Alison thought waspishly. He could have written ahead to one of the ports—had he wished to. The next moment hope did a nose-dive. He's proud. He would never be the first one to give in after they had parted for good. But now that Jo has made the effort the way is clear for him.

"I do want you to teach me, Craig." Who would have believed that Jo's dominating tones could be so sweet and appealing?

"Sorry, but you'll have to wait." Craig didn't sound unkind, merely matter-of-fact. "I've got to go out drafting steers this morning and it's going to take me most of the day."

Alison guessed that the refusal would do nothing for Jo's temper, always on a short fuse. But her answer when it came was honey-sweet. "Just as you say, Craig. Seems I'll just have to wait until you get time to teach me. Unless you put off the silly old drafting? Couldn't we start today, Craig?" Alison could see Jo's hand caressing Craig's bronzed arm. She was smiling up at him beseechingly. "*Please*!"

Apparently, however, Craig was unimpressed—or more likely, Alison thought wryly, his mind was on the steers. "Why don't you ask Alison to give you a few lessons? She's a crack rider and she'll see that you're started off in the right way. If you ask her nicely she might even let you have a go on Banner."

Alison was aghast. Allow any novice to mount Banner! The next moment, however, she realised that her fears were groundless.

"Take lessons from her? That'll be the day!"

"Okay, it's up to you," Craig told her, and moved away towards the stables.

Alison couldn't help a sneaky feeling of satisfaction that for once Jo wasn't having things all her own way. When she had finished grooming Banner she took the mare back to her paddock and went to wash in the bathroom. She was in the kitchen, stirring red jelly crystals in a basin, when the door was flung open.

"So there you are!" The words cut across the silent room and Alison found herself facing a girl who clearly was beside herself with anger. No doubt the fury Jo was feeling towards Craig, the disappointment and frustration, was now turned on Alison, whom for some reason she blamed for the coolness of her welcome. "I wanted to have a word with you," Jo's low voice throbbed with emotion. "There are a few things we have to get straight. You might think you've been pretty clever hanging around here, getting in everyone's way. You seem to forget you're not family like the rest of us." The emotion-charged voice rushed on before Alison could argue the point. "So if I were you I'd make some excuse and get going. You're not wanted here and I'm warning you, *get out*! You'll get something to do. If you like," the round eyes were empty of expression as tinted glass, "I'll fix you up with something in the domestic line myself."

"Don't bother." A tide of anger rose in Alison and with it the old stubbornness. Resolutely she lifted her rounded chin. She refused to be tossed out like a—a sack of dog-nuts!

"Well," prompted the icy tones, "I'm waiting."

"So am I, until Frances gives me notice, tells me she doesn't want me here. Until then—"

"Oh, *you*—!" Savagely Jo spat the words out.

"Don't worry, I'll take off when Craig tells me to."

Jo stared at her. "Craig? So that's it?"

Alison felt cold at the pit of her stomach, but she held her ground even though she could see that Jo was almost choking with rage. For a dreadful moment she feared the other girl was about to strike her. "You little fool! You don't really think Craig wants a kid like you hanging around here? That he *wants* you to stay? You must be out of your mind! Don't you see that he's been forced into keeping you on for a while because of the car accident? He feels under some obligation to you because of that, and he isn't one to dodge his responsibilities. You've put him in an awkward position. Now that I'm here to take over things at the house he doesn't need you any more, but he's trying to do the right thing. Surely..." a pitying look, "even you can see that. Or is it that you don't want to?"

The thoughts whirled through Alison's distraught mind. Could it be true what Jo had said? The next moment she thrust the thought aside. Craig would never pretend. Whatever his personal thoughts concerning her, there was no doubt about his needing her help at his home.

Before she could make an answer Jo had hurried away. "Don't say I didn't warn you!" she flung over her shoulder. Alison went on stirring the jelly crystals. It was a moment or two before she realised that her hands were shaking.

It was the following afternoon when once again Jo came into the kitchen where Alison sat slicing fresh beans into a basin. In that one lightning glance she realised that Jo looked paler than usual and her eyelids were puffy, as though she had been weeping. Jo swung herself up on a corner of the table, swinging her sandalled foot with its gleaming pink toenails. Even without looking up Alison was aware of the other girl's silent scrutiny. Now what? "I've just been down to collect the mail." Jo began sorting out letters addressed to herself and Frances, business letters, farming magazines and circulars addressed to Craig. Her tone was deceptively casual. "You never get any mail, do you?"

"Not yet," Alison was choosing her words carefully, "but you never know your luck!"

"You don't write letters either." And before Alison could think up a satisfactory rejoinder, "You're really an awfully mysterious sort of person." The intent gaze probed Alison's downcast face. "How come you never let on about yourself, where you come from or anything?"

"Why should I?"

"It makes folks suspicious, that's all. Seems like you've no people of your own, no boy-friend, no girl-friend even, except Mary, and I gather you only picked her up on the way here. Frances doesn't seem to have a clue as to where you worked before you turned up here or who your previous employer was. Anyone would get the idea," Alison found she was holding her breath, "that you were covering up, hiding away under another name. Just a girl from nowhere!" Beneath the words Alison sensed a warning—or a threat. The next moment she told herself that Jo couldn't possibly know anything of her past life—*but she was doing her utmost to find out.* "Who but Frances," Jo was saying, "would take anyone into her home on trust, someone who just walked in off the street without any credentials? I mean, you could have been anybody—"

"Nonsense, Jo!" Neither girl had noticed that Frances had switched off her transistor radio and now her loud voice echoed from the adjoining room. "Frances didn't care about anything but being offered a helping hand by a stranger, and that's the truth! It was a miracle to me, Alison walking in with Mary that day. They just seemed like angels from heaven!"

"Pretty funny angels!" sneered Jo. Aloud she said crossly, "Oh well, Frances, I suppose if you don't mind taking a risk—"

"Mind!" came the exasperated tones. "I *love* having Alison around. I just don't know how I'm going to get along without her when she goes."

"*When* she goes." Only Alison caught the low meaningful words.

When Jo had left the room Alison's thoughts were in a turmoil. Happily Frances' intervention had had the effect of bypassing Jo's persistent questioning, until next time. What if in some manner she ferreted out the truth? It was unlikely that Jo would be interested enough to make inquiries, and yet...the niggling sense of unease remained at the back of her mind.

"You'll have to forgive Jo for the things she says," Frances told Alison when she carried in the afternoon tea. "I can always tell when she and Craig have had another of their rows! He's got that strained look around his mouth today and she looks as though she's been crying all night!" Alison found it difficult to imagine Jo giving way to tears, and yet...she remembered the puffy eyelids. "It was too bad of her to take out her bad temper on you. You won't take any notice of what she said, will you?"

"Of course not." Alison was thinking that at least she must have convinced Craig that he had nothing to be concerned about regarding her past life, for he appeared to be satisfied with her evasive answers to his inquiries. Oh, why not face up to the truth and admit to yourself that he's simply lost interest in your affairs now that he has Jo here with him!

Thoughtfully Frances sipped her tea. "I wonder," she remarked thoughtfully, "what the trouble was between Jo and Craig this time. *You*, probably."

"Me?" Alison attempted to cover the betraying squeak with a careless laugh. "I don't see—"

"Oh, he's always talking about you," Frances stated calmly. "He thinks you're wonderful."

"In what...way?"

"Every way, according to him. He likes the way you keep house, says it seems to be no effort to you to have everything done and meals always ready on time no matter what time he happens to come home. No clutter anywhere and the children so well cared for. Outside too... he says when it comes to mustering and drafting you're as good as a man."

"Oh," Alison could feel her spirits dropping back to their usual heavy position these days, "those sort of things."

Frances looked surprised. "They mean a lot to a man on his own, especially now that I've gone and developed this stupid sore leg."

"I guess he thinks I'm handy to have around the place," the brave words belied the pain shadowing her eyes. "Handy"—but it was Jo with her voluptuous body and dominating personality who fascinated him.

ONE AFTERNOON a strange car pulled up in the driveway and Mary strolled along the path escorted by a tall young man with dark eyes and a pleasant expression. Alison felt sure this must be Tony Vasanovich. A different Mary, this, Alison couldn't help thinking, for her friend radiated a sense of happiness and the sleepy eyes were brilliant. After a time Craig, calling back at the house, took Tony out to the paddocks to see a new foal and Jo, uninvited, hurried after them.

Mary's gaze followed Jo as she trailed alongside the two men. "Things are just the same here, then?" She took in Alison's pale face and shadowed eyes. "You're not overdoing it, are you, with all the extra work?"

"No, no, I'm just losing a bit of my tan. It comes of being inside so much."

Mary was altogether too perceptive. "No more riding with Craig these days?"

"I've got far too much to do indoors," Alison said quickly, "I haven't a hope of getting outside."

"Well, at least you're sticking it out and proving a match for you-know-who."

But not when it comes to love. Swiftly she made to

change the subject. "How about you? Are you one of the family yet?"

Mary sent her a startled glance. "Oh, I see what you mean. It's funny," she gazed dreamily over soaring sheep-threaded hills, "but it seems like home to me over there, has done ever since the first moment when I walked in at the door."

"Are you sure," teased Alison, "that you'd like it so much at the Vasanovichs' if Tony weren't there?"

"Tony?" Suddenly Mary was confused. A dull pink suffused her face and she played nervously with a cuff-button of her denim blouse. "Whatever makes you think he has anything to do with it?"

Alison laughed. "There must be some attraction, and you're always talking to me about him over the phone. Not that I blame you, he's very good-looking. Tall like you, nice manners, the sort of man you couldn't help liking."

"He's okay." Mary's voice was muffled and she jumped to her feet. "I'd better have a word with Frances. She's sure to have oodles of typing ready for me by now. Isn't it lucky that all the farmers seem to have an ancient typewriter kicking around the office?" She smiled reminiscently, "Who would ever have dreamed that I'd land in New Zealand and right away start on becoming an authority of Maori proverbs?" She tossed her long dark hair back from her shoulders. "I do miss Frances and her proverbs. She could always produce one to fit the occasion." She giggled. "D'you remember her telling Jo that you were her 'little bit of greenstone'? I don't think Jo appreciated it very much. Come to that, I don't imagine Jo likes anything here very much, except Craig, of course. I must fly—"

Mary rang through on the following day, her tone so warm and alive with happiness that Alison found herself saying wistfully, "You still seem to be enjoying yourself over there."

"Oh, I am! I am!"

The two chatted for a time, making arrangements for

Alison to visit Mary on the following evening, then Mary broke off—"Wait a minute, Nick's here beside me. He wants to have a word with you, but only, and I quote, if you want to speak to him."

"Of course I want to speak to him." Poor Nick, in her troubled state of mind she had all but forgotten him.

"Alison! Can you forgive me for what happened the other night?" She caught the note of distress in the low tones. "I've been wanting to tell you, to come over and make it right with you, but it didn't work out." She recalled Craig's warning to Nick that he was to keep away from her. "I tried to get through on the phone, but had no luck—" So he had been unfortunate enough to have had his call answered by Craig. "But that doesn't mean to say I haven't been worried stiff about you. Mary tells me you're all right, but I can't help wondering—"

"Of course I'm all right. I'm fine, no harm done. How about you?"

"Oh, all I copped from the smash was a stiff ankle and the odd bruise. Nothing bad enough to keep me from entering in the rodeo events next month."

"And your car?"

"Tony's car, you mean. It's still in the garage in town. Tony's not being very co-operative about that. He tells me I've got to pay the repair bill even if it takes me the rest of my life to settle it. I wouldn't put it past him," he confided morosely, "to add interest on the money as well. No pity, no brotherly love…"

Alison laughed. "Fair enough."

"Oh, forget old Tony. It's you I'm interested in. It seems an age since—Look," all at once he was excited, "Mary tells me you're coming over here tomorrow night." Urgency laced the boyish tones. "You will make it? Promise?"

"I'll come."

"That's all I wanted to know. You've made my day. Bye."

She replaced the receiver and swung around to meet

Craig's grave, intent gaze. "Who was that on the blower?"

She hesitated for barely a second. He would scarcely be interested in young Nick, not now, so why trouble with explanations? "That was Mary on the phone. She rings me most days. She's invited me to go over there to see her tomorrow evening."

"Mighty! It'll get you out of the house for a bit. A good idea."

A good idea for whom? For him and Jo, to enable them to make up their recent disagreement in privacy?

He said, "I'll run you over there and pick you up later."

"But there's no need," she protested. "I've got the Mini. I've scarcely used it for ages and the battery..." the words died into silence beneath his brooding stare.

"I'll take you." The tense lines around his mouth relaxed a little. "It's a date, then?"

"I guess." A date for him and Jo? An opportunity for them to be alone together? The thought came to torture her for a few hours at least Craig wouldn't be forced to carry on his love affair under the eyes of a silly romantic girl who had read into his light caresses a depth of feeling he had never intended. She felt the prick of tears behind her eyelashes and was glad that Frances, calling to him at the moment, summoned him away.

That evening at dinner Jo's strong accents dominated the conversation. Could it be Craig's withdrawn manner, Alison wondered, that was causing the other girl to run on like this, as though she couldn't bear silence? Jo was describing in some detail her travels overseas, the varied exotic foods she had sampled during her short stay in distant lands. Always the anecdotes would conclude with a light and laughing reference to the many men she had met during her travels, the attentions lavished upon her by influential friends and the escorts who had competed for the pleasure of taking her dining and dancing.

Even in the midst of heartache Alison was aware of a note of over-excitement running through the monologue. Who was Jo trying to impress? Frances, seated on a couch nearby, injured leg propped up on a stool and tea-tray balanced on her ample lap, appeared suitably awed by the mention of well-known names, but Craig said little and the discourse appeared to be passing him by. There must indeed have been a bitter quarrel between these two, but they would make it up again. Hadn't Frances told her they always had in the past?

As she passed around mugs of steaming coffee Alison was only half aware of Jo's superior tones. "Of course everyone knows that travel broadens the mind, gives one a wider outlook. I've been lucky, I suppose, everyone can't get around the world as I did. Take Alison now—" why must Jo speak of her as though she weren't in the room? The slightly protruding eyes with their suspicious expression were fixed on Alison's downcast face. "Bet you've never been far from your own little corner of the world, wherever that is. Where do you come from, anyway?"

Alison, pouring coffee into a pottery beaker, pulled herself together. "Me? Oh, just down country a bit—" Unfortunately she couldn't control the trembling of her hands and coffee spilled over on to the cloth. If only no one had noticed. Apparently, however, someone had, for Jo's avid tone quickened. "You sound awfully vague about it." A wicked light like a tiny bulb burned in the blue eyes.

"It's such a small place, scarcely on the map even. You would never have heard of it."

"Try me," challenged Jo. "I've been over most parts of the country one time or another."

Alison didn't answer and Jo's glance moved from Alison's flushed cheeks to Craig's closed face. "I suppose Alison has always worked with sheep and cattle," somehow she contrived to make the activities seem distasteful, "wherever she came from? Come on now, Alison, don't be so secretive—where was it?"

"Nowhere important." Why was she such a colossal fool when it came to lies and deception? Why couldn't she have made mention of a name previously, any name, and thus avoided this interrogation which she felt sure was being staged with a deliberate attempt at planting suspicions in Craig's mind.

He was stowing away the makings, tobacco and flimsy papers, in the pocket of his cotton shirt. "It wouldn't ring a bell with you, Jo. Anyway," he drawled, "it's not where she comes from that matters. It's what she does that counts around here."

Jo shot Alison a glance of pure hatred. "I wouldn't know, never having been domestic."

Alison had never seen Craig's eyes look so hard. He rose to his feet, pushing back his chair. "If you'll excuse me, folks, I've got to get cracking."

CHAPTER NINE

ALISON HAD BATHED the twins and put them to bed before she showered and changed into an ankle-length dress of flower-patterned cotton. She was moving down the hall when Craig joined her. "All ready?"

"Ready and waiting, sir!" He paused, taking in her sweet young face with its wistful expression. Did she imagine a softening of the harsh lines of his face?

The next moment Jo opened her bedroom door, her resentful tones shattering the moment of silence. "I don't see why you have to go out tonight, Craig. Surely Alison's got her own car in the garage?"

"She doesn't know the way," he explained briefly. "Besides, I've got to make sure she gets home safely."

Alison turned away with a forlorn droop of her shoulders. Of course...his right-hand man.

Out in the purple dusk car-lights beamed down the winding track as they swept down to the gates. Alison jumped out of the car to open and close them, then they were out on the main highway. A single star glittered low in the darkening sky and cicadas piped their endless summer song from the sombre bush at the roadside.

"This is new territory to you, isn't it?"

"That's right." How distant was his voice, as though she were a stranger to whom he was giving a lift. To break the strained silence she heard herself chattering wildly. "I—haven't been out anywhere lately. I've been sticking close to home—" Did that sound like a complaint? "With one thing and another." Heavens, now he might imagine that she was criticising Jo for the other girl's lack of co-operation.

His thoughtful glance underlined her suspicions.
"You've been working flat-stick lately. Not much fun,
but it won't be for long now."

"No." Anguish like a dark cloud enveloped her
spirit. If only he weren't so devastatingly attractive! If
only she had insisted on driving her own car tonight.

The well-shaped hand on the wheel was firm and he
drove swiftly and competently. Presently he began to
speak of nothing things, farming procedures, local history, the names of the hills rising in the distance. The
miles flew by and before long they were turning off the
main road and taking a winding drive that led towards a
comfortable-looking, red-roofed house half hidden
amongst tall native trees.

He let her out at the entrance to the house. "What
time shall I pick you up? Eleven, twelve? Just say the
word."

Flustered, she said, "Eleven will do."

"Right. See you." He swung around in the driveway
and she ran up the front steps, the long folds of her
dress falling around her ankles.

Before she could put a finger to the door chimes
Mary had opened the door and was drawing her inside.
"Lovely to see you!"

"You too!" They strolled down the long hall with its
shelves of trailing plants.

Mary said, "How's everything over at Craig's place?
Jo still throwing her weight about?"

"You know Jo."

"And Frances, how is she?"

"Oh, she's ever so much better. She—" Alison's
words were drowned in a gale of voices as the two girls
entered the big old-fashioned lounge room. Nick's parents greeted her warmly, as did Grandmother Vasanovich. Around her pressed a group of tall muscular men,
all with dark hair and eyes, all welcoming her at once in
their loud voices. Someone asked her to sit down on a
couch, then the babel of voices broke out again, inquir-
ing after her health. Was she okay after the accident?

Young Nick, his older brothers assured her, would never get away with that sort of thing again, especially with her in the car, they could promise her that! A young man who appeared to be only slightly older than Nick told her his name was Ivan and offered her wine.

Presently she became aware that Nick had squeezed into the seat beside her. "Gee, I'm sorry about the smash—" He did indeed look crushed, Alison thought, and no wonder, with the constant reprimands of his brothers.

"Forget about it," she smiled, and turned her attention to Tony, standing nearby. "How badly was the car damaged?"

"It wasn't too extensive after all." He had an attractive voice, she mused, quiet, well-spoken in contrast to the wild exuberance of his brothers. "Not that it mattered so long as you and Nick haven't any serious injuries."

"Only his pride," put in the mischievous-eyed Ivan. "Do you know what he said about you?" She realised Nick was frantically trying to signal his brother to silence, to no avail. "He told us you were the most fantastic girl he'd ever met in his life! He said he'd never met anyone like you and then he'd gone and blued his chances! He was feeling so low about it he was thinking about shooting himself, but when we offered to do it for him he seemed to change his mind all of a sudden."

In the guffaws of laughter Nick edged nearer to Alison. "You really mean that, about it being all right now? You don't hold it against me?"

Looking down at his downcast young face, she felt a prick of compassion. "Of course I don't."

Nick's expression cleared. "Tremendous! I can't believe it! I was coming over to tell you I was sorry about it all, ask you to let me off the hook—"

"Why didn't you?"

Nick looked acutely embarrassed and it was Ivan, listening unashamedly to the conversation, who answered. "He's scared stiff of your boss, that's why! He

says the guy's nuts about you and he'd eat him alive if
he as much set a foot in the place.''

Nuts about you! If only it were so!

"It's true, isn't it?"

She became aware of Nick's anxious gaze. Swiftly
she gathered together her wildly-flying thoughts.

"What's true? That Craig was mad about the crash?
He was rather," her lips curved in a sad little smile,
"but only because he seems to have an idea you're a
menace on the road—"

"Not any more! You've got to believe me—"

"You're not going to trust *his* word," came Ivan's
jeering voice. "You just don't know him like we do."

Nick wasn't listening. "But it was *you* he was so het
up about."

She shook her head. "Craig would have been concerned about anyone in the car that night." How weak
the statement sounded! But the alternative was so fantastic, so utterly improbable it didn't bear thinking
about.

Oddly, Nick persisted in the ridiculous supposition.
"You can't tell me that guy's concern was for any old
body. It was the way he looked—"

"Forget him." The talk about Craig was making her
embarrassed and stupidly happy, raising hopes that had
no possibility of fulfilment. All that, she reminded herself, was before Jo's arrival at the house.

It seemed no time at all before she was urged into
the old-fashioned kitchen where a huge spread was laid
out on the long kauri table. "This isn't just supper?"
Alison whispered to Mary, looking in surprise at the
assortment of foods.

"They were so pleased about you coming tonight,"
Mary whispered back. "They're trying to make up to
you for what happened, you know?"

"Nice of them." But she found herself wishing that
the family could have expressed their good wishes in
some other way. At the house she tried to disguise the

fact that she had little appetite. How could she pretend beneath these watching eyes?

At last, however, the plates were emptied, coffee cups taken away and Mary drew her away to the privacy of her own room.

"All that supper!" groaned Alison. "I can scarcely move."

"I know, but they meant it kindly."

"I like your room." Alison was taking in the spacious bedroom with its gleaming floors of polished wood and scattered fluffy sheepskin rugs, the plain old chest of drawers and long picture windows. She dropped down on the neatly made bed with its yellow spread. "I've brought you the latest instalment of Frances' proverbs. Hope you're not too busy to type it out for her."

"No, no, I'll do it." Absently Mary took the clipped folder Alison extended towards her. She said with studied carelessness, "What do you think of Tony?"

"The quiet one? I like him a lot." Alison reflected that Tony would be an ideal mate for Mary. Tall and dark with a nice manner, confident yet not too confident and of just the right age. She knew that Craig had taken a liking to him too and somehow that was what counted. Aloud she murmured. "You told me about him the first time you came to his home. He's the clever one who's a fully fledged barrister."

"That's him, that's Tony. I thought you'd like him. Look," she was speaking rapidly, nervously, in a most un-Mary-like manner, "he gave me this." She lifted the tiny translucent heart carved from amber swinging from a leather thong around her neck.

Alison eyed the smooth little shape.

"It's kauri gum! Is it made from gum dug up around here?"

"Is it ever! It's quite old, actually. Tony's grandfather carved it out of gum he dug up in the district when he first arrived here from Yugoslavia. Seems he made some sort of living from the gumfields, living in a tent until he could afford to build a house. They say there's very little of the gum about the district, now that the kauri trees have mostly been cut down or burned." She seemed to be running on. "Tony wanted to give me something else." Restlessly she fingered the small heart shape. "A ring, his grandmother's engagement ring, but I couldn't take it." A frown etched itself along her smooth forehead and there was a worried note in her voice. "I just couldn't! I mean, how could he love me—*really* love me, so soon?"

"It's happened before." There was no need to ask if Mary loved him, Alison thought. It was there for anyone to read in the low unsteady voice, the words that were tumbling from her lips in an obvious attempt to ease her own uncertainty of mind.

"Was it because of the ring?" Alison queried gently. "Didn't the family approve of your having it?"

Mary stared back at her. "Oh no, nothing like that. They wanted me to have it. That was the trouble."

Alison looked bewildered. "I don't get it. If the family are happy about the idea and so are you and Tony—"

"The family! The family!" Suddenly Mary's usually composed tones were rising out of control. "They're so close, they do everything, but *everything*, together. Grandmother Vasanovich's word is law, you wouldn't believe it! How do I know," Mary cried passionately, "he really loves me, wants me *himself* and not just to please his people. Don't you see what I mean? Here they all are, living in this practically womanless community, and one day in I walk with all the right qualifications. Mama Vasanovich is a darling. I'm fond of her, but she tells me I'd make a perfect wife for one of her sons. She probably wouldn't care which one. How do I know he loves me for myself?"

"But hasn't he told you—"

"Of course he has, lots of times, but I don't know whether I can believe him. I keep remembering that he spent years and years studying for the law and then tossed it all away—and why? Simply because the family had taken over a bigger property and could do with his office training as well as his help on the land. Doesn't that go to show that his family comes first and his own feelings way behind?"

Alison hesitated. "Problems, problems. Well," she said with conviction, "I think you should believe him."

You think, jeered a small inner voice from somewhere deep in her mind. Who are you to hand out advice to another girl? Didn't Craig tell you that he loved you? Did you believe him? That was different. So *you* say. The small niggling voice refused to be silenced.

Craig arrived at the house promptly at eleven o'clock and despite pressing invitations from the Vasanovich family to stay, even if only just long enough to drink a glass of wine with them, he insisted on leaving at once. Because of Jo waiting at home, Alison wondered bleakly, getting into the car. As they moved away she put on her gayest smile and waved to the group gathered together on the long verandah.

The blue-blackness of the night sky was pricked by scintillating stars and a soft wind caressed her face. She was reminded of one of Frances' expressions, "the soft west wind of love." Love...She stole a glance towards the stern masculine profile at her side.

She must be dreaming. His strained expression, the set line of his jaw, scarcely indicated a man who was happily reunited with his lost love, but then there had been a quarrel between him and Jo. Tonight he made no effort to throw an arm about her shoulders. Why should he bother with make-believe when he had the reality at hand? Could it be that his hard angry look had something to do with herself? Maybe he was remembering those brief moments of tenderness between them, asking himself how best to put an end to any romantic feelings she might happen to have on his account. With a shame-making feeling of humiliation she remembered his mention of that expressive face of hers.

"Had a good time tonight?' He didn't lift his gaze from the road ahead.

"Oh yes," she roused herself to answer him, "it was super meeting them all. Mary seems to have really settled in over there—"

His voice was steel. "You didn't go making any arrangements with young Nick to see him again?"

"No, no, I didn't!" Too late she thought up a better rejoinder. "What is it to you if I did?" In the darkness her lips quirked in a wry smile. And Nick had actually got the idea that this man, this dark angry man seated beside her, had been crazy about her!

He drove in silence and the miles fell away on the long straight road where there seemed nothing in the world but the dark bush at either side of the highway and the beam of the headlamps illuminating a fragment of roadway ahead. Lost in her thoughts, she was surprised when suddenly he braked to a stop, pulling in at the side of the lonely bush-fringed road.

"What's wrong?" she jerked herself upright. "Not trouble?"

He turned to face her, the line of his jaw set in the dim light of the dashboard. "Big trouble—no, not the car," as her eyes widened in alarm.

"Then what—" For no reason at all she felt the heavy thud-thud of her heart.

"Alison, there's something we've got to get straightened out—"

"You don't have to tell me," she was in a flurry of pain. A sick sense of humiliation made her rush on. "It's okay, you know."

She was aware of his startled look. "What do you mean?"

Idiot! By forcing the subject she had got herself into an embarrassing position, but she had no course but to follow it through. "Oh, nothing, just about you and Jo—"

His voice was dangerously quiet. "What about it?"

"Oh, you know what I mean." Confusion carried off

whatever sense she had left. "Frances told me all about you and her."

"You don't know." His voice was very low.

"Enough." She scarcely knew what she was saying. "You don't have to spell it out." She only knew she must cling to whatever remnants of pride she had left. "I understand."

"Damn it all, you don't!"

Before she realised his intention his arms were around her and he gathered her close, close. The old betraying sense of wild excitement took over.

"It's you I love, Alison." His lips sought hers in a kiss that sent her pulses leaping wildly in response.

At last, shaken and trembling, she drew away. Her heart was thudding madly. "Don't!" she whispered brokenly. Madness to believe his protestations of love with Jo waiting for him at home. Once again his dark good looks and masculine magnetism had betrayed her into forgetting all the important things, the things that mattered, like Jo's assured position in his home, her planning of renovations to the house where she would soon be mistress.

"You don't expect me to believe you?" Her voice had a high wild note, but evidently the message got through because his arms fell away from her.

"Why shouldn't you believe me?"

"You ask me why, with Jo—"

"Forget Jo!" he said roughly, and made a move towards her, but she was on her guard now against the betraying magic of his touch.

"Sorry, but I can't, not even to please you!"

Anger flared in his tone. "Look, you might give me a chance to explain."

"You might have told me about Jo," she said very low, "before I made a fool of myself. I'll go," she told him nervously, unhappily, "just as soon as—"

"You won't, you know! You'll stay until I can get you to understand a few things I can't seem to get through to you."

"It's no use—"

"Right!" His low angry tone cut her to the heart. "I've told you how I feel. If you choose to think differently, if that's what you want to believe—" Savagely he thrust a hand towards the starter and they shot forward.

What she wanted. Oh, Craig, if you only knew!

She huddled in a corner of the seat as far away from him as possible. Craig never drove in this manner, recklessly and wildly. She had really upset him this time, but it was no more than he deserved. Imagine thinking he could make a pretence of loving her while all the time he and Jo were planning their future life together! Well, she had made it plain to him that she wouldn't play his game and there was no doubt he was angry, surprised too. But what could he expect her to do in such circumstances? Funny—moisture stung her eyes as they swept on in the darkness—you would imagine that having done the right thing you would feel better about it, that it would be a load off your mind, yet she felt no such reaction, only a terrible anguish that seemed to be tearing her apart.

For a crazy moment she was tempted to take him on any terms, but almost immediately the thought died. Anyway, he was no longer interested in her, you could tell that from his stormy dark face, the hard set of his jaw. She swallowed and bit her lip to stop the trembling. If only Jo hadn't come to spoil everything she might have had a chance of happiness. Craig's "It's you I love" might have been true.

The uneasy silence seemed to her to last for ever, but at last they were turning in at the homestead gates. Alison wrenched herself from unhappy musing, realising that although the rest of the house was in darkness, lights streamed from the windows of the room where the twins were sleeping. As Craig braked to a stop at the garage, she let herself out and hurried away. "I'd better see what's wrong with the kids."

He made no answer and she fled into the house. In the lighted room two red and tear-stained faces looked up at her, then the twins were hurling themselves towards her.

"She wouldn't read us a story!"

"She wouldn't let us have the light on. She took away my lamp." Patrick was terrified of the darkness and Alison had made a special trip to the township to get him a tiny light with a low-powered bulb. "She says she's going to throw it away in the gully tomorrow," howled Patrick. "She called me a baby to want it."

"She wouldn't let us get up to get a drink of water!" Sue added her complaint.

The two indignant voices were shouting in unison, "But we got a drink of water when she went out for a walk with Uncle Craig!"

"Yea, and two biscuits." Triumphantly Patrick concluded the triumphant recital. "An' we got back into bed and she didn't know."

"Well, you'll be all right now. Look, here's your little light." Alison picked it up from beneath the bed and fitted in the plug, then switched off the bright centre light.

When she returned to seat herself on the bed the little girl's freckled arms went around Alison's neck. "We love you, Alison."

Patrick hurled himself towards her and she was half-smothered in a bear-hug. "You won't ever leave us again, will you, 'cause we love you and we hate you going away!"

"We won't let you!" Another embrace from Sue.

Something, some sense of being watched, made her look up to meet Craig's brooding gaze. How strange he looked, so stern and forbidding. Yet when he spoke his voice was gentle. "That'll do, you two. Let Alison get some sleep."

She straightened the top sheets, rolled into balls, and pulled the bedclothes over the children. "Go to sleep now. See you in the morning."

"See you in the morning," echoed two sleepy voices.

Leaving the dim light burning, Alison turned away, aware all the time of Craig standing in the doorway. What was he waiting for, and where was Jo?

"Alison—" She avoided his gaze. There was one thing she must remember, and that was not to let herself be alone with him. Resolutions were fine in their way, but she knew that he had only to hold her in his arms once again and it would be harder than ever to make herself remember the important things, like Jo.

"'Night, Craig." She hurried past him and fled up the passage. In the turmoil of her heart she was vaguely aware of the sound of someone sobbing, a sound that came from Jo's room. So the walk she and Craig had taken tonight hadn't mended their recent quarrel? Difficult to imagine Jo crying into her pillow. Anger, yes, retaliation too, but tears...

Lying in bed a little later, she told herself she had done the right thing in refusing to be led into a midnight talk alone with Craig. Only if it was the right thing, why did it hurt so much?

As the days crept by Alison found herself living from day to day, if you could call it living. Really it was existing, watching for Craig, listening for the deep tones of his voice as in the evenings he spent the time at the telephone, deep in discussions with stock agents, veterinary surgeons and carriers. At these times Jo would glance impatiently at the clock, wriggling in her chair and at last, with an angry expression, go to her room. To Alison it seemed a strange courtship between Jo and Craig, but then, she reminded herself, there were countless couples who appeared to thrive on disagreements and reunions. If Craig was happy...certainly he showed little evidence of contentment. Had the deep lines always etched themselves down his lean cheeks, his face been set so grimly? Could be the trouble lay in herself, a third party in his home, but he had refused to let her go and she knew she was bound by the ties of love that held her here until Frances was able to look after the household herself. By that time Jo and Craig might have set a wedding date. The thought was never far from her mind.

It was a relief to escape occasionally from the house, to jump into the Mini and drive over to visit Mary—for at the Vasanovich home her welcome was always warm and uncomplicated.

"Here she is! She's here!" Mama Vasanovich would cry as the little car paused in the driveway. "Mary! Where are you? Alison's come to see you!" By the time Alison was inside all the family would be there to welcome her, all talking at once telling her the latest news of family and farm doings. Always there would be Nick hurrying towards her, his face glowing as if a lantern had been lighted behind the dark eyes, the words spilling excitedly from his lips in the pleasure of seeing her once again.

Today, however, Mary appeared to be acting strangely, waving an arm in the air and sending silent messages over Alison's head to others in the room.

"We'll have to tell her," Mary cried at last, "she's never going to notice!" Only then did Alison realise that on Mary's third finger gleamed an antique ring set with rubies and pearls.

"Mary! I didn't notice!" Her own heartache must have blinded her to the ring that had been repeatedly pushed beneath her gaze. Everyone talked and laughed at once. Tony came out of his office and stood at Mary's side, proud and happy and smiling, accepting Alison's congratulations. Papa Vasanovich opened a bottle of wine, the precious vintage reserved for special family occasions and toasts were drunk to the newly-engaged couple.

It was only after a huge lunch had been eaten and cleared away that the two girls escaped to the privacy of Mary's room.

"I'm glad for you," Alison told her friend, "It's wonderful that things worked out right after all." Her eyes glimmered with a teasing light. "I knew you loved Tony—"

"All the time," Mary's serious face glowed with a

deep inner radiance, "more than anyone in the whole world! What I was worried about was, did he love me?"

"Oh yes, the family—"

"But it wasn't at all like I thought. Tony did give up his training for law, but it was his own idea and he had plenty of family opposition to contend with."

"He told you about it?"

Mary shook her head, her gaze fixed on the jewelled ring encircling her finger.

"It was Mama who put everything right for me. She told me that Tony had never wanted to be a lawyer or to live or work in the city. All he had ever wanted to do, right from childhood, was to work on the land with his father and brothers. It was his parents who set their heart on his following a career. It seems he was very clever at school and they followed the principal's advice at the college and insisted on his having training for law. To please them he stuck it out, he even worked at it for a time, but the family took over a bigger holding and there was need of his trained mind to keep an eye on the business side of things, need of another man too on the farm, he saw his chance to get back to the work he loves. Grandmother Vasanovich had lots of arguments with him about it, but he held out for the sort of life he wanted—and got it." She smiled her secret smile. "And got me as well." For a moment her face grew serious. "If only things could have worked out for you too!"

"Your wedding," Alison cut in quickly, "when is it to be? You'll have to give me time to get something ready to wear."

Mary's sleepy eyes saw entirely too much and an understanding heart supplied the rest.

"We haven't decided yet. Things are just the same, then, with Jo and Craig?"

Alison looked away. "They've known each other... for a long time."

"Too long, maybe. Craig doesn't strike me as a man

who's madly in love—at least, not with Jo. There's nothing more dead than a burned-out love affair, one that's really finished. Jo's wasting her time trying to revive it.''

Alison didn't know that her eyes were lighted with a wild gleam of hope. "Do you really think so?''

"Ask yourself. Especially as everything's different now.''

But Alison wasn't listening. The surge of hope had died away leaving her with the old sick feeling of misery, the hopeless longing. Wishful thinking will get you nowhere. She jerked her thoughts away from thoughts of Craig and said, "Frances wanted me to give you the last chapter of her proverbs book to type.'' She took from her suede bag the folded sheets of handwriting. "She just made it in time. She'll be on her feet pretty soon with lots to do—''

"And you'll be moving on?''

"Don't worry, I'll keep in touch.'' Alison raised a tremulous face, "Wherever I am I'll be back for your wedding.''

They went on to discuss details of the forthcoming wedding and Nick's car that was due to arrive on the following day.

"He's determined to behave himself from now on,'' Mary told her. "Craig's laying it on the line that he wasn't to come near you at his home really hit him hard. He can't wait to prove what a reformed character he is.''

Alison laughed, "Poor Nick!'' but she wasn't really concerned.

The next morning began as usual. She followed the usual routine into which she had fallen since Jo's arrival. First there were breakfasts to be attended to, then the usual household chores and Frances to be comfortably settled for the day. After that came the part of the day she most looked forward to, when she went up the slope to the paddock not far from the house, saddled Banner, then went flying over the gates and up and down grassy slopes encircled with the tracks made by a myriads sheep. Black steers grazing on the hills scattered madly at the approach of the small copper-headed figure mounted on the graceful white mare and sheep milled wildly ahead of the flying hoofs.

There were times when she would catch a glimpse of Craig as he repaired a boundary fence or mustered sheep on the hills, but although every nerve in her body strained towards him she would guide Banner in the opposite direction. No sense of multiplying the memories—and the anguish.

Today as she emerged from a bush track through a gully she caught sight of Craig a short distance away. He was mounted on Pax, one of the stock horses, and gestured to Alison to join him, but she shook her head and went on, urging Banner to a fast canter.

A shout made her glance back over her shoulder to find Craig in pursuit. Well, if he wanted a race he should have it! She leaned forward and encouraged Banner to a faster pace. Ahead loomed a steep slope, but the mare didn't hesitate. Now Alison could hear behind her the thud-thud of galloping hoofs on the turf—but he hadn't caught up with her yet. Half way down the incline rose a seven-barred fence. She heard his warning call but took no notice, clinging with her knees to the white flanks. The fence was directly ahead. "Come on Banner, you can do it!" The mare gathered herself together spread out and sailed effortlessly over the barbed wires running across the hillside. Another minute and Craig's horse landed on the ground directly behind her, then he was riding level grasping her rein. At last flushed and laughing with exhilaration, she drew Banner to a halt.

"You didn't tell me," surprise and delight mingled in his tone, "you were a top show-jumper!"

Caught in the pleasure of the moment, she forgot everything else and turning a smiling face towards him. "You didn't ask me!"

"That's done it!" He turned towards her as the

horses paced surefootedly down the steep incline. Suddenly his eyes were ablaze with excitement, almost... elation. Surely what she had done didn't warrant such a look! "I've got news for you! How would you like to go with me to an A. & P. show they're putting on at the showgrounds on Saturday? Enter Banner in one of the hack events?"

"Fabulous!" Her face was alight with pleasure. "Oh, *could* we?"

"Why not? You get Banner ready for showing and I'll see to everything else. We could put the mare in the truck." Enthusiasm rang in his tone. "We'll enter Banner in the Champion Hunter event and see how she does. You'll know what to do, you've done it all before."

"Lots of times." Today she couldn't lie to him. "I brought my saddle with me."

"Tremendous! The way I look at it, it's a chance to find out what she's capable of." Craig glanced towards her as the horses moved side by side in the bright hot sunshine. "I've only had Banner for a short while and I haven't a clue as to how she performs in the show ring. For all I know the hurdy-gurdy music might scare her stiff or the fluttering of the flags around the arena put her off. I told you before, the mare doesn't belong to me."

"You did say something about it." Alison daren't raise her glance for fear he would read the truth in her eyes.

"So I'd be interested to find out her capabilities in the ring. This is your chance, Alison, yours and Banner's. Win the Champion Hunter event and you'll collect a silver cup and be in the money to the tune of seventy odd dollars. What more could you want?"

What more? The wild surge of excitement ebbed, leaving only the ache of longing. "You seem to have an awful lot of faith in Banner?"

"In *you*, Alison." How deep and vibrant was his tone, almost...caressing. Had she not been aware of the relationship between him and Jo she could almost have imagined...He said softly, "Didn't I ever tell you?"

A little more of this, she thought in panic, his warm expression, the tenderness in his tone, and she would be lost. With an effort she forced herself back to sanity. "You're wrong, you know. Banner is a horse in a million, the sort you only come across once or twice in a lifetime. I just let her have her head." Belatedly she realised she was speaking of the mare as though she had known her for a long time. She added quickly, "If you feel like that about her why don't you ride her yourself at the show?"

"Aha—!" Craig's eyes were dancing with a teasing light and all at once a terrible fear shot through her. He couldn't possibly have discovered the truth about Banner and her previous owner, he couldn't! She found she was holding her breath.

"It's just," he was saying, "that Banner has been used to being ridden by a girl. Chances are she mightn't perform as usual if I took her around the show ring. Like I said, I want to get a true picture of what she can do."

"I see." Somewhere deep inside her a tightly coiled spring seemed to unwind. So he didn't know. It was only her own sense of guilt that had lent significance to his words. Reassured, she looked up into his face and felt confusion, wild and sweet, sweep through her. "Come on, race you to the big tree down there!" She urged Banner forward and the two mounts took off along the straight and galloping side by side, reached the tree at the same moment. As she and Craig pulled in Alison caught sight of the school bus moving along the road far below. "Golly, I've got to get back. Frances will be wanting her afternoon tea and the twins—" The words trailed away as she turned her mount.

"Don't forget—day after tomorrow's Show Day!" Craig called after her.

"I won't! Goodbye!" She pressed her heels to Banner's sides and was away, escaping from the temptation of falling deeper in love with a man who wasn't for her. She risked a swift backward glance. He sat motionless, looking after her. Was he waiting to see her safely over the barbed wires of a sheep-fence looming ahead? There was no need for anxiety on her behalf. Hadn't she and her mare taken countless more difficult jumps at shows and local hunts? The mare performed faultlessly, clearing the top wire easily to land safely on the grass at the opposite side. As Banner moved on Alison allowed herself one more backward glance. He was still looking towards her. She saw him raise his hand in a salute. Just ordinary politeness, of course, he would have done the same for any girl rider who had safely negotiated a difficult jump.

Craig was home early for dinner that evening and it was he who brought up the subject of the forthcoming A. & P. Show to be held in the showgrounds of a neighbouring township at the weekend.

"An A. & P. Show! Super!" Jo's excited voice cut across the laconic tones. "I haven't been to one in years. Maybe," her beguiling smile and melting look was beamed in Craig's direction, "you'll be able to educate me yet in preferring country life to city attractions."

"Sorry, Jo," he sounded polite but uninterested, "but I need Alison with me this time. Special request. Someone's got to stay here with the old lady and keep an eye on her."

"Can we go with you, Uncle Craig? Can we? Can we?" The twins eyed Craig beseechingly. "We've only been to a show once," shouted Patrick. "Once isn't very much, is it?"

"It'll be on again tomorrow. I'll take you in then."

"Goody! Goody!" The twins began pushing into their mouths the heaps of green vegetables pushed to the side of their plates.

Jo's face with its dark and angry expression was turned towards Craig. "I don't see why Alison—"

"I need her to take Banner over the jumps."

Jo said, "You mean that white horse up in the paddock, the one you wanted me to learn to ride?"

"That's her, that's Banner. I'd like to see her in the show ring, get a line on whether she goes wild at the sight of the crowd or keeps her head and clears the jumps. She's used to being taken over the hurdles by a girl rider. If only she stays as cool in the arena as she does around here going over the jumps—"

An expression of pride leaped into Alison's eyes. She cried happily, "Oh, she does! She does!"

Everyone glanced towards her, but she was aware only of Craig's deep intent look. "How do you know, Alison?"

Too late she realized the blunder into which her own enthusiasm had led her. 'I—" she groped wildly in her mind and came up with something at least feasible. "I've seen her perform once or twice at shows, down south. At least," she heard herself babbling wildly, "it was a white mare and it looked...like her. I'm sure that her name was Banner." Beneath Jo's suspicious gaze she could feel the betraying colour rising in her cheeks.

"Well, what d'you know!" Disappointment and envy tinged Jo's strong tones. "Alison has actually told us something about herself. She's been to shows somewhere. At least that's something—"

"Thing is," Craig cut in smoothly, "if you could help me out tomorrow with Banner, Alison?" The words were politely spoken, yet somehow, Alison thought in confusion, he made is sound like an order.

Apparently Jo thought so too, for she snapped, "I don't see why we can't all go tomorrow. Frances could sit in the car and watch—"

"Oh no, dear, I'm afraid not." Alison had expected Frances to grasp eagerly at an opportunity to leave the house for a time, yet here she was displaying a reluctance to fall in with Jo's suggestion.

"It's my leg," she explained with a wince of pain.

"It's been playing up all day. I really wouldn't feel like risking a day out, not without checking up with the doctor, and he won't be calling this week. I'm sorry, Jo, but I do need someone at home with me and Alison could do with a break. She's been really housebound lately. It will do her a world of good to get out for a day and forget all about cooking and cleaning and looking after children—"

"She likes us!" wailed Patrick.

"Of course I do," Alison's smile placated the small distressed face. "I love looking after you both."

"There's something you've all forgotten," Jo's voice held a ring of triumph, "and that is that you won't have any riding gear, Alison. How can you ride in a show? Don't you need jodphurs, hard hat, shirt, jacket, things like that?"

Alison's face fell. It was true. How could she have lost sight of such an essential detail? All she had with her was her beloved saddle.

"It's all right," Craig spoke with careless confidence. "It's all taken care of. I've been ringing around the district and got on to the Smiths. Seems they have four daughters, of varying ages but all show-jumpers. They're all married and away now, but their mother told me she has oodles of their gear lying around the place. She's bringing an outfit over tonight."

"You did?" Alison's face lighted up. She reflected that when it came to Banner's appearance in the show ring at the weekend Craig refused to allow any difficulty to stand in his way.

Apparently Jo's thoughts were running along the same lines. She asked curiously, "How did you know the right size to ask for?"

"I knew." Craig's gaze was on Alison's face and something deep unspoken yet terribly important passed between them. Like a secret message, she thought, or caress.

Apparently, however, someone else had tuned in on that flash of impact, for Jo was pushing back her chair with a scrape. "I've had enough!" The chair fell with a crash to the floor, but she left it there and hurried from the room.

Frances from her seat on the settee looked after her worriedly. "I don't know what made her get so huffy all of a sudden."

Alison wished she didn't know. In spite of all her resolutions to the contrary a secret traitorous happiness was taking over. Tomorrow...tomorrow she would be with Craig. She darted a glance towards his impassive face, but he was rolling a cigarette, apparently engrossed in the task. What electricity leaping between them gave her the secret knowledge that, in spite of his calm appearance, he felt it too?

THE FOLLOWING AFTERNOON she was on her knees in the back porch, newspapers spread out around her cleaning and polishing her saddle and bridle when Jo came strolling in the door. She said, "I've just been down to collect the mail," and something in Jo's tone alerted Alison to danger. There was a malignant sparkle in the prominent blue eyes.

Alison turned back to her task. For something to say she murmured, "Nothing for me?"

"No," Jo paused at her side, "but then there wouldn't be any, would there? You never get any mail ever, *and I know why!*"

Alison felt as though someone had punched her in the stomach. So Jo had discovered who she really was and intended to use the knowledge to her advantage. There was no doubt of it, or why did Jo look so triumphant all of a sudden? She bent her head and went on polishing. "How do you mean?"

"You know what I mean! You're not Alison Wynyard at all! You come from Te-o-nui and you were known there as Alison Carter. You see, I know all about you, how you were forced to give up the house and property when Craig inherited it from the couple who had taken you in." *Taken her in*, that hurt, that

really hurt! Dot and Jim had been her parents in everything but the matter of birth, they had loved her.
Had—for all that was over. Now she was on her own
and about to be unmasked as a liar and a cheat, even
something worse. She could read the accusation in Jo's
angry eyes.

"I suppose you thought you were pretty smart,
worming your way into Craig's home, making up to
him, trying to get him to marry you. Oh, you were determined to get your property back, one way or another, even though it had never ever belonged to you.
But Craig wasn't taken in by your schemes and neither
was I. It just happened that I was a bit smarter than you.
Wait until I tell Craig how you've been pulling the wool
over the eyes of everyone here."

She raised panic-stricken eyes. Her voice was very
low. "How did you find out?"

"It wasn't hard once I got an idea that something was
going on." Jo bent down until her eyes were on a level
with Alison's face. Angry, accusing, *triumphant* eyes.
"Last year when I was staying at the house I met an
aunt of Craig's. I remembered her telling me about
you. She said you had curly red hair and you were en-
grossing in show-jumping and a white horse you had
called Banner. It wasn't much trouble to write away to
the aunt and check up on you. I made an excuse that I
wanted to buy your mare and needed some details of
the owner. I got the answer back today. She fell for the
story and told me what she knew. It wasn't much, just
that you seemed to have vanished after the house and
property were sold up, but that was enough for me. Too
bad about your schemes, but they wouldn't have
worked, not with Craig. My advice to you is to get going fast, before I tell everyone here, starting with Craig,
how you made a play to get your property back, *the easy
way*."

The colour had drained from Alison's face. She got
to her feet. "You wouldn't!"

"Watch me!" Something about the other girl's set

angry face told her Jo would have no hesitation in carrying out her threat. "It's what you deserve, living a lie like that! Oh, it was a good idea, it might even have worked. You're running enough with that little-girl-lost voice of yours and all the rest of it. I'll keep it to myself, but only if you make yourself scarce. I'll give you until after the weekend and then—out! Is it a deal?"

Alison said very low, "I can't leave them."

"Why not? No one is indispensable, especially you. Craig will soon find someone else to give him a hand outside and if he doesn't, I can always help you out. You can easily make some excuse, anything. Tell him you've got a sick mother."

Alison winced and Jo had the grace to look a little ashamed. "Tell him anything, I don't care, as long as you get going!"

Alison's thoughts were whirling in turmoil. Why did her presence here mean so much to Jo? She couldn't be jealous, not on her account—or could she? Should she make a confession to Craig herself, tell him who she was and how it had all happened that she found herself here? Would he believe her? It was scarcely likely, because Jo would leave him in no doubt as to the truth or otherwise of the story. He would be told that she had been pursuing him for her own gains and anything would be preferable to that, even flight. Frances won't need me here in a matter of a week or two and the twins will soon forget. Craig... but it didn't do to think of Craig. She would like him to remember her once in a while, remember her not as a scheming little money-grabber but just... Alison.

"Well," demanded Jo harshly, "have you made up your mind? What's it to be?"

Alison said slowly, "I haven't any choice, have I?" The words were wrung from some deep well of pain. "Not really."

"Hello, what goes on?" Craig, looking happy and carefree, pushed his felt sombrero to the back of his head as he came whistling up the path. "You two are looking pretty intent on something or other. What is it, girl's talk?''

Alison didn't dare look up for fear he would glimpse the anguish in her face. It was Jo's cool tones that made answer. "Something like that. You wouldn't be interested."

"How do you know?" He went on into the house and Jo followed him.

Alison gathered up polish and brushes and stowed them in her woven flax pipi-kit. Now that she had lost everything and her last hope of happiness had fled a wild recklessness took over. She had a day, one day left from the wreckage of all those crazy dreams. Even Jo couldn't cheat her out of those few hours alone with Craig away from the other girl's jealous accusing eyes.

As she took her saddle and bridle into the shed she made up her mind that tomorrow she and Banner would give their best performance ever! Banner...the thought struck her with a sense of loss that she could never claim her mare now. Faced with that deeper deprivation, however, even the prospect of losing Banner faded into insignificance.

All at once she realised that Craig was moving towards her. "Here, let me do that." He lifted the saddle up to a bracket. "All set for tomorrow?"

She nodded, unable to trust herself to speak, thankful that in the dimness of the old shed he couldn't see the tears that blinded her eyes.

Nonchalantly he leaned against a shelf, his gaze on her averted face. "How was the gear from Smiths? Fit okay?"

"Oh yes, yes!" She prayed he wouldn't catch the unsteady note in her voice, "I tried it all on last night and even the jodphur boots were the right size. I don't know how you knew—"

"Don't you?" The caressing note in his low tones went straight to her heart. His gaze rested on the slim young figure and turned-away face and she felt his hand on her head, ruffling the tumbled curls. "I know a whole lot about you, Alison."

She gave a shaky laugh. Thank heaven he didn't!

All at once his tone was casual. "We'll load Banner on to the truck early, about seven—did you want something, Jo?"

"Nothing." Jo's glance darted from his laconic face to Alison's tremulous lips. "Just a handkerchief. I must have left it somewhere else."

CHAPTER TEN

ALISON SLEPT LITTLE that night and it was a relief to get
up very early in the morning, a day of soft cloud where,
as so often in this part of the country, sky, sea and land
mingled in an atmospheric effect. The rain that hovered near yet never seemed to fall hovered overhead in
grey cottonwool clouds streaked with sunshine. Like
my life, Alison mused. So soon she would be parted
from Craig for ever, but today was her own, shot with
golden gleams of excitement.

When she went to catch Banner to groom her for the
show the mare was already at the gate nickering to her
as she approached. Yesterday she had worked up a
soapy lather and rubbed it into the white coat. Now,
however, it was clear that the mare had rolled in the
grass, for the white legs were streaked with green. "Oh,
Banner, how *could* you?" Alison scrubbed the legs
down, plaited the neatly trimmed mane and tail and
rubbed oil into the hooves.

She returned to the house to change into the borrowed riding gear, now pressed and immaculate. The
bald patches on the hard hat she had touched up with
black boot polish, a trick she had often resorted to in
the past. When she was dressed and ready she was
struck once again by the perfect fit of the garments.
Who would have guessed that Craig would be so observant concerning herself? Thinking of Craig brought
back the surge of wild inexplicable happiness that had
bemused her at intervals since yesterday. He's only taking you to a local show, she reminded herself, and that
only because of Banner. Didn't he tell you that he

wants to try her out against competition? There's nothing personal in his invitation, how could there be?

So why did she feel this way? It was no use, no amount of rationalising could avail against the high tide of excitement and anticipation, and all the time the feeling of recklessness persisted. She was tired of pretending, sickened of being treated by Jo as someone who apart from her duties was of little account in the household.

Presently, in jodhpurs, white blouse and green tie with the bright curls brushed away from her face, she went out to help load Banner into the waiting truck. Craig was there already, freshly-shaven, oddly unfamiliar and terribly attractive in lemon shirt, checked sports jacket and slacks. Or was it the expression in his eyes when he greeted her that was throwing her into this state of wild confusion?

"I'm so lucky you got me the gear to wear today," she told him breathlessly, "though I still don't know how you guessed the size so perfectly."

"I told you, I notice everything about you—especially the way your hair curls up like this." Once again he put up a hand to touch the coppery-red waves and curls. "Don't put the helmet on yet. Why hide hair like that?"

Because this was dangerous territory in which she couldn't afford to linger she said hurriedly, "The truck would hold a couple of horses." She remembered the glittering array of silver trophies arranged along the mantel. "Why not change your mind and enter for some events yourself today?"

"Can't do that. Sabre's let me down badly, he got caught in some barbed wire last night and ripped a nasty gash in his leg. I'll get the vet to come and have a look at him. Anyway, it's your day today, Alison!"

"And Banner's!" He didn't appear to hear her.

Although in the past when taking Banner to shows and gymkhanas the mare had been no problem at all to get into the horse-float, today she showed a reluctance to enter the truck. At last, however, with a lot of heaving and pushing, plus appeals by Alison and a certain amount of strong language on Craig's part, they got her up the ramp and into the vehicle.

A hurried cup of coffee and slice of toast at the house, then they collected the picnic hamper Alison had prepared in readiness for the outing and they were out in the yard once again. The others were still in bed, but the twins wandered out in their sleeping suits, watching with interest as Alison climbed up to the high seat and Craig secured the doors of the vehicle.

"Goodbye! Goodbye!" The children were still waving enthusiastically when Alison got out of the truck to open the last gate before they turned into the main road.

"It seems mean not taking them with us," she murmured as she climbed back into the truck.

"Take them!" Craig threw an incredulous glance. "After all the trouble I've been to to get you to myself for once."

Her pulses leaped, then steadied, and she glanced towards him uncertainly. He didn't mean what he'd said, of course, it was all just a game to him, part of the day's outing. "You're joking!"

"I never lie to you, Alison," his voice softened, deepened. "If you like I'll prove it to you."

Again the wild sweet happiness. "I believe you," she said hastily. And so she did—almost. No doubt he did mean what he said, at the moment. To change the subject she said, "Tell me about the place where the show is being held. Is it far?"

"Roughly an hour and a half's drive from here. It's an annual event and from what I gather they get a great attendance. They tell me the crowds get bigger every year and so do the show attractions. There'll be the usual chop, merry-go-round and all that stuff for the kids, with a rodeo on the second day. The ads feature something new to me. Seems a farmer somewhere up north has kept some bullocks and trained them as a

team. Quite a novelty these days. Ever come across a
bullock team in your part of the country?"

"No." Any mention of her past life brought with it a
feeling of defensiveness that was becoming a habit with
her. Wait for it. Next would come the inevitable query.
"Where *do* you come from, Alison? You've never
really let on."

Surprisingly, however, he did not pursue the subject
and she relaxed in her seat. "Will you buy me some
candy floss when we get there, Craig? I've got a weakness for it."

He slanted her a teasing grin. "Not that sticky pink
tack? You don't mean to tell me you like it?"

"Love it."

"It's just a lot of nothing."

Like my happy day with you, Craig, that seems so
perfect, yet underneath it's all as unsubstantial and
airy-fairy as candy floss. "I like it," she persisted stubbornly.

"Then you shall have it. And anything else you
want."

Anything else? Oh, Craig, don't torture me. She
forced her mind back to her surroundings. To the long
straight bordered with raupo and blowing flax and the
green hills all around them with their long shadows
chased by the wind. Craig was driving carefully with
concern for the mare and as they went on they could
glimpse in the distance a Land Rover towing a horsefloat, followed by a long stock truck and trailer. Other
vehicles too were heading in the direction of the show
grounds. Above them the swiftly-changing skies were
darkening. Great gunmetal clouds collided with a thunderous roar and big drops splashed against the dust of
the windscreen. Another minute and rain streamed
down the windows. Alison, peering ahead, could scarcely see ahead because the road was almost obliterated by
the sudden deluge. Then as abruptly as it had started the
pelting cyclonic downpour cleared, the clouds drifted

away and the sun was shining hotly, adding a fresh sparkle to tea-tree and flax that lined the roadside.

They passed through a small country township where modern attractive shops lined the main street, sped past a picturesque old timber hotel, a petrol pump on the corner. Ahead of them was a long line of vehicles and clustered around the entrance gates of the large area of the show grounds were trucks and Land Rovers, horse-floats and stock carriers. As they took the track towards the grassy enclosure where horses and vehicles were assembled Alison caught glimpses of tents and open stalls. She watched the ferris wheel as it circled high in a washed blue sky and heard the carnival music grinding out from the merry-go-round where excited children clung shrieking to their wooden mounts. Then Craig was guiding the truck in a space between the parked caravans and tethered horses. To Alison it was a familiar scene with children anxiously attending to their ponies, parents hovering around cars and horse-floats, a voice on a loudspeaker calling for competitors entered in a pony event.

Craig led Banner from the truck and tethered her to the side of the vehicle. "I'll go and put in your entry. What's it to be?"

She glanced up from grooming the mare. The mood of recklessness still possessed her and she looked back at him levelly. "The Champion Hunter of course, what else? She can do it!"

The expression of pride and excitement that crossed his face was worth a lot. "That's my girl!"

Oddly she didn't feel in the least perturbed in anticipation of competing in the champion show-jumping event of the afternoon. It was the sort of day when anything could happen. And Banner, she knew, was an outstanding show-jumper.

When Craig had moved away in the direction of the tent where two women were taking names for the hack ring events, Alison took her saddle and bridle from the truck. She had complete faith in Banner, especially as she knew she could trust her mount not to allow excitement to get the better of her. Had Craig but known, the mare was quite at home amongst the crowds and general bustle of the show. Hadn't Banner won for herself endless rosettes, red ribbons and silver trophies at similar gatherings over the past few years? Not the Champion Hunter event—well, not yet, but Alison was going to see that today Banner gave it a darned good try!

What puzzled her was that Craig showed no surprise at her confidence in the mare's jumping ability. Another odd thing was the confidence he appeared to have in her as a rider. One would have expected him to question her regarding previous events in which she had taken part, but he hadn't done that. Had she not known such a thing was well nigh impossible she might almost have suspected him of knowing all about her. At the thought her heart almost stopped. Then she told herself not to be absurd. How could he know? For a moment she stood motionless. *I wish he did know. I wish there was nothing between us, no secrets, no Jo.*

"It's all fixed." Craig came striding towards her over the wet grass. "Your event isn't on until late." How happy and animated he looked! Much too happy for a man parted from his love? Nonsense, he was merely enjoying the day, excited over the possibilities of the performance of the white mare in the show ring, for it was clear that his faith in Banner's show-jumping abilities matched her own, and she *knew* what Banner could do. Of course that was the explanation of his high spirits. "You'll have swags of competition," he told her as he came back to join her. "There's a mob of entries for that event and the jumps are high, particularly the brush ones. Come along and take a look." He tucked her arm in his and they threaded their way between parked caravans and stock trailers as they moved towards the arena. For a time they stood watching the entrants assemble for the next event but Alison was aware only of Craig's nearness, his touch. Presently they moved away to the roped-off area separating the hack and pony rings, Alison, however, was finding it difficult to concentrate on the field. She was much too conscious of his nearness and it was only vaguely that she realised that the brush jumps were high indeed and so was the wire jump in the centre of the field. A tiny voice that she knew she shouldn't trust echoed deep in her mind. As though anything could go wrong today!

They watched the event, waiting as the judges adjudicated points and announced the winners. Then they turned their attention to the field on the opposite side of the track where children mounted on ponies were moving in a ring. One small girl with a mop of red ringlets was evidently finding difficulty in controlling her restive mount, because she trailed a long way behind her competitors.

"She looks like you," observed Craig. "All those curls—or weren't you like that at eight years old?"

Alison laughed. "I guess I could have been—a bit. I know I was about that age when I first started taking my pony to the local show." *Careful now*, Alison.

He didn't follow the lead she had given him, thank heaven. She said smilingly, "I hope I give a better account of myself today than that!" For the small rider had slipped to the ground and was sobbing bitterly.

"You will." It was amazing, the confidence he had in her considering that all he had to go on was seeing her clear the farm fences or take Banner over the jumps she had made for herself in the paddock.

As they made their way amongst happy family groups and excited children Alison mused that it was fortunate both she and Craig were strangers to the district. Otherwise they may have found themselves drawn into a picnic party or a group of young farmers. But they strolled on unchallenged until suddenly raindrops pelted down once again and they hurried back to the shelter of the truck. Alison didn't mind rain today, not when it meant she could sit in the front of the vehicle with Craig, screened from everyone by the cyclonic shower. All at once it was over, the sun struggled through cloud and once again everything was a-glitter.

In the fitful sunshine they dropped down from the truck and hand in hand like children, they leaped over rain puddles on the path as they made their way towards a wood-chopping event in the ring at the entrance to the pavilion. They watched as one competitor after another mounted a tree to wield a flashing axe with speed and precision as the chips fell around. At last they moved on, passing the sheep pens under the trees and the sheep-shearing pavilion where muscular men with sweat running down their shoulders worked against the clock as the heavy fleeces fell to the floor. Then they wandered away to watch the teams of marching girls, preceded by a military band playing from the cramped shelter of the official stand. Still hand in hand they stood watching the grand parade headed by a team of bullocks patiently plodding around the ring. Behind them came the glossy horses and prize-winning stock, then the cars, tractors and motor cycles on display.

When it was over they strolled towards the stalls, mingling with the crowd while the age-old carnival melodies around them formed a background to all the fun of the fair. Craig bought a hot-dog for himself, but when he asked Alison to have one too she shook her head. "You promised—"

"Oh yes, the candy floss." They found a tent nearby where a girl was bending over the whirling candy in a drum and he presented Alison with a cornet of pink fluff.

They returned to watch the riding events in the ring until the announcer declared a break for lunch and they made their way back to the truck. The day, her precious day, was flying by so fast!

With appetites sharpened by the fresh air they enjoyed the man-sized hamburgers Alison had prepared. The freshly-baked buns filled with ham and salad were a welcome change from the usual diet of mutton which she prepared in various ways. Afterwards she poured coffee from a flask and they bit into crunchy red apples plucked from trees in the orchard that morning.

When the show-jumper events were resumed Craig helped her to saddle Banner, Alison leaped up lightly, and waited for the signal to enter the arena. It came at last and as she alerted the mare Craig was beside her, his hand warm and encouraging as he clasped her fingers. "Good luck, Alison!"

"Thanks, Craig." He came with her as she rode Banner towards the high brush jumps. As she warmed her own mount up other riders entered one at a time. One horse, excited by the crowd and waving flags, shied away from the first fence. A big bay hunter refused suddenly at the huge brush, tipping his rider on to the ground. She realised it would not be easy. There had been no clear rounds at all.

CHAPTER ELEVEN

"Alison Wynyard!" She heard her own name called, the name to which she was getting accustomed. No longer did she do a double-take before realising it was her own. As she entered the grassy enclosure the look on Craig's face stayed with her. When he looked at her like that she felt she could do anything, anything!

The confidence born of the moment persisted. Or could it be pride in her mount that prompted this feeling of assurance? For Banner, with her long steady stride and unflappable nature, was progressing without a fault. As one brush jump after another loomed up she took exactly the right sized stride beforehand, then spreading herself out, sailed over, to land perfectly on the other side. The crowd that had gathered to witness the main event of the day crowded close to the rope. As Alison swept around once again she was tempted to look for Craig for she knew he would be watching her progress, but long training held and she fixed her gaze ahead on the high brush jump.

Over...then another...over...no trouble at all. Now there remained only the last hurdle, the wire jump in the centre of the field, to surmount. A hush fell over the watching crowd as the girl mounted on the graceful white mare moved towards the final jump, a coppery-haired girl who was leaning forward in the saddle. She could feel Banner gathering herself and spreading out. They were up, up and over, a faultless performance completing a clear round.

A cheer broke from the crowd as Alison on Banner cantered away, but she was scarcely aware of the groups pressed against the rope barrier. She only knew that Craig was there, Craig looking at her in a way he had never done before, elated, with wildly shining eyes. He hurried towards her and as she slipped down from the saddle he caught her close. "You made it, Alison! You made it! I knew you would!" His eyes said a lot more, said things she dared not interpret. *Why fool yourself, it's Banner's success he's so excited about!*

She became aware that strangers were approaching her, offering congratulations, shaking her by the hand. It was a victory for her and Banner—not the one she wanted, but nevertheless a victory, and there was no doubt they meant it kindly.

"Good show!"

"Great performance you put up, Miss Wynyard!"

"Have you shown Banner often?"

"What else have you won with her?"

The questions and congratulations fell around her until the voice of the judge echoing over the loud-speaker called her away. "The winner of the Champion Hunter Event is Alison Wynyard on Banner. The prize is a cheque for seventy dollars as well as a silver cup donated by Lord Westerbury of England."

Alison moved forward to accept the trophy and prize money. She thanked the sponsors and the judge. Then when the prizegiving was over she made her way back to Craig, waiting on the outskirts of the crowd. They were examining the silver trophy together when the judge, a tall alert-looking woman of middle age, walked across the grass to join them.

"That's a great mare you've got there!" she said to Alison. "I can't think why I didn't recognise her right away. This is the second time I've awarded her first place in a hunter event. Last year at a gymkhana in Te-o-nui, remember? It was your name that put me off the track. Alison Wynyard was unfamiliar." Her friendly glance went to Craig, standing tall and attentive at Alison's side. "I didn't know you were married, my dear. This is your husband?"

To Alison the terrible shame-making moment seemed to last for ever. "No," she gasped, "I—"

Something of her distress must have got through to

the woman. She said quickly, "I just took it for granted. I'm afraid I've made an awful mistake—"

"No mistake," Craig's cool tones cut across the embarrassed accents. "You're a bit early, that's all. Carter's my name, and I'm going to make it Alison's too—"

"*Carter*?" The expression of the judge's sun-weathered face changed from one of surprise to complete bewilderment. "But that was—I don't get it."

"You will!" Craig assured her in his easy tone.

"Sorry to butt in," a man in riding gear touched the woman on the arm, "but they're waiting for you in the judge's tent—"

"Not to worry," Craig told her with his friendly grin, "we'll explain it all later. Better still, we'll send you an invitation to the wedding!"

"Wedding!" Alison tried to speak lightly, but she didn't make much of a success of it. How much had Craig understood of the judge's words? Enough to make him realise that she was living under an assumed name, or what must appear to him to be an assumed name. "That poor woman," she was speaking wildly, running on in panic, "she won't be in a fit state to do any more judging today with your spinning her a tale like that."

"But we *are* getting married—if you'll have me!" He spoke so softly, yet all around her bells seemed to be ringing. The next moment she came back to reality with a jolt.

He was teasing her, of course. His talk of marriage had been an impulse thought up on the spur of the moment to cover her obvious dismay and confusion, what else? He couldn't really mean it. All at once she felt utterly deflated. "You don't understand, what she said about me is true. Here, take these—" she thrust towards him the silver trophy and the cheque. It was finished, this stupid masquerade of hers, all over in one minute. She pulled herself up in the saddle, said wretchedly, "You see, I did have another name when I was given a red rosette at a gymkhana last year." She pulled on the rein.

"I know," he said calmly, "it was Carter."

"You—knew?" She spun around, incredulous.

He took hold of the bridle and there was no avoiding his direct gaze. "I've known about you for a long time."

"But how—? I didn't say a word."

"Didn't you?" It was odd, but he didn't appear disillusioned and angry or even disgusted with her. And how calm was his tone, she thought bewilderedly, not at all the sort of reaction one would have expected from him now that her trickery had been exposed. She wrenched her mind back to the deep tones.

"Remember the night of the smash? The time you flaked out when I was taking you home? You gave yourself away, you know, you told me yourself."

Her eyes were wide in dismay. "But I couldn't have!" she cried incredulously. "I didn't say anything."

"You said it all in five little words. 'Take me home to Te-o-nui.'"

"And that was how you knew?"

A twinkle of amusement flickered in his eyes. "Oh, there were plenty of pointers along the way. Remember that first day when you caught sight of Banner? No girl would get all that excited over a strange white mare. And Banner's welcome to you was pretty obvious too. Besides, you did clam up every time I brought up anything to do with your past life. You looked guilty as hell into the bargain. I told you," he reminded her gently, "that your face is a dead giveaway every time!"

"But I didn't know," she told him in her sweet young voice. "I had no idea when I called at your place with Mary that it was *your* home. Truly, Craig, you've just *got* to believe me!"

For a moment he was silent, regarding her with an expression she couldn't interpret.

"I didn't go there for the reason you think," she

cried defensively, and felt the hot colour flooding her cheeks. "You don't need to feel—"

"Come on, Alison," he said softly, "take Banner away and give her a drink and a brush-down. Then we'll shove her back in the truck and take off."

"Take off?" Her spirits plummeted. He had hidden his feelings well, but underneath it all it was all too clear that he couldn't wait to be rid of her. Dispiritedly she turned away.

Suddenly his compelling tones were deep with emotion. "We'll go somewhere where I can tell you how I feel about you."

Alison began to tremble inside. He didn't speak like a man who never wished to set eyes on her again. *Could he possibly have meant those words about a wedding?* The next moment she wrenched her mind back to sanity. Things like that didn't really happen.

When they reached the grassy enclosure competitors who had been taking part in the jumping and flat events were already loading their mounts into trucks and horse-floats, coloured ribbons fluttering from the cabs of vehicles. To everyone else as well as Craig this was no more than the end of an enjoyable day, while to Alison it meant the end of everything she held dear.

Heavy-hearted, she led Banner up the ramp and into the truck, tossing the silver trophy carelessly on to the seat. What matter a silver cup now that she had lost the real prize in life?

"Why so sad?" Seated in the high seat at her side, Craig had his hand on the starter. Was it his uncanny perception concerning herself or that too-revealing face of hers that enabled him to divine her feelings so correctly?

Hastily she composed her features into a pleasant mask. "I'm not really." She gazed unseeingly out of the window. The giant ferris wheel was stilled, a tracery against a grey sky, and the muddied pathway leading to the gates ahead was jammed with slow-moving trucks and transporters, horse-floats and dust-spattered cars.

At length they were out on the main road joining in a long procession of vehicles winding in the direction of a small township ahead. As they came nearer she could glimpse water tumbling over a rocky cliff into a river below and presently they were approaching a small colourful township with hilly streets and clean attractive stores that lined the highway. As Craig pulled up in the main street she glanced across at him in surprise. "Why are we stopping here?"

He didn't answer for a moment. A look of controlled excitement flickered in the dark eyes, excitement... and something else. Alison said uncertainly, "Is there something you want?"

"*Is* there?" How strange he sounded, so quiet and intense, as if it were something that mattered terribly to him, something like— Again the look of secret excitement that made her heart give a crazy upsurge. Was it possible that incredible story he had told the woman judge hadn't been just a fun-thing after all, could he really have meant it for real? The next moment she pulled herself up. He was probably referring to some part of machinery he needed for the truck or tractor which he intended buying from the garage opposite. There she went again, reading impossible things into his gaze.

"I'm hoping I'll get what I want tonight. Let's see, shall we?"

Obligingly she leaped lightly down to the footpath and once again Craig clasped her hand in his. "Come on, this happens to be important!" It *must* be a part for the truck.

They waited while a great stock-transporter thundered past then he led her into the door of a restaurant. She looked up at him in surprise. "But you said—"

"Let's eat first." Once again she was aware of his air of suppressed excitement.

She hesitated. "What about the others at home? Jo—"

"Forget about Jo!" *Forget about Jo!* Alison could

scarcely believe her ears. "This is our night, just us, you and me."

So the day wasn't yet finished after all, the magic still endured. Why not take the reprieve she had been offered, multiply the memories? Another hour or so with him would be something to remember in the lonely years that stretched ahead. She preceded him down the long carpeted aisle of the dimly-lighted room and without waiting for the waitress who was moving towards them he led Alison to an isolated table in a quiet corner away from the main body of diners. He saw her seated, then flung himself down opposite her, handing her the menu. "The fried schnapper they put on here is recommended, probably caught this morning right here in the harbour."

"That'll be fine." At this moment she couldn't have cared less what variety of food was served to her. It would all taste heavenly, eaten here with Craig. All at once it came to her how seldom they had been alone together during the past week or so. Her own fault really, seeing that since Jo's arrival at the house she had resisted all attempts by Craig to speak with her in private. Tonight was different, tonight she would take what fate offered.

He gave the order and when the wine steward approached their table, ordered champagne.

"Champagne?"

At her expression of surprise he leaned over the table, his eyes dark and intent. "Why not? It's a celebration. Special!"

Then she remembered. Of course, he was referring to the Champion Hunter trophy she had won today.

Mindful of the mare waiting in the truck outside, they did not linger over the meal. When they emerged from the restaurant the amethyst haze over the hills had darkened to a soft darkness, pricked with a handful of stars. As she climbed back into the truck Alison reflected that she was glad they had interrupted the journey to eat at the restaurant. It had given her a little more time and, for her, time was running out. As they moved away into the night Craig threw an arm around her shoulders and she found herself wishing the journey could last for ever. At intervals they passed clusters of lights that were small townships along the highway, then all too soon they had left the smooth bitumen and had turned into a rough metal road, where the only sign of habitation was the glow of an isolated farmhouse set high on a hill. Presently she caught the glimmer of lake water at the side of the road and before long the sombre pine forests rising on either side of the winding track told her they were nearing their destination.

She was very quiet as they approached the turn-off and soon she was getting out to open the gates. When Craig pulled up in the yard she slipped down from the high seat and soon they were unloading Banner. Alison led the mare away while Craig garaged the truck.

The moon had risen, a silver ball in a luminous dark-blue sky. In the moonglow she led the mare up the silvered pathway winding up the slope. As she closed the gate in the paddock a dark shadow was coming towards her and a moment later Craig was beside her...a different Craig this..."Alison!" He caught her close and kissed her forehead, the tip of her nose, her throat, and last of all, her lips. At last he released her, whispered hoarsely, "I've wanted to do this for a long time, but you never gave me the chance—"

The poignant forbidden happiness was taking over. "I know I know—" Then sanity came back with a rush. "But Jo—"

He caught her once more in strong arms, holding her closer than ever. "You can forget about Jo, put her right out of your mind—"

She stirred, said on a sigh, "If only I could!"

"It's over, my sweet. Whatever there was between us is dead and gone." His wild exultant laugh echoed in her ears as once again his seeking lips were on her own.

When she could speak... "Over!" Dazedly she stared

up at him, unable to take in the electrifying words he had said, "You mean, there's nothing between you and her?"

"I mean there never was anything real with Jo and me, and whatever there was was all washed up a long time ago. It was a bit difficult...I was hoping she would get the message and shoot back to the South where she comes from, but in the end I had to spell it out, tell her the truth. I guess she had to have it straight, especially as she was spreading the word around about staying on with me for good."

He drew a little away, his eyes dark and thoughtful. "We had it all out last night, late. It wasn't too pleasant, but there were things that had to be got out in the open. I don't think she was too surprised really. She must have known we were through with each other a year ago. That was the reason she took off on the tourist trip. I happen to know that she was planning a wedding when she got back from the cruise, an Australian she'd met on the trip. But something happened, a story got around that he already had a girl of his own back in Sydney. Anyway, Jo found herself out on a limb. It was a situation she couldn't take. Her pride had taken a pounding and she got the idea of salvaging something out of the wreck of our old relationship, such as it was. There was a time when just for a while—" He broke off. "No need to go into that. Jo would never have meant anything to me, even if I hadn't been lucky enough to meet you."

His words were ringing bells again all over the place.

"Did Jo...say anything about me?"

"Oh, she tried to tell me some story about you and your name, nothing I hadn't known already."

Alison stirred in his arms. "You didn't think I'd done it deliberately, coming here, I mean?" and held her breath for the answer.

"I—know—you, Alison." His kisses punctuated the words. "Jo's raking up the old ashes didn't mean a thing to me. She'll thank me one of these days when she meets someone more in her own line. The country life was not for her, or a country man either." His voice softened, deepened. "Not like my girl."

"What is she like?" Alison whispered.

"Oh, she's really something! I was so lucky to find her! So pretty...so very lovely..." He twined around his finger a clinging copper-coloured tendril of hair. "You wouldn't believe that a girl so lovely could be so knowledgeable."

She raised a flushed face. "Only because I like working with you."

He said softly, "There's more to marriage than work, you know."

"Marriage?"

"I've had it on my mind for quite a while," he whispered close to her ear. "There's just one real love in my life, and I've found it right here amongst the sandhills. Once you came into my life, that was it!" All at once the deep tones were warm and tender. He caught her closer and once again his lips sought hers. "Marry me, say you'll marry me and I'll never have to let you go again—ever."

"The answer's 'yes,'" she whispered, the remainder of the words lost in his caress. She was swept by elation she had never known existed. The stars seemed to be whirling overhead and her whole being rose on a great wave of happiness.

After a time she murmured contentedly, "If only I'd known that with you there was no secret to worry about!" She stirred in his arms, reaching up to trace the lines of the beloved masculine face. "Why didn't you let on when you first knew about me?"

He put his fingers to his lips. "I wasn't going to risk losing you. I was all set to get things cleared up as soon as you were well again after the accident. Then Jo breezed in to ruin everything and I didn't want to push my luck. I knew what might happen if I let on to you about knowing all about you right then, with Jo talking about house alterations, making out everything was set

and all she had to do was plan the wedding. You'd have
taken off, you know you would, and I'd have had to go
and find you all over again. The way I look at it it was
easier to let things ride, mark time until I got matters
straightened out with Jo.'' Once again his kiss started a
trembling in her. "Everything sorted out now?"

"Oh yes, yes," she whispered. "It's so wonderful to
have no more secrets, especially your knowing about
my coming here being a mere accident—'' She raised a
tremulous face. "You do believe me?"

"Not really." She caught his low exultant laugh. "I'd
call it fate!"

Alison felt inclined to agree with the verdict. "You
knew, though," she murmured, "the moment I mentioned Te-o-nui?"

He held her close. "There's only one place of that
name I've ever heard of, only one girl with coppery-
coloured hair, a girl called Alison, who disappeared
from there, vanished so completely that my inquiries
with her lawyer came to a dead end and all my letters
failed to catch up with her. They were sent back to me
by the Post Office, address unknown."

"You wrote to me?"

"Half a dozen times. I wanted you to share the inheritance with me. I made it plain that we'd be
partners—but now," passion and urgency were in his
kiss, "I've found a better way. That's why I'm asking
you to stay with me for ever." His hand traced her soft
cheek. "I love you." Then she was caught in his arms,
close, close. His voice came muffled, hoarse with emotion. "Right from the start when you walked into my
life I couldn't think of anything else, I couldn't get you
out of my mind. The thoughts of you going out with
young Nick nearly set me raving mad."

"You needn't have worried. How do you think I felt
when Jo turned up out of the blue?"

"Oh, Jo." The lack of interest in his tone told her
how mistaken she had been in ever imagining that any
embers remained from forgotten fires. The next mo-

ment he whispered close to her ear, "There never was anyone else but you, there never will be."

"Me too." She had no doubts, no fears, only this rapturous sense of happiness and fulfilment.

"It's you and me together from now on." All at once his tone softened. "It's a pretty rugged life you'll be taking on with me, little one, especially when a man happens to be working on his own. There'll be times when I'll have to call on you to give me a hand with mustering. You'll need to cook for gangs of shearers as well as feed all the other bods that turn up to stay. Farm cadets, duck-shooters, wild pig hunters, the odd fisherman—"

Alison put a hand to his lips. "I'll love it all—with you."

When she could think constructively once again she murmured, "I wonder what Frances will say when she hears our news? I know she'll be surprised—"

"You reckon?" Amusement tinged his tone. "The old lady's been on at me from almost the first day you arrived at the house for not letting you slip away. It wasn't Jo whom she'd picked out for a daughter-in-law, not once she'd met you."

"Jo—" she linked the bronzed fingers in her own, "she really did seem to think she'd be your wife before long—"

For a moment Craig's face sobered. "She'll get over it. Don't worry about her."

Alison was too wildly happy to feel over-concerned about the other girl. "She did *try*."

"She didn't have a hope." The restless wind endlessly blowing over dark sandhills ruffled his soft dark hair and tossed her clustered curls back from her forehead as once again he bent to kiss her. "Let's go and tell the old lady. You know what she'll say, don't you?"

Alison laughed softly. "How about, 'Blame it on the soft west wind of love'?"

When they went into the house a light burned in

Frances' bedroom and together they went into the room.

Frances, who was sitting up in bed, put down the detective novel she had been reading.

"We've got something to tell you," Craig said.

His mother's gaze went from Alison, flushed with excitement and happiness, to the unmistakable expression of pride on her son's lean face. His arm thrown lightly around Alison's waist, he drew her close and there was no mistaking the depth of feeling in his low exultant tones. "Alison isn't leaving here ever, are you, sweet?"

Her denial was a tremulous whisper. "We wanted you to be the first to know."

"But that's wonderful news!" An expression of incredulous delight rang in Frances' strong tones. Her eyes suffused with most un-Frances-like tears of emotion. "Alison dear, I just can't tell you how pleased I am about this!" Throwing back the covers, she jumped out of bed. Her long nightgown flapped around her ankles as she ran across the room and throwing her arms around Alison kissed her heartily. When she had assured Alison over and over again of her delight in gaining the daughter-in-law she wanted she crossed to the wardrobe and taking out a serviceable red woollen dressing gown, pulled it around her.

"Oh dear," she clapped a weather-roughened hand to her mouth. "I almost forgot. It's Jo! She's gone! She came in to see me just after you two had left the house this morning and told me she had just had an urgent message calling her back to the South Island." Frances' eyes were thoughtful. "Funny, I didn't hear the phone ring. Anyway, she came out of her room carrying her suitcase, rang for a taxi at Dargaville to come and collect her and just—went. She didn't even say goodbye to the twins. She just took off."

Alison's gaze went to Craig and his gaze signalled back a message. You see, it's all over. You've nothing more to worry about from Jo.

Alison let out her breath on a long sigh of relief, but on another level something clicked in her mind. What was it Frances had said about the children? "The twins—who's been looking after them all day?"

"I have." Frances gave her rakish grin. "They were no trouble at all, the darlings!"

"Frances, you're a fraud! You're walking around all over the place without even a limp. Know what I think? You've been up and about for the last couple of weeks, when no one was looking." Enlightenment dawned on her. "So that was why you wouldn't let us call the doctor to come and see you for a final check-up?"

"She's right, you know," joined in Craig. "You may as well come clean and tell us about it now that you've given yourself away. What was the idea of putting one across us, making out you were a helpless invalid? It couldn't be that you liked being waited on hand and foot by Alison, I know you better than that."

"I had my reasons." Frances couldn't quite hide the expression of smug satisfaction that had spread over her craggy features. "How else," she demanded of her son, "could I get Alison to stay on? I had to think up something to keep her here until you came to your senses and did something about asking her to stay on for ever. You see, I knew," she added complacently, "that it was just a matter of time." She swung around to Alison. "You will forgive me for my little deception, won't you, love?"

"*Forgive you*?" Alison laughed her clear young laugh with the catch in her throat. "It's the best thing anyone has ever done for me in my whole life. Talking of deceptions," her dancing glance went to Craig's glowing face, "shall we tell her?"

His eyes were tender, loving, amused.

"Might as well. You'll never keep anything from the old lady for long."

Frances glanced bewilderedly from one to the other. "Tell me what, for heaven's sake?"

"Just," explained Craig with a grin, "that her name

happens to be Carter already. Alison Carter—does it ring a bell with you?''

Frances gasped. "You don't mean *that* Alison Carter?''

It took quite a time to explain the whole story, but at last Frances understood all that had happened. Moving to a drawer, she began rummaging amongst the oddments for pad and ballpoint.

"Another proverb?" Alison asked smilingly.

"Oh no, dear, not this time. I've just been thinking about the wedding. We'll have it from here, of course. Just a small affair. Mary could be your bridesmaid. You did say you have no folks of your own?''

Alison flushed and smiling, glanced from Craig, his eyes warm with love and tenderness, to Frances' weatherbeaten face. "Oh, but I have!" she protested. "I've got all I want," she murmured contentedly, "right here."

When they had left the room Craig said softly, "I should have warned you that the old lady would start thinking up names for wedding invitations the minute we passed on the news. Do you mind?''

"I don't mind." All that mattered to her was Craig, close at her side, loving her, needing her—for keeps.

THE AUTHOR

Gloria Bevan lives in New Zealand. She's been writing stories, she says, "ever since I can remember," but now, with her three daughters grown up, she has more time for writing. She and her husband explore the countryside to capture for her novels the unique magic of New Zealand and Australia.

The Land
of the
Lotus-Eaters
Isobel Chace

The Land
of the

Sarah had always put her sister's interests ahead of her own. So, although Sebastian de Hougement offered Sarah the chance of a lifetime photographing his archeological expedition, she knew she'd have to turn him down.

Then Philomena's wedding was called off, and the two sisters set off to Tunisia together.

Much to Sarah's dismay, instead of resenting Philomena's intrusion, Sebastian seemed to regard her presence with a little too much pleasure.

CHAPTER ONE

SARAH FEANEY was apt to find breakfast with her family rather an ordeal. Usually she made sure that she had already finished by the time they got up and gave herself just time to offer both her mother and her sister a peck on the cheek before she fled out of the house to the sanctuary of her work. Sarah was the clever member of the family and the odd man out. Her mother had both wit and charm and her sister, Philomena, had a fragile beauty as well which she emphasised very cleverly with just the right amount of make-up. Sarah found them both impractical, and, though she loved them very dearly, rather taxing because they always managed to make her feel guilty in some way, which was ridiculous but nevertheless a fact.

On this particular morning Sarah was late. She heated the coffee with impatient hands, frowning over the headlines in the newspaper.

"Have you got the mail?" Philomena called down the stairs to her.

Sarah rescued the toast from the grill.

"Not yet," she shouted back.

"Be a dear and have a look. Edmund promised to write last night! Oh, Sarah, *darling,* you have no idea how romantic he is!"

Sarah thought crossly that that was probably true. And, as Philomena had not come in until well after midnight, she wondered how she could possibly expect any letter from her escort to arrive in the first post the following morning! But she went to the front door as asked and collected the mail from the letter-box, sorting it out in her hand as she went back to the kitchen.

"There's nothing for you—sorry!" she called up to her sister.

Philomena came flying down the stairs.

"Are you sure? Here, let me look!" Tears appeared in her eyes. "How could he have forgotten?" she demanded.

"I don't suppose he did! It will probably come in the next post," Sarah replied comfortingly. "Come and have a cup of coffee."

"We-ell," Philomena began doubtfully, "I really ought to finish getting dressed, but you don't know what a comfort it is just to talk about him! Sarah, you know this time I really have fallen in love! He's perfect!"

Sarah struggled with her own doubts. "Is he going to marry you?" she asked abruptly.

Philomena's face shone.

"He asked me to last night! I'm so happy I could cry! It will be a gorgeous wedding, with me in white and you as my bridesmaid."

Sarah looked even more doubtful. "But what about the expense?" she hazarded gently.

Philomena smiled sweetly.

"Blow the expense! You're such a darling, Sarah, and I expect if you were to write a special article or something we could manage, with what Mother has saved."

Sarah bit her lip. "Articles on archaeology don't really pay at all! I could try with some photographs—"

"And I'll be your model!" Philomena put in excitedly.

Sarah laughed. "That'll be the day! When I start taking cheesecake photos! You are an ass! I meant sell the rights to some of my past efforts. If I sold enough I might be able to make fifty pounds."

Philomena's face fell. "But that wouldn't pay for the dress!"

Sarah squared her shoulders, fighting down her urge to agree to anything her sister wanted.

"It may have to!"

Philomena's rather pale eyes darkened suddenly. "It's not just *anybody* whom I'm marrying, Sarah! It's *Edmund*!"

Sarah sighed. "I expect he'll understand," she said hopefully. "He must know we haven't very much money."

"No, he doesn't," Philomena contradicted her flatly. "I told him you earned a lot!"

Sarah glanced across at her thoughtfully.

"Well, I don't suppose that he believed you. Museums and libraries are notoriously bad payers."

"Of course he believed me!" retorted Philomena. "He believes everything I tell him."

More fool him! Sarah thought. She carried the coffee to the table and filled the toast-racks with toast. If she didn't hurry she would be late for work and that would put her out for the whole day. She sat down in her accustomed place and reached for her own letters. Two of them were bills; the grocer and the butcher. Sarah stared at them with something very like rebellion. Why should she pay them? Philomena was working too, but she never paid anything. Sarah was the elder sister and her mother depended on her to help keep the house which was all that her father had been able to leave them. Possessions, her mother had said sadly, brought responsibilities. She might own the house, but the rates still had to be paid and there was very little money in the family kitty, and so Sarah had buckled to and helped all she could.

It was only after she had finished her toast and marmalade that Sarah allowed herself to open the third letter. She couldn't recognise the handwriting on the envelope, and it most certainly wasn't another bill because it wasn't that kind of shape. She ripped it open and took out the letter, glancing immediately down at the signature. Sebastian de Hougement, she read, and with a growing sense of excitement, she turned the letter over and began to read it.

"Dear Miss Feaney," it began, "your name has been given to me as the author of an article which appeared recently in *The World Before History*. The photographs were particularly interesting and of a very fine quality. Upon enquiry I find that you have had training in this kind of work and do a great deal of it in your spare time. At the moment I am engaged in a project for the Tunisian Government on the Isle of Djerba, connected with the discovery of a Roman ship which was wrecked there probably in the reign of the Emperor Caligula. We have not yet filled the position of photographer to the expedition and I wondered if you would be interested in coming with us, provided you can get the necessary extended leave from your present employers.

"If you are interested in this suggestion, I shall be in England for the next week at the address I have given above. I should be most interested to meet you and discuss your work in any case. Yours truly, Sebastian de Hougement."

Sarah knew a rising sense of excitement. De Hougement was a great man in his field, and that he should want *her* to work for him was something like a miracle! It was the chance of a lifetime and she would grasp it with both hands before it slipped away from her.

"What's your letter about?" Philomena asked petulantly.

"I'm going to Tunisia," Sarah said dreamily.

Her sister stared at her with wide eyes.

"You're *what*?"

Sarah pulled herself together. "Sebastian de Hougement wants me to be the photographer on his expedition in Tunisia," she explained.

"Oh, *work*!" Philomena exclaimed. "Well there's no need to go all gooey about that! You can't possibly go anyway!"

"Why not?" Sarah cried out.

"Oh, Sarah! Have you forgotten already? I'm getting

married! There'll be less money than ever if you take yourself off. Mother will never agree to it!"

Sarah put the letter carefully back in its envelope.

"But I want to go," she protested. "I want to go terribly badly!"

Her sister giggled.

"Wanting is free!" she said lightly. "As long as you can see that you can't actually go!"

Sarah swallowed down the last of her coffee.

"We'll see," she said, but she knew that she was already more than half defeated. "I'll talk to Mother about it."

IT WAS EASY enough at the museum to slip down to the library and turn up some of Professor de Hougement's articles. Sarah had read most of them before, but she studied them now for quite different things than their content. She wanted to know what the man was like in himself and what he would be like to work for. Looking up, she caught sight of herself in one of the imposing looking-glasses that decorated the reading-room and she wondered what he would think of her. She was tall and thin, with a bony face and fair hair that she wore in a knot on top of her head. She thought she was very ordinary, missing the charm of her dark grey eyes and the beauty of her fair complexion. Her looks were not as obvious as her sister's, who was everybody's beauty, but she had a loveliness that was more enduring because it was held in a fleeting expression and the easy way she liked almost everybody she met.

She bent her head and concentrated more fiercely on the articles before her. There was an honest quality and a certain humour which were unusual in continental writings on the subject. It was devastatingly clear that she was going to like him, like him very much indeed! There was no harm anyway in going to see him, she thought. It would be tantalising, for there were few people with whom she could really discuss her work and she would love to have half an hour with him for that alone, but there was another reason for wanting to meet him, a reason that she would scarcely admit to herself. Somehow, something which he might say might make it easier for her to go to Djerba with him, to the sun and the hot golden sands and work that she could really enjoy. It would be bliss!

She penned a letter accepting his invitation to meet her and posted it on her way home that evening. That, at least, could do no harm to anyone and she wouldn't tell her family about it at all. That way they could hardly spoil it for her and she wouldn't feel guilty about it. That way nobody could take the moment away from her.

MRS. FEANY HAD BOUGHT a new hat. She put it on for her daughters' admiration, turning this way and that so that they could see it in all its glory.

"It was only two guineas, Sarah! Imagine that!"

Sarah was visibly relieved. She had thought that it was much more expensive than that, and she could think of nothing else but the cost of the coming wedding.

"It's lovely!" she agreed generously. "It suits you and it's very pretty!"

Mrs. Feaney gave herself a satisfied look in the glass.

"You don't think it would suit Philomena better?" she asked.

Sarah shook her head positively, ignoring the frantic nods of her sister.

"I don't think so at all! And, even if it did, Philomena isn't going to need a hat for the wedding and you are."

"I'll need a going-away hat!" Philomena protested.

Sarah gave her a cool stare.

"I thought you said hats weren't in," she said calmly.

"It depends on the occasion—" began Philomena sulkily.

"Perhaps it is a little too young for me?" Mrs. Feaney dithered anxiously.

"It looks very nice," Sarah told her firmly, but Mrs. Feaney was still unconvinced.

"But you're not always a very good judge, are you, dear? I mean you don't *follow* the fashions like Philomena does, do you?"

Sarah shrugged her shoulders placidly.

"I suppose not, but I still think it's just your hat! I should keep it, if I were you. Philomena has dozens of hats already."

She went into the kitchen to start preparing the evening meal and, as she went, she could hear Philomena's voice, clear and very young.

"You don't have to worry, Mother. Sarah is in a sulk because I'm getting married before her, and just when she wanted to leave us and go to Tunisia on some jaunt—"

"Go where?" her mother asked faintly.

"To Tunisia. Didn't she tell you?"

"Where *is* Tunisia?"

Sarah closed the door so that she couldn't hear any more. If she had been able to tell her mother herself there had been just a chance that she might have understood why she wanted to go so badly, but now she knew the damage was done. Philomena had called it a "jaunt" and to her mother that would mean only one thing, the kind of sudden excursion her father had taken when he had wanted to get away from his womenfolk and his responsibilities. It would be quite useless now to explain that she wanted to go to Tunisia for very different reasons.

She cooked the meal in a dream and went to call the others when it was ready. They were both sitting on the sofa, chatting to each other. To Sarah, they looked peculiarly alike, both of them dark and vivid and very much alive.

"We can eat," she told them.

Lazily they stretched and got to their feet.

"Lovely," said Mrs. Feaney. "I'm really hungry for once! Tell me all about this idea of yours for going to Tunisia, Sarah."

Sarah smiled at her very gently.

"Professor de Hougement wrote and asked me to be the photographer on his expedition there," she said. "It's a very great compliment—"

"I'm sure it is!" her mother agreed warmly. "But of course with Philomena getting married—"

"Of course," Sarah agreed wearily.

THE MUSEUM gave Sarah the day off to see Professor de Hougement. They were frankly pleased that anyone on their staff should have attracted his attention and were all agog to know what the great man was like.

"You must tell us all about it tomorrow, Sarah!"

"Fancy him asking to see you! It was a lovely article, of course. I showed it to all my family!"

Sarah grinned to herself. The museum and the library were home to her in a way that her own home could never be. She liked the elderly, spare man who was the chief curator at the museum, she liked the librarian and she liked the rather silly girl who stamped the books in the library but never read one herself.

"I will," she promised. "I'll tell you all about it."

She took the tube to St. John's Wood and then consulted the address that the Professor had given her. It was only a short walk from there to the block of flats where his sister lived and she set out gaily, hoping she was going in the right direction. It was not long before she reached the right address, a large, modern block of pleasing proportions on the corner of a large, shady avenue.

The porter directed her to the lift and pressed the button for her. Smoothly, she was carried upwards and deposited on the right floor, just opposite the number she required.

With a thudding heart, she rang the bell.

The door was opened by an obviously French woman in a black dress.

"Miss Feaney? Come in, please. My brother is expecting you. I am Mrs. Leslie, by the way." Her English was perfect and Sarah immediately felt at home with her.

"It's very kind of you," she began.

The Frenchwoman laughed.

"But my brother insisted!" she smiled. "He likes your work very much," she added in almost a whisper. "Come and meet him."

The drawing-room was empty, to Mrs. Leslie's obvious surprise.

"Men!" she exclaimed disgustedly. "Isn't that typical to disappear at the critical moment? But please sit down, Miss Feaney. Will you have some tea?"

Sarah hesitated. The French, she thought, did not drink tea either often or willingly. She smiled uncertainly and was relieved when Mrs. Leslie rescued her from the dilemma.

"I am having tea myself," she said. "I am an Englishwoman now, you know. Besides, I find it most civilised to have conversation over the teacups!"

Sarah laughed.

"To tell the truth so do I!"

Mrs. Leslie picked up the telephone and ordered tea to be brought up. Sarah, who had never lived in a service flat, was impressed, though more at Mrs. Leslie's simple manners than at her wealth.

"It must have made a big change in your life, coming to England," she said.

Mrs. Leslie laughed, with a great deal of self-satisfaction.

"Marriage is a very great adventure! You should try it!"

Sarah blushed. "I'm not sure—" she prevaricated. She recovered herself. "My sister has just got engaged," she added.

"Do you like him?"

Sarah was a little shocked. She had never dared to consider whether she liked Edmund or not. He was Philomena's choice and that was that.

"I don't think I do—much," she said with some surprise.

Mrs. Leslie chuckled.

"How nice it will be for Sebastian to have you with him!" she said. "I am so glad, because I was a little bit worried about his asking you. You know what it can be when you take women on an expedition like this? But you could not be better! I am quite happy about it now."

Sarah wondered whether she should be complimented or not, but at that moment a man came into the room, so like his sister to look at that it was amazing, the only difference being that he was as masculine as she was feminine.

"What Antoinette means is that you will not deliberately upset all the men, not that you have no sex appeal," he said dryly.

Mrs. Leslie got slowly to her feet, her eyes mocking her brother.

"Miss Feaney is not stupid, *mon frère*. She must be aware that I should not suggest that anyone as pretty as she had no sex appeal!"

Sebastian de Hougement allowed himself to take a good look at his visitor.

"Very pretty!" he agreed with satisfaction.

Sarah blushed. She was not used to such frank speaking and was not even sure that she entirely approved of it. Valiantly she tried to change the subject.

"We have just received your latest book in our library, *monsieur*," she told him.

His eyes twinkled. "What did you think of it?" he drawled.

She felt caught in a cleft stick.

"It—it only arrived yesterday," she admitted humbly. "I haven't seen it properly yet."

He laughed.

"Well, let me tell you that the illustrations are deplorable. I'm afraid you're not going to be at all impressed with the quality of any of the photographs!"

Sarah was immediately all concern. She knew what poor illustrations could do to a book.

"What happened?" she asked.

His very French eyes crinkled slightly at the edges.

"It was not a very successful expedition," he said carefully. "Hence my sister's interest in who I take with me this time. Of course, being on the Mediterranean will probably add to my difficulties rather than otherwise. The last lot was in the middle of a desert!"

Sarah blinked.

"I've never done any field work outside of England," she said.

Antoinette Leslie walked casually towards the door. "I shall come back," she said, "when you have tied up all the details. We shall have tea then."

Her brother stood up for an instant as she went and then turned all his attention on to Sarah.

"I am not, at this moment, worried about your comparative inexperience," he began abruptly. "I want to know first if you want to come."

She looked down at her hands, wondering desperately what she should say.

"My sister is getting married," she burst out. "I *can't* go! My father is dead, you see, and the family depend on the money I bring in."

She thought that if he had had any tact at all he would not have looked at her in quite such a manner. She felt that his eyes would never leave her face and that the truth of how much she resented having to stay behind would be plain for him to see.

"Philomena is younger than I," she added.

"I see." He went on to talk about technical matters to do with photography. Filters were the important thing, he understood, as they showed up the different textures of the soil and the objects. Would this be true under water?

Sarah, to whom photography was an exciting challenge which had to be kept under strict control because it was so expensive, became engrossed in the whole venture. Carefully she explained the different films that could be used and how to protect the cameras from the sea. It was important to measure distance accurately under water, for it was impossible to guess. She *envied* the person who would have all the fun of actually doing it.

"I have not despaired of your coming yet," he replied calmly. "We have time to decide. Go home and think about it for the next week, that will be time enough to tell me."

She thanked him warmly. It was a very generous offer and she knew it.

"I can't think why you should want me," she exclaimed, flustered and looking charmingly pink.

His look was frankly amused.

"I think the spice of your femininity will add interest," he remarked dryly.

She was outraged.

"If I do come it will be because of the work!" she told him hotly.

"Of course," he agreed maddeningly. "Why else?"

SARAH TIMED HER ARRIVAL home so that it would coincide with her normal time for getting back from the museum. She knew that something was wrong the instant she put the key into the lock. There was a silence inside that was ominous. The glow that her talk with Professor de Hougement and his sister had given her fell away and she was suddenly aware of how weary she felt and that her back ached.

"Is anyone home?" she called out. There was no answer.

Feeling decidedly let down, as one can when one expects to be met by people and is greeted only by silence, Sarah went into the sitting-room and turned on the light because it was already beginning to get dark. Her mother and sister were sitting, in complete silence, at either end of the sofa. They were both in tears.

"What's wrong?" Sarah asked them sharply, anxiety welling up inside her.

Philomena began to sob.

"Now, now, dear, you *must* stop!" her mother said helplessly. "Sarah, did you have to start her off again?"

"I'm sorry," Sarah apologised. "What happened?"

"It's Edmund!" Philomena screamed. "He's going to marry somebody else!"

Sarah stared at her with disbelief.

"Since when?" she demanded.

Mrs. Feaney gave her elder daughter an impatient look.

"Darling, you have as little tact as your father had! Can't you see that this is *not* the moment to ask silly questions? Philomena is very upset!"

Sarah thought Philomena looked more angry than upset, but she didn't like to say so.

"I'm very sorry," she said instead.

"Why?" Philomena burst out. "You're *glad*! Now you can go off to Tunisia with a clear conscience! Why should you be able to have all the good times? All that sun and lovely surroundings, while I'm stuck here in a dead-end job! It isn't fair!"

Sarah winced away from them both. She hated these endless discussions on which of them had the better job and why, even though Philomena appeared to derive a certain satisfaction from it.

"Does it matter?" she asked. "I've already told Professor de Hougement that I can't go. He'll have found someone else by now."

Philomena stopped crying immediately.

"Sarah! How can you say such a thing? You're so deceitful! You went to see him today, didn't you?"

Sarah bit her lip, annoyed that she was going to have to share the experience with her family.

"Well, yes, if you must know, I did. But he understood that I wouldn't be able to go with him."

Mrs. Feaney waved an impatient hand at the two girls.

"Then you'd better telephone him and tell him that you'll go. I have a little money put by and that will pay for Philomena to go with you. It will be much better for her to be away from England for a while, and you can look after her."

"But what will you do?" Sarah asked her anxiously.

Mrs. Feaney looked smug.

"I have friends to go to," she said vaguely. "Go and telephone him now, Sarah, before either of you can think up any reasons why you shouldn't!"

Sarah was only too willing, but she was too practical to do so without finding out exactly how much money her mother had.

"It will cost quite a lot," she said carefully.

"More than three hundred pounds?" Mrs. Feaney asked.

Sarah gasped. *"Three hundred?"*

Mrs. Feaney looked hurt.

"I don't see why I can't give it to anyone I like!" she said crossly. "I *want* to give it to Philomena. She deserves to have a good time! Look how hard she has been working recently, and now this on top of everything else! The girl *deserves* a holiday!"

Sarah said nothing. She was hurt that her mother had said nothing to her about having as much money as this behind her before. Philomena on the other hand excitedly kissed her mother.

"Oh, *Sarah!* Don't just stand there looking disapproving! Go and ring your Professor. I can't afford to send *both* of you to the sunspots."

Later on, Sarah thought, she would be hurt, as she always was, by her mother's casual dismissal of her. Only now all she could think of was the sheer glory of the moment. It didn't matter how or why it had happened. It didn't matter at all. She was going to Tunisia after all, and she thought she would cry with the sheer joy of it.

CHAPTER TWO

THE BLACK MEDITERRANEAN, disturbed only by silver glints of reflected moonlight and the lights of an occasional ship, gave way abruptly to the land of Africa, and the massed lights of fairyland that gave away the positions of all the towns and villages as they fell behind them. Sarah leaned across her sister to see them better.

"Isn't it heavenly?" she exclaimed.

Philomena painfully opened her eyes.

"Do you *have* to?" she asked crossly. "You're squashing me horribly, and I may as well tell you that I feel quite unwell as it is!"

Sarah chuckled.

"You look all right to me," she retorted. "If you'd take an interest it wouldn't seem such a long ordeal."

Philomena sighed. "If I had known—" she shuddered.

Sarah ignored her. Her own excitement was almost a pain within her and she couldn't believe that her sister didn't in some way share her pleasure in the long journey. That would be Algeria below them now. It would not be long before they would cross the border and be over Tunisia itself, and then it would be only a few minutes before they would begin to make their landing at Tunis Airport. It felt very foreign and strange, and not even the fact that they had left London only four hours before could dispel the impression that they were entering into a completely new world.

When they did begin to go down, they dropped sharply, and Philomena shut her eyes again and groaned. The light over the door came on asking all the passengers to fasten their safety belts. Sarah fastened both her own and her sister's belt with impatient fingers. She had seen a flash of the landing lights and she could hardly wait to get out of the aeroplane and take her first look at Tunisia.

Nor was the moment in any way an anti-climax. A member of the crew threw open the heavy doors and the first of the passengers began to make their way down the portable steps to the tarmac strip outside. Sarah hurried forward, pulling Philomena behind her. She paused for an instant at the top of the steps and looked about her. It was indeed a different world—an Arab, dressed in the old-fashioned camel-trousers that were like a skirt, caught and dragged up forward between his legs, and a scarlet skull-cap perched on the back of his head. His womenfolk stood a little behind him, veiled and mysterious. It was exactly what she had imagined it would be.

But the illusion was speedily lost as the rest of the airport buildings came to life and a group of efficient, modern-looking officials came swarming out to deal with the plane-load of tourists and businessmen that had just arrived. It seemed to Sarah no time at all before they were standing in line waiting for their passports to be checked and for their luggage to be passed through the customs. It gave her a childish pleasure to see the Tunisian stamp on her passport, made incomprehensible by the flowing Arab script. It made her feel cosmopolitan and important, and she found herself smiling back at the man with rather more warmth than she might have done otherwise.

Philomena tugged at her sleeve.

"Sarah! There are other people waiting!" she complained. "What do we do now? Do we have to carry our suitcases ourselves? Because I don't think I can manage mine."

Sarah looked about her. A number of porters came rushing forward, anxious to be the one to be chosen to transport the cases outside.

"Taxi? Madame?"

Sarah hesitated. Until that moment she had not given any thought to whether they would be met or not. She had received detailed instructions about every stage of their journey, but at this point it had only said: Night in Tunis. Continue to Djerba the next day on Tunis air flight as arranged. She bit her lip, and Philomena sighed.

"As a holiday—" she began.

Sarah felt quite hot with a mixture of temper and dismay.

"It isn't exactly meant to be a holiday!" she said sharply. When she thought about it, she still felt embarrassed by the conversation she had had with the Professor on the telephone.

"I'm coming!" she had burst out with as soon as she had heard his voice.

There had been a short silence at the other end, but when he had spoken she had heard the smile in his voice.

"That is very good to hear," he had said gently. "And what of your sister?"

She had swallowed, knowing that this was one of the most difficult moments of her life.

"Philomena isn't—isn't getting married after all," she had said.

"Oh, and what is she doing?" he had drawled.

Sarah had not been deceived by the smoothness of his voice.

"M-Mother's sending her with me—on a holiday," she had managed, wondering desperately how she could decently cover the bare facts of the arrangement her family had landed her with.

"I see," he had replied abruptly. "Well, see that you keep her under control!"

She had known then it wasn't going to be easy. Looking at Philomena now, weary from travelling and already bored with her immediate surroundings, she knew that it was going to be impossible. To her great relief, at that moment, her sister saw a fair young man who was obviously looking for somebody and smiled at him. He came over immediately.

"My name is Roger van Hueck," he announced shyly. "Are you by any chance Miss Feaney?"

Philomena looked pleased and nodded.

"I expect you want my sister, actually," she said. "Everybody always does. She's the important one, you see."

Mr. van Hueck coloured slightly.

"I'm sure that is an exaggeration," he replied gallantly. He returned to Sarah with anxious eyes. "The Professor asked me to meet you. Shall we take a taxi to the hotel?"

Sarah put her annoyance with Philomena firmly behind her.

"It's very nice of you," she said warmly. "I'm not much good at coping with this sort of thing and I was just beginning to get worried!"

Roger van Hueck grinned. He was, it seemed, excellent at dealing with luggage and taxis, and he certainly managed to load all the suitcases into one of the tiny taxis and get all three of them into it as well, with himself sitting beside the smiling driver.

"We'll be in nice time for dinner," he told them cheerfully.

"Good," said Philomena. "Now that I have my feet back on Mother Earth, I'm absolutely starving!"

Sarah thought she was too excited to be very hungry. She stared out of the window of the little taxi, afraid that she might miss something if she took part in the light conversation of the other two. The royal palms were just what she had been led to expect and the beds of flowers seemed right and proper, though the mixture of plants was very strange indeed, for here the seasons had catapulted into one another and roses and daffodils flowered side by side with dahlias and lilies.

Philomena nudged her fiercely. "He is asking you a question!" she said sharply.

Sarah started. "I'm sorry," she said. "I was dreaming!"

The young Dutchman eyed her almost affectionately.

"It is you who is the member of our expedition?" he asked her. She liked the faint accent that was the only thing that betrayed the fact that he was not an Englishman and she looked at him with greater interest.

"Yes, I am," she admitted. "It's the first time I've ever done anything half as ambitious as this! I'm rather excited about it," she added naively.

He nodded enthusiastically. "We are lucky!" he agreed. "I'm the recorder, you know, so most of your work will be done with me."

Sarah was pleased. He would be easy to work with, she thought, and she knew what a difference this could make when one had to work closely with anyone over a period of time.

"Have you been in Tunisia long?" she asked him.

"Truly no. I was in Djerba for perhaps a week when I was asked to come back to Tunis for you."

"Djerba?" Sarah repeated. "Is it really such an exciting island?"

He laughed and thought about the question.

"No, it is not at all exciting to look at. It is very flat and covered with palm trees, but it does have this strange magic, that is true. It is still the isle of the lotus-eaters!"

Philomena frowned.

"What on earth are you talking about?"

Sarah chuckled.

"Some people think Djerba was the land of the lotus-eaters, whose people lived on the fruit of a flower. When Odysseus sent some of his most trusted men ashore to find out if they were friendly, they ate some of the fruit and wanted to stay there for ever. They had to be taken back to the ship in irons."

Philomena looked at her with caustic disbelief.

"That's just one of your stories!" she said flatly.

"Oh, hardly mine!" Sarah chided her gently. "It's attributed to Homer."

Roger van Hueck swivelled round in his seat so that he could see both girls.

"When one is there, it is easy to believe that it is true," he said quietly. He smiled at Sarah with all the delight of a small boy. "How nice that you should know such a legend!" he said.

Philomena sighed, more than a little annoyed that this quite presentable young man should be willing to pay any attention to Sarah. Who cared what somebody had written thousands of years ago anyway? Nobody she knew ever had!

They had come into Tunis itself now, a city that could have been any provincial town in the south of France. Only the mosques and the flat roofs of the Arab quarter made one aware that one was now on the African side of the Mediterranean. Sarah returned to her day-dreaming, her imagination playing on the strange walking bundles that turned out to be women and the laughing groups of men, a favour of jasmine tucked behind one ear and as likely as not a cigarette in one hand aiding the most sensitive gesture of meaning. Once she saw a donkey, its face turned towards the wall, happily munching at some food. It was these things that made the difference between Africa and Europe. It was these things that caught at her heart and made her fall headlong in love with Africa.

The hotel was a small one, run by a French family who had sensibly combined European comfort with the best standards of African service and hospitality. They had no rigid times for meals and were pleased to serve dinner for the three of them out on the balcony.

It was a happy meal. The lights were sufficiently subdued for them to be able to look right across Tunis in the moonlight, a myriad of blurred street-lights and shadowed buildings. It smelt, Sarah thought, of whitewash, dust and strong cigarettes. The food too was excellent and the Tunisian wines, mostly produced by the White

Fathers, seemed as good to her as many of the French wines her family had experimented with on special occasions at home. It was sheer bliss, she thought, to be alive! And it was on the same note of complete contentment that she finally went to bed, to sleep very much better than she had for a long, long time.

ROGER VAN HUECK rounded them up for breakfast at a very early hour. Sarah had left Philomena still sleeping and crept out of the hotel into the gardens beyond, anxious not to miss a moment of her time in the city. A woman, dark from the southern sun and completely unveiled, came towards her, holding her hand out for money with a furtive air, knowing that all begging was now forbidden. Sarah had fallen to the temptation of giving her a coin, more because she wanted to see the heavy jewellery that hung low over the forehead than because she looked hungry. The woman snatched the coin away from her and buried it somewhere in the front of her dress. She hurried off before anyone else should see her, leaving Sarah alone in the gardens and feeling slightly guilty at having encouraged her.

The Dutchman came quickly over to her.

"Is your sister ready?" he asked. "The aeroplane to Djerba leaves in just two hours. If she requires breakfast, it would be as well to have it now."

Sarah left the gardens reluctantly.

"I'd better go and call her," she said.

Roger put a friendly hand on her shoulder.

"Your sister will soon be one of us," he comforted her awkwardly. "It must be strange for her at first."

"Oh, it is!" Sarah replied thankfully. It was true, she told herself sternly, that none of the jobs that Philomena had ever had had been anything like her own. It was different when one worked just for the money, quite different from working because the work was in one's blood and the money only incidental. But, even so, she couldn't help wondering how she was going to entertain Philomena all the time she was working. And

Philomena wouldn't suffer in silence! It was a niggling anxiety that refused to be silenced. Deliberately, Sarah shrugged her shoulders. Her sister was old enough to look after herself and no doubt she would, and she wouldn't want any help from Sarah.

Actually she looked young and very charming when Sarah tried to shake her awake.

"Go away!" she said distinctly.

"I can't," Sarah pleaded with her. "We shall have to leave for the airport at any moment. Breakfast is now!"

Philomena sat up sulkily.

"I'm not going on any more aeroplanes! So there isn't really any hurry, is there, darling?"

Sarah's eyes widened anxiously. "But you must! It's all arranged!"

Philomena smiled. "I expect you can rearrange it, if you try. Tell that young Dutch type of yours that you fancy going by car. I don't think he'd object very strongly."

Sarah bit her lip. "It's more than five hundred miles," she explained patiently, "and we have to be there today. This morning in fact."

Philomena pulled the bedclothes over her head.

"Speak for yourself, darling. *I* don't have to be anywhere at any time."

Sarah regarded her helplessly.

"Well, I do," she said at last, "and I'm going by plane as arranged. Mr. van Hueck will be leaving in about three-quarters of an hour, I should think. If you want to go by road, you'll have to arrange it for yourself!"

She was shivering as she went down the marble stairs to the dining-room below, her joy in the morning destroyed. Roger van Hueck stood up as she approached his table and drew out a chair for her.

"Everything all right?" he asked her.

She forced herself to smile.

"Philomena doesn't greatly care for flying," she told him lightly. "I don't suppose she'll risk any breakfast."

He sat down again.

"She is probably wise. It will not be a very big aeroplane going to Djerba, for the airfield there is rather small."

Sarah chuckled. "I can't wait to see it all!" she exclaimed.

There was, at least, nothing the matter with her appetite. She chose one of the crusty rolls and ladled herself a generous portion of the apricot jam, pleased to see that it was home-made. She made it last for as long as she could, because she didn't want to go out to the hall and not find her sister there. It wouldn't be easy to leave her to find her way to Djerba. She might not even try to make any arrangements for herself and then she, Sarah, would have to come all the way back for her. She couldn't abandon her in a foreign city! Anxiously, she looked across at Roger van Hueck, half hoping that he might somehow provide some solution.

"Do you think I should send someone up to my sister—to bring down the suitcases?" she asked him.

He looked thoughtfully at his watch.

"I shall go up myself," he said finally.

Sarah watched him go up the stairs, grateful to him for taking so much trouble. When he appeared a little later with Philomena leaning on his arm and smiling up at him, she was more grateful than ever.

"Roger is going to sit next to me in the plane," Philomena said cheerfully. "I shall feel so much safer with him beside me!"

Sarah raised her eyebrows. "Good," she said dryly. She was more amused than anything else by the complete way that her sister took the young Dutchman under her wing. He seemed to like it too, making a great deal of fuss about seeing her into the taxi and later on even more fuss as to whether she was quite comfortable in the aeroplane. Sarah didn't mind being practically ignored. She was accustomed to standing on her own feet and to looking after herself and she thought that she even preferred it.

The flight was a marvellous experience. Somewhere she had read that the north coast of Africa had once been joined to Europe and that it had been a comparatively recent convulsion that had thrown up the mountains of the Alps on the one side and the whole Atlas range on the other, causing the Mediterranean to appear between them. Looking down now she could see the Tunisian end of the range of mountains that separated the fertile northern areas from the Sahara to the south. Great terra-cotta heaps of rock and sand, slashed by purple shadows of majestic proportions, stood out from the semi-fertile land that was in the process of being reclaimed. She could see the terraced slopes and the thousands of young, newly-planted trees that it was hoped would hold the fragile soil and bring more rain to the area. Everywhere there were signs of where men had been working, pitting their new knowledge and skills against the old, old enemy—desert.

From there the land grew progressively poorer until they were over the salt flats and the desert proper, broken only by the occasional oasis, a splash of green and date-palms against the rough reddish yellow of the surrounding sand. And then there was the sea. Djerba was set on a shelf that kept the water shallow from Tunisia to the most northerly part of Libya. From a height it was the most glorious shade of greeny-blue, edged by golden sands and the odd flash of white foam as one wave, bigger than the rest, broke against the gentle shore.

Then suddenly there was Djerba, attached to the mainland by a seven-mile-long Roman causeway, now restored but still resting on the same foundations of so long ago. The small plane circled over the main town of Houmt Souk at the northerly end and then dropped from the sky on to the tiny airfield below. Philomena gave a small, feminine shriek and grabbed at Roger's hand. Sarah, sitting behind them, felt the comforting support of the safety belt and took a deep breath to break the sudden popping in her ears. The wheels squealed as they hit the ground and a few seconds later they were taxiing across the bumpy surface towards the single building that governed the few aeroplanes that came and went from the island.

Roger was the first one to release himself from his belt and stand up.

"So here we are!" he exclaimed. "And I see the Professor himself has come to meet us!" He grinned at the two girls. "Home for the next few months. How do you feel about it?"

Philomena looked indifferent.

"It looks a trifle short of mod. cons., if you ask me," she said.

Sarah frowned at her.

"You haven't even seen it yet," she protested. "It looks quite marvellous to me! I can hardly wait to take a look around. Did you see those terrific beaches over there?" She waved her hand vaguely in an easterly direction. "I'm glad I brought a swimsuit," she added with satisfaction.

Roger laughed. "You'll never be out of it!" he told her flatly. "I hope you can swim, because you'll need to be able to, playing around with the Professor's ship."

"Of course I can swim!" Sarah claimed. "I can swim very well."

"But I can't!" Philomena wailed. "Roger, you will have to teach me!"

"You don't need to swim," he teased her. "You're pretty enough to sit and do nothing! It is your sister who has to work for her living!"

Sarah was hurt, but she was determined not to show it. Her sister looked satisfied at any rate, and that was something now that at last she was going to have to introduce her to Professor de Hougement. She had the oddest feeling that he was not going to be amused by Philomena's helplessness, that he wasn't even going to like her very much.

They hurried down the steps out of the aeroplane

and followed Roger's eager stride over to where the Professor was standing waiting for them. He gravely shook hands with each one of them.

"You are very welcome on Djerba," he told them. Then suddenly he smiled and he was more as Sarah remembered him. "Your plane is exactly on time."

The whole party went through the small airport building and the two men loaded up the waiting car with the cases.

"Sarah had better sit in the front with me," the Professor directed with finality. "I wish to talk with her, to explain the arrangements."

Fortunately Philomena was only too pleased with this plan.

"You and I are dismissed to the rear," she said to Roger, but without malice. "Are you sorry?"

His fair skin burned scarlet.

"How could I be?" he protested.

Sarah jumped into the right-hand front seat beside the Professor and took note of her surroundings. The car was a Citroen Safari model and was both capacious and comfortable, but it was the scenery which fascinated her. She had never seen hedges made of prickly pear, nor the long-legged, aristocratic camels that strode down the narrow roads. Otherwise there were only palm trees and olive trees so old that five men would have had a job to hold hands around their girth, and women in woven witches' hats, burned brown by the rays of the sun.

"It's beautiful!" she exclaimed softly.

The Professor smiled. "I think so," he said.

Sarah giggled. "It seems quite impossible to believe I'm really here!"

"You'll believe it soon enough when you see the hotel where we are all quartered," Roger broke in from behind. "It's an Arab hotel."

The car swung off the main street and into an extremely narrow lane, where the pedestrians had to jump into the doorways for safety as the car went past.

"Here it is," the Professor announced.

The hotel was very small and shabby, with a door straight out of the Arabian Nights, painted blue and studded in geometric designs with large black diamond-headed nails. The inside looked cold and bare and not very inviting.

"Well, speak for yourself," said Philomena.

CHAPTER THREE

THE HOTEL HAD BEEN BUILT round an inner courtyard with most of the rooms facing inwards. The courtyard itself was a mass of flowering and sweet-smelling plants that were diligently watered every day, though nothing was done to prune them or to keep them under any sort of control. They gave a lush, damp appearance to the place, which was fostered by an ancient statue, propped up in one corner, that was quite green from a mixture of damp and age.

The upper floors were reached by a handsome marble staircase on the steps of which more pots of green plants stood waiting to trip up the unwary. Above them hung singing birds in cages, shattering the silence with their different songs, some of them black, some yellow, and some a peculiar shade of brown.

The rooms themselves were small and old-fashioned, with brass bedsteads and Victorian washstands that had been empty for so long that the water had caked round the inside edges of the porcelain in grimy streaks. They were clean, but it was some time since anyone had touched up the decorations and the original green had faded into a sickly shade of yellow clashing madly with the greeny-blue of the shutters.

The two girls had been given adjoining rooms Philomena glanced around hers with contempt.

"Are we really expected to stay here?"

Sarah went over to the window and opened the shutters wide, allowing the sound of the birds' singing to come pouring into the room.

"It isn't so bad," she said. "In fact I rather like it. Have you seen the gorgeous rugs on the floor? And *have* you seen these blankets? Aren't the patterns marvellous?"

Philomena looked at the cracking paintwork and sniffed.

"Some holiday!" she commented briefly.

Sarah shrugged.

"As far as I am concerned it isn't a holiday," she reminded her sister gently. "Don't you think you might grow used to it?"

Philomena shivered.

"*Used* to it? We shall probably be murdered in our beds—if we don't die of pneumonia first! I'll bet those beautiful blankets of yours are wringing wet!"

"Nonsense!" Sarah retorted stoutly. "They feel perfectly dry to me, and anyway, I expect they're most particular as to whom they murder when it comes to it. I hardly think they would think that we were worth their while."

Philomena disliked anything that smacked of sarcasm, especially from her sister.

"I hate narrow little streets!" she said.

Sarah smiled wryly. "I can see you're going to have a lovely time!" she said. "I'm going next door to unpack my things. I'll get somebody to put some hot-water bottles in the beds to air them, if you like."

But Philomena didn't bother to answer. Instead she sat on the edge of her bed and lit a cigarette. Even the cigarettes, she thought, were strange and nasty, with almost black tobacco and a strong aromatic taste that displeased her. It was going to take quite a lot to reconcile her to all this!

Sarah's room was almost an exact replica of the other one, but far from disliking it she thought it had a certain rather stark charm. Apart from the design of the rugs and blankets, she had noticed the fantastic ceramics that covered part of the walls, intricately patterned with geometric trees and animals that looked quite Persian in origin. She had noticed too the ornate carving on the bedside table, which may at one time have been polished, but now appeared to have been firmly washed, not once but often, in soap and water. Later she was to realise that she never saw any furniture polish the whole time she was in Tunisia, but at the time she merely thought it was rather peculiar.

She put her clothes away with care, hoping against hope that what she had brought with her would be suitable. She had always chosen her clothes with care, so that they would be useful both for her work and on the few days she had at home. By a careful use of accessories she had discovered how to turn average dresses into "round the clock" creations and, although she couldn't hope to compete with Philomena either in quality or looks, she had been quite pleased with the results. What had been more difficult was to know what she would need in Djerba. She wondered briefly whether Philomena had had the same problem and thought how odd it was that they had never discussed it, indeed, they had hardly mentioned the trip at all unless their mother had done so. Perhaps it had been her fault, Sarah reflected. Perhaps she should have made it easier for her sister to talk to her. But the truth was that she had wanted to bury herself in the professional details of her new job without any interference from her family. She sighed. Put that way it sounded a rather selfish reaction.

Her unpacking did not take long. With a well-practised movement she flipped the suitcase up on to the top of the wardrobe and looked about her with satisfaction. The room already looked quite like home. There was a desk for her to work at and a whole cupboard that was free and in which she could store her photographs and other data. She had, she thought, everything she needed here, and if Philomena was content there was no reason why they shouldn't both have the time of their lives.

There was no sound from Philomena's room as Sarah went past it to the stairs and she didn't bother to knock on the door to find out if her sister was still upstairs. It would be pleasant to have a few minutes for exploring on her own, to get to know the layout of the hotel and perhaps even to find her way around this extraordinary little town of Houmt Souk.

A young Negro stood in the middle of the hall below and he grinned at her, muttering something quite unintelligible. Sarah returned his greeting in French, which he quite obviously didn't understand, but his grin grew broader and he made signs for her to look through the door to where both the Professor and Roger were standing.

"Settled in?" the Dutchman asked her cheerfully.

She nodded her head. "I'm very comfortable!" she exclaimed. "I can hardly wait to get started!"

The Professor smiled slightly. "Good. We will take you out to the site after lunch." He turned briefly to Roger. "Perhaps you could arrange to have the *kamaki* ready?"

Roger van Hueck smiled happily.

"Now you really have got a treat in front of you," he said to Sarah. "These boats are my greatest delight here. They have huge orange sails and yet they are so easy to handle—You wait and see!"

Sarah was quite willing to be enthusiastic about any boat. There was enough breeze to make for speed which would be wonderful out on the water, but which here in the town was uncomfortable in the way that it sought out the fine white dust on the streets and blew it into the houses, through the doors and across the windowsills.

"Shall I bring a camera?" she asked.

The Professor watched her closely. "You may as well," he said.

Lunch was a cheerful meal. They sat round a long refectory table which the Professor thought must have been left behind by a Spanish ship in search of conquest—because who hadn't attempted to conquer Djerba at one time or another?—the carving on it was so fine and the proportions so exact. He himself sat at the head of it, quite at home acting as host to the party, making an occasional gesture to the man who was serving them to make the meal go more smoothly. It was a good meal, too, of local fish and vegetables, followed by dates from the mainland, sweeter and more satisfying than any that can be obtained in Europe, and oranges of the large, seedless kind.

Sarah enjoyed it all very much. She liked the faintly masculine flavour to the conversation, the talk of previous digs and Roman ships and history. She would have enjoyed it even more if Philomena had looked happier and less as though she was going to cry at any moment. She gave her a quick look of sympathy as they got up from the table and was met by an answering stare of disapproval.

"Feeling a bit down?" she asked her bravely as they mounted the stairs to their rooms.

Philomena quickened her pace.

"Mother said it was going to be fun!" she said fiercely. "But nobody cares that I'm here at all! Who cares about their beastly Roman boats?"

"Well, I do," Sarah replied.

Philomena's eyes swept up her sister's dress, taking in every detail.

"That's what I mean! You're *built* for the intellectual pursuits, but most girls like their lives to be spiced with something very different!"

Sarah flushed and was silent. Philomena had a way of destroying her confidence in herself, but, this time, she couldn't afford to allow her to do so. This time it was her bread and butter and she would have to ignore her sister's discontent. But she had a feeling that it was going to be easier said than done.

"I'll see you later," she said with unexpected firmness when they reached Philomena's door. "It would be silly for you to go out into this heat as you don't have to. Perhaps I shall be back in time for us to go swimming later."

"If I'm still here!" Philomena retorted.

Sarah refused to give any thought to this particular parting shot. Determinedly, she put her sister right to the back of her mind and began to think of her work. She changed into a swimming-suit and dressed again, picking up the camera that was easiest to carry and was the one she thought would be most suitable for any preliminary photographs she might take, and then she hurried down the stairs again, anxious not to keep anyone waiting.

The Professor was already there. She came up behind him and was able to see how easily he stood, looking foreign to her eyes and subtly powerful; certainly she could never imagine him losing confidence in himself. She could see too the quality of his drip-dry clothes and the gold flash of his watch and strap which she was quite sure were the real thing. In an Englishman she might have had doubts about the vividness of everything about him. In a Frenchman she found it different and exciting, the more so because she knew his true solid worth from his work.

"Roger will have gone on ahead to the harbour," he drawled. "What have you done with your sister?"

Sarah blushed and was cross with herself because of it.

"I thought I might go swimming with her when we get back," she said tautly.

The Professor held the door open for her so that she went before him out into the hot, dusty street.

"I imagine you may find leading a double life rather exhausting in this heat," he remarked without any change of expression. "I hope that *my* work is going to come first?"

Sarah felt quite indignant that he should feel it necessary to ask.

"Of course!" she said with a touch of hauteur.

He smiled at that.

"Good. Seeing that we have that quite clear let us go off and enjoy ourselves. I am afraid you will be disappointed when you see all that remains of my ship. I am hoping that we shall find that it is buried beneath the sands, waiting for us to reveal their secrets."

Sarah smiled. "What do the local people think of it all?" she asked.

He threw back his head and laughed.

"Their collective memory is very long!" he said slyly. "Some of the older people I have talked to actually remember it going down!"

Sarah chuckled also. "Perhaps long life is one of the other effects of the lotus flower," she suggested in much the same tone of voice.

The Professor grinned.

"We shall have to feed you on it in that case," he teased her. "We could perhaps capture you, just as you are, for ever and ever."

She made a face at him, still laughing.

"I think that would be rather dull!"

"Mmm," he agreed. "I can see you are the sensible sister." A comment which thoroughly annoyed her and kept her busy thinking of the perfect retort the whole way to the harbour. Once there she forgot it immediately, however, for the sheer beauty of the boats on the water, the classical faces of the young men who stood about and talked, and the whole surmounted by the ruined fort that at one time guarded these lovely shores.

Roger was waiting for them, sitting in the bottom of one of the local boats with a happy expression on his face. He stood up immediately he saw them and leaped easily ashore to join them.

"Mustapha is all ready to go," he called out to them eagerly. "Most of the others seem to have gone out fishing."

The Professor cast the young Tunisian boy a quick, hard look.

"Don't you want to catch fish?" he asked him.

Mustapha stood foursquare, holding the end of the painter.

"I want to go fishing for pots with you," he said. He

grinned suddenly. "I can go fishing any other day."

Sarah was amused by his frankness. He looked scarcely more than a child to her, with strong classical features and a fair skin tanned to the palest shade of coffee by the fierce sun. When he turned to stare at her in return she was surprised to find that his eyes were as blue as periwinkles. But then this was White Africa, she reminded herself, where the people were as mixed in their breeding as there were countries surrounding the Mediterranean. This Tunisian could as easily have been a Roman or a Greek, or even a Spaniard; he could match the pride and vivacity of any of them, with only a subtle gaiety of his own to mark him out as one of Bourghiba's boys in the New Tunisia.

She allowed Roger to help her into the boat and sat down quickly on one of the cross-seats as it lurched dangerously beneath her weight. It was a moment or two before she could bring herself to relax, so strange was the feel of the rippling water below and the insecurity of the fragile craft. But gradually it felt rather less necessary to grasp the wood of the seat to keep it still and she could even look about her and enjoy the sights of the harbour from this unusual angle.

A group of Berber women stood gossiping just within her sight. Unlike their Arab countrywomen they didn't wear the veil, finding it enough to turn their heads if a man should look at them too closely. They carried some enormous pots between them, shaped to a point that could be dug into the ground, and with two large handles which made them easy to carry. Sarah stared at them with disbelief—amphoras, no less! Perfectly shaped and exactly the same as those used in the time of St. Paul.

The Professor jumped neatly in beside her and sat down in the same economical movement.

"They haven't changed, have they?" he remarked. "Look hard at those amphoras, Sarah Feaney, you'll be seeing some more of them in a minute."

She dragged her eyes away from the women and

glanced across at his face to see if he was serious. The dark strength of his features struck her anew and she looked away again hastily before he could see the naked appreciation in her eyes. Philomena could get away with the obvious, but she was more easily embarrassed and she wasn't prepared to take any chances where her employer was concerned.

"I read somewhere that they often give the position of these wrecks away," she said. "It will be rather fun to actually see for myself!"

He leaned forward until his face obscured her view of the quay.

"It will be rather fun showing them to you," he said.

"I'm so glad you think so!" she said tartly.

He exploded into laughter, not a whit put out. "Is Philomena ever sentimental?" he asked her.

She fingered her bony chin thoughtfully, disliking this reminder of her sister.

"I've never really thought about it," she compromised.

"Well, at any rate, she hasn't your astringent quality!" he said, looking ostentatiously foreign and very masculine.

She coloured and pulled her skirts primly down over her knees to give herself something to do, to ward off the hurt that she was sure his words were going to inflict if she let them.

"No, she hasn't," she said abruptly. "She's a much more social animal altogether."

His body bent to the angle of the boat, his eyes on the sails.

"Why should you care? I imagine you have the brains of the family?"

"Oh yes," she admitted bitterly, "I'm the clever one!"

"Then why resent it when it shows?" he asked.

She gave him a look of passionate dislike.

"I don't!" she said sharply. "And it wouldn't be any of your business if I did!"

His smile was disarming.

"*Touché*, my dear. Move over and let Roger sit down."

It was something, she supposed, that it was Roger and not the Professor who sat next to her. His large frame took up by far the greater part of the seat and she could feel her ribs pressed hard against the gunwale. She took a deep breath to make sure that she did in fact have room to breathe and the smell of canvas and warm sea filled her lungs and gave her an unexpected feeling of contentment. Mustapha hauled the sails up into the wind and they cracked excitedly as they filled with a sudden gust of hot air that sent them scurrying out to sea.

It was terribly hot. The sun had a look of old pewter all around it, blazing down on the sea beneath. Even that water was warm, warmer than she had ever known seawater to be, and beautiful, the ripples a pure jade green set off to perfection against the white wake of their boat. It was the most perfect day that Sarah could ever remember.

From a distance the shore looked pale and romantic. The palm trees that bespeckled the island looked almost squat and the olive trees no more than a delightful green haze in the distance. Sarah imagined that she was sailing with Odysseus and gaining her first sight of the island. It was a strangely attractive place, drawing one's heart like a magnet. Was it something in the soft air? Or something more tangible? She didn't know. She only knew that when the time came she was going to be very sorry to leave.

Mustapha touched the tiller and the boat reeled over in answer to his command. Sarah's fingers curled round the wood of her seat again and a sudden excitement gripped her as the spray brushed across her face. They were travelling fast now and it was a most exhilarating sensation. She had not known that boats were such exciting things; it was almost as though they had a life of their own, scurrying across the surface of a sea that had borne their kind for as long as man had ventured to leave his natural element of the land.

"The wreck is over there," Roger told her, pointing it out from some mysterious bearings on the land. "We shan't be long now!"

There was little enough to tell them they had arrived. The Professor had arranged to have a line of small buoys strung round the site, partly to make it easier to find and partly to keep the fishing boats away so that they would not disturb it any further.

"We had a lot of fun with the suction equipment," he said with a laugh. "The whole island came out to watch and we scarcely had room to breathe. We sucked away enough mud to make sure that there was a ship down there, then they took it away again. It will be back again tomorrow and we'll be able to clear away the rest of the muck and take a good look at it."

Sarah peered down into the blue waters, hoping to see some shape below that would be recognisable as a ship. But there was nothing. A few fish swam lazily into her sight and out again, but there was nothing more.

"Have you got your swimming things on? Do you want to go down and take a look?"

Sarah's hands went up to her hair, pulling at the pins and scattering it over her shoulders.

"Yes, I want to," she said.

"Have you ever been long under water?" asked the Professor.

She shook her head reluctantly. "But I can hold my breath for ages!" she exclaimed. "And I'm very good with a snorkel."

"I think we can spare you some compressed air—if you're good!" he smiled.

She wasn't entirely pleased. She had never used diving equipment and she would have preferred to have experimented alone, or at any rate somewhere away from the probing eyes of the two men.

"I don't suppose there is all that much to see as yet,"

she said indifferently. "I think I've changed my mind about taking a look!"

The Professor looked displeased.

"You'll have to go down some time," he warned her.

Her eyes met his. "Then I'll go now," she said bravely.

It took courage to allow herself to be strapped into the harness that carried the cylinders of compressed air. It chafed her bare shoulders and she was sure that the Professor had done the straps up too tight, though she didn't say anything because it was quite bad enough to feel his strong, neat fingers against her skin. It didn't mean anything, of course, but she was horribly aware of him all the same and unexpectedly shy of what he might be thinking.

He handed her her mask and she busied herself with dipping it over the side to make sure it was wet.

"Spit in it," he advised her, "and make sure it grips you properly."

She did as she was bidden and then sat and waited as the men got themselves ready too. Roger was the first one over the side and she followed him, clumsily, unaccustomed to the extra weight of the equipment.

Once in the water a new world opened up to her. She thought she had never seen anything so beautiful in her life before. It was true that it bore some resemblance to the coloured photographs she had seen in magazines, but they were distorted in some way because they were still. Here it was all movement and glancing lights. She plunged downwards, following Roger as he struck out for the bottom. It was difficult to remember to breathe, but fascinating to watch the bubbles of their breath dancing up to the surface. She tried to remember all that she knew about refraction under water and the difficulties of judging distances. Her job was not going to be easy. She landed with a bump on the bottom and groped her way towards where the two men were already standing. A needle-fish, a cheerful extrovert with an endless nose and a great many small teeth which, happily, he kept to himself, came up to have a look at her. She pulled it backwards by its tail and it shot off indignantly, only to return to take another look at her from a different angle.

The Professor beckoned her over to where he was standing and scraped away at the sand with his hands. She watched with interest as the top of the main mast came into view. It was marvellously well preserved and caught at her imagination, making her wonder how the rest of the ship would be. Parts of it might even be recognisable, with barnacles holding fast to the bottom. She did a bit of scraping for herself, but she wasn't very successful. Earnestly she wished she had her camera with her for a first shot of the Professor bending lovingly over his find. The strange light gave his tough body an added glamour and the strong angles of his face shone beneath his mask. She turned away from him deliberately and contemplated Roger instead. It was not, after all, the men she had come to photograph but the ancient Roman ship.

When it was time to come up to the surface she was accustomed to the peculiar sensations of being beneath the sea. It no longer seemed odd to be able to chase the fish in their own element, or to watch the strange crustations of the coral, or to grasp the occasional sponge that men had dived for from this coast for as long as man could remember. There didn't seem to be many about now and she wondered if this was yet another crop that had been over-harvested in recent times, stripping the accessible parts of the sea of their valuable assets.

She came up easily, meeting the sudden heat of the atmosphere outside with a sense of surprise. Her movements felt restricted after the freedom of the water and the equipment was suddenly unbearably heavy and she couldn't get rid of it quickly enough.

"Had fun?" the Professor asked her. He was stand-

ing on one of the seats in the boat, rubbing his hair
with the casually efficient movements of the born ath-
lete. When Sarah hoisted herself on board too, he very
nearly went over, and she laughed.

"Lovely fun!" she said with satisfaction. "I wish I'd
brought a camera with me."

He nodded to Mustapha to get under way as Roger
also landed in the bottom of the boat.

"There'll be plenty of time for that," he assured her.
"Tomorrow we can all start in earnest."

She nodded happily. A warm breeze was blowing,
drying her skin without chilling her at all. She flicked
her fingers through her hair so that it too would dry
more quickly and pulled her dress back on over her
swimsuit. She was blissfully content and she looked it.
She tucked her long legs beneath her and sniffed at the
salt in the wind and the spray. What more could any
person want beyond a job that held their interest and
surroundings like these? The sandy beaches of the island looked white in the fading sun and the palms
stood tattily against the green horizon that turned to
blue only directly above them and there it formed the
perfect background to the orange sails of the boat and
the white clean ropes.

She was still dreaming as they came into harbour,
and she didn't notice that her sister had come to meet
them until long after Mustapha had lowered the sails
and they had come right up against the side of the quay.
She waved to her as soon as she did see her and sprang
ashore, eager to tell her all about the ancient wreck and
the delights of diving. But Philomena turned away and
walked quickly up towards the ruined fort.

"You'd better run after her if you want to catch
her," Roger told her. "We'll finish here."

She glanced uncertainly at the Professor, but he was
already gathering up the equipment from the bottom of
the boat.

"Well, if you're sure?" she said uncertainly.

"I'm sure," Roger grunted.

Sarah wasn't entirely happy about it, but she ran after her sister all the same.

"It was super!" she called out to her.

Philomena turned and met her eyes coolly.

"You look a mess!" she said. "And if you plan to do that to your hair every day, you'll ruin it completely!"

Sarah tossed her salt-sticky hair behind her shoulders, refusing to care.

"I'll have to buy a cap," she agreed indifferently. She fell into step beside her sister, linking her arm with hers. "Isn't this a beautiful place?" she exclaimed.

But Philomena pulled away from her.

"I'm glad somebody is enjoying herself!" she said bitterly.

CHAPTER FOUR

HER BED, Sarah discovered, had that indefinable sense of discomfort that French beds are apt to have. It was something to do with having a bolster instead of a pillow and the way that the blankets were tucked in seemed more open to draughts than the more staid English method. She awoke with a crick in her neck from the uncompromising roundness of the bolster and an eager feeling of anticipation in the pit of her stomach. It took her a moment or two to remember where she was. The peeling yellow paint appalled her and the smell of camel from the blankets was unusual and made her want to sneeze. She pushed the bedclothes away from her and turned over, glorying in the sudden remembrance of the hot sun and the water and the feel of both on her body.

There was no sound from Philomena's room as she went past. Sarah hesitated outside the door, wondering if she should wake her sister, but she decided against it and went on downstairs by herself. Only the servant seemed to be up and about and he was busy watering all the plants. His grin was wider than ever when he greeted her, and she wished that they had some language in common so that they could converse. Perhaps he was one of the descendants of the slaves who had once been brought up from the south, though now he seemed to be as much a Tunisian as anyone else.

He beckoned her to go into the dining-room and seated her in solitary state at the table.

"*Café*," he suggested, pleased with his one word of French.

She smiled back and nodded. "*Café!*" she repeated.

He was gone for some time and she was tempted to leave the table again and explore the neighbouring rooms to find out what they contained, but at that moment Philomena came in and sat down opposite her.

"Thanks for waking me!" she said abruptly.

Sarah looked up, startled.

"Why, did you want me to?" she asked.

"Well, I didn't want to be left on my own again. This isn't exactly a woman's country," Philomena added dryly.

Sarah's heart sank. "What do you mean?" she asked with determined cheerfulness.

Philomena patted her hair into a better shape.

"I shouldn't have thought it was necessary for me to put it into words! People look at you if you're on your own—I noticed it yesterday."

"Nonsense!" Sarah retorted bracingly.

Philomena tightened her mouth into an unattractive line.

"How do you know? *You* weren't here all afternoon. Anyway, I knew you wouldn't believe me!"

Sarah tried to ignore the familiar feeling of inadequacy that her sister was apt to give her.

"There's nothing I can do about it now," she said tautly. "I have to do my work."

Philomena shrugged her pale shoulders that contrasted so well with her black hair.

"Then I'll have to come with you," she said.

Sarah wondered if she could leave it to somebody else to explain why that would be impossible. She wished long and hard that her mother had not had this brilliant idea of sending Philomena just here for her holiday when she would probably have enjoyed it so much more at some exotic centre where everything would be laid on for her.

It was something of a relief when the men came in to join them. Roger van Hueck's look of ruddy health made Sarah suspect that he had just come from a cold bath and an uncomfortable shave. By contrast the Professor smelt strongly of after-shave lotion and the stuff he put on his hair. It was difficult not to smile at the contrast between them—and difficult too not to suspect the Professor of a certain dandyism, but perhaps it was just because he was a Frenchman and therefore couldn't see why a man should not smell like a bunch of flowers!

They greeted Philomena with the special courtesy that all men reserve for a pretty, if useless, woman, and nodded to Sarah with rather less enthusiasm before they sat down. Philomena expanded visibly under the treatment.

"We were just beginning to get bored with one another!" she told them sunnily. "I suppose it's because we got up so early!"

Roger van Hueck looked sympathetic.

"Is your sister such an early riser?"

"You don't know her? She was always the one to get to school early—I'm afraid I was almost invariably late!"

Despite herself Sarah found herself remembering those mornings when her mother had called out from her bedroom:

"You're to take Philomena with you, Sarah! She's younger than you are and I won't have her crossing that road by herself!"

Sarah could remember now the pleading in her voice.

"But I'll be late again!"

Her mother had never been able to see her point.

"Nonsense, dear! Your classes don't begin any earlier than Philomena's!"

And so they had both been late, and Sarah had been too proud to complain at the extra essays and the lines of poetry learned in punishment for slipping into prayers late, or even for skipping them altogether. She had always taken her work seriously, impatient to learn and to escape from the prefabricated ideas in which she was being brought up.

"I expect I was a bit of a prig," she admitted aloud

with a half-smile. "It always upset me to think I was doing something wrong!"

Philomena preened herself happily.

"It still does, sweetie!"

Sarah was very conscious of the Professor's eyes upon her.

"I dare say," she said uncomfortably. She tried to think of some way of changing the conversation and clutched gratefully at the day's work ahead of them. Impulsively, she turned to Roger as being the more sympathetic of the two men. "Have you thought that we ought to take some aerial shots?" she asked him.

Van Hueck looked completely blank, and it was the Professor who came to the rescue.

"We shall have to suck most of the mud away first to reveal the ship. When we have done that you will have to tell Roger and myself what shots you want to take and we shall try to oblige you."

Sarah flushed with pleasure. "It might be rather expensive—" she warned him tentatively.

"That isn't your worry," he said firmly. He smiled suddenly. "I'll take you up myself if you promise not to be air sick!"

Roger laughed heartily. "Philomena is the one who doesn't like flying!" he said.

"I suspect I haven't sufficient sensibility to notice the hazards!" said Sarah demurely.

The gleam in the Professor's eyes rewarded her.

"No," he agreed, "there's nothing in the least Victorian about you." And although she wasn't quite sure what he meant by that she found that she didn't mind the bantering tone in his voice at all. In fact she rather liked it.

WHEN IT CAME TO IT Philomena didn't want to go out in the boat after all. She stood on the edge of the harbour wall looking cool and beautiful in her yellow cotton frock. Sarah heaved a sigh of relief as they rounded the edge of the point and hit the open sea.

"What is she planning to do with herself?" Roger asked her, enjoying the picture that the younger sister made against the ruined fort.

"I don't know," Sarah replied tautly. "She didn't say."

The Professor looked back at her over his shoulder.

"We'll have to find her some playmates before she gets bored," he said thoughtfully, "or our butterfly will escape us."

Sarah looked up at the flapping orange sails, not daring to let herself dwell on that remark. She had to remember that the Professor was her employer and that she couldn't let fly at him as easily as she would have done with anyone else.

"Philomena is hardly a butterfly," she said with obvious restraint.

He grinned at her.

"A very pretty butterfly," he acknowledged. "I like having her around!" Which somehow didn't succeed in pleasing Sarah either, so she busied herself with her camera equipment, experimenting to see how the camera fitted into its waterproof casing.

The suction plant was already in position, held in place by rafts, like some gigantic household cleaner sucking away the mud and sand from around the sunken ship. It was being operated by the other two members of the team, neither of whom Sarah had met as yet. She knew that one of them was a Tunisian called Sinbad el Haruch, which had made her wonder what his surname meant and whether it could really be Sinbad the Sailor! The other, an Italian, was well known in the field of Roman sailing methods. Sarah had read several articles by Giuseppe Torri and was looking forward to meeting him.

It took only a few moments to strip off her dress and to be eased into her diving equipment. Oddly, she did not feel at all nervous this time at the prospect of descending into the depths below. She dangled her feet over the edge of the boat to get the feel of the cool water and then splashed over the side in an ungainly movement that landed her in the water.

It was as beautiful as she had remembered it. She kicked out, using the black rubber flippers on her feet to the best advantage, and streaked through the cool water. The sensation gave her a feeling of power and control. She had never known anything quite like it before. The colours were fantastic and the whole underwater world was strange and enchanted.

Sarah struck out for the ship, seeing the shape of two men already there, holding the nozzle of the suction equipment for the delicate task of unveiling some of the objects which had been left on the deck so long ago. The men greeted her with a wave of the hand and signalled for her to be careful of where she put her feet. Some of the ancient pots were very fragile. The sea was muddied by the flying sand and it was more difficult to see what she was about. She peered through the murky water and saw that already one side of the ship was easily recognisable. She would have to go back for her camera and start work in earnest.

It was more difficult to persuade the Professor to halt operations for a few minutes to allow the sand to settle.

"Can't you take them later?" he asked.

But she stuck to her guns.

"I want a series, showing the ship slowly coming into view." Gently, she smiled at him. "Nobody can stay down for very long. Couldn't we have a bargain that I take a picture every hour—or so?"

"Or so!" he grunted crossly. "Are you sure it's necessary?" He wasn't the kind of man to appreciate that a photographer always had doubts.

"Absolutely," she assured him solemnly.

"Then you'd better go and tell Roger. He'll call the others off for you."

Roger was a much easier proposition.

"Do you want the finds of each level lined up too?" he asked.

"I'd rather do those back at the hotel, except for

large things to add interest. Some of the small stuff might get lost until I'm completely in control of the camera. It's difficult to judge what things will show and what won't with the naked eye."

He nodded.

"It's your job," he reminded her softly.

"I know. As a matter of fact I think the results are going to be pretty good! The water is so blissfully clear when they're not stirring up all that mud!"

Roger's eyes slid over her, rather obviously enjoying the picture she made as she stood, dripping, before him.

"You're enjoying it, aren't you?" he said.

She flicked her hair back behind her shoulders. "Yes, I am."

He prodded her camera with a thoughtful finger. "Good."

From then on the day seemed full of measurements and worries about whether the film she had chosen had enough light to make the pictures clear and brilliant. Once she got distracted and took one of the needle-fish whose curiosity had brought it within inches of her nose. It was her bad luck that it happened to be at that moment that the Professor came down himself to see how she was getting on. He frowned at her through the water and she hurriedly went back to her proper job and took him against the now clearly revealed wreck of the ship.

Sarah was tired when they came to the surface for the last time. She dried herself off rapidly and pulled her cotton frock over her head, subsiding on to one of the seats in the boat, pulling her collection of films towards her to make sure that they were still all intact.

"When can we see some of the results?" the Professor asked her.

She glanced up at him, immediately worried because she knew that she ought to develop the films that night and she wasn't sure what Philomena would want to do and whether she would have the opportunity.

"I—I don't know exactly," she compromised. "I'll be as quick with them as I can."

He looked at her steadily, the hint of a smile in his eyes.

"I'll take your sister out," he promised her. "She'll be out of your hair for a while—and I shall enjoy her particular brand of feminine charm."

It was so hot that she felt stifled. She longed for the sail to be raised and to feel the slight breeze against her cheeks as they made for harbour. Anything would be better than to feel the atmosphere like a cloud on her head and to be hardly able to move. But when the sails did spread to meet the wind it was very little better. The breeze was as hot as the still damp air.

Later on she had no time to worry about either the heat or Philomena. She blacked out her room carefully and set up her equipment for developing films, a little agitated because these were the first she had done for the Professor and she wanted them to be perfect. If she shut her eyes, she could imagine some ghastly happenings such as none of them coming out properly, and then she would never forgive herself. The Professor would be distant and kind and she would feel like crying inside. Or, even worse, he would make some biting remark that would be funny enough to make her laugh, but the sting would linger for a long, long time, so long that it might be for ever.

Her hands trembled slightly as she pulled the precious records out of their cachets and dropped them into the fluid. If she were lucky—if she were very lucky, some of them should be almost perfect and then she could relax, knowing that she was on top of her job. She would know then too that she was pulling her weight on the expedition. With Philomena there it gave the whole place a kind of holiday air that wasn't valid for her and she had to remember that, consciously, all the time. She glanced down at her watch. Another few seconds to go.

When at last she dared to look at them, her breath

caught with excitement. They were very clear and well defined and as far as she could see they were well centred without too much inessential detail or useless space. She was almost sure that they were a success.

The printing came easily. She was no longer aware of the heat or the time. All she knew was a mounting delight in the pictures she had taken. The wreck showed clearly and she noticed things about it that she had not even noticed when she had been down there looking at it. The intricacies of the scrollwork that led up to where the figurehead had once been, but was no longer, were fine and delicately patterned from vine leaves and bunches of grapes. Perhaps that had been the trouble, she thought, that Neptune had been envious of all this attention paid to Bacchus and wanted the ship for himself. She smiled at her own silliness and went on to the next print. Both the Professor and the needle-fish had come out well, but of the two of them the fish had the broader smile.

When she had finished she took the top copies of the prints and the book she was reading downstairs to wait for the others to come in. The waiter came hurrying over to her to see if she wanted anything. She wondered how she could order a pressed lemon drink from him and went through an elaborate pantomime of what she wanted. He laughed delightedly and went off to fetch the drink for her. When he came back he caught sight of the photographs. As eager as a child, he reached out for them, chuckling with glee as he recognised the various shapes and realised what she had been doing.

He was still looking at them when the others came in. Sinbad el Haruch said something to him in Arabic and he handed over the photographs with an appreciative glance at Sarah.

"What does he say?" she asked Sinbad as the waiter said something to him.

The Tunisian shot a glance at the Italian and smiled sheepishly.

"He wanted to know who had taken them," he admitted. "He doesn't believe that a woman would have an eye for such things!"

Sarah joined in the general laughter. She suspected that neither Sinbad nor the Italian, Giuseppe Torri, had really thought that a woman could do the job either. Women were all very well when the archaeological site was on land and in full view—a proper "dig," in fact—but it was a very different matter to have a woman diving with them and holding up their operations while she took photographs. They would have preferred a man to have been on the other side of the camera, but they bore her no grudge and were pleased that her first shots had turned out so well.

"Will they do?" Roger asked her. He looked tense and worried and she wondered what was the matter with him.

"Have a look," she suggested, and held out the prints to him.

He went through them with the careful eye of an expert.

"Yes, very nice," he said at last. "What relevance has the fish?"

She bit her lip.

"Don't you think he's rather attractive?" she asked him.

"I should hide it before the Professor sees it," he rapped out. "He won't approve of your wasting film like that!" His usually mild blue eyes sparked dangerously. "Nor will he care for this one!" he added, producing the one of the Professor.

Sarah bit back her first retort.

"The fish was just for fun," she said tautly, "but the one of the Professor was necessary. He will need more than just the pictures of the ship for his book."

Roger gave it a last disapproving look. "You've made him look quite a pin-up boy in that!" he exclaimed.

Sarah looked at it over his shoulder.

"He is quite handsome," she said critically. "He has a nice shape. You can see it better in his swimming trunks, that's all."

"Is that what it is?"

She didn't know why she took his scorn so seriously, but it hurt and embarrassed her because she didn't understand it.

"Where is he, anyway?" Roger demanded of the company at large.

Sarah took back the photographs and stacked them neatly on the table. "He's with Philomena," she explained.

"Why?" he snapped.

So that was it! Suddenly, the reason for his displeasure was quite clear to her. She gave him a warm, sympathetic smile and was rewarded by a rather bleak smile in return.

"What are you drinking?" he asked her.

She waved the pressed lemon drink under his nose. "Why don't you have one? It's very refreshing!"

"I need something considerably stronger than that," he grunted.

She wondered briefly if the Tunisian would mind, but he didn't appear to, merely translating the orders of the others so that the waiter could get them for them. He himself joined Sarah in having a soft drink.

"Sometimes I have a glass of wine," he told her in answer to her unspoken enquiry. "But we are very modern in Tunisia. It is not uncommon nowadays."

They all sat down in a friendly group at one end of the dining-room. To Sarah it was a completely new experience to find herself so much at home in such a cosmopolitan gathering. Giuseppe sat himself down beside her with a comical look at any possible rivals.

"We are very lucky to have you here," he said with open satisfaction. "You must come and meet my second cousin, the potter, when we are next free, and he will make you a charming pot all for yourself."

The Tunisian looked at him reproachfully.

"He is not your second cousin," he objected slowly.

"But of course he is my cousin! We come from the same village."

Sinbad shrugged his shoulders. "Prove it!" he said charmingly.

Giuseppe was decidedly put out.

"He is my cousin—he is not my cousin! What does it matter? He makes fine pots!"

"The very finest," Sinbad concurred courteously.

"There you are! So you see," the Italian went on quickly, turning back to Sarah, "how wise you would be to come with me to meet him. He has the same name as myself," he added in a fierce undertone.

"Of course he is my cousin!"

Sarah laughed. "Do they really make pots here in Djerba?" she asked.

"As fine as any that came out of Rome," he assured her.

She was astonished. "You, an Italian, can say that?" she teased him.

He spread out expressive hands.

"We took the shape from the Greeks, why should we complain when the Arabs take the shape from us?"

Sinbad sat up indignantly. "And the Egyptians? They had these pots long before either of you had them!"

Giuseppe pursed up his lips. "The ancient Egyptians? Were they exactly the same?" he pondered.

"Shall we say a Mediterranean shape?" Sarah interposed hastily. "Do you always argue like this?"

"Yes, they always do!" a very French voice said behind her, and she turned quickly, just in time to see the Professor drop Philomena's arm as they came right into the room. Philomena's face was glowing with excitement and pleasure and she looked prettier than ever. "They quarrel all the time. It is a part of their life here."

"It proves we are good friends," Sinbad drawled carelessly.

The Professor smiled at him. "Yes, you are good friends," he agreed.

Philomena chose a high chair, hitched up her skirt above her knees and sat down negligently.

"This," she announced, "is the most wonderful town I've ever been in! Sarah, I've had the most gorgeous time! Sebastian took me into the *souks* and I bought a camel blanket—I'll show you after. Then we drove out of town to some hotel and sat around on the beach. Did you know that there were springs of water all over the island? There was a hot one right on the beach. Some of the people had dammed it up!" She stretched herself exotically. "Oh my, this is quite a place!"

Sarah was glad to see her looking so happy. She relaxed into her chair and felt happier herself. It had been kind of the Professor to entertain her sister, she thought, but then he was both kind and considerate. She felt his eyes on her and looked across at him, meeting his eyes squarely.

"Well?" he asked her.

But she couldn't thank him. He had prevented that by his attitude earlier when she had tried to show him she was grateful.

"I—I wanted to show you the first photographs," she said.

Immediately he held out his hand for them, but it was Philomena who took them from her.

"Why," she explained joyfully, "here's one of you, Sebastian! It's too, too glamourous!" She wound her arm round the Professor's. "May I keep it?" she asked him.

He released himself with gentle fingers.

"If you like," he said.

CHAPTER FIVE

PHILOMENA PAUSED on the landing as the two sisters were making their way to bed.

"Are you coming to see my purchases?" she asked Sarah.

Sarah was immediately enthusiastic.

"I should love to! I'm dying to hear all about the *souks*. Are they as romantic as they sound?"

"Well, no," Philomena had to admit. "They're very dark. A maze of passages with all the shops being no more than holes in the wall. I can't think how they see to work at all!"

"Did you get your blanket there?" asked Sarah.

Philomena nodded her head.

"We went to have a look at them being made. Sebastian seems to know all the local craftsmen. Look what he found for me."

She held open her hand to reveal a small silver Arab brooch with a geometric design that was pleasing to the eye and not too complicated. Sarah took it from her and held it up to the rather dismal light that hung, naked, from a tatty piece of wire in the ceiling.

"It's lovely!" she said. "Was it expensive?"

Philomena snatched it from her, looking coy.

"Well, I should hardly know that, should I?"

So the Professor had given it to her, Sarah thought, and wondered why the knowledge should hurt her. It was nothing to her whom Philomena wove her charms over! Why should it be?

"Very nice!" she said aloud, crisply. "He seems to have given you a very pleasant afternoon!"

"Oh yes, he did!" Philomena agreed. She looked

like a kitten faced with a jug of cream, just before the first gorgeous lick. "He did indeed!"

There wasn't much that one could say to that. It seemed to Sarah that her sister's self-confidence had never been at a higher level. It was impregnable. And that, she told herself, was a very desirable state to be in, so there was not the slightest need for her to be so down about it.

"Good, I'm glad," she said with what she hoped was sincerity. "I'm glad you're beginning to like it better here too!"

Philomena shrugged her shoulders.

"People always mean more to me than places," she said calmly. "Just as with you it's always been the other way about!"

Sarah wondered if that were true. She thought she had always been content wherever she had been, but she was learning things about herself that she had never known before. She had never thought before that she could be jealous of Philomena's easy conquests, and yet she had been very nearly wishing that her sister had had a perfectly horrible afternoon and for no good reason that she could see.

"Aren't you going to show me your blanket?" she asked brightly.

Philomena unwrapped it slowly, untying the knots in the string one by one so as to delay the process. It had been beautifully done up in brown paper, making it look a great deal smaller than it really was. Spread out, it practically covered the floor of the small bedroom. It was a rich green in colour with the traditional Moslem geometric designs woven into it in brown, black and white.

"It has a funny smell," Sarah complained.

"It's new," Philomena explained patiently. "And it's made of camel wool. Probably it hasn't been very well washed."

Seeing that there were still one or two burrs clinging to the wool, Sarah thought that that was only too likely.

But it was beautiful. The colours had a simplicity that only natural dyes could give—and the black, the brown and the white had not been dyed at all, but were the natural colours, carefully sorted into their own batches. It had been woven on a hand-loom of the simplest sort, with the ends knotted together and ended off in green woollen baubles that finished the blanket nicely. Originally it might have been used to add comfort to a camel-saddle, but now they were mostly made to boost the tourist industry, though happily it had not yet occurred to anyone to make them in any way different from those they had been turning out for generations.

"It's very nice indeed!" Sarah exclaimed with appreciation. "We must have a look some time and see if we can find one for Mother."

Philomena sniffed. "They're three or four *pounds,* you know!" she said.

"I imagine they are! All the better. You'll want to take her back something nice."

Philomena laughed. "Oh, good heavens! She didn't give me the money to squander on her! She wants me to have a good time here, not scrimp and save so that I can take presents back to her."

"Well, perhaps," Sarah admitted, "but you'll have to take her something."

"Oh, I may not bother," her sister said airily. "You'll go back laden with more than enough stuff from the two of us. You always do that sort of thing!"

Sarah felt suddenly quite tired of all the things she "always did." She made a swift mental calculation of the amount of money she could expect to save in the next few weeks and vowed to herself that she would take her mother a single, luxurious item and it would be quite clear that it came from her alone! But then it was only because Philomena was young that she was so heedless. She loved her mother just as much. It wasn't really selfish, just thoughtless. Sarah glanced across at her and wondered again at her strong, petulant beauty which was so like their mother's. Her own fairness seemed bare beside it and her seriousness dull against her sister's gay frivolity. Involuntarily, she sighed.

"Well," she said, "I'm for bed." She stretched herself and went towards the door. "What are you doing tomorrow?" she asked.

Philomena's smile grew wider.

"I don't share that sort of knowledge, remember? I never did!"

Sarah sighed again. No, her sister had never shared any of her activities with her family, resenting any interest that they might have shown in her romantic affairs. It was something that Sarah had always been able to sympathise with, because she too had liked to keep all that was really dear to her, and that was her work, away from the prying eyes of those she loved, so it was all the more bewildering to realise that she was resenting her sister's attitude now.

"I suppose he's taking you out again?" she hazarded tentatively.

Philomena gave her a long, blank stare.

"So what?" she asked. "You don't own him, you know."

Sarah took a deep breath.

"No," she agreed softly. "And really, I'm awfully glad I don't!"

She lay awake for a long time that night, and it was all the more irritating because she knew she was tired and that there would be much to do in the morning. When morning came, however, she was still tossing and turning and the bolster seemed as hot and as uncomfortable as ever. Tonight, she vowed, she would open the shutters wide, no matter what, to catch any breath of air that happened to be passing there, for there was no doubt about it, it was the abominable heat, which had been keeping her awake.

THE PHOTOGRAPHS WENT QUICKER that day. From her darkened room upstairs she could hear a transistor radio being played downstairs. The music sounded strange and it was difficult to pick out the melody, but she didn't quite dislike it. At intervals it stopped and the harsh, guttural accents of the Arab language would flood the silence around her in unrecognisable syllables and she was left wondering what it was all about. Then the music would sound forth again in what seemed to be exactly the same song as before.

It helped her to work. She found the rhythm, complicated as it was, invaded her being and made it easier to concentrate. In quite a short time she had the rolls of film developed and had started to print them, her heart hammering with anticipation in case they weren't as good as the day before. But when she had finished, she didn't think anyone would have any cause for complaint. They were clear and sharp and they were meticulous in showing each stage of the unveiling of the ship. If there were rather too many of them, that was only to be expected.

When she had done she put the prints on her dressing-table and considered what she would do with herself before it was time to join the others for the evening meal. She had a whole precious three hours to herself, which was a treat indeed. A little guilty just in case her sister was in her room after all, she crept past her door and ran lightly down the marble steps, almost tripping over the radio as she did so. The Negro put out a huge hand and rescued it from beneath her feet, grinning at her as he did so. Carefully, he put it beside one of the pots, humming the same tune under his breath. It was the first time that Sarah had looked at all carefully at the plants that littered up the steps, but now the pot that held a large, bushy green thing held her attention. The markings were original and the varnish thick and splodgy. It was not really a very well made pot, but it had an unexpected charm lent by the restraint of its colour scheme.

The Negro was pleased at her interest and tried to tell her something about it, but she couldn't understand him.

"Guellala?" she asked him hopefully, repeating the name of the local pottery village, hoping that it was a local piece.

He nodded vigorously. "Guellala," he repeated.

She would just have nice time, she thought, to go there. She didn't think Giuseppe Torri would really mind her stealing a march on him and going to see for herself. She felt a growing excitement at the idea of seeing something of the island for herself, and clutching her camera to her she set off down the narrow street that separated the hotel from the main square.

It was cooler than in the full heat of the day and all the inhabitants had come out into the streets to gossip and to trade. The houses belonged very much to the women, where they entertained each other and lived out their mysterious lives; the men haunted the cafés and the sidewalks of the streets, their long robes flowing about them and more often than not with their heads swatched in a piece of turkish towelling. They watched her pass with good-mannered interest, only too pleased to direct her to the spot where she could catch the Guellala bus.

The bus, when it came along, was a French one, typical of the long, straight country roads of France, with an impertinent-looking front and a rickety ladder at the rear that led up to the luggage rack on top. Flung haphazardly on to this rack were a couple of bicycles, several crates of fruit and three baskets of local fish. Two small boys, reluctant to pay the normal fare for travelling inside, clung perilously on top of the lot, giggling happily every time the bus lurched round a corner in the road, almost dislodging them.

Sarah got in with some trepidation and seated herself quickly on the nearest vacant seat. One or two of the women, unveiled because they were Berber rather than Arab, smiled tentatively at her and were delighted when she smiled back. With soft, exploratory fingers, they touched the material of her dress and laughed excitedly between themselves. Even her camera didn't disturb them, though they shook their heads when she asked if she might take a photograph of them. Instead they offered her a share of the marzipan sweets they were eating and tried to introduce her to the complicated family relationships between them. In the end she was sure of only one thing, that they all came from the same village and had gone into Houmt Souk to take their newly washed wool to the market there. She was so intrigued with them that it came as a shock to her that they had arrived at Guellala and that she had hardly noticed the surrounding countryside at all.

She felt very alone, standing in the white dusty road after she had waved her new-found friends goodbye. The road was edged with a hedge of prickly pear that reached taller than her head and the only other thing she could see was a stretch of olive trees that reached as far as she could look along the road ahead, great gnarled trunks in fascinating shapes topped by the distinctive almost silvery leaves. There was no sign whatever of the pottery centre. Disconsolately she walked to the corner and was relieved to see the village ahead of her, bigger than she had expected and more spread out, an array of houses that had been highly decorated to advertise the potters who inhabited them. Some had trained in Italy and France and had the most impressive-sounding diplomas, and there was one who called himself Carlo Torri and, as he was the nearest to her, she went to visit him first.

There were pots everywhere. Many of them exactly the same as those which they had rescued from the depths of the sea leaned against the white walls. Others, of a less happy design, filled the blue painted windows and the niches in the wall, while yet more stood in groups on the concrete floor.

"Madame?" a young man greeted her. He looked every inch an Italian, with soft black curly hair and almost black eyes, but all the Mediterranean races are so mixed that he could have been anything.

"Monsieur Torri?" she asked hesitantly.

He nodded excitedly, his interest caught.

"Your cousin—" she began.

He broke into delighted laughter.

"But of *course*! You come from the expedition? My *cousin* will have sent you?"

"Well not exactly," she compromised. "He told me about you, but he said he'd bring me himself."

The Tunisian Torri laughed with wicked good humour.

"How wise of you to come by yourself!" he commented dryly. "Now, let me see what I can find to offer you. Or perhaps you only came to look and admire? I am not one of those who will do *anything* to make an honest *dinar*!"

Sarah was amused.

"I've come to buy," she assured him, "but it will have to be something small and cheap because I can't afford a great deal."

He considered her seriously for a minute.

"It doesn't have to be expensive to have charm," he said at last. "I will make one or two suggestions and then you can look around and see if there is anything you like better. Poke about where you please. Everything is for sale, sooner or later."

Sarah took him at his word. She delighted in examining all the different shapes he had made. Some were frankly hideous in both conception and execution, covered with shells and highly coloured, but others were both fragile and dainty. There were a number of hanging gardens, made in the shape of pots, but with diamond-shaped holes cut out of them, and it was on a small one of these that Sarah's eye fell.

"I'll take that!" she said.

He was doubtful that it would carry without breaking, but said he would wrap it carefully.

"How much is it?" she asked him rather belatedly.

His dark eyes flirted with her.

"For you? A very special price, no? Shall we say the privilege of escorting you around the village? You will want to see the ovens and the other shops, will you not? And you must be able to report to my cousin that I looked after you properly!"

Sarah felt confused. She knew she was blushing and that made her cross, but it was nice to know that he wanted to escort her even if she didn't think that she ought to accept the offer. She bit her lip, wondering what to do, and was glad when she was rescued by someone else coming into the shop.

"Hullo, Sarah."

She blinked, even more annoyed with herself that she had not noticed who it was who had come in.

"I—I'm sorry, you were against the light," she stammered.

Sebastian smiled at her, more gently that he usually did, and picked up the piece of pottery she was buying.

"Is this for your room?"

She took it from him, admiring again its fragile lines.

"I'm not sure. I want to take it to England with me."

He looked amused.

"Women always do want to pack the most impossible things!" he said. He reached for his wallet and turned enquiringly to the potter. "I'll pay for it," he told him with decision. The smile played on his lips again. "A present from the expedition, if you like," he explained.

She accepted it without really knowing what to say, the gesture was so unexpected.

"Thank you very much," she said awkwardly.

His eyes were cold as he looked at her and she was almost sure that he was comparing her artlessness with her sister's feminine grace and chatter, and that made her less sure of herself than ever.

"Monsieur Torri said he would show me round the village," she announced, forcing herself to break the silence.

The Professor was quite unperturbed.

"How nice of him, but I know my way around pretty

well, so I don't think that will be necessary, do you?
What do you want to see first?"

Clutching her parcel as a kind of talisman, she was
swept off in his wake to do a complete and efficient
tour of the village. He pulled her in and out of one of
the ovens which was not being used and demonstrated
to her exactly how it worked. In a short while she forgot
she was nervous of him and began to argue heatedly
about the relative merits of the pottery which was on
sale.

"The old isn't always better!"

Sebastian picked up a handful of wet clay and
squeezed it dry.

"I imagine this is more the trouble," he said. "It's
coarser than the stuff they used to use."

"Locally?" she asked.

"Ah, that I don't know," he admitted.

They stood and watched one of the potters throwing
a pot, admiring the way he kept the wheel turning with
his feet as he shaped the vase with his fingers, pausing
every now and then to dip his fingers in a bowl of
muddy water. Finally he cut it free from the wheel with
a wire and put it on one side to dry. It all looked very
easy and satisfying. Indeed, he told them, it was easy,
provided that the clay was well centred on the wheel
right from the start. After that it grew beneath the
fingers, now taller, now squatter, exactly as one had
first planned it.

Sarah dipped a finger into the muddy water and
grinned at him.

"Did you train in France too?" she asked him.

He shook his head. "I went to Holland, I meant to
stay, but like all Djerbans I had to come back in the
end."

"The isle of the lotus-eaters?"

He laughed, "I ate the lotus when I was still a child.
Perhaps I am immune?"

But the Professor was quick to deny this heresy.

"No one is immune. I should think it works its

magic on Djerbans more than anyone else. You all come back here as soon as you've made enough money to do so!"

The potter was delighted.

"It's true. Over here is oblivion. This is the happy isle. What more is there to say?"

They bought a pot from him too, exactly like the one they had just watched him make, and walked out into the strong sunlight again. The shadows were long in the evenings, but the heat was still present until long after the sun had actually set. It was impregnated in the white walls of the buildings and in the hot white dust of the roads. Sarah wiped a bead of sweat off the end of her nose and wondered what it was that was so delightful about the Professor's company. She eyed him covertly and thought about it carefully. He looked more foreign than ever in casual clothes, and his shirt collar was rubbed in places, in a way that could have been mended quite easily if someone had taken the trouble. And yet he wasn't shabby. All his clothes had the same good cut, only it wasn't the cut of Savile Row, the cut she was used to. Perhaps it was this strangeness which intrigued her?

"How did you come here?" she asked him.

"I came in the car." His eyes looked very French as he looked at her. "Or did you mean *why* did I come?"

She coloured slightly, aware that she had no cause to think that he had come because he had somehow learned that she was there.

"I thought you were taking Philomena out," she explained.

His expression did not encourage her.

"Your family take up quite a lot of your time, don't they?" he said at last.

Feeling rather foolish, she nodded her head.

"But one's family should, don't you think?" she insisted.

He shrugged his shoulders, looking bored by the discussion.

"I wouldn't know," he remarked casually. "I mostly take mine for granted."

She felt snubbed, though she didn't quite know why. Without much effort she could dislike him almost as much as she liked him, she thought. With a sudden change of mood she handed him the parcels to carry and rushed off before him to peer down the village well. It was not at this moment working, but it was easy to see the lengthy track where the camel walked back and forth, lowering the leather bucket into the water and pulling it dripping with water, up to the top again. Sarah leaned on the edge of the small wall that surrounded it, thoroughly content with her surroundings, and smiled over her shoulder at Sebastian.

"Don't you wish you could stay here for ever?" she asked him.

He didn't reply immediately.

"I'm not sure," he said finally. "There is something unsubstantial about an enchanted island. I prefer to know that the magic around me will last!"

"What kinds of magic?" she asked dreamily.

He smiled down at her, his eyes crinkling at the edges.

"All kings of magic. The magic of work and the magic of love—"

"But they would last longer in an enchanted land!"

"Do you think so? I think it lasts longer when built on a few solid foundations!"

"In the full light of day?" she teased him.

"Why not?"

Her amusement died at something in his eyes and she turned back to the well quickly to hide the rising tide of emotion that fountained up within her and which she couldn't even begin to put a name to.

"I think we should be starting back," he told her.

She followed him willingly to his car, glad of the comfort it offered compared with the bus she had come on. Gently he eased it out of the village along the narrow road edged with prickly pear.

"Would you like to go back beside the sea?" he asked her.

She had never seen anything like the Djerban beaches. The sand seemed to stretch for miles, edged by an army of palm trees that went as far as eye could see in whichever way one looked. And they were empty, with no more than an occasional shepherd sitting motionless on a hillock guarding his sheep. Even the places that had been turned into tourist centres had room and to spare on the hotel beaches. Once a caravan of camels came along the road in the opposite direction and the owner stopped and stared at them, grinning a greeting, his *chechia* set at a rakish angle on his head, his face burned brown in the sun. Sarah waved back at him and the camels arched their aristocratic necks and looked down their long noses at her. They were fatter than she had expected and she was secretly delighted by their disdainful manners.

Houmt Souk came upon them suddenly, the buildings ruddy in the fast-fading light. They went through the square with its little groups of men sitting on the iron tables and drinking the sweet Arab green tea, or the equally sweet cups of Turkish coffee, and a minute later drew up outside the hotel.

"How are today's lot of pictures?" the Professor asked as they got out of the car.

"I'll show them to you at dinner," she responded immediately. It was a mundane ending to the excursion, she thought, to be asked about her work. It all went to show that the magic was only the enchantment of the island after all. Back at the hotel, Sebastian was the leader of the expedition and she no more than its photographer. It served her right for dreaming dreams and seeing visions of impossible things which she didn't really understand herself. She stood awkwardly in the hall and thanked him for the piece of pottery he had given her and for the lift home. She felt suddenly and unexpectedly weary as she mounted the stairs to her room and not at all in the mood to start explaining to Philomena where she had been.

But in the end that wasn't necessary. Philomena was sitting hunched over the desk in her room, writing a letter.

"I've been taking your words to heart," she greeted her sister. "I'm writing to Mother!"

Sarah looked guiltily at the thick pile of pages all covered by Philomena's generous sprawl.

"Oh? What are you saying to her?" she asked.

Philomena chewed on the end of her pen, eyeing her sister with a slightly malicious expression.

"I'm suggesting that she should come out and see it all for herself," she drawled. "She can use that bit of money that she's always saving for a rainy day."

"But she might need it!" Sarah exclaimed.

Philomena grinned.

"Oh, quit worrying, Sarah. You're such a drag when you go on about money. Mother has some and she might just as well spend it coming out here and keeping me company. It will be *good* for her!"

Sarah sat on the edge of the bed.

"But I'm supposed to be working here."

"Work away!" her sister instructed her calmly. "Mother won't stop you!"

Defeated, Sarah tried to consider the whole idea calmly, wondering how she would ever explain it all to Sebastian that yet another member of her family was joining them. And yet there was no reason at all why her mother shouldn't stay at a local hotel if she wanted to. It would be fun having her close at hand.

"She won't come!" she said aloud.

Philomena signed her name with a flourish.

"Of course she'll come," she said.

CHAPTER SIX

SARAH CHANGED for dinner in a turbulent frame of mind. She unwrapped her piece of pottery and set it carefully on her desk where she could see it. Just looking at it gave her pleasure, the more so because Sebastian had given it to her. It was difficult not to sit and gaze at it, dreaming of this and that. She wondered if her mother would find the people here as delightful as she did, or whether she would find the Professor too much of a Frenchman and a foreigner really to appeal to her. Somehow it was terribly important that her mother should like Sebastian.

She was glad that Philomena thought her mother would have enough money put by her to be able to come. If the worst came to the worst she might be able to help a little and so prolong her stay. The only difficulty was going to be in trying to explain the situation to the Professor. She could imagine it in her mind and the picture didn't give her any confidence.

"My mother is coming out to stay," she would say. And he would reply—but there her mind boggled. Only one thing was certain and that was that he wouldn't be pleased. He had wanted a photographer for his expedition, not an army of Feaneys, all wanting this and that!

She picked up the piece of pottery again, picking out the squiggles of the pattern with her finger. Dimly she heard the gong ring down below for dinner and roused herself to do her hair and to put some powder on her nose.

"Are you going to tell Sebastian tonight?" Philomena asked her as they went downstairs together.

"Tell him what?" Sarah hedged uneasily.

"Why, that Mother will be coming out!"

Sarah shook her head.

"She may never come. I'll tell him when I have to."

Philomena gave her a quick look.

"I'll tell him if you like," she offered.

To her surprise Sarah found she resented the suggestion.

"I shall tell him myself!" she said quite crossly. "But only when I'm absolutely sure that Mother is coming!"

Her head was held high and there was more colour than usual in her cheeks as she went into the dining-room. If she had but known it, she looked almost beautiful.

THEIR MOTHER, when she wrote, wrote to the two of them. She was, she said, looking forward to paying them a visit and had already seen about her flight out. If she had got it all right, she should be with them in less than a week, and they were to make sure she had somewhere to sleep on arrival and that they both had plenty of spare time to be with her and to help her enjoy herself.

Sarah read the letter through twice, wondering what she should do. There was no doubt now but that she would have to tell the Professor that she was coming, and her heart sank at the prospect. She was already behind with her work and although he had said nothing she could tell that he had noticed. Roger had made matters worse by trying to conceal the fact that their records were not up to date and had received one of the sharpest comments Sarah had ever heard the Frenchman make. He did not easily tolerate sloppy work.

Philomena snatched the letter from her.

"I told you there was sufficient money!" she exclaimed. "Let me read it again!"

Sarah shrugged her shoulders.

"I hope she knows how expensive the hotels out here are," she said thoughtfully. "I think one of us

should find out the exact price so that we know exactly
what to expect.''

Her sister gave an excited wriggle.

"Of course, if you want to," she agreed. ''You'd better go when you've finished this evening.'' She looked
up through her eyelashes in a pretty movement she had
learned about in a magazine. "I have a date," she said.

"With Sebastian?" Sarah asked before she could
stop herself, but her sister had already danced off to
her room, taking the letter with her. Oh, how glad she
would be, she thought, to see her mother! Her face
softened as she anticipated the moment when she
would step off the aircraft and see the island for herself.
Would the enchantment work for her too, tying her
with invisible cords to the place? That would be quite
something to see, for her mother liked the familiar
ways of her life and usually it took a great deal to up-
root her and make her set out for foreign parts.

There was no opportunity to tell the Professor that
afternoon. They had reached the final stages of un-
earthing the sunken vessel and they were all working
harder than ever. Sarah began to feel that she spent as
much of her time beneath the water as she did above it.
They could crawl right into the wrecked boat at last, but
it was so dark inside that she had to take down some of
the heavier lamps so that she could see what she was
doing.

"I think we shall have to use infra-red," she said to
Roger.

He made a face at her.

"Well, if you have to, but it does come rather more
expensive.''

In the end there was no help for it because the lamps
cast curious shadows across her best shots and the Professor was getting increasingly impatient as it took her
longer and longer to get the necessary records.

"What's holding you up?" he called across to her
almost as soon as she had surfaced. With an effort
Sarah dragged herself up on to the edge of the raft and

sat there, panting with the exertion. Under water her equipment was part of her, making it easier for her to move around, but once she was out of the water it was a very different story and she could hardly move at all.

"It's getting darker all the time," she said disgustedly. "I shall have to take down another lamp to balance the other two. I'm sorry to hold you up, but it isn't easy now that we've got inside the ship."

He gave her one of his rare, sweet smiles, that were quite different from his more usual ones.

"Shall I help you?"

She hesitated, thinking how much easier it would be to have him holding one of the lamps for her. On the other hand it seemed terrible to think that she couldn't manage better alone.

"Which one shall I take?" he asked.

She pointed it out to him, admiring the easy way he slung it over one shoulder, standing there, looking down at her.

"Do we need anything else?"

She shook her head.

"Are you sure?" She couldn't really believe that he was prepared to help.

Again that smile flashed out.

"I am quite sure! We must get this moving somehow!"

He dived first, plunging down into the green water with an ease born of long practice. She had a mental picture of him, at home in his native France, playing on the sun-drenched beaches of the South, surrounded by his sister and a selection of lovely French girls all vying for his attention. Carefully she spat into her mask and washed it in the sea, replacing it over her face, and followed him into the cool water.

Every time she went through the ancient hatches she had a peculiar sensation of excitement. How long had it been since anyone had made their way along these ancient decks or used the small cabin or eaten their meals in the confined space? She went in head first, somersaulting on to her feet to stand beside the Professor who was already struggling with the lamps.

It wasn't easy to hitch them up and to hold them steady. Little eddies of currents, mostly made by their own movements, shook the lights and gave a series of dappled shadows across the walls and floor. Impatiently, Sarah set up her camera and waited for the eddies to settle. She could feel Sebastian close beside her, hardly breathing at all in his efforts to keep still. Only the very occasional bubble of air escaped them, pushing its way upwards.

At last she could press the button and the shot was taken. She gave him a triumphant wave of the hand and between them they gathered up the equipment and floated up to the surface. Willing hands grasped the heavy lamps and the cameras, enclosed as they were in heavy waterproof cases, and dragged them up on to the raft. The Professor and Sarah followed, easing off their masks and their flippers and shaking their bodies dry in the hot sun.

"I think that will be all I need for the moment," Sarah said. "We still have most of the recording to do, but that's really writing it up from our notes."

Sebastian looked at her enquiringly.

"Can you and Roger get it done tonight?" he asked.

For an instant she hesitated, thinking about the room she ought to be finding for her mother.

"I expect we can do most of it," she answered at last.

The Professor's eyes met hers.

"What's the matter? Were you planning to do something with Philomena?"

It was on the tip of her tongue to tell him that she knew that he was taking Philomena out, but she didn't say anything because her reason told her that it wasn't any of her business. They could do as they liked and she wouldn't care! Of the two men she much preferred Roger anyway, because he didn't worry her and make her care about what she said and did, guarding her words and actions like an actress at her first film test.

"No, it isn't that." Now, she supposed, was her opportunity to tell him, but even as she was searching for the words he turned away from her and began to towel himself down with the enthusiastic energy of the very fit. She picked up a towel and began to dry her ears and the back of her neck. The sun was very hot and she could feel it burning her fair skin. If she sat in it for long she would get that glorious, lissom, lazy feeling that spelt death to intelligent work. When she had finished drying herself, the moment had gone and he had moved away from her and was talking to someone in the boat who was hidden from her by the great pile of orange sails.

A breeze suddenly cavorted over them and stayed with them the whole way back to Houmt Souk, filling the sails and rippling its way over the calm, green sea. They could feel it on their hot skins and they rejoiced in its light caress.

"It's going to be a lovely evening," Roger said with appreciation.

The Italian Giuseppe Torri smiled at him.

"I should think it will be, as you are going to monopolise Sarah for most of it."

Sarah laughed. "I met your 'cousin' in Guellala," she told him.

"So I heard. And after I had promised myself the delights of your society for the occasion too!" He looked as mournful as a spaniel.

Sarah gave him a look of apology.

"I hoped you wouldn't mind, but I did so want to see it all for myself and I had some spare time, so I went."

"And I hope you had a lovely time!" he exclaimed. "It is sad that you don't have the same freedom as your sister!"

Sarah grinned at him, well aware that under his light touch he was not very fond of her sister.

"On the contrary," she said sweetly, "Philomena is between jobs—I actually have one! A much more comfortable position, don't you think?"

"Maybe." He looked at her curiously. "Is it true your mother is going to pay you both a visit?"

Sarah's air of content fell from her in sudden ruins. "How do you know?" she asked sharply.

"Philomena told me, who else?"

"Did she tell anyone else?"

Giuseppe pulled down the corners of his mouth.

"Now how can I say? But it might be as well to put in a word in the right quarter first, don't you think? Not that it is any of my business."

Sinbad nodded gravely, just catching the end of the conversation.

"The man's right. The Professor won't appreciate hearing it from anyone else."

Sarah sighed. "To tell the truth, I don't think he's going to appreciate it anyway," she said. "It would be different if we were way ahead of schedule, instead of several days behind."

The Tunisian eyed her solemnly.

"Are you afraid of the man?" he asked.

She wriggled uncomfortably.

"Goodness, no! Not *afraid* of him! It isn't that at all. It's just that it all happened so suddenly and I'm not even sure where my mother is going to stay."

The two men considered the point.

"You'd better do a round of the hotels," they suggested. "There's a French hotel in Houmt Souk," Sinbad added. "But the best ones are the new ones which have just been built along the coast."

Sarah picked up her camera and the rolls of film she wanted to develop.

"Yes, I shall have to go and look at them," she agreed. "If only I didn't have to work this evening!"

Actually, as soon as she started work, she forgot all about her family. There was so much to do. Because she had been out at the site all afternoon she still had all the developing to do, and then there was the more laborious task of recording all the finds they had made and exactly where they had been discovered, as well as a survey of the ship as it was gradually coming to light, with its measurements, the thickness of the decks and the bottom, and anything else that was relevant to how it had been built and by whom.

Roger came up to her room to work with her. He stood by the window, smoking restlessly, as she put the finishing touches to her pictures.

"Have you noticed the horizon here is quite green at night?" he asked her.

She smiled at him over her shoulder.

"It starts green, then it goes purple and all the houses turn pink and look as if they were made of sugar!"

"You have a great deal of imagination," he said sourly.

"Oh, not at all! Have you really looked at the houses?" she demanded. "They whitewash them so often that none of the lines are quite true any longer— like a slightly melted marshmallow—not even the doors are properly centred! I like the elegant tracery on the roofs and windows too and the strange patterns they paint on the walls to keep away the evil eyes."

"Is that why they do it?" he remarked. "And why so many hands?"

"On the walls and doors? They're the 'hand of Fatima.' Sebastian thinks they are older than the Prophet's wife in actual fact and have just been wished on to her."

"So!" he exclaimed crossly. "Sebastian is the reason for all this information! I might have known you hadn't read it in a book!"

She stared at him in surprise.

"But I might just as easily have done!" she said.

"Oh really? And Philomena too?"

Sarah laughed. She hadn't meant to, but the irresistible urge to giggle grew somewhere within her and burst suddenly into joyful mirth.

"Philomena?" she repeated with a snort of laughter. *"Philomena?"*

"Yes, Philomena."

"Nonsense," she said when she could. "Philomena wouldn't occupy herself with details like that!"

He gave her a rather sour smile.

"Wouldn't she? She was full of it earlier today!"

Sarah giggled again. "What on earth were you talking about?" she asked him.

He blinked, and she saw with surprise that beneath his anger lay a real hurt.

"She was telling me about your mother coming. She's looking forward to it very much, isn't she? I suppose it's been boring for her here on her own, but we did our best to make it interesting for her."

"It sounds to me as though you succeeded!" she teased him.

He came up behind her, putting a hand on either of her two shoulders.

"I could wring your neck for making fun of me like that!" he said in a fierce whisper. For a moment she was quite afraid of him and her laughter left her as suddenly as it had come.

"I'm sorry," she said. "I didn't know you were serious."

"I'll tell you about your sister," he went on grimly. "She's bone selfish and she doesn't do a thing she doesn't want to. And yet she can eat the heart out of a man almost before he is aware."

"You mean you've fallen in love with her?" she said softly.

He pulled himself together with a jerk.

"It's an idle fantasy, isn't it? With Sebastian filling her head with pretty stories!"

Dumbly, she stared down at the photos she was touching up, wondering what to say.

"Couldn't you tell her pretty stories too?" she asked at last.

Roger dropped his hands to his sides and she shivered slightly with relief that he was no longer touching her.

"No, I couldn't!" he said sharply. "It was all right when she thought you were interested in me, but now she is equally sure that you are not!"

Sarah could feel her cheeks buring.

"I hope she never thought that!"

For a second he looked amused.

"Well, she did. I'm not saying that I didn't encourage her in the impression—"

"Oh, did you?" she said coldly. "On what grounds?"

He looked very fair, very young and very vulnerable.

"It could have been true," he said helplessly. "The fact that I am a Dutchman would make me different from the other men you have known, no?"

"In what particular?" she asked dryly.

"Because English people always find an accent very attractive—and that sort of thing," he ended lamely.

"And now she doesn't believe you?" she prompted him.

"She can see for herself that you are more interested in your cameras!" he said sulkily. "Or even in the great Sebastian!"

Again Sarah could feel her cheeks burning.

"There would be very little to see there!" she said icily.

"Oh, I agree," he said, almost too easily to please her. "That is what she finds so annoying. If you insist on loving only your work, there is no competition for her."

Sarah made an impatient gesture.

"But *I* don't want to compete!" she argued. She wondered if anyone but herself would ever know that to be a lie. But it was true in one respect, she didn't want to *compete*, she wanted to *win*! And not some very young Dutchman but someone much more sophisticated. Someone with an accent, it was true, and who could never be mistaken for an Englishman, if only because of the way he put on his clothes. Someone—who was not for her, her reason finished for her. Bother Roger! Why couldn't he get on and do some work?

"But surely," he said persuasively, "it would be interesting for you to provide just a little tiny bit of competition?"

"No," she said positively.

"Just to bring her eyes to me! You could not deny me that?"

She eyed him wearily. "What do you want me to do?" she asked.

He smiled triumphantly.

"It will be so simple, you see! I shall stand beside you and admire you very much. And she will hate us both!"

"That," said Sarah, "is the only part of all this I can believe!"

THE FAITHFUL WERE BEING CALLED to prayer. The high-pitched, guttural cry came clearly through the still evening air. Sarah stretched herself.

"Is that a signal for calling it a day?" she asked.

Roger shook his head.

"There is still more to be done." He smiled across at her. "Feeling hungry?"

She was. She remembered that the meal was going to be late that evening and glanced down at her watch. It was already half-past eight. She bent over her work again, struggling with the figures that wouldn't work out.

"Do you think the boat can be breaking up?" she asked Roger in despair.

He looked both worried and incredulous.

"It can't be!"

She pushed over the two drawings of the ship she had been doing, each one recording the finds at one particular level and the exact location of each object.

"Then our measurements must be wrong," she said.

He stared down at the two diagrams, checking each drawing from the figures they had taken. There was no doubt about it. The two outlines of the ship didn't match.

"Well, we can't go back and take them again," he sighed. "What makes you think she's breaking up?"

She pointed at the differences in the two drawings.

"It's only here and here that there is any difference," she explained. "Couldn't that be explained because the sides are falling outwards?"

Roger groaned.

"Wait until I tell the Professor this! We'll have to take another set of measurements first thing in the morning to be sure."

"And meanwhile these drawings will do?" she asked him.

He shrugged helplessly.

"They'll have to!"

She finished the second drawing, adding a few final remarks in her neat, scholary script, clipping to it the relevant photographs so that it would be easy to sort out one layer from another later on.

"Have you seen the renovated pots that Sinbad has been working on?" Roger grunted. "He's a very fine workman, you know."

Sarah thought of the pile of broken pottery that had been handed to the Tunisian to work on and wondered how he had managed to fit the pieces together so quickly.

"He mentioned that he had one particularly interesting pot," she said.

Roger swore fluently in Dutch as his pen slipped. He tore up the graph he was doing and took another piece of paper from the pile.

"That's right. He wants you to take a picture of it some time. It has some rather interesting figures on it."

"Greek or Roman?"

Roger yawned.

"I think not. He thought it might have come from somewhere else. Fascinating, really, to think how it came to be on board."

At that moment the silence was shattered by the

gong going for dinner. Roger looked down at his ink-stained shorts and made a face.

"Just as well we are not expected to dress," he remarked.

Sarah grinned at him. "I daresay Philomena would appreciate your changing," she suggested meekly.

He looked at her suspiciously, convinced that she was teasing him, but she looked as if she meant what she said.

"Okay, I'll go and put on a clean shirt," he said helplessly.

She chuckled.

"I'll see you down there!" she told him. "I'm making straight for the food!"

The hot smell of the *briks* came up to meet her. It was one of her favourite Tunisian dishes, of eggs mixed with herbs folded unbroken into an envelope of the finest pastry, so fine that one could read through it if one took the trouble to lay it out on a newspaper. The waiter greeted her with his usual broad grin, knowing that she was pleased to find the dish on the menu.

Sinbad and Giuseppe were already at table. They rose as she entered and pulled a chair out for her.

"Where's Philomena?" she asked them.

The two men exchanged knowing glances.

"She will be here," they said soothingly. Giuseppe winked at her. "It is too nice an evening to be inside," he added meaningly.

Sarah felt her neck prickle with annoyance. Philomena, she thought, would have been a great deal better employed finding their mother a room. Her absence was all the more marked as the Professor's chair also stood empty at the top of the table.

She ate her *brik* with care. The egg was apt to run down one's chin and the crusty envelope was so stiff that it couldn't be used to mop up the escaping yoke. She had just managed to cram in the last mouthful in triumph when the door outside slammed in anger and the Professor appeared in the doorway.

"Sarah!"

She took a deep breath and choked. Giuseppe patted her solicitously on the back, but there was nothing in the least sympathetic about Sebastian's expression.

"Sarah, I want to speak to you—*now!"*

She took a sip of water and brushed away her tears with the back of her hand.

"What about?" she asked.

"Need you ask?" he asked nastily. "But what I want to know is why wasn't I told?"

The hot colour slid up her cheeks. So he had heard that her mother was going to pay them a visit.

"It—it isn't certain," she whispered. "I haven't even found a room yet."

He still looked quite unbelievably angry.

"Then you'd better start looking after dinner," he said grimly. "You and Philomena *together!*"

She nodded humbly, inwardly cursing whoever it was who had told him.

"It will be nice for Philomena," she explained breathlessly. "You see, she has so much time on her own—"

She came to a hesitant halt and he smiled at her. It was just like the sun coming out after rain.

"I see exactly," he said. He looked about him. "And where is Philomena?" he asked.

Sarah blinked, feeling more than a little shattered.

"I don't know," she said. "I thought she was with you."

CHAPTER SEVEN

IT WAS RIDICULOUS to be so pleased that Philomena had not been out with the Professor. Sarah told herself firmly that she was being small-minded, but even so it was difficult to keep the smile out of her eyes and the lilt out of her voice.

"It was Philomena who told you, wasn't it?" she asked him impulsively.

He nodded curtly.

"I met her in the square. You'd better tell her that it would be as well if she didn't sit there by herself. Everybody knows she's a foreigner, but it still might be misunderstood.

Sarah flushed. "I don't see that it's any of our business where she sits," she objected.

It was Sinbad who answered her.

"In Tunisia our women stay in the houses," he told her quietly. "We are used to foreign women doing strange things on the beaches and in the European style hotels, but Houmt Souk itself is not a very sophisticated town."

Sarah bit her lip.

"I'll tell her," she said sulkily. She wasn't looking forward to the task, though. Philomena would think she was fussing again—and so would her mother when she arrived. Quite suddenly it came into her mind how Sebastian had first greeted the news that Philomena was coming with her to Tunisia. He had not sounded particularly surprised, but he had told her that it was up to her to keep her sister under control. The trouble was that Philomena had a mind and a will of her own, and who but Philomena ever knew what she was going to do next?

The Professor's *brik* was brought to him and they all sat there, in silence, waiting for him to finish so that they could go on to the next course. He refused to be hurried, though, and took his time, apparently enjoying every mouthful. Sarah envied him his aplomb. When he looked up and caught her staring at him she was hotly embarrassed—and yet she liked to look at him, at the planes of his face and the foreign setting of his eyes and brows.

Afterwards she wondered why she hadn't started to worry about Philomena then. The meal dragged to its close with everybody except the Professor feeling tense and awkward. When it was over they all disappeared to their rooms, leaving an air of relief behind them. It was only then that she realised that Philomena had still not come in and that she had no idea where she was.

"I really thought Philomena was going to be with you," she told Sebastian almost accusingly.

He smiled without much sympathy.

"You'd better see what you can do about getting your mother a room and let Philomena look after herself!" he retorted.

She dithered in the doorway, wondering whether to take his advice.

"She should have come to dinner by now," she sighed.

He looked impatient. "I daresay she decided to eat somewhere else. Why do you worry so?"

"Well, for one thing, she's younger than I am," she explained.

To her surprise he laughed.

"My dear Sarah, Philomena is as old as the hills compared to yourself. It's you who still has to grow up!"

She was more astonished than anything else.

"But you don't understand!" she exclaimed. "I've always looked after my family, ever since my father died, more or less."

His eyes softened unexpectedly.

"I suppose you have," he agreed. "Perhaps that's why you haven't had time for other things and they'll probably catch up with you soon enough!"

She would have liked to have asked him what things. Perhaps at another, braver moment she would have done, but just now she was a little afraid of him in case he asked her for any further explanation of her mother's proposed visit.

"What have you done with your pot?" he asked her.

She started and blushed again.

"It's in my room."

He looked pleased about something and she thought again how foreign and incomprehensible he was and that she didn't really understand him at all.

"Shall I come with you round the hotels?" he suggested gently.

She was passionately grateful. She knew that she had been putting off the moment of asking him if she could borrow the car and that she hadn't been looking forward to dealing with the hotels either. Her French was good, but she was always afraid that it would break down and prove to be less than adequate.

"Oh, would you?" she said thankfully.

"I was only waiting to be asked!" he teased her.

The night was black and beautiful. Sarah enjoyed the almost liquid feel of it against her skin and the tantalising coolness of the breeze. She sat beside the Professor and allowed herself to be hypnotised by the shadows and the stretch of white road that showed up in the headlights. On both sides of the road were palm trees, some of them torn by the wind, but others, in the more sheltered places, tall and elegant, making beautiful silhouettes against the night sky. Occasionally too they would pass the shape of a house, or one of the rounded tops of the mosques, the minaret pointed and not quite upright, almost as if it were rather a child's drawing than a real building.

"Doesn't it seem far away?" she said aloud.

"It always surprises me that one can see so few lights

on the island," he replied. "Look now, we can't see a single light anywhere."

Obediently, she looked about her.

"I don't suppose many of them have electricity," she suggested.

"Indeed they do! And a splendid disregard for its dangers! Of course the voltage isn't very high, but even so, in a thunderstorm—!"

She laughed.

"I don't want to see it," she said. "I'm nervous of all such things."

He gave her a quick look.

"I don't think you are short on courage," he commended her.

She felt warmed by his words and relaxed against the seat. She was surprised to discover that she was enjoying herself.

The hotel was a long flat building with the public rooms in the centre and two long strips of bedrooms going out at either side, so that each room had the same view of the sea on one side and the sand and palm trees on the other. It stood out against the darkness in a blaze of light. Reluctantly Sarah got out and waited for the Professor to join her on the tarmac drive.

"It looks expensive," she whispered.

He grinned at her.

"It is. But I'm told, on the very best authority, to ignore the price!"

She felt a little prickle of annoyance.

"Philomena?" she asked sharply.

"I expect she knows," he said easily.

"Well, she doesn't!" she insisted. "Our mother has only a widow's pension to live on. It doesn't go very far!"

He didn't argue with her as she had more than half expected, instead he turned back to the car.

"Do you want to find somewhere cheaper?" he asked her.

She came to a quick decision, hoping that she wouldn't regret it later.

"No," she said. "Let's go in. My mother will only be here for a week or so and I expect if she can't manage it, I will be able to."

He gave her one of his unexpectedly gentle looks.

"I don't suppose she would be coming if she couldn't really afford it," he suggested quietly. "I shouldn't offer any help until you're sure."

She smiled back at him. "No, I won't," she said.

The inside of the hotel was spacious. One or two wrought-iron pictures hung on the white walls, sharing the space with some Tunisian tourist posters. From the entrance one could see right through to the sea and the wide, silver sand beach, ghostly in the moonlight.

"Can I help you, *madame, monsieur*?"

Sarah looked hopefully at Sebastian, but he had found something intriguing to read on one of the posters. *Men*, she thought, and took a deep breath.

"I am with the expedition—" she began.

"Ah *yes, madame*!"

Her eyes twinkled. There were few people on Djerba who had not heard of the expedition. The fishermen came as near as they dared to see what was going on and everybody else took a lively interest in the pieces they had found and had brought home to clean and reassemble. The whole island was pleased that such a thing should have been found off their shores, eccentric as they considered all this interest to be.

She began again.

"The thing is that my mother is coming to Djerba," she exclaimed.

"And you wish to find a room for her?" he prompted. "One which overlooks the sea and where you can be sure she will be quite comfortable?"

"Yes," she said, "that is exactly what I want."

The Tunisian went behind his desk and flipped over a few pages of a ledger.

"I think we can manage that for you. When will she be arriving?"

"In about a week's time."

He nodded gravely and wrote something down on the ledger.

"What name is it?" he enquired.

Sarah told him and he scribbled it down beside his other entry.

"Thank you very much, *mademoiselle*." He bowed to her, bringing the conversation to a polite conclusion. "Perhaps you and the *monsieur* would like to go through and have a drink while you are here?"

Sarah was keen to have a look around. She looked hopefully at the Professor and found his eyes already on her. She wondered if he had listened to every word that she had said, and knew that he had when he commented briefly:

"You didn't enquire how much the room would be."

The Tunisian pushed over a piece of paper with the official charges printed on it. Sarah put it in her handbag and was pleased when Sebastian took her arm and led her into the public rooms.

"Do you think Philomena will be waiting for me?" she asked him anxiously. "I wish I knew where she has gone."

He shrugged off all knowledge or interest.

"There are other people on the island besides the members of the expedition," he reminded her. "Leave her alone. She'll come home when she's ready."

It was easy for him, she thought; he didn't feel responsible for a pretty younger sister. Philomena wasn't even really a member of the expedition. Nor did he know how easily she could fall from one scrape into another and how she would expect her, Sarah, to do something about it.

"It's very tiresome of her," she said aloud.

"Very!" he agreed emphatically, and they both laughed.

The room, Sarah thought, had been cleverly designed. The dining tables had been arranged round the outskirts of the room, with a large space in the centre for dancing or, alternatively, a space where casual tables and chairs were placed for people to sit and have a drink, or just to sit and talk. It was to one of these tables that Sebastian led her, pointing out the local paintings that were hanging on all the columns as they went past.

"There is quite a colony of artists in Tunisia now," he told her.

She studied some of the pictures with interest. They were colourful and full of new ideas, if not very sophisticated.

"I thought Muslims were not allowed to make representations of living objects," she said.

"They're not," he agreed. "Some of them consider it is taking over the creative faculties of God. But even strict Muslims are much more liberal in their thinking nowadays."

Sarah found one picture which she really admired and liked.

"With very happy results," she commented happily.

"Sometimes," he grinned.

The barman came for their order and brought the drinks across to them on a silver tray. It was very pleasant, Sarah thought, to be civilised again and in a comfortable hotel, but somehow she could have been anywhere in the world, whereas their own Arab hotel had a flavour all its own and for her summed up Tunisia.

"I think my mother will be very happy here," she said, looking about her with appreciation.

His eyes met hers over the rim of his glass.

"I am afraid she will not be seeing as much of you as she might hope," he warned her.

She smiled, only faintly abashed.

"She'll have Philomena," she reminded him.

"Mmm." He looked doubtful. "I'm not sure that that is why she is coming," he said at last. "But we shall see." He laughed suddenly. "For a working girl you certainly have the knack of gathering your family about you!"

She flushed scarlet. "But I didn't ask *either* of them!" she denied hotly.

"Forgive me," he said, "but it's that which makes it all rather funny!"

She smiled reluctantly.

"I suppose it does," she admitted. "I love them both dearly, you know."

He took another sip of his drink. "Yes, I know," he said.

A whole party of Germans came in from the beach, clutching their beach-robes around them. There was some discussion as to whether they would change before they had a drink or not. The men looked at their watches and expressed their surprise at finding it so late. In the end they decided it was not worth the effort of getting into their formal clothes as they would soon be going to bed. Sarah watched them with interest, getting a vicarious pleasure out of their frank enjoyment of life. She wished she could understand what they were saying and thought she must have been mistaken when she thought she heard her sister's name.

"Have another drink?" Sebastian asked her.

A little sleepily, she shook her head.

"It's been a long day," she said. "I think I ought to get back to bed."

Obligingly he finished his own drink and rose lazily to his feet.

"Come and take a look at the sea first?" he suggested.

She went with him because she couldn't resist the silver light of the night. It was so beautiful outside that she could have wept. The palm trees rustled gently in the light breeze, their tall silhouettes exotic against the star-filled sky. Below were the undulating dunes of sand, the quiet sea and the curved lines of the lit-up hotel. She reached down and took off her shoes so that she could walk more easily on the fine sand.

"It's still warm from the sun," she announced with surprise.

He took her shoes from her and carried them easily in his right hand. With his left hand he took a firm grasp of her arm and drew her close beside him.

"It's perfect, isn't it?" he said lightly.

She smiled up at him.

"You've eaten the lotus," she accused him.

"Could be! And what of you?"

She didn't know how to answer him. The night, she thought, was tinged with a magic she had never known before, and she was almost unsurprised when he paused, putting his arm right round her shoulders, and kissed her gently on the lips.

"What was that for?" she asked him seriously. Later on, she knew, she wouldn't be able to believe that he had actually kissed her.

"Do you mind?"

She shook her head. On the contrary, she had liked it, even though she couldn't understand it.

"No, I don't mind," she said.

He held her tightly then and kissed her in a quite different manner. When he finally released her she was breathless and shaken. She had seldom been kissed in her life before and certainly she had never been kissed like that. She could see the gleam of his eyes in the moonlight and knew that she was in danger of losing her head. Reluctantly, she pulled away from him.

"We ought to go back," she whispered.

He shook his head at her, smiling.

"You will need to give a better reason than that before I let you go, my sweet," he told her. "You are lovely in this light! Did you know that?"

It was delicious to hear, but she couldn't quite believe him.

"You must take another look in the full light of day—"

"Now that," he chided her, 'isn't very civil, my love!"

She couldn't tell him how bewildered she felt. That she was more than a little in awe of him, and that she really didn't think he meant anything more than the lightest flirtation.

"It's only—" she began, and stopped because he was kissing her again.

"It's only what?"

She stared up at him, trying to put her feelings into words.

"Let's go home," she pleaded.

He released her immediately.

"Of course, if you wish."

The whole way back to the hotel she strove to find the right words to explain her feelings. It had all been so unexpected that he should kiss her, and she had not been ready for her own delight in his touch. It wasn't as if he had ever thought of her as anything but a photographer before. It was the beauty of the night and the slight coolness of the breeze, she assured herself. Any girl would have done in those circumstances, for any girl would have looked beautiful in that silver light.

She wasn't pleased when they came up to the car, though. She didn't want the magic to end and she knew that it was her own fault that it now was spoilt. She felt gauche and very young and she was almost sure that he thought she was being silly as well. As she reached out for the handle on the door, she was more miserable than she could ever remember having been before. It seemed to her to be the final humiliation to find Philomena waiting in the car.

PHILOMENA WAS SITTING in the front seat and she had been crying. Her smile was brilliant, though, as she greeted the Professor.

"I knew you wouldn't mind giving me a lift back to the hotel," she said sweetly. "I recognised your car."

The Professor opened the rear door for Sarah and waited for her to get in. Judging by the impatient set to his shoulders he was tired of both the Feaney sisters and, really, Sarah could hardly blame him.

"Where have you been?" she demanded crossly of her sister.

Philomena looked decidedly sulky.

"I told you I had a date!"

It was partly reaction to her own evening, but Sarah felt decidedly cross. To her dismay her anger made her feel cold and shivery and she thought that it served her right that she had been put in the back seat like a child while her sister made the most of the short time she had beside the Professor.

"How comfortable your car is," Philomena was saying to Sebastian. "You don't know what springs can do for a girl's morale!"

He chuckled. "I can guess!" he retorted.

She put her hand on to his bare arm.

"You didn't mind my coming home with you, did you? What are you doing here? I didn't see you inside."

"We came to book a room for your mother."

Philomena started prettily.

"How awful of me!" she cooed softly. "Do you know, I'd forgotten all about her coming. I do hope you've got her a nice room. She wouldn't be a bit happy in the dump where we're staying!"

The Professor didn't answer, and Sarah sat in an unhappy huddle in the back, disliking herself pretty thoroughly. The magic had gone from the night and the narrow streets of Houmt Souk were dark and sinister. She was glad when the Professor stopped the car outside the front door of the hotel to let them off before he put the car away. She slipped out on to the street almost before he had stopped and turned to go into the hotel.

"Goodnight, Sarah," he called out to her.

Belatedly she remembered her manners.

"Goodnight," she replied. She licked her lips, clenching her fists to give herself courage. "It was very kind of you to come with me," she said.

She couldn't see what he was thinking in the darkness which was probably just as well. She could feel the tears in the back of her throat, but there was nothing she could do about it now. He would never again want to kiss her, and who could blame him?

"I enjoyed it," he said with surprising decision. "Shall we do it again some time?"

She gasped, quite speechless. There was nothing tongue-tied about her sister, however.

"Don't the French always give you that nice feeling?" she asked loudly of no one in particular. "They have such beautiful manners!"

Sarah's misery returned.

"I—I don't know," she said.

Philomena grabbed her roughly by the arm.

"Come on!" she said sharply. "This day has gone on too long!"

Sarah turned to wave at Sebastian, to assure him again how much she appreciated that he had gone with her, but he was already slipping the car into gear and was certainly not looking at her.

"Yes, I think it has," she agreed, and followed her sister into the hotel.

Philomena ran lightly up the stairs to her room. She turned at the turn in the stairs and looked back at Sarah.

"What were you really doing with Sebastian?" she asked abruptly.

Sarah shrugged. "We went to look at the sea in the moonlight."

"What was he aiming at? Showing me he didn't care? Well, don't take him seriously, sister dear. He's a hard nut to crack, and you'd only get hurt!"

Sarah almost missed her footing on the steps. She glanced down at her stockings and was annoyed to see that she had jagged one of them on one of the many plants that cluttered up the stairs.

"He was only being kind over finding Mother a room," she said. She could feel the tears dissolving against the back of her throat in a painful lump and she swallowed hard to keep them at bay.

"Frenchmen are never kind!" Philomena warned her lightly.

Sarah passed her without speaking. She had to get to her room and the luxury of being alone.

"Don't you want to know where I've been?" Philomena taunted her. With her head on one side, her dark hair falling against her face, she looked unbelievably pretty.

"I don't think so," Sarah replied and, truth to tell, she no longer cared.

"You look tired," Philomena went on as though she hadn't spoken. "You get undressed and I'll come and sit on the end of your bed and tell you all about it!"

"Won't it wait?" Sarah asked. "Tell me about it to-morrow."

But Philomena didn't want to wait.

"I'll give you ten minutes," she said brightly.

Sarah's room was unbearably hot although the window was wide open. Automatically she checked to see if she had left any of her photographic equipment on by mistake and was annoyed to find that Roger had left the lights on in the small space she had set aside for making enlargements and other such things. Enclosed as it was, they had got hotter and hotter and had gradually heated the entire room.

"As if it wasn't hot enough!" she grumbled to herself as she unhooked the lights. She tried to open the window wider, but that was impossible. The only answer was to leave her door open and hope for a through draught.

She undressed quickly, leaving her things on the floor where she had dropped them, and rushed into a nightdress and a lightweight nylon wrap. Someone was already in the bathroom for she could hear the taps running and the sound of someone cleaning their teeth. Impatiently she waited in her room until the door slammed and the sound of footsteps went away down the corridor to where the men were sleeping.

The water was delightfully cool. She stood in front

of the basin and allowed it to play over her wrists until she was cool all over. She was beginning to feel better. It would all be different when her mother arrived. She wouldn't have to worry about Philomena and she would be able to concentrate more fully on her work. And that, she told herself doggedly, was all that she wanted to do—ever!

Philomena was waiting for her when she got back to her room.

"Have you had a fire on in here?" she asked, wrinkling up her nose in distaste.

Sarah explained about the lamps.

"It's getting cooler—I think," she added. "I'm going to leave the door open till it clears."

Philomena made a face.

"Well, I'd rather you than me!" she said frankly. The secret look descended over her face again, masking her eyes and making her a stranger. "Did you get a decent room?" she asked.

Sarah nodded.

"I think she'll like it. It's expensive though."

Philomena looked up with a touch of bravado.

"As a matter of fact I may join her over there," she said. "I've made friends with some people—" She hesitated. "I haven't wanted to tell you, but it's awkward being here with all of you. Sebastian would like it very much better if he didn't have all of you watching us all the time. You know how it is?"

Sarah hooked back the shutters to make sure they didn't bang in the light wind.

"But you weren't with Sebastian tonight!" she said sharply.

Philomena chuckled.

"Of course not! It wouldn't pay to let him have everything his own way! And why do you suppose he took you to the hotel if it wasn't to keep an eye on me?" Her eyes lit up with suppressed excitement. "Oh yes, Sarah darling, he's all mine! Every bit of him!"

CHAPTER EIGHT

SARAH GRASPED HER PURSE firmly in one hand and approached the little knot of people who had gathered in the fish market. Sitting cross-legged on the marble counter was the auctioneer, his face proud and impassive as the people pressed in on him. With a slight smile he held up a single fish and the bidding started in earnest. It was impossible for Sarah to understand a word of what was going on, for it was all in Arabic, and she was just pondering on whether they were selling the fish one by one or in larger lots when Roger came and joined her.

"You haven't forgotten your promise, have you?" he reminded her anxiously. He was standing too close to her and she moved away from him surreptitiously.

"Of course I haven't!" she said without thought.

He caught up with her and put a familiar arm around her shoulders.

"Good! Because she's over there, looking at us now!"

Sarah wriggled free.

"Oh, really, Roger! It's too hot for that sort of thing!"

He looked so crestfallen that she felt sorry for him. Perhaps, later on, she would suggest they had a cup of coffee in the square, but at this particular moment she wanted to watch the auctioneer. He had started on the squids now. They looked singularly unattractive and it was difficult to believe that they could be turned into a truly delicious dish.

"Can't we go and talk to her?" Roger pleaded in her ear.

"Oh, if you must!" she agreed impatiently. She pushed her way through the crowd, mildly surprised to notice that all of them were men, their white robes pulled up out of the water that kept the floor so beautifully clean.

"Don't any women do any of the shopping?" she asked Roger.

He shrugged his shoulders.

"How should I know?"

Perhaps the women couldn't count, she thought. It was only in the last few years, since Independence, that they had been admitted to the schools, and if they couldn't manage the figures it was natural, she supposed, that the men should have taken on the job of getting in the family stores. It seemed quaint, though, to her Western eyes. Lucky women, she thought.

Philomena was sitting on a low wall just outside the market itself. Like every other building it had been whitewashed until it blazed in the sunlight, and she made a very pretty picture, with her coloured skirts against the clear white. At her feet were a collection of wrought-iron ornaments and a few burnished copper and pewter pots made locally by the Jewish community. In the far distance a Djerban rug had been hung on the wall of a shop as the simplest form of advertisement. It was very effective. In the centre of the street a whole pile of pots clustered together for support, some of them large enough to store oil or wheat, some of them ready to be used for carrying water or milk, and some of them no more than cooking utensils, roughly shaped and sometimes bearing the fingerprints of their maker.

"Well?" she greeted Sarah.

"You should have come inside," Sarah told her. "They're holding an auction. If I could speak any Arabic I would buy us some fish for lunch!"

"Thank goodness you can't!" her sister retorted. "You'd buy a whole boatload by mistake!"

Sarah laughed. "Very likely!" she admitted.

Roger came forward and held out his hand to Philomena in the Continental manner, bidding her good morning. Philomena smiled at him and ignored his hand.

"Why aren't you two working?" she asked pleasantly.

Roger's fair skin flushed.

"We are waiting for some film to come from Tunis," he explained sulkily. "They're flying it down this morning.

Philomena looked amused at his discomfiture.

"You don't seem to work very hard," she drawled. "Compared with my sister, shall we say?"

Roger flushed again. "You're not very kind this morning," he replied.

Philomena giggled. "Who wants kindness?" she asked.

Sarah thought that she did, but apparently Roger rather enjoyed Philomena's caustic humour and was prepared to put up with more of it.

"If you are not doing anything in particular, I thought we might all go and look at the museum," he suggested shyly.

Philomena considered the invitation without enthusiasm.

"All right," she said. She rose negligently to her feet and smiled at both of them. "But don't walk me miles, because I have high-heeled shoes on."

As far as Roger was concerned, this was good news. It provided an excuse for him to take her arm and he looked thoroughly pleased with himself as he led the two girls down the street towards the wide avenue that housed the museum. They arrived at the old Arab house that spread back from the avenue, its heavy, ornate door the only thing that hinted at the splendours within. A couple of pepper trees shaded the entrance, but even so the sun had caused the paint to peel a little and had dulled the ironwork on the windows.

Roger paid for the three of them. An elderly man

with quick, darting eyes, dressed in the traditional camel-trousers and with a towel wrapped around his head, accompanied them inside.

"There is a great deal to see—" he began hopefully.

"We can take ourselves round!" Roger cut him off brusquely. Sarah saw the disappointment in the old man's eyes. It was probably the way he earned his money. She smiled at him and slipped him a silver coin, and Philomena gave her a mocking smile.

"Roger can take me around, I guess," she said. "You can go with your friend!"

Roger gave her an ecstatic smile which Philomena accepted with a bored look and Sarah with resignation. She watched her sister allow herself to be helped round the room and wondered wryly how she managed it. The Arab guide looked at her enquiringly and she smiled at him and said in her best French: "Where do we begin?"

It didn't take very long to go round the museum. The costumes interested Sarah the most. Each village had its own distinctive dress, most of them with the twine-coloured witch's hat that was so distinctive of the women of Djerba. She was just struggling to memorise the differences between the colours of the Arabs and the Jews when there was a disturbance as another visitor came into the museum. Sarah's guide went darting off to see if he could double his custom and she was left alone with the display of costumes. She looked up when she thought he was coming back and was surprised to see the Professor coming towards her.

"Are you alone?" he asked her.

She had thought she would be embarrassed when she saw him, but he was so normal himself that she forgot her shyness.

"No, Philomena and Roger are somewhere about," she answered.

He came over to where she was standing and studied the Jewish dress that she was looking at.

"Did you know that the Jewish community here is possibly the oldest in the world?" he said.

"Really? *Here?*"

He nodded.

"Some say they came here when the Israelites were carried off to Babylon. Of course they say that one day they will go back and the last one to leave, one of the family of Cohen, for they have that privilege, will throw away the key to the synagogue and shout aloud 'We have kept Thy Covenant, O Lord!'"

"But will they really go to Israel?" she asked, intrigued.

He laughed.

"More likely to New York or Tunis, or stay where they are. They have a place of honour in Djerba. No one would want to see them go."

The guide came back, bringing with him Roger and Philomena. He was quite obviously annoyed with the two of them and berated them soundly in Arabic as he firmly escorted them across the heavily carpeted floor. Philomena took one look at Sebastian and ran the last part of the distance, throwing herself into his arms.

"You came!" she exclaimed. "You actually came!"

Sebastian allowed himself to be kissed and then disentangled himself.

"I told you I would, if I had the time," he said.

Roger gave the two of them a look of almost comical dismay, the joy going out of his eyes and his smile.

"Were you just filling in time with me?" he asked Philomena angrily.

Her eyes danced as she looked at him.

"What of it? You had Sarah, didn't you?" She hooked her arm around the Professor's. "I'm ready when you are!" she announced.

They left without a backward look, and Roger glared angrily after them.

"Where are they going anyway?" he demanded.

Sarah shook her head, saying nothing. She was hurt herself, but she knew she had no reason to be, for hadn't Philomena told her herself that the Professor was hers, every bit of him?

"How about a cup of coffee?" she suggested. The suggestion had been bound to come sooner or later and, in the face of their mutual dejection, now seemed to be the moment.

Roger ignored the offer.

"I can't understand her at all!" he said finally.

Sarah, who had never been able to understand her either, regarded him helplessly.

"I—I think she really likes Sebastian," she offered.

"Then she shouldn't kiss and flirt with the rest!" he retorted.

"Isn't that a little harsh?" she asked.

Roger laughed roughly.

"Is it? Then why do you suppose the little Arab was so cross with us? It seems that in Tunisia people do not go around kissing in public!"

Sarah could hardly believe him. Philomena was her younger sister and she had never thought of her in any other way. But of course she would love to tease and enjoy herself, and she would expect everyone else to understand. Very probably they usually did. It was just unfortunate that Roger should have taken her seriously.

"I'm sorry," she said awkwardly. "But Philomena doesn't mean any harm. She never does!"

"Then it's time someone taught her a lesson!" he said viciously. He pulled himself together with obvious difficulty. "Cheer up," he said more gently. "It's not your fault I got burnt!" He paused, his eyes still angry. "Did you mention coffee?" he said at last.

As a suggestion she thought it had fallen rather flat, but she agreed hastily that she was longing for something to drink and allowed herself to be hurried out of the museum, conscious of the bewilderment of the guide who could not understand the free and easy ways of the West and who was obviously very glad to be rid of them.

The square was practically deserted as they sat down on two of the uncomfortable iron seats. A waiter, with a *chechia* perched cheekily on the back of his head, came over for their order.

"Are you having a pleasant holiday in Djerba?" he asked them socially.

Sarah agreed that they were while Roger stared into the middle distance, pretending he hadn't heard the question.

"When is your mother arriving?" he asked abruptly.

"On Thursday," she said.

He sat back in his chair, letting the reflection of the sun dance in his eyes.

"Good! I suppose Philomena will join her at her hotel?"

"Possibly," Sarah replied cautiously.

"Better still," he said with satisfaction. "I shall find it difficult to share my meals with her after this."

Sarah stirred uncomfortably and removed an insect from her skirt. For just one brief moment she wished she was back in the dull security of her library at home.

THE DAWN that Thursday was particularly lovely. The sun came up over the sea so slowly and casting such an array of light and colour that it almost broke one's heart to watch it. The sea was silver, green and gold and the sky magnificent in its greys and purples and the sudden, bursting yellow of the naked sun. A single boat, its orange sails spread wide to catch the faltering breeze, tacked in and out of the path of the sun, watched only by the silent palm trees and the mysterious, slumbering island.

Sarah watched it from the high land that overlooked the little harbour of Houmt Souk. Behind her was the ruined Spanish fort, that now housed nothing more dangerous than a few rats. She sat on a hump of dew-laden grass that had made a foothold for itself in the fine sand. She could feel the damp slowly seeping through her clothing, but she didn't care. The moment was as near perfection as any that she could ever remember. Natural beauty meant a great deal to her, and this was completely unspoilt by any man-made monstrosity to mar the wealth set out before her. It was a banquet of colour and peace and it had brought a calm to her that had been hard to find in the last few days.

To begin with they had discovered that her figures had been quite correct and that the ship really was slowly breaking up now that it no longer had the silt of ages to support the ancient timbers. Sebastian had ordered that they should build a framework around it to hold it together and for three days they had all of them spent their time struggling with wet ropes and irresponsible bits of wood that refused to stay put. Now, they thought catastrophe had been averted, but it had delayed their work and had meant long hours of extra drawing for her, marking the exact position of the supports and making sure that the frame of the ship was now steady.

There had been a mounting tension between the members of the expedition too. Roger, almost impossible as he snapped at everyone, openly walked out of any room that Philomena came into, and the rest of them watched him covertly and wondered why the heat and the food should suddenly get on their nerves. Only Sebastian remained impervious to his surroundings, demanding work and still more work from his team with the same charm of manner. Sometimes Sarah wondered if he was a human being at all and at other times she would resent how easily he could charm the heart out of her, leaving her bereft and vulnerable to his lightest word.

An Arab boy and his black sheep came slowly up the slope towards her. He greeted her with the dignity of his race and sat down a short distance away from her, pulling the blanket he wore as a cloak over his feet. In silence they watched the sun burst over the horizon and the day begin. Other fishermen joined the boat that had already put out to sea and the harbour suddenly came alive below them as scores of young boys ran down the quays in an excess of energy before they disappeared into the schools for the day.

"It is a fine morning," the shepherd said gravely in French.

Pleased that they were able to communicate, Sarah nodded.

"It was worth getting up early for," she replied.

He smiled with amusement. "I see it every day."

Sarah chuckled, accepting the rebuke.

"Where do you live?" she asked him.

He whistled to his sheep to come closer.

"Under the sky. My father is a rich man and we have many sheep to watch."

Sarah might have taken his family's riches with a pinch of salt, but she had heard stories of Djerban money and was realistic enough to know that the boy beside her could probably buy and sell her several times over. He went back into his previous silent reverie and she was loath to interrupt him. She settled herself more comfortably on her damp tussock and relapsed into silence. They were still in the same attitude when the Professor came to find Sarah.

"Have you had breakfast?" he asked her.

She shook her head and solemnly introduced him to the shepherd, who wished him peace and whistled for his sheep again.

"I was so excited by the thought of mother's arrival," she said, "that I came out early to greet the dawn."

He smiled.

"It's a pleasant thought! Is Roger not with you?"

"Roger?" she laughed. "You ought to know that nothing gets Roger out of bed before the streets are well aired!"

He gave her a lopsided grin.

"Don't special circumstances warrant special measures?"

She laughed because he did, but she didn't really understand the joke.

"I'm hungry," she complained. "You shouldn't have mentioned breakfast!"

He pulled her to her feet and laughed as she made a face at the damp patch on her skirt.

"Come and eat, then! I'm not stopping you!"

They said goodbye to the shepherd and ran down the slope towards the town. The strange white shapes that were the houses looked almost windowless and were broken only by the spiky minarets of the mosques and the green of the pepper trees that shaded the narrow, dusty streets.

"Whoever would have thought it could have become so familiar?" she panted.

He stopped and waited for her to catch up with him.

"It doesn't with everyone."

Sarah was pleased by the compliment and it showed. She put a hand up to her knot of fair hair and pressed home one of the pins that held it there.

"Doesn't it to you?" she asked.

"To me?" He seemed surprised that she should make the question so personal. "Yes, it seems familiar to me. Why not? I used to come here as a boy."

"Did you?" She was immediately intrigued to know what kind of a boyhood he had had. "Did your sister come with you?"

He nodded.

"Oh yes! We used to lie on the sand and dream of how great we were going to be! Then one day we heard tales of a wrecked ship out from the coast there. From that day on I knew what it was that I was going to be."

She was caught up into the dream and it brought the tears to her eyes.

"And now you are here again," she said softly.

"But I'm not crying about it!" he teased her.

She smiled rather mistily at him.

"Nor am I really," she denied. "It's more a leftover from getting up so early!"

He took both her hands in his and there was something in his eyes that made her heart beat very fast, but whatever it was he had had in mind, he dismissed it quite casually and said instead:

"I thought you were hungry. I'll race you back to the hotel!"

She was almost as fast as he. There are some advantages in being tall and one of them is a good length of leg. She dodged down the nearest street and tore through the *souks* hoping to gain an advantage, but he knew the terrain better than she and was there before her, grinning at her efforts to avoid an astonished pedestrian.

There was fish for breakfast. Through the open doorway Sarah could see them being cooked over the charcoal fires. The waiter was fanning the embers until they were red hot, then he rubbed the skin of the fish with roughly ground black pepper, placing them on sticks to grill over the blazing fires. It was worth being hungry, for when they came to the table they were delicious, eaten with large hunks of home-made Arab bread and butter.

No one else was up yet, so they had the whole dining-room to themselves. The waiter greeted them delightedly and gave them the two largest fish he had cooked. The fish from the Djerban waters were the best in the world, he told them with a few gestures of his expressive hands. They must eat a lot of fish and they will grow happy like the Djerbans.

"Very good advice!" Sebastian commented as he neatly filleted his fish and removed the backbone.

"They say just the same of the oranges and the dates," she answered. "I wonder what really was the lotus flower?"

He shrugged his shoulders.

"They say it's the edible part in the centre of the leaf of the date palms. I tried some once. It was perfectly horrid!"

She laughed.

"Oh, I do hope my mother likes it here!" she exclaimed.

The gentle look was back in his eyes.

"It won't be your fault if she doesn't," he said.

THE TWO GIRLS SAT side by side in the café, dressed in their frilliest dresses and with matching white hand-bags and neat white sandals. Philomena had also brought a sunshade to protect her dark beauty. Sarah privately thought this rather affected, but she didn't like to say so. The sun and the sea had roughened her own skin and, rather to her surprise, she had gained a healthy-looking tan despite the fairness of her skin and hair.

"The plane is late," Philomena said flatly, looking at her watch.

Sarah searched the horizon for anything which might be her mother's aeroplane.

"I do hope Mother hasn't found the trip too long," she fussed. "She should have stayed a couple of days in Tunis."

"Good heavens," said Philomena, "she's not ready for her grave yet!"

"That isn't exactly what I meant," Sarah said hotly.

Philomena gave her a cool look and flourished her sunshade with an expertise that Sarah could only envy.

"I don't know why you're always wrapping Mother up in cotton-wool. She doesn't appreciate it, you know."

Sarah was silent. She could feel her dress sticking to her back and she prickled with heat. The airstrip was a shimmering sheet of glass and the patches of vegetation on either side were dry and brown from too much sun. Away in the distance a coloured sausage rose and fell in the inconstant breeze to show the pilot which way the wind was coming from.

"I think I can hear it," she said at length.

The silence was almost unbearable as they strained their ears to listen.

"Nothing!" said Philomena. "Why don't we go across and join the men?"

Sebastian had come as a matter of course. He had apparently taken it for granted that Mrs. Feaney's arrival was as much his business as anyone else's and had found out the time of the aeroplane and had made arrangements to meet it long before anyone else had really got used to the idea that she was coming. Sarah could only just see him from the car. His trousers fitted him exactly and his scarlet shirt had been tucked in for the occasion, showing to the full the breadth of his shoulders and the leanness of his hips. She had been nervous that he would look too foreign and strange and that her mother might not like him, but she couldn't see how anyone could possibly fail to find him attractive and, somehow, that was a relief to her. Roger, who had come for some reason of his own, looked flabby beside him and as hot as Sebastian looked cool.

"Do you think it's any cooler over there?" Sarah asked doubtfully.

Philomena opened her door. "It could hardly be hotter than here," she said.

"She's late," Roger said as the two girls came up to them.

"I daresay it's Mother's excess baggage," Philomena said calmly.

Sarah cast an exasperated glance into the sky.

"She wouldn't need to bring very much with her," she said.

Philomena laughed.

"That's all you know! My guess is that Roger should have stayed behind and then we might have got it all into the car!"

Sarah sighed. She wished her sister and the Dutchman would leave each other alone. It made things so uncomfortable when they were forever making pointed remarks to each other.

"Oh, shut up!" she said rudely. "It's too hot to quarrel!"

Philomena raised her elegant eyebrows.

"Who's quarrelling?" she asked dramatically. "Sebastian darling, you tell her! Do I ever quarrel with anyone?"

The Professor looked amused.

"Not often, certainly—" He broke off and pointed into the sky. "There she is at last!"

The black speck grew steadily larger until it flashed overhead, banked and came down towards them again to land. The tires screeched their protest as they hit the hot landing strip. They bounced upwards and hit the tarmac a second time. Almost immediately the note of the engine changed and the small craft taxied across to the airport building and to where they were standing.

Philomena jumped up and down excitedly, waving madly at the small windows where the passengers would be sitting. Behind her, Sarah felt faint and almost sick. She stood very still, letting the heat and the excitement pour over her. The Professor glanced at her anxiously, but she managed to give him a reassuring grin. Someone brought up some steps and the door of the plane was flung open. A few seconds later Mrs. Feaney appeared, looking exactly like a slightly older edition of Philomena, her eyes darting about her as she looked for her daughters.

It was Philomena who ran to greet her.

"You look gorgeous!" she cried out. "Isn't it exciting?"

Her mother hugged her.

"You look gorgeous too! I can see this island agrees with you!" She freed herself from her daughter's arms and came slowly down the steps. A little tentatively Sarah went forward to meet her.

"Darling!" her mother said as she kissed her. "Let me look at you too!" She made a comical face of dismay. "My word, the sun has caught your nose, hasn't it?" She gave Sarah an extra hug. "Never mind, a good cream will soon put that right!"

Sarah blinked and smiled.

"Mother, I want to introduce Professor de Hougement," she said carefully.

Mrs. Feaney looked at Sebastian with an undisguised interest and took his hand in hers with a smile.

"I've heard so *much* about you!" she said.

He grinned at her, looking very French and foreign. "Then you'd better call me Sebastian," he said.

CHAPTER NINE

LUNCHEON WAS A VERY GAY AFFAIR. They all went to Mrs. Feaney's hotel and took possession of the largest table there, and laughter was almost as much a part of the meal as the food. Philomena was at her very best and her witty sallies brought forth an eager response from the men. Sarah herself was more silent, enjoying the noise all about her and beginning to relax a little. Her mother was obviously going to enjoy her stay, and then it would be worth all the expense so she wouldn't worry any more about where the money was going to come from. She looked up and found the Professor's eyes on her and she smiled at him.

"The sun *has* caught your nose!" he told her.

She rubbed it with one finger, a little embarrassed.

"I hadn't noticed," she said.

"It has a certain appeal," he teased her.

"I don't know so much," she said awkwardly.

Her mother leaned across the table towards her.

"It's a great pity you didn't inherit your skin from me instead of from your father. Neither Philomena nor I ever have the slightest trouble!"

"A great pity!" Sarah agreed dryly.

Sebastian gave her a look which confused her, for of course she knew very well that he had succumbed long since to Philomena's more striking looks—as whoever had not?

"You'll be getting freckles next!" he said.

She made a face at him.

"That would be the last straw indeed!" she admitted.

It was left to the Dutchman to say that he rather liked freckles and nobody really believed him. It was funny really, but Sarah was far more inclined to believe Sebastian when he said it had a certain appeal. It was comforting that he thought so and even more comforting that she could believe him. She cast him a covert look from beneath her eyelashes and was amused to see the way he was setting out to charm her mother. She could see too that Philomena didn't like it very much, but one would have had to have known her very well indeed to have been able to tell. It was no more than a slight tightening of the neck and a certain rigidity around the mouth. Poor Philomena, Sarah thought, her mother would provide more competition than the rest of them put together!

When lunch was over the Professor and Roger went back to Houmt Souk, leaving the two girls with their mother. Sarah offered to go back also, acutely conscious that she herself was not on holiday and that she would be expected to do her fair share of the work.

"Not this afternoon," Sebastian decided firmly. "We have a heavy day tomorrow and you'll see little enough of your mother then, I'm afraid."

Mrs. Feaney came close to her daughter, putting her arm around her shoulders.

"Philomena is going straight out on to the beach," she said, "so I'm hoping you will show me my room and where everything is, dear?"

Sarah nodded. "I hope you'll be comfortable," she said. "This hotel is nice, isn't it?"

"Very nice!" her mother agreed warmly. "It was clever of you to find it, darling. Philomena isn't very keen on where you are, but I suppose you have everything you need there."

"It's convenient," Sarah said quietly, "and I like it."

The Professor looked anxiously from one to the other.

"It's better for us all to be together," he put in. "We can't afford to waste any time at all."

Sarah smiled at him. "I like it," she said positively. "It's of the country. This hotel is more comfortable, but it could also be anywhere in the world!"

Mrs. Feaney shrugged her shoulders. "I *like* my comfort," she complained. "And why shouldn't I?"

The Professor laughed. "No reason at all!" he assured her.

They went out into the hot sun to see the men go off. As the car disappeared down the made-up road, it seemed suddenly lonely. There was only the hotel and the sea behind them. Inland there was only date-palms for as far as they could see, apparently growing in the dry sand that covered their roots. Unless one knew that there were more than two thousand springs of clear, fresh water on the island, it could well be a mystery as to how it was so fruitful with only the sea, apparently, to sustain it.

Mrs. Feaney turned to Sarah and hugged her again.

"Darling, I can't tell you what it means to me to be out here with you both!" she whispered eagerly.

Sarah hugged her back.

"It's lovely to see you!"

Her mother looked at her curiously. "I had the suspicion that you were just a wee bit doubtful about my coming?" she asked. "But, truly, I don't mean to be extravagant!"

Sarah laughed softly.

"How terribly mean you make me seem," she said. "Of course I want you to enjoy yourself, but—"she hesitated—"how much money have we got, Mother?"

Her mother made an airy gesture with her hands.

"I don't know *exactly*, dear. You know that's not the sort of thing I'm any good at working out! Philomena told me it would be enough."

Sarah sighed. "Then Philomena knows what you have?" she asked.

Her mother bit her lip.

"Oh dear! You're not hurt, are you, dear, that I

didn't tell you about this little nest egg? You see, it was mine and I wanted to spend it on myself! Is that so very selfish?"

"Of course not! I'm delighted that you could manage to come!"

Her mother's face clouded over.

"Of course I don't suppose it will pay for *everything*," she said sadly. "Do you think I should have let the house while we are all away?"

Sarah's lip twitched with sudden amusement.

"How long have you come for?" she asked.

Mrs. Feaney looked both secretive and very naughty.

"Well, dear, I thought if I found the fare, you might be able to find the cost of the hotel. Is that possible?"

Without any regret Sarah said goodbye to the savings she had been so carefully keeping for some future occasion.

"That sounds a very good idea," she said warmly.

They walked slowly down the long covered corridor towards Mrs. Feaney's room, stopping at intervals to admire the whiteness of the sand against the vivid, cheerful blue of the sea.

"I thought at first the scenery was rather dreary," Mrs. Feaney remarked, "but it isn't, is it? It's grown on me already."

Sarah looked rather dreamily out to sea.

"The land of the lotus-eaters!" she said.

Her mother laughed. "Well, I shouldn't want to take those old stories too seriously! Think of the discomfort they went through!"

"But the lotus-eaters were rather sweet!" Sarah objected.

"And are the Djerbans 'rather sweet'?" her mother asked her.

Something in the tone of voice brought the colour flooding into Sarah's cheeks.

"Yes, I think they are," she said.

Mrs. Feaney regarded her daughter thoughtfully.

"You must tell me all about it," she invited. "*And*

about the fascinating Professor! Philomena's letters were full of him. Such a relief, don't you think? I was so worried that she wouldn't get over the other disappointment."

Her mother's room was, she thought, very nice. It was furnished in the Scandinavian style, with a minimum of waste space. But everything was there. A comfortable bed, two chairs, a basin with hot and cold water, and a small space that had been carved out of the room and which held a shower, curtained off by a plastic material in a modern design. The whole effect was light and pleasant even if it had lost any particular North African character.

Mrs. Feaney dropped down on to the edge of the bed. "Will this Sebastian be kind to her?" she asked.

Sarah hesitated. "I don't know," she said at last.

"What do you mean?" her mother demanded sharply.

"I mean," Sarah replied, "that Sebastian makes his own running. He won't like it if Philomena reads more into—things than is actually there."

"And do you think she is?" Mrs. Feaney asked.

Sarah swallowed, a peculiar dejection overtaking her. "No," she said.

Her mother looked very pleased with herself.

"No, I didn't think so either," she preened herself. "That was really why I came."

Sarah swallowed again. "I see," she said.

A LITTLE WAY ALONG the beach from the hotel a warm spring gushed its waters out across the white sands. Philomena had spent the afternoon damming it up and was sporting herself in the quite large swimming pool she had created. Sarah found her with something like relief.

"I shall have to go now," she said. "Will you come and keep Mother company?"

Philomena splashed the warm water over her shoulders.

"Why do you have to go?" she demanded. "Did Mother say anything?"

Sarah shook her head.

"Of course not! What would she have said?"

Philomena cast an experienced eye over her sister's face.

"I thought she might have been rubbing you up the wrong way by asking you about your love life," she said frankly. "Let's face it, nothing irritates you more."

Because she didn't have any? Sarah almost finished for her. It wasn't true, not quite. She had feelings and likes and dislikes just like everybody else. Only she didn't want to talk about it all the time. Especially not now, when her whole mind and heart was filled by Sebastian whether she wished it or not, and even her mother could see that he had quite other ideas. It was that that hurt, she admitted it, but she didn't want the whole world to know she was hurt.

She smiled, a little amused.

"Actually," she said, "it was your love life we were talking about."

Philomena gave a contented sigh.

"That sounds more interesting! Was Mother telling you all the latest about Edmund? What he's doing and how dastardly he is?"

Sarah laughed. "I don't think he was even mentioned," she retorted. "As if you care!"

Philomena chuckled. "I did at the time." An awful thought struck her. "Sarah, do you think I may be fickle?"

"Very likely!" Sarah agreed callously.

"How dreadful!" Philomena said comfortably, quite unperturbed by the prospect. "I must ask the Professor what he recommends as a cure."

"Yes, I should," Sarah said evenly.

Philomena gave her an interested look.

"Or shall I ask Roger?" she asked brightly.

Sarah began to walk away, back to the hotel.

"Ask anyone you please!" she said.

HER OWN ROOM HAD LOST a great deal of its charm for her. Sarah struggled with the charts that Roger had left on her desk, but her mind kept wandering to the peeling paint and the faded colour on the walls. It was peculiar, she thought, how much one's reaction to the things around one are a matter of mood. There was so much work to be done, and all she could think about was her mother's conviction that Philomena had fallen in love with Sebastian. Cross with herself, she drove herself on to get all the paperwork finished and when Roger came up to her room to consult with her about the photographs that would need to be taken the following day, she had practically cleared the lot.

"I thought you were having the afternoon off to be with your mother," he said.

She turned in her chair and smiled at him.

"I did."

He glanced over her shoulder at the finished pile of work.

"Phew! You should do it every day!" he commented.

She coloured slightly. "I didn't want to think about something else," she admitted. "Work is a wonderful panacea!"

He looked justifiably dubious. "I've never found it so!"

Her eyes went to the great, untidy piles of photographs that littered up her room.

"Is Sebastian pleased with what we've found?" she asked.

The Dutchman shrugged.

"Who knows what the Professor thinks? I know he's expecting a great deal more stuff in the forecabin."

"What sort of things?"

Roger looked bleak.

"Good Lord, you don't think he takes *me* into his confidence, do you?"

"Why not?" She faced him squarely.

He looked sulky and his eyes slid away from her face.

"Okay, I guess it's my fault. I haven't been exactly forthcoming myself. Philomena likes to see us all at one another and she plays her cards well, doesn't she?"

"I can't see that it has anything to do with her," she said.

"Then you must be blind!" he retorted.

It was something of a relief when the gong rang for dinner. She slipped into her bathroom and washed the ink off her fingers and did her best to repair the damage the sun had done to her nose. Her hair, too, was quite white where the sun had caught it and the continual drenching in salt water had made it dry and difficult to manage. She thought of the television advertisements for shampoos at home in England and giggled. In their never-world of almost make-believe all she needed was the right shampoo and the world would be hers. In her own world, though, the world belonged to Philomena.

The Professor was already behind his chair when she entered the dining-room. She slipped into her own seat and all the men sat down, their eyes curious as they watched her serve herself from the bowls of salad that had been placed on the table.

"We thought you would eat with your mother," Sebastian told her kindly.

She nodded, not resenting their interest. It was funny that in the dining-room she felt quite at home, as she had not in her own bedroom.

"I had so much work to do," she explained.

Sebastian smiled at her, his whole face crinkling with amusement.

"And have you done any?"

She nodded gravely. "Have you noticed that some of the pots aren't Roman?" she asked him.

He was delighted as a cat with a mouse, playing with the idea in his mind, this way and that.

"Most of the pieces seem quite Roman to me," he said at last. "One or two Greek pieces, of course."

"And one or two Egyptian," she went on. "Only

they aren't Egyptian—at least, I don't think they are.
They're rather intriguing."

"Persian perhaps?" he suggested.

She shook her head.

"I don't know enough to tell. Shall I get the photos?"

"Please."

She was rather pleased to be busy, to set her mind
firmly on the impersonal problem of the origin of some
nice impersonal pots. She found the photographs without any difficulty and ran down the stairs again with
them, arriving breathless at her own place.

"They're all here, I think. Sinbad first did this
one—" She handed the Professor a handful of prints.
"He was doubtful about it, so I took quite a number of
shots of it."

They all peered at the prints, tracing the intricate
markings with their fingers, trying to make the pot fit
in with any others they had ever seen.

"Etruscan?" Sinbad suggested.

"Never!" the Italian answered him. "I've seen
enough of this stuff to recognise it in my sleep."

The Tunisian flashed him a smile.

"What other suggestion have you got?"

"It could be local."

The Professor looked up, his eyes alight with interest.

"Could it?"

Giuseppe grinned.

"Why not? It is heavily influenced by Egypt, it is
true, but it is not Egyptian. It is interesting that some
forgotten ancestors in the Canary Islands used to mummify their dead. Some people think the custom spread
slowly west from Egypt. Other things could have spread
also."

"It's possible, but we shall need a great deal more to
go on." The Professor threw back his head and for a
moment he was truly handsome. "It all depends on
whether we find anything else in the fore-cabin."

"And you think we may?" Sarah prompted him.

His face creased into a smile.

"We can always hope," he said.

SARAH HESITATED before going up to bed. The servant began to lock up, shutting up all the windows and the blue wooden shutters that Sarah outraged everybody by throwing open all day long. She made signs to tell him that her sister was not in yet and that she would lock the front door herself. It took some time to explain and when he did understand he seemed reluctant to leave her. When he finally disappeared into the kitchen there was nothing but the shadows on the wall to keep her company. They came and went as the glowing cinders in the open-style oven in the kitchen fell into ash and nothingness. The electric lighting, ever uncertain, made a feeble attempt to light the book she was reading, but when the power dropped towards midnight even that failed, leaving no more than a single red twist of light in the bulb.

It was late and Sarah was tired. She sat on the edge of her chair in the darkness trying to keep awake, but gradually she slipped back into it and fell asleep. It was a deep chair, with a couple of cushions placed over the wooden structure to give an illusion of comfort. When she awoke she was stiff and the wooden edge of the arm was eating into her ribs. There was still no sign of Philomena.

She stood up, muttering to herself about the pins and needles in her legs. Perhaps, she thought, Philomena had already slipped in and had gone up to bed. It was worth going up to see and she struggled up the stairs, wincing away from the pain of the blood returning to her limbs. But Philomena was not in bed. She glanced down at the luminous hands of her watch and saw that it was after three o'clock. Where on earth could she be?

She knocked over a pot-plant going down the stairs again. She picked it up carefully and replaced it on the step, staying quite still for a moment to see if she had disturbed anyone, but there was no sound from any of the rooms upstairs and so she went on down to the front door.

It was as black as velvet outside. A single light lit the end of the street, casting a mysterious shadow on the white wall and the lucky sign of the "Hand of Fatima" stood out in the dark against the lime wash. In the daytime it was no more than the imprint of a woman's hand in blue paint; in the blackness of night it was an emblem of a strange land. Sarah shivered in the light wind and tried to make herself think it was as ordinary as a No Parking sign in a street at home, but the curious light remained to threaten her and in spite of herself she was afraid.

She shut the front door with a bang and locked it securely, leaning on wooden supports for comfort. She daren't go to bed, she thought, leaving Philomena alone out there. She would have to go back to her chair and wait for her. With a sigh she pushed herself off from the door and at the same instant the lights came on, blinding her for a moment, and a hand reached out for her and held her, helpless, against the hard frame of a man.

"Let me go!" she whispered fiercely.

She was freed immediately.

"Little fool!" the Professor exclaimed. "What on earth are you doing prowling around in the dark?"

She swivelled round to face him.

"I wasn't," she denied. "The power failed and so I turned the lights out."

"The power failed," he told her dryly, "more than three hours ago!"

"I've been asleep," she explained.

He looked down at her crushed clothes and the lines from the back of the chair which still marked her cheek.

"So I see."

She struggled helplessly to find the right words to explain to him why she was not in her bed without implicating her sister.

"Have you been out?" he asked her sharply.

She shook her head. "I'd be afraid to," she admitted breathlessly. "When the door is open you can see the light at the end of the street and the markings on the wall—"

"And the dust making curious patterns on the narrow street?" he finished for her.

She was mildly surprised that he should understand so well.

"Yes," she said, "it's silly, isn't it?"

He smiled, his teeth very white against his suntan.

"Silliness can be a form of wisdom. At least it stopped you going out to look for her!"

She flushed, annoyed that he should have seen through her so easily.

"She's probably with Mother," she said.

"Very likely," he agreed. "Is that any reason not to let you know?" He pulled the front door open and they both stared out into the street in silence, which lengthened until it became almost unbearable.

"I could wring her neck!" he said viciously.

She smiled irresistibly.

"To tell you the truth," she said, "so could I!"

He laughed and then quite suddenly he stopped laughing and put his hands down hard on her shoulders.

"And I could wring your neck too," he said. "You need your sleep like everybody else. Go up to bed, and I'll wait up for Philomena."

But Sarah shook her head.

"She's my sister," she objected. "I'm really quite all right and not in the least tired."

"Is that so?" he drawled. The imprint of his hands on her shoulders became almost painful. "Is that why you can hardly keep your eyes open?"

She opened her eyes wide.

"Nonsense," she said tartly. "Really!"

He grinned. "Yes, really!"

He came very close and she was quite unsurprised

when he kissed her. With an effort she pulled herself free.

"That wasn't very kind," she said.

"Was it not?" He looked apologetic but not in the least repentant. "I rather enjoyed it," he said.

She gave him a desperate look because nothing would have induced her to admit that she had enjoyed it too.

"That isn't the point!" she exclaimed.

"Isn't it?"

"You know it isn't!"

"I? I know nothing of the sort!" he laughed.

It was foolish to try and explain it to him and she knew it was, but somehow she could hear herself trying.

"It must be because you're French!" she ended helplessly.

"It's a possible explanation," he agreed.

She was tempted to stamp her foot at him, mostly because she wanted him to kiss her again.

"It wouldn't be so bad if you *meant* it!" she exploded.

"What makes you think I don't?"

There was a sudden noise in the street outside and a car jerked to a stop outside the hotel. Philomena got languidly out and came towards them in the open doorway, a half-smile on her lips.

Sebastian rounded angrily on Philomena and his temper showed exactly how anxious he had been for her.

"And where the devil have you been?" he asked.

CHAPTER TEN

WHEN SARAH AWOKE and dressed herself, Philomena was still fast asleep. Sarah gazed down at her sleeping sister and thought how lovely she was. She slept as quietly as a child with one hand tucked behind her head and the other almost hiding the half-smile on her face. Even asleep she looked confident and sure of herself, as though she knew where she was going and was delighted to be going there.

Sarah thought back to the scene earlier that morning when Philomena had at last come back to the hotel. It hurt her to remember, but she couldn't keep her mind away from the subject. Sebastian had begun by being angry, but he had ended by being amused.

"Where have you been?" he had repeated.

Philomena had smiled up at him.

"Oh, *darling*," she had purred, "I didn't know you cared!"

Sebastian had looked as if he could have slapped her.

"Philomena—" he began.

"I've been dancing," she had pouted. "Everyone here doesn't go to bed at midnight, you know."

He had softened visibly.

"Perhaps they have their own door keys," he had suggested silkily.

She had laughed softly.

"You could always present me with one." She had twitched the wrap off her shoulders and had looked up at him in the prettiest way imaginable. "Darling, I don't know why you should be so angry. I was only enjoying myself!" She had taken a quick step forward and had kissed him hard on the mouth. "There! Better now?" she had asked.

And he had laughed.

"Baggage!" he had said in tones of warmest affection. "For heaven's sake go to bed now and let the rest of us get some peace." And laughing, with Sarah quite forgotten, they had all gone up the stairs to bed.

Now, looking at Philomena sleeping, it was easy to see how she had managed to charm the anger out of Sebastian, or any man. It was just chance that he had happened to be flirting with her when Philomena came in—it was just chance that she had been on the verge of taking him seriously and now knew that she could not.

It was still early, though the men had already breakfasted. She buttered herself a roll and waited for the coffee to be heated up. Her eyes felt sandy from lack of sleep and she was worried about her camera which kept sticking. It was not, she felt, going to be a very good day, and she tried to throw off the feeling, knowing how easy it was for one's own mood to invite a disaster.

As soon as she had finished her second cup of coffee, she grabbed her cameras and started walking towards the harbour, but the men were not yet ready to go and so she walked off by herself down the beach, dreaming of finding half a dozen pots that would put their ship in the forefront of the archaeological finds of the century.

The women were already out washing the wool. They stood in little groups, knee-deep in the sea, washing the fleeces again and again in the sandy water, until they were soft and quite free from grease. Afterwards they left them to dry on the sand, as white as snow and quite ready for use. It was a picturesque scene with the women's colourful skirts, their off-white enveloping veils, caught back and stuffed into their belts, and with their straw-coloured witches' hats perched on the tops of their heads.

They stopped work and smiled at Sarah as she went

past. She lifted her camera and showed it to them, but they one and all shook their heads. Because she was a woman they were prepared for her to go among them and some of them, being Berber rather than Arab, might have allowed her to take a picture of them in the distance, but they were afraid of anyone capturing their image, an attitude they had learned through their religion and through half-forgotten tribal memories of magic and conquest.

"Hey, Sarah!" Roger came running across the sand towards her, waving a paper over his head. "Hey, Sarah, did you leave this out for me?"

She walked towards him, squinting into the sun.

"What is it?" she asked him.

He handed it over to her and she glanced down at it. It was a single photograph from a series of a statue she had taken. In the corner, marked in her neat script, were the letters R4.

"It was found in the rear-cabin," she said.

"But do you remember anything about it?"

Sarah shook her head. "There were so many things," she explained.

"But surely you can remember *this* one!"

"I'm sorry."

"It's important," he prompted her. "Look at it closely."

She looked at it again more closely. It was of a beautiful little statute, a warrior with his hair combed up into a pillar above his head and with a long flat spear in his hand.

"It isn't either Greek or Roman," she said humorously.

"That's the whole point! Would you say it was Egyptian?"

"Well, no," she said doubtfully.

He snatched it from her, gazing down at it.

"I'd given anything to know!" he exclaimed. "I can't wait to open up that other cabin."

She grinned cheerfully at him.

"Well, with any luck, we should make a start today," she said.

It was terribly hot. As the boat slowly drifted towards the rafts that marked the site of the sunken ship, the orange sails flapped idly, vainly seeking sufficient wind to send them hurrying across the water. The Tunisians laughed and turned on the inevitable transistor radio and the latest Egyptian pop songs rang out across the sea, a little more nasal than its Western counterpart, but with an equally fierce and obvious beat. Then, just when they had resigned themselves to rowing, a frolicking breeze caught the sails and sent them scudding forwards. The shock of the sudden movement could be felt right through the timbers of the boat and the heat seemed more bearable again.

Sarah was the first to set foot on the anchored rafts. With leisurely care she made herself ready to dive, going through the now familiar actions of powdering herself before putting on the thick rubber shirt and making sure that her flippers were securely on her feet.

"Are you ready to go?" Sebastian asked her.

"Yes."

He helped her into the harness that held the cylinders of compressed air and tested the apparatus to make sure it was working properly.

"Okay," he said, "you're away!"

He shook hands with her very formally and she was chuckling to herself as she made her way to the edge of the raft and jumped into the clear water. She allowed herself to fall like a stone to the bottom, completely relaxed and enjoying the feel of the water against her skin. This was the best part of every dive, she thought, when there was time to look about and see all the wonders of the seabed and watch the bubbles of oxygen flattening into ovals as they floated upwards to the surface.

The wreck loomed up, an enormous shape quite different from when they had first started exploring her. Sarah put her hand on one of the struts that was holding up the rotting side of the ship and pulled herself nearer the gap they had made for easier access. It was darker inside and, as always, it took a second or two for her to get used to the gloomy interior. Down one side it was difficult to recognise that it was the inside of a boat at all. With careful movements she made her way towards the fore-cabin and got her camera ready for the first shots. Two other shapes came up behind her and she knew that Roger and Giuseppe were ready to pull away the ancient doors. It was a moment of acute excitement and her hands were trembling as she held the camera ready.

Giuseppe put his two hands against the door and pulled. It came away so easily that he almost fell over backwards. Sarah pushed her way up to him and beckoned to Roger to bring up the arc lamps. It was better than the other cabin, possibly because it was nearer the shore and had not had to take the strain of the current or the sudden battery of storm that could blow up so suddenly in the Mediterranean. It was quite possible to make out the framework of two bunks that had practically fallen to pieces, almost covered with sand and silt, but full of promise of what might be buried with them.

Sarah took her first shots and then helped haul the arc lamps away again so that they could ease their way inside the confined space. The beams creaked ominously, sounding eerie when magnified by the water. The men started moving the sand and immediately the atmosphere grew thick until it was almost impossible to see across the narrow space. Sarah pulled her camera closer to her and left them to it. Immediately she pulled herself out of the wreck she could see the sunlight filtering down through the water, magnificently gold and green. She allowed herself to float gently to the surface and came up just beside one of the rafts.

Sebastian was waiting for her. He helped her to haul herself up beside him and undid the straps of her harness.

"How long will they be?" he asked.

She wrinkled up her nose.

"They're stirring up a lot of sand and muck," she said. Her voice took on a new note of excitement. "Oh Sebastian! It's in a very good state—what we can see of it!"

He was far more phlegmatic about it than she had expected. He took her camera from her and put it carefully in the bottom of the boat. When he came back to her she was shaking her hair loose so that it would dry more quickly.

"Aren't you going down to look for yourself?" she asked him.

"No, I think not. I shall wait for them to clear it out a bit and then go down with you. I shan't see anything much before then."

She didn't answer him, though she wondered how he could wait so calmly. She herself was in a turmoil of expectancy. He came and sat down beside her, dangling his feet over the edge of the raft into the water.

"Shall I oil your back?" he offered. "It's in danger of peeling as badly as your nose."

She tried to get a glimpse of it over her shoulder, knowing even as she did so that nothing would induce her to allow him to touch her.

"It doesn't hurt," she said with an attempted cheerfulness.

"It won't—yet!" he retorted.

She twisted her neck round to have another look and retreated to the safety of an awning that someone had spread out to save the equipment from the worst of the hot sun.

Sebastian watched her with lazy eyes.

"Was Philomena awake before you left?" he asked her.

Her eyes were cool as she looked at him.

"I don't think so," she said.

"Your mother was asking for her," he explained.

She was startled. "Mother was?"

He nodded. "She rang up. She wanted to know if Philomena had got home all right."

Sarah swallowed. Her back was smarting after all.

"How lucky that you were able to tell her all about it," she said smoothly.

He grinned, looking pleased with himself.

"Yes, wasn't it?" he agreed.

SARAH COULD hardly recognise the cabin when she next saw it. The silt had been gently sucked away, revealing an odd collection of objects. There were a couple of wine jars, a brooch, so encrusted that it was impossible to see of what it was made, a small figure of Neptune, with his nose broken, which gave him a curious devil-may-care expression. With care she photographed each exactly where it was lying and marked it on the plan she was carrying. It always gave her an odd feeling to be writing several feet under water, but so far the pen had never failed her, though it baulked when she tried to use it on dry land.

The brooch was probably the most interesting of the finds. She played the sand through her fingers around where it had been lying, hoping to find something else of similar worth. But there was only sand right down to the rough boards which had once formed the bottom of the ship, but were now a mass of barnacles and weed growing from the few remnants of the original timbers.

Perhaps a little further forward, she thought. She inched her way to beyond where the men had cleared, allowing her fingers to sink in and sift the shifting silt. At first she could find nothing, but then her fingers felt the edge of something hard. She signalled over her shoulder to one of the men to come up to her and help her clear it, but they had their backs turned to her, carefully packing Neptune away into a basket. She gave the object a gentle tug and was answered by a whining noise all around her. She stood quite still and waited, but there was only the usual sounds of the running sea and her own breath escaping into bubbles. She gave an anxious look behind her, but neither of the two men had looked up.

Very gently, she pulled again. She knew a second's triumph as the object came free in her hands, but at the same instant the whining started again and a large part of the wall of the boat began to sway behind her. Desperately she tried to prop it with whatever came to hand, but a large part collapsed and there was only darkness. She tried to force herself to move, but her muscles were frozen into inactivity. It came to her as something of a surprise to discover that she was afraid.

The seconds ticked past into a full minute and there was still only blackness all around her. There must, she thought, be a glimmer of light from the arc lamps somewhere. She forced herself to edge back to where the wall had caved in. There was no light anywhere and everywhere she could reach was hard and unyielding to her touch. She was trapped.

She spent all of ten minutes pushing against the fallen side, but nothing happened. Tired and panting, she sat back and took stock of her position. She had little compressed air left and the harder she breathed the more quickly she would use it up. She was shaking now with the chill of fright. She breathed very slowly, counting her breaths in and out until she felt quite dizzy. There was nothing to see and nothing to hear and only her panic to keep her company. It would be all right, she told herself again and again. It would be all right because Sebastian was there.

She couldn't see the pressure meter, but she knew when the cylinders were failing. It was harder to breathe than it had been, and it might have been her imagination, but it tasted different and it made her want to cough. When it gave out entirely it was the silence she first noticed. An unbearable silence, broken only by the echo of her thudding heart against the weight of the sea.

SHE DIDN'T know anything about the way they tore away the rotting timbers that were holding her. She knew even less of the sudden light that flickered over her.

Nor did she remember anything of the way they lifted her and brought her up to the surface. Her first conscious moment was a painful coughing and the feeling that her lungs were going to burst.

"And again!" Sebastian's voice came calmly through to her.

She struggled against his hands.

"I'm not going to be sick again for anyone!" she objected harshly.

He laughed. "Wait for it!" he said.

She tried to tell him just what an unfeeling, unsympathetic brute she found him. She wanted to hurt him as he was hurting her, but she was too busy gasping for breath.

"There!" he said, and to her ears he sounded unpleasantly triumphant. "Doesn't that feel better?"

To her annoyance it did, much better.

"I thought you were never coming," she gasped.

"Did you?" he asked gently.

She turned over on her back and let the sun bake right into her bones. "What happened?" she asked.

He leaned back, apparently satisfied that she was better.

"You pulled the whole boat down about you, that's what happened!"

She sat up, appalled. "But, Sebastian, I couldn't have done! I was pulling at some object, but it was quite loose in the sand!"

"Is that it?" He nodded to a small object beside her.

She pounced on it eagerly and then wasn't sure.

"I don't know," she said doubtfully.

"Well, certainly nothing would part you from it!" he grinned.

She picked it up with interest, trying to guess what it might be. "Are you suggesting this held up the whole ship?" she demanded hotly.

"Not exactly."

She smiled. "Then I shall reverse my defence!"

The men laughed, and Roger ruffled a hand through

her hair with an air of possession that dismayed her.

"I don't think it will come to that," he smiled at her.

Her eyes flickered to Sebastian's face and back to her own feet.

"I'm not so sure," she said. She rubbed the object gently against the side of the raft, but it was useless, only a chemical would release it from the bonds of the crust that had grown up all around it. It looked to her like a small ornamental knife, but she didn't like to say so because it was no more than the wildest of guesses.

"The ship will be all right—won't it?" she asked Sebastian anxiously.

He shrugged his shoulders. "We'll manage somehow," he said.

A WHOLE PARTY of skin divers came out from the hotel that afternoon. They descended on to the raft with whoops of joy.

"We thought we'd never make it!" one of them cried out. "It's further out here than it looks!"

Sarah, recognising that they were nearly all Frenchmen, sought for the right words to discourage them from actually landing.

"Please be careful of the equipment," she said. "Some of it is very valuable."

They looked at her curiously. "Are you part of this outfit?" they asked.

She nodded, secretly rather pleased that they should ask her.

"I'm the photographer," she told them.

One of the men half pulled himself out of the water and looked round at the cylinders of compressed air and the carefully wrapped up finds.

"There was a rumour at the hotel that you had trouble out here this morning?"

Sarah tried to look quite normal, but she could feel the colour creeping up her cheeks.

"What sort of trouble?" she asked.

"That one of you was almost drowned!" a younger

man put in. "That's why we came out really, to see for ourselves.

Sarah sighed impatiently.

"Perhaps you'd like to speak to the leader of the expedition?" she asked grandly. "He'll be up in a minute."

"Then nothing happened?" they pressed her.

"Nothing serious."

At that moment Roger came up to the surface with a look of thunder on his face.

"We can't shift it!" he burst out angrily.

Sarah tried to warn him that he had an interested audience, but he paid her not the slightest attention. He was far too intent on kicking off his flippers and unbuckling his harness.

"Then you did have an accident!" one of the Frenchmen demanded of him.

Roger looked around at their expectant faces.

"I'll say! Sarah nearly drowned herself down there! And now we can't get into the cabin at all!"

The Frenchmen looked accusingly at Sarah.

"I thought you said that nothing had happened!" they accused her.

"Well nothing did," she denied. "I look all right, don't I?"

"Philomena had a feeling—"

"*Philomena?*" She didn't know why, but she was upset that her sister should have had anything to do with them swimming out to the wreck.

"She's an English girl at the hotel," he explained. "She said she had a sister out here."

"Yes, she has," Sarah said. "I'm her sister." She wished urgently that Sebastian would come and rescue her from her predicament. "What kind of a feeling?" she asked sharply.

The Frenchmen looked embarrassed.

"It was more a rumour that was going about at lunchtime. The waiter said that there had been an accident and Philomena rather dramatically claimed that she had had a feeling all morning that you were in trouble."

"What nonsense!" Sarah said sharply. She looked at the Frenchman more curiously. "How well do you know Philomena?" she asked.

He grinned, suddenly very cheerful.

"I'm getting to know her better!"

"I see," she said quietly. "I hope my mother wasn't told any of this rubbish?"

The Frenchman lost his smile.

"She was there," he said. "Perhaps I had better introduce myself. My name is Marcel Martin."

They shook hands gravely while Roger watched them in disgust.

"Philomena seems to have got to know a lot of people mighty quickly!" he remarked acidly.

The Frenchman met his eyes squarely. "She is popular," he said guardedly.

"With you too, I suppose," the Dutchman grunted.

"Yes, with me too," Marcel agreed smoothly.

For a moment Sarah thought Roger was going to push the Frenchman back into the water and start a fight, but instead he dived in himself and swam off, away from the rest of them, where he stayed until Sebastian and the other man came up to the surface.

It was impossible to tell how serious was the damage done to the ship from the Professor's attitude. He greeted the unexpected visitors with his usual calm good manners, stripping off his rubber shirt and carefully stowing his equipment away as he always did, unlike the others who were far more apt to leave it lying about until they had recovered from their stint under water.

"It was a pretty good swim, coming right out here," he congratulated them.

Marcel acknowledged the compliment with a gesture from his outspread hands.

"One can walk nearly half the way," he said. "It is so shallow all round the coast here."

"Still, I expect you will be glad of a lift home?" Sebastian smiled at them. "We'll take you to Houmt Souk."

The little boat was pretty heavily laden by the time they had all scrambled on board. The captious wind came and went and the orange sails flapped back and forth. Other boats came in close, calling a greeting in Arabic across the still waters. One and all had heard of the morning's incident in that way that Arabs seem to, plucking the knowledge out of thin air.

"You're quite a heroine," Marcel said with a grin.

"I'll *feel* more of a heroine when I know how the boat is," she replied grimly.

"Your mother thinks you are one, anyway!" he laughed.

She turned quickly and caught Sebastian's eyes on her. It was difficult to know what he was thinking and her own discomfort made her read disapproval into everything. She flushed.

"Mother gets carried away very easily," she said gruffly. The frown increased between Sebastian's eyes and she wished she didn't care what he thought of her quite so much. "It wasn't as though anything *happened*!"

It took them a long time to sail into Houmt Souk. The white town looked like a faded photograph in the late afternoon sun. It would be like that for another hour and then suddenly it would come to life and the universal blue paintwork would be dazzlingly bright and the glaring white buildings would take on a softer pink from the setting sun.

Quite a crowd had gathered on the small quay. Tunisians pushed each other out of the way in their eagerness to be first to catch the painter of the boat. Even one or two women had threaded their way daintily through the crowd to stand and watch the excitement. Sebastian went ashore first and it was only then that Sarah saw her mother and Philomena standing a little way back from the others, looking both nervous and excited. Too late she wished she had taken the trouble to do her hair and to cover up her still pale face with make-up. She waved to them, but neither of them waved back.

Willing hands helped her on to dry land and she loaded herself up with her camera and the films she wanted to take to be developed. Out of the corner of her eye she could see her mother approaching.

"Sarah, Sarah darling! Are you sure you're all right?"

She smiled as calmly as she could.

"Of course, I'm fine."

Her mother looked about her with an air of great determination.

"Well, I may as well tell you, here and now, that you're never going down to that wreck again!" she said. "Nearly killing yourself! Sarah—Sarah! Are you listening to me?"

CHAPTER ELEVEN

"Oh, Mother, really!" Sarah protested.

"Yes, really!" her mother insisted. "I'll speak to your Professor about it myself," she added grimly. "I'll not have it!"

Sarah gave her a quick hug.

"Of course you won't do anything so silly! I'm quite all right and, indeed, nothing really happened at all."

Mrs. Feaney looked at her daughter with tears in her eyes.

"You look pale."

Sarah made a protesting noise.

"And when have I ever looked anything else?" she asked pertly.

Her mother responded with a wavering smile.

"I think I'll talk to him all the same," she said. She pushed her way through the knot of people towards Sebastian and Sarah was left, a little apart from the rest, completely on her own. She looked about her to see if she could warn the Professor and tell him not to pay her mother any attention. It was humiliating to be discussed as though she were no more than a teenager and not responsible for herself. But she needn't have worried, because unwittingly Philomena came to the rescue. She looked lovelier than ever in a close-fitting white linen dress that showed off her dark tan to perfection. The contrast between the two sisters could never have been plainer.

"Sebastian, my dear, how *tiresome* my family seems to be being to you! Never mind, you may take me to the square and buy me a drink and I'll make it all up to you!"

Sarah froze, waiting for Sebastian's reaction, although she already knew what it would be. His worries fell away from him and he laughed with genuine amusement, looking deep into Philomena's eyes.

"What a marvellous idea!" he said.

Sarah wondered if Marcel, or even Roger, would make any objection, but the Frenchman only watched her sister with his hands on his hips and a smile in his eyes.

"What a fickle heart!" Marcel teased her, flicking her dark hair.

Philomena tossed her head idly, her eyes sparkling.

"Why not?" she said. "Nobody's going to tie me down—yet!"

Roger was the only one who didn't laugh, didn't say anything. He just watched her go with the Professor in a brooding silence. Then he turned angrily on Sarah.

"Don't just stand there!" he barked at her. "You have work to do!"

THAT EVENING the sunset was almost perfect. Sarah watched it from the window of her room, letting the riot of colour seep into her soul, for she could still see that frightening blackness whenever she shut her eyes and feel her lungs bursting for lack of air and the awful desire to cough. The pepper tree on the corner, dusty with the hot, summer days, made a splash of silver green against the white houses, all uniformly painted with blue. Except, she noticed with amusement, for one individualist who had decided on a vivid green. Almost every window was covered with wrought-iron work, bulging out towards the bottom so that the women could lean out of the windows and still be protected. It was a beautiful scene, with the odd, narrow streets that led higgledy-piggledy into one another under beautifully shaped arches or through minute alleyways that divided the houses. From where she was standing she could see the dome-shaped roofs, varied sometimes by long squares or others shaped like the top of a Nissen hut, but all of them gleaming white as though they had been painted with lime only the day before.

"I wish you'd come and look," she wheedled her mother.

Mrs. Feaney sat on the edge of the bed, an expression of acute disapproval on her face.

"I'm not surprised Philomena wants to come to my hotel," she said at last in a faint voice.

Sarah smiled cheerfully.

"It's not so bad! The bed is comfortable and I have everything I need for my work."

Mrs. Feaney sniffed. "And that's all you want?" she asked.

The question took Sarah by surprise.

"I don't know," she admitted. "I like it here, though—" She looked round the room—"I like it despite the peeling paint."

"But the peeling paint is only one thing," her mother objected. "Frankly if I had to face that colour first thing in the morning I shouldn't get up at all!"

Sarah laughed.

"I hardly see it at all now," she assured her. "Generally speaking I'm too busy when I'm up here to notice anything much."

Mrs. Feaney sighed.

"Darling, I wish I could see where it was all leading to. I've always understood what Philomena has wanted, but you—" She hesitated. "Sarah, is there anything I can do?"

For a brief instant Sarah wondered if her mother had guessed that she had fallen in love with Sebastian.

"I suppose I want the usual things," she said at last, in a tight voice that she could scarcely recognise as her own. "I want to marry and have children." She laughed harshly. "I have the usual, normal ambitions!"

But her mother didn't laugh with her.

"I think I was wrong to suggest that Philomena came here with you," she said thoughtfully. "I didn't realise that it meant so much to you." She looked at her daughter reproachfully. "You could have told me, you know. I would have tried to understand."

Sarah smiled very gently.

"I know you would," she said. "But I didn't know myself until I got here quite how exciting it would be."

"And the Professor?" Mrs. Feaney asked.

Sarah blushed. "He helps to make it exciting," she admitted.

"And Philomena?"

Sarah bit her lip. "Philomena is in love with him," she said.

Her mother stood up, a look of sadness on her face.

"I am so sorry," she said. "How awkward for you! But you don't have to go on with this job, do you, dear? You can always come home with me and go back to that library of yours. You'll get hurt if you stay!"

Sarah tightened her jaw with determination. "I may do," she agreed.

Mrs. Feaney sighed. "Oh dear, how I wish your nose *didn't* peel in the sun!" she said agitatedly. "I'm sure it would help!"

Sarah laughed. "I'm sure it would!" she agreed.

Her mother was somewhat mollified to find that she had been invited to dinner. She peered anxiously into the primitive kitchen and wondered aloud how any meal could possibly come out of it. Later, when she saw the servant lighting the charcoal fire out in the yard, fanning madly at a pile of embers in a small enamel bowl, she asked dryly if they couldn't install some better system for him.

"I think he likes it that way," Sarah said vaguely.

Her mother flatly refused to believe it. She insisted that the adjoining door should be kept open so that she could watch the meal being prepared, astonished that so much could be heated and cooked over a single flame.

"He would certainly win the economy stakes!" she said at one point.

Sarah leaned forward and glanced through the open door. The smell was delicious and very Tunisian and she was glad that her mother was to have one of the traditional dishes rather than something quite international and well known.

"They eat everything all together in one dish, meat, vegetables, everything! Usually rather highly spiced."

Mrs. Feaney sniffed appreciatively.

"I only hope it's half as good as it smells," she said.

They were drinking wine, from a local vineyard that had been started by the Wine Fathers, when Sebastian came in. He was alone.

"Has Sinbad found out what your object is yet?" he asked Sarah.

"I don't know," she admitted. "I haven't seen him at all."

"And the photographs?"

"They're drying," she murmured.

"Any good?"

She nodded her head.

"They're clearer than I thought they'd be. The light was very poor."

Mrs. Feaney bristled to her daughter's defence.

"I don't know what more you can expect!" she snapped. "You work your team very hard, young man."

Sebastian's eyes twinkled.

"Maybe," he admitted, "though actually today my team have been working me pretty hard!" He threw himself into a chair. "It's been a long day!"

Mrs. Feaney was outraged.

"Is that all you can say about Sarah's experience?" she asked haughtily.

"I expect I shall say a *good* deal more when I've got over the shock!" he retorted. His eyes slid over to Sarah. "How are you feeling?" he asked her.

She lifted her head proudly.

"Fine!"

His eyes mocked her, but he said nothing. She felt a

gushing warmth for him throughout her being, and was afraid that it might show, so she sat there looking down at her hands and knowing that the deep colour was rushing into her cheeks.

"Where's Philomena?" she asked at last.

"She stayed on in the square."

She found herself hoping that this time her sister would come in at a reasonable hour. She was so tired that she felt quite light-headed. She drank her wine more quickly, as if it were water, and felt a bit better. She would feel better still once she had eaten, she thought.

Indeed dinner was a success. Sinbad had a reed whistle which he had bought from an old man in the desert and he entertained them by playing and singing some of the songs of the island. A number of Djerbans came and stood at the open front door, and after a while, when they became less shy, they came right inside and joined in the singing and even managed one or two dances, tough dramatic affairs that reduced them to a breathless shuffle after a while.

It was late when they had all gone.

"I'll drive you home, Mrs. Feaney," Sebastian offered.

"I'll come too," Sarah said. It would be nice, she thought, coming home in the dark with only the moon to light their path, in the gorgeous comfort of his car. But he shook his head.

"You're practically asleep on your feet! It's bed for you!"

She opened her mouth to argue with him. She wanted to go.

"Are you planning on diving tomorrow?" he asked her lazily.

"Of course," she said, ignoring her mother's anxious expression.

"Then go and get some sleep!" he retorted.

It was lonely when they had all gone and there was only the dirty glasses and the cigarette smoke still heavy on the air to tell of their having been there. The smoke was strongly scented from the black tobacco that the Tunisians use and unpleasant. Sarah flung open all the windows to get rid of it, regardless of sorrowful shakes of the head from the servant. Sebastian could close them when he came in, she thought, if he remembered. But he would probably have Philomena hanging on his arm and would have other things on his mind. Angrily, she slammed shut the front door and went to bed.

SINBAD WOKE EVERYBODY with a shout of pure joy.

"Come and see! It's beautiful!"

Sarah pulled herself out of her deep sleep and jumped straight out of bed, feeling for her dressing-gown. They all met on the stairs, laughing as they bumped into each other in their hurry to get to the bottom.

Sinbad was out in the *patio*, a tub of chemical in front of him. Very carefully he lifted out the object that Sarah had grasped so firmly the day before.

"Don't breathe on it!" he warned them. "It's very fragile."

It was indeed quite lovely. Once it had been a knife as Sarah had suspected, but the blade was held together now only by the chemicals that Sinbad used on it. It was thin and jagged and in some places it had given way altogether. But the handle had been preserved almost intact. It was a lovely object, intricately wrought of gold and other precious metals, it was in the shape of a human being with the head of a jackal.

"Egyptian!" Giuseppe said with satisfaction.

Sebastian looked at it more closely. "It could be," he agreed.

The Italian looked up sharply. "Why the doubt?"

Sebastian made an impatient gesture.

"It isn't a doubt, more a feeling. The jackal doesn't look like a jackal to me."

Giuseppe made a face. "It looks like Anubis to me," he said positively.

Anubis, Sarah remembered with a little spurt of excitement, was the Egyptian god of embalming.

"But surely—" she began.

"Look at the ears!" Sebastian said disparagingly.

"Look how many years it's been down there!" she retorted, quite heated.

He laughed. "There spoke the dispassionate scientist! I still don't think it's genuinely Egyptian. I think it's a copy."

Sinbad looked over his shoulder with a smile.

"It could be," he agreed. "It would tie in with the other finds. If we ever get inside that cabin again we may get some other pieces that would make sense."

Sebastian nodded. "We'll get back inside," he said grimly.

He was as good as his word. They spent most of the morning rigging up a hoist so that they could move the heavy supports that they had sunk deep into the seabed, but which were now preventing them from getting at the fallen walls of the cabin. Sarah forced herself to go down to look for herself. She didn't want Sebastian to know how scared she was, so she asked Sinbad to help her into her equipment. The cylinders seemed heavier than ever and she was shivering from fright as she stood at the edge of the raft and tried to will herself to jump in.

She shut her eyes as the water closed over her head. When she opened them again the worst was over. The familiar sensation of the water was not frightening at all. She took a deep breath, completely filling her lungs and was reassured when she breathed out and the familiar bubbles swept past her towards the surface. As soon as they started to tie the thick ropes round the supports, she forgot all about her fears and yesterday might never have been. She worked as hard as any of them and was astonished at how quickly the time went before she had to return to the surface herself.

Coming up, she could see the bottom of a strange boat tied up to the raft and she wondered idly who would have made the trip out. It was not one of the local Djerban boats because she could see a propellor at the back. It was funny, she thought, how strange things looked from an unaccustomed angle. This boat looked like some enormous monster! She came up beside it and was almost surprised to find it was really quite small with an outboard motor hanging over the back.

Laboriously, she climbed up the rungs of the ladder that Sinbad had fitted to the raft, tearing off her mask as soon as she reached the top. The dazzle of the sun on the water nearly blinded her and she blinked several times before she could see who had come. She was somewhat surprised to see her mother sitting on a pile of cushions and Philomena standing behind her, idly smoking a cigarette.

"So the heroine returns!" she drawled.

Sarah undid the buckles of her harness and struggled out of it.

"Hullo," she said.

Philomena raised her eyebrows. "I suppose that's as good an answer as any," she commented.

Sarah turned her back on her.

"What brought you out here?" she asked her mother.

Mrs. Feaney stirred on her cushions. "I couldn't resist it!" she said comfortably. "I wanted to see it all for myself—and we had the offer of the boat!" She looked guilty. "Well, to tell the truth, Philomena charmed it away from its owner."

"Marcel?"

Her mother nodded, laughing softly.

"He wanted to come out with us, but Philomena wouldn't hear of it!"

"Why not?" Sarah asked her sister.

Philomena shrugged. "I had other ideas." She took up an even more careless stance. "Want to pick a quarrel about it?"

Sarah sat on, in an uncomfortable silence. She wished as she had never wished before that she knew what Philomena was thinking about. Marcel must have quite a lot of money if he could bring his own boat all the way from France. She wondered what Philomena really thought of him and how she had managed to persuade him to lend it to her.

Philomena threw her cigarette into the sea and frowned. After a minute or so she came over and sat down beside Sarah.

"I'm sorry," she said. "You ought to know that I don't mean half of what I say. Don't take it so seriously!"

Sarah smiled willingly.

"I don't!" she teased her sister.

Philomena made a face. "I wish I could believe you. Sebastian has been taking me to task for being selfish. He says you're worn out with looking after me."

"Do I look worn out?" Sarah asked, amused.

Philomena considered her.

"A trifle peaky, perhaps." She hesitated. "Then it's all right between us?"

"Of course!"

"Then that's all right!" Philomena looked decidedly relieved. "I had the impression that I was getting quite unpopular!"

Sarah looked genuinely astonished.

"Don't be silly! *That* will be the day!"

Philomena raised one eyebrow.

"How lovely it would be if all the world were as naive as you!" she said dryly. "Not everybody is bluffed by a pair of sparkling eyes, you know!"

Sarah's easy sympathy was instantly aroused.

"Sebastian's bark is worse than his bite—"

Philomena cut her off.

"It depends if his interests are challenged, honey."

Confused, Sarah changed the subject.

"I ought to get back down below," she said. Neither her mother nor her sister made any objection, in fact Philomena went so far as to help her connect the fresh cylinders of compressed air to her breathing apparatus and was busy helping her into her harness when Sebastian came up to the surface. Sarah waited as he came up the steps, shaking himself like a young puppy.

"We've got back inside the cabin," he said as soon as he could. "Have you got the cameras ready?"

She nodded. "How's the light?" she asked.

He laughed. He looked tremendously pleased with himself now that they could get on with opening up the cabin.

"Terrible! Couldn't be worse! You'll just have to do what you can."

She checked that she had the fastest film possible in the camera and put it back into its waterproof capsule ready for use.

"Did you see anything inside?" she asked.

Sebastian's eyes shone with excitement.

"I have a theory that whoever was in that cabin was a pretty important person," he said. "Definitely *not* a Roman himself, not by birth at any rate. He may have been a Roman citizen, of course."

Mrs. Feaney opened her eyes wide. "Then what was he?" she asked.

"We don't know. He might have been an Egyptian, but we're not very pleased with that suggestion."

"We're hoping to find something else that will tell us," Sarah added.

"That's right," Sebastian agreed. He changed his cylinders with the speed of an expert. "See you later," he said.

He and Sarah jumped in together. The coolness of the sea was glorious after the humid heat on the raft. Sarah let herself slowly sink, enjoying the smooth sensation against her skin. Beside her she could see the dark shape of Sebastian gathering momentum as he somersaulted and struck out strongly, making the most of his flippers. Lazily she followed him, striking out more strongly as she came nearer the ship, anxious to see what they had done.

When she got closer she could see that they had torn

away the whole of what remained of the deck and had opened up the supports so that two or three of them could be lowered at a time into the close confines of the cabin beneath. Standing well back, so that she could get the whole ship within her lens, she began to photograph the changes.

It was less easy inside the cabin. She waited for Sebastian to bring the lights up exactly where she wanted them and spent the time looking about her. She could see the place where the knife had stuck and how she had managed to pull the rotten side in on top of her. It was less easy to see anything else, although they had succeeded in dredging away most of the sand. She took one or two tentative steps forward and looked down at her feet, clumsy-looking in their enormous flippers. For an instant she thought she caught a glimpse of something gold, but it disappeared immediately and the space was too confined to do much in the way of an examination.

Sebastian was better with the lights than Roger. He was far more sensitive to the needs of the camera and far less likely to allow them to cast strange shadows across the object in view. Sarah gestured to him to show him what she wanted and as she did so pushed away some sand with her foot and caught a glimpse of the gold again. She pointed down to her feet, hardly daring to breathe. Sebastian pushed the lights back and very carefully squatted down to examine the spot. His fingers lightly brushed the sand away and then, when he thought even his sensitive touch might do some damage, he took a paintbrush out of his pocket and worked away with that.

Slowly and carefully he revealed a gold case which had once held a scroll that had long since been dissolved by the sea. It was very fragile, but it appeared to be complete. With gentle hands he lifted it and took it nearer the lights. It was almost completely covered with a strange script—strange at least to Sarah. Certainly it was none of the languages with which she was most familiar and which they might have expected, such as Latin, Greek or even Etruscan.

Sebastian made a motion to show he was going up, taking their find with him. Sarah followed eagerly and they both arrived at the surface out of breath and quite dizzy from the sudden ascent. Sarah went up the steps first, tearing off her equipment as she went. She flung her harness, heavy with the cylinders of compressed air, down on the raft and tore off her flippers. Then carefully she reached out for the scroll casing from Sebastian. It lay, shining in the sunlight, across her palms, beautiful and intricately worked.

"What a lovely thing!" Mrs. Feaney exclaimed. "What is it?"

Sarah explained how it worked, showing how the roll of parchment would have fitted inside so that it could easily be pulled out and read, winding itself back into a second case. Some of these 'books' might be extremely long.

"How interesting!" Mrs. Feaney exclaimed, her attention already wandering. "And is it valuable, do you think?"

Sarah smiled.

"It depends which way you look at it," she said, smothering her amusement. Her eyes glinted with laughter as she returned the case to Sebastian. He gave her an answering grin and they sat down amicably, side by side, and examined their find more closely.

"I've been thinking," Sebastian said finally. "I wonder if the writing isn't Hebrew. It's certainly from around that area, but unfortunately I'm not an expert."

Sarah frowned down at the scroll-case.

"Sinbad? Giuseppe?"

He shook his head. "Sinbad is the more likely," he said, "but neither of them know much about the fertile crescent."

"Then how are we going to find out?" she asked anxiously. It had become a personal challenge to her to solve the mystery of the mysterious passenger.

Sebastian grinned.

"We'll take it to the Jewish village and ask the Rabbi. He's quite a scholar and will soon be able to tell us. Pack it away, Sarah, and we'll take it over this evening."

As always when she was excited, Sarah couldn't find any words with which to express herself. She took the case and wrapped it gently in cotton wool, making sure that nothing could harm it. It was left to Philomena to fling her arms around Sebastian's neck.

"Oh, *darling!*" she exclaimed. She kissed him warmly on the lips. "Are you terribly pleased?"

He released himself with a touch of annoyance.

"It was Sarah's find," he said abruptly.

"But the credit is yours," she insisted.

He ignored her, his eyes firmly on Mrs. Feaney.

"I think you'll find eventually it will be written down as a de Hougement find!" he said humorously, and laughed at the puzzled glances they gave him. Sarah, completely bewildered, said nothing at all, but she felt that her mother had understood and had been shocked by the unexpected knowledge she had gained.

CHAPTER TWELVE

MRS. FEANEY WAS COMPLETELY SILENT the whole way back to Houmt Souk. At intervals she cast worried looks at both her daughters, but she said nothing until they had actually landed and were all standing on the quay watching Sebastian bring the scroll-case ashore.

"Poor Philomena!" she sighed.

Sarah frowned at her.

"She looks all right to me!" she said with a touch of impatience.

Mrs. Feaney smiled meaningly.

"Poor darling! She's obviously destined for another romantic disappointment! How unkind life can be!"

Sarah was more puzzled than ever.

"What on earth on you talking about?" she demanded.

But her mother chose to look mysterious and very sad, dabbing at her eyes with a handkerchief.

"She isn't tough like you are, Sarah," she said by way of explanation.

Sarah smiled, her whole face taking on a gleam of naughtiness.

"Nonsense, Mother," she said bracingly. "She's as tough as nails and we both know it!"

Philomena came nearer to them, looking unbelievingly beautiful in the hot sunlight.

"Did I hear you correctly, sister dear?" she asked smoothly.

"I suppose you did," Sarah admitted.

Philomena shrugged elegantly.

"What terrible expressions you find to use in the

cause of accuracy," she drawled. "Tough I may be but I could prefer a more feminine comparison!"

"What would you suggest?" Sarah grinned at her.

Philomena smiled mockingly. "Diamonds?" she suggested casually.

They all laughed and Sebastian looked up to see what the joke was. Sarah ran eagerly forward and took the precious package from him so that he could step ashore more easily.

"Are we going straight away?" she asked him.

He glanced down at his watch.

"If you like. Perhaps you'd better come and carry it." He smiled at her enthusiasm. "But you can't come dressed like that! You'd better change into a dress— and bring a head covering of some sort!"

So they went first to the hotel. The two sisters ran straight upstairs to Sarah's room.

"You'd better let me choose the dress," Philomena suggested. "Something frilly and feminine and open to adventure, don't you think?"

Sarah stared at her sister.

"No, I don't," she said coldly. "And anyway, I haven't got anything like that, as you very well know!"

Philomena laughed.

"I know only too well!" she agreed sadly. She stuck her head in the wardrobe and came out with a dress that Sarah occasionally wore in the evenings.

"How about this?"

The dress was no more than an ordinary dressed cotton. It had cost very little, but it had always been one of Sarah's favourites. It was largely the colouring which so appealed to her. It was full of browns and golds and an occasional squidgy green that was very nearly khaki and it made her hair look fairer than ever and had a certain elegance that hid the occasional awkwardness of her movements.

"It has short sleeves," she objected.

Philomena considered.

"You can wear a cardigan in the synagogue if you

have to," she said finally. "It probably won't be necessary, and if it is you'll just have to suffer! You haven't anything else that's half as nice!"

Sarah allowed herself to be pushed into the dress in record time and even submitted to Philomena taking down her hair and doing it for her.

"Aren't you coming?" she asked her in puzzled tones, for she could never remember her sister doing anything like it for her before. "You haven't left yourself much time, have you?"

Philomena pulled her hair.

"No, of course not. What possible interest would it all be to me?"

Sarah sighed. "They're the oldest community of Jews in the world!" she said.

Philomena looked bored.

"My dear, they could have been there before the Ark for all I care. Have you any perfume?"

Sarah looked vaguely about her at the pile of papers that rested on the desk she was also using as a dressing-table.

"Somewhere," she said.

Philomena gave her an exasperated little slap.

"You're quite impossible?" she exclaimed. "You'll have to have some of mine. It's heavier than anything you ever use, but that won't be such a bad thing!"

She went into her own room and came back with a pretty cut-glass bottle of scent that she sprayed liberally about her. It had the sharp tang of a really expensive perfume with nothing to cloy the nostrils.

"You never bought that?" Sarah exclaimed.

Philomena remained calm.

"Of course not. I've never bought scent in my life!"

Sarah giggled, beginning to enjoy all these preparations.

"Sebastian will think I've gone mad!" she said with a certain pleasurable anticipation.

Philomena looked down at her sister with the wisdom of the ages in her eyes.

"I hope he does," she said sardonically. "You keep your head on far too many occasions—"

"Philomena!" Sarah exclaimed, shocked. "You're throwing me at him! I thought you wanted him yourself?"

Philomena's eyes sparkled.

"Why, so I do! *Amongst others!* So you'd better make sure of him while you can. At the moment I'm playing the reformed character, but I don't suppose it will last long!"

Sarah looked at her sister in the looking-glass. The contrast between the two of them was as obvious to her eyes as ever. Her sister's dark beauty gave her own fairness a faded look and her vivacity was the exact opposite of her own shyness. But, for once, there was a colour in her own cheeks which was probably only the sun but which was very effective all the same, and her eyes were alight with an excitement that she still couldn't entirely believe or understand. She tried to thank her sister, but Philomena would have none of it.

"Don't be silly! I'm only doing it because he said he would skin me alive if I didn't fuss over you for a bit—"

"Sebastian did?" Sarah repeated in complete disbelief.

Philomena made a face at her.

"What did you think it was all about? The goodness of my nature?" she demanded.

Sarah smiled a little shakily.

"Something like that," she said. "Actually," she added, "I still think so whatever you might say."

Philomena shrugged her shoulders.

"The more fool you!" she retorted.

SEBASTIAN WAS waiting for her in the car. She felt awkward and she wouldn't look at him as she climbed in beside him.

"What have you done with it?" she asked.

"It's on the back seat."

She glanced over her shoulder and saw the box carefully placed in the centre of the seat where there was no chance of its falling off.

"Isn't anyone else coming?" she asked.

He started the car, a slight smile playing on his lips.

"I hope they're going to get on with some work," he said dryly.

She flushed, more uncomfortable than ever, wishing earnestly that she could get her sister's remarks out of her ears and forget all about them. She pulled her cardigan on to her knee and played with the sleeve in her fingers. It was terribly hot and she could feel her hands getting hot and sticky. The silence grew until she could almost touch it and she searched desperately for some remark that would break it, but at that moment everything she could think of seemed either trite or stupid. The perspiration crept down her back and she pushed her cardigan away again impatiently.

"Do you know the synagogue well?" she asked.

There was a slight lifting at the corners of his mouth.

"Reasonably so. The old Rabbi and I used to be great friends, but he died a few years back."

"And now they have a new one?"

"Yes. This one has travelled quite a bit, unlike his predecessor. He went to university in the States and has been to Israel. But he stays with his people now as the leader of the community."

There were in fact two Jewish villages in Djerba and two synagogues, but it was the Ghriba, the one belonging to the smaller village, to which they were going. The Ghriba which is possibly the only Jewish place of pilgrimage, where Jews from all over the world come to celebrate the Day of Atonement, packing the hostel and changing the rather sleepy village with its Old Testament character into a meeting place of the centuries, the most modern mingling with the Prophet like inhabitants who welcomed them with a gentle courtesy.

At the moment the village was practically deserted. The street was the same to look at as any other; the lime-white houses with their blue painted wrought-iron and woodwork and the women with their Grecian beauty and distinctive traditional dress. Sarah was delighted to see the man who had supplied her with film in Houmt Souk standing just outside the synagogue, dressed like all the other men, in baggy trousers, bare feet and with a kind of turban over his head.

"Miss Feaney, have you come to see the synagogue?" he asked with evident pleasure.

She smiled at him, casting a swift look at Sebastian.

"Why not, while we're here?" he said. "I'll lock the car."

"Do you think it will be quite safe?" she asked.

Her Jewish friend smiled at her.

"We have no robbers here on Djerba," he said gently. "Not even the dates are stolen from the palms."

She wasn't entirely sure that she believed him, but Sebastian seemed perfectly satisfied with the situation and so she walked between the two men to the entrance of the synagogue, where they came to a dead halt.

"I'm afraid you'll have to take your shoes off," the Jew said. "While you're doing that, I'll go and get the Rabbi and ask him to show you the Torah."

The Torah, the Law, is always held in special honour in any synagogue and Sarah knew that it was an honour to be allowed to see it. She slipped off her shoes and put them neatly at the side of the door and then waited while Sebastian took his off in a more leisurely fashion, leaning against the building as he did so.

"You're in luck," he said. "The Torah here is famous for its age and beauty. The scroll is written on a gazelle's skin and is housed in a silver cylinder."

"As beautiful as ours?" she demanded.

He laughed.

"I shouldn't care to say. In this case I have a feeling beauty is very much in the eye of the beholder!"

The Rabbi was a very old man. His thonged sandals

moved cautiously when he walked and his long flowing white beard practically hid his face. He looked so like a picture of Abraham that it was difficult to imagine that he could also be a graduate of one of the most modern universities in the world. He extended a frail hand to Sarah, seizing her own hand and shaking it with a vitality that surprised her. He greeted Sebastian with a French-styled hug, poking him in the ribs and whispering something in his ear.

"You only come when you have work for me to do!" he complained aloud. "I suppose I must forgive you, though, when I see the company you have been keeping." His eyes twinkled with sudden amusement and, without waiting for any reply from either of them, he led the way into the synagogue, leaving his sandals beside theirs at the doorway.

It was very ornate inside. The walls were covered with old ceramics, in various geometric patterns, and were divided by marble arches and intricate carved doorways that are a delight everywhere in the Arab world. The furniture by contrast was very simple, no more than a few wooden seats, on which the worshippers perched themselves, crossing their legs before them, most of them reading the sacred scriptures aloud to themselves, the ancient Hebrew words taking on a sing-song sound that was very attractive. On the floor were a few rush mats.

The old man pattered across the mats in his bare feet, nodding here and there to the stares of curiosity from men almost as old as himself. The few young men kept very much in the background, poised for flight, as if they knew that theirs was a dying way of life and that at any moment they would have to leave and find a living in Israel, the States, or even in the main cities of the north where their relations had gone before them and where they would find a welcome.

Sarah followed the two men more slowly. She liked the feel of the mats on her bare feet and she wanted to see everything, without hurrying through and missing half the detail. She paused to admire the pulpit in the inner room and read the stones on the wall commemorating the dead. Then bells rang, a clear silver sound of pure metal, and the doors that hid the Torah from the eyes of men flew open. The Rabbi approached first, going down on his knees before the ancient scrolls. Sarah took her turn, kissing the ancient book. The writing was absolutely superb and the skin was as white as ever, as beautiful as it was old.

The Rabbi watched her closely.

"So," he said, "you appreciate beautiful things?"

Sarah nodded.

"Look closely at the cylinder, then," he told her. "The Jews have always been renowned for their metalwork." He held it out to her and she studied it closely. To her untutored eyes it looked very like the one they had brought with them. She looked excitedly at Sebastian and he grinned at her.

"They do look alike, don't they?" he agreed.

The Rabbi shook his head at them.

"No one knows the artist who did this," he warned them. "There are two theories about how we come to be here. Some say we are part of the remnant who fled from Jerusalem at the time of the Babylonian captivity. Others, less romantic, say we are no more than Berbers who were converted many centuries ago."

"And which do you believe?" Sarah asked him.

He chuckled.

"I? I believe that we came from Jerusalem. We have the grave of an unknown Jew here and that certainly is very old, too old to allow for any other theory."

"And afterwards, was there any traffic between you and Jerusalem?" Sebastian questioned.

The old man shrugged his shoulders.

"Who knows? It is probable. People travelled round the Mediterranean far more than we imagine."

The bells rang again and the doors shut. Grunting, the Rabbi got to his feet and led the way back into the sunlight.

"And now," he said, "how can I be of service to you?"

He was as excited as they were when they showed him their cylindrical scroll-case. Methodically he examined the patterns that were still clear, comparing them with others, centuries old, with which he had become familiar. Sebastian told him briefly of the other finds they had made and he clicked his teeth in disapproval that a Jew should have had such articles.

"It is likely, though," he said at last. "The prosperity of Egypt and later Rome was always a temptation to us. It is very likely that your mysterious passenger was a Jew." He gazed down at the cylinder again, his whole being concentrating on the search. "Ah!" he exclaimed, pointing at a minute flake of gold. "That is Hebrew! I have no doubt at all that you are right and that this once held a copy of the Torah!"

Sarah and Sebastian looked at each other in triumph. He held out his hand and she took it shyly, pleased at the contact.

"I cannot tell you the exact age," the Rabbi went on. "I have not the equipment here to make a proper examination, but I am quite sure it once held the Law."

He watched them pack it away again, as pleased and as excited as they were. Afterwards they went to his house and he gave them each a glass of the very sweet green tea that was such a favourite in Tunisia. He entertained them on the *patio*, plying them with oranges and dates and suggesting that they should return some time later for a meal, which they accepted eagerly, longing to meet the other members of his family.

"And now," he said at last, "you will be wanting to return to Houmt Souk." His eyes twinkled as he looked at Sarah. "The little one will be in a hurry to return to her family!"

Sarah gave him a startled look.

"To tell them the good news," he prompted her.

To her dismay, the colour poured into her cheeks. She was dismally aware of the surprised expression on the two men's faces, and that Sebastian's changed to a look of complete triumph that made her blush all the more.

The Rabbi patted her gently on the shoulder.

"My wife says it is the lot of women to be made uncomfortable by their menfolk," he said gently. "It is only too true, I'm afraid. Is there some other good news that you would wish to tell them?"

Sarah completely tongue-tied, sought in vain for the light answer that would make them all laugh and relieve the situation. She felt stupid and obvious and she hated her own ineptness with words and her lack of social grace.

Sebastian took her firmly by the hand.

"I think we'll take the long road home," he said.

She said goodbye very prettily to the Rabbi, glad to be able to retreat from her confusion into good manners. With elaborate courtesy he came to see them off, opening the door of the car for her and making quite sure that it was properly shut.

"It is good for you to have such a charming assistant!" he called out to Sebastian. It was impossible to tell whether he was smiling or not because of his beard.

"You'd think more highly of her still if you could see her work!" Sebastian replied, his eyes resting on Sarah's face. "She's an artist with a camera."

The Rabbi frowned.

"Photography, eh? Are you expecting me to approve of that!" He laughed suddenly. "And a very fine worker, I'm sure! I shall be most interested to see the other finds you have made—any time!"

Sebastian smiled and nodded, getting into the car himself. A minute later they had left the village and had turned off the main road towards the sea. The prickly-pear edging to the road also marked the boundaries of the various olive groves. Occasionally they could see a farmer tidying up the weeds around the trees, with either a donkey or a camel in patient attendance.

"I'm surprised the Rabbi doesn't miss the comforts of America," Sarah hazarded by way of conversation.

"Are they so important?" he asked.

"I don't know," she admitted. "I've never had to do without them for long. I don't think it would worry me much, but he's so much older!"

Sebastian chuckled.

"But you think you could manage?"

She considered the question carefully, sensing that he was giving it some hidden importance.

"Yes, I could manage," she said.

He drove off the road into one of the olive groves and stopped the car. It was a shady spot beneath two of the gnarled old trees that could well have been standing there when their ship had been wrecked all those centuries before.

"Perhaps it will be third time lucky with me," he said with a smile.

She looked at him enquiringly.

"The third time?" she asked.

He ran a finger down the line of her jaw and throat and she sat so still that she could scarcely breathe.

"The third time I've kissed you," he said. He pulled her into his arms and kissed her soundly. For an instant she strained against him, but he was much stronger than she, and anyway she didn't really want to be free of him at all.

"Are you sure?" she asked him when she could.

He didn't answer, merely kissing her again.

"Like it?" he asked her eventually.

She sighed. "Very much!"

"Darling!" He looked very well pleased with himself.

She laughed. "Philomena made me put on my prettiest dress for you," she told him. "Did you know that?"

His eyes crinkled with amusement.

"Sometimes I quite like that sister of yours—when I don't want to smack her!"

"Oh, surely not!" she exclaimed.

"Often!" he assured her remorselessly.

"Oh, but, Sebastian—"

"Often! And she knows it!" He grinned amicably. "It's quite half my attraction for her!"

"Philomena doesn't mean half of what she says," she explained uneasily.

"Probably not," Sebastian agreed dryly. "She's thoughtless rather than plain selfish. It won't do her any harm to have to think a little!"

"But—" Sarah began.

"But nothing! Your family is absolutely charming, my love, but for me you are the most important member and I prefer that everybody should know it."

She was silent, digesting this pleasing bit of information, then she kissed him experimentally on the chin. In answer, he hugged her hard against him and kissed her in a way that was not experimental at all, but masterly.

"I'm afraid you're as prejudiced as I am!" she said sadly when she could. She liked to feel his chuckle beside her even when she couldn't hear it. It gave her a confidence that she had never thought to have.

"And just how prejudiced are you?"

She screwed up her nose at him.

"It wouldn't be good for you to know!"

"Is that so?" he drawled. He watched the colour come back into her cheeks and knew that she was regretting her lighthearted remark. "Then perhaps I had better tell you how prejudiced I am."

She didn't answer. She had thought for so long that it was Philomena who attracted him that she still felt doubtful of her own ability to hold his interest. It was an entirely new and delightful sensation even to have him to herself.

"Darling, will you marry me?" He put a finger across her lips to silence her. "No, wait, I haven't done! You may think that this is no more than a spell on me in this witching island, but that isn't so! I was very sure that I wanted to know more of you from the

day we met in my sister's flat. But it will not be an easy
life—"

She escaped from his finger, holding his hand away
from her face.

"I'd love to," she said simply. "I can think of nothing I should enjoy more than being with you. And I
don't care if you have been eating the lotus!" she
added generously.

"I'm very much in love with you," he said.

She smiled, completely happy.

"And I with you," she told him gravely.

IT WAS A LONG TIME before they started back to Houmt
Souk. The sun had set and it was no longer hot, but
there was a sudden coolness in the air and a number of
thick black clouds came spinning across the sky and
retreated towards the mainland.

"Will it rain, do you think?" she asked dreamily as a
single drop fell on the windscreen.

"It's too early in the year."

But the people of Houmt Souk didn't think so. They
had pulled the awnings down over the shops and the
streets were almost deserted. Sebastian drove up outside the hotel and let Sarah get out.

"I shan't be a minute, I'll just put the car away."

She nodded, but she stood in the doorway and waited
for him because she didn't want to go in alone. When
he came back to her she was cold from the wind that
swept round the corner and had put on her cardigan.

"Did you see them?" he asked her.

"See who?"

He grinned.

"Roger and Philomena."

"What, *in the rain*? Where are they?"

His grin grew broader.

"Walking. It could be that Philomena is beginning to
see his worth."

Sarah laughed. "Oh, hardly his *worth*!" Her eyes
shone. "Poor Marcel!"

He put an arm round her shoulders and held her close to him as he opened the door. Inside it was completely deserted. They looked at each other and laughed again. Who cared what everyone else was doing? Sarah reached up and kissed him, and as she did so, the waiter came into the hall from the kitchen. He took one look at them and a pleased smile broke over his face. For a couple of seconds he sought for some words to wish them joy, some few words they would understand, but he had no French and they no Arabic. His two hands went to his head in defeat and then very shyly he said, *"Bon soir!"*

Sarah and Sebastian smiled back at him.

"Bon soir!" they echoed. It had, after all, been a wonderful evening.

A Cure
with Kindness
Ruth Clemence

It was a mystery to Rosabel why her brother, a respected Highland physician, would take into his home a disreputable-looking stranger. Although she theorized that a little love often helped patients more than most medical treatments, Rosabel, couldn't hide her disapproval of Robert Carr.

His blackouts, she suspected, were firmly linked to the amber liquid he so often consumed. And more disturbing, a strong instinct warned Rosabel that his presence would eventually disrupt all their lives....

But a marriage proposal! Nothing she'd learned about him had prepared her for that!

CHAPTER ONE

ROBERT CARVER SWORE SOFTLY under his breath as he turned the last corner and saw the long straight village street stretching out before him. It was so obviously the dead end he had suspected it might prove to be. He shifted the worn knapsack to try and ease his aching shoulders before drifting over towards the wall which bordered one side of the road.

The river ran parallel with the road and lapped at mud banks beneath him. He guessed that at high tide the water would reach half-way up the wall on which he was leaning. He cursed himself again for a fool. Three miles back he had suspected that he had taken the wrong road. He should have asked his way then. Now he felt almost too tired to take another step, and it wasn't as though he hadn't been warned. There was no point in leading this kind of life if he forgot the object of the exercise and overtaxed himself.

A few minutes later he straightened up and looked around. He certainly couldn't walk back to where he'd taken the wrong turning this evening. It was too late. He wore no watch, but he judged the time to be about seven-thirty. If he was going to find somewhere to stay the night he'd better start looking right away.

He turned his back on the wall and looked across the narrow country road to the cliff which rose sharply on the opposite side. It was thickly wooded with firs of various kinds, but he could see a gateway farther along and he made his way across the road again. A small wooden arrow pointed upwards with the words, "The Golf Hotel" printed in neat white capitals. "Not for me!" Robert remarked below his breath. He was in no shape to climb the steep zigzag footpath to which the arrow pointed.

He began to walk slowly on down the road. First he came to a row of terraced cottages, their backs snugly fitting almost into the cliff face. Then came a small petrol station and garage, followed by the village pub, standing alone, snowcemmed a clean-looking yellow shade and with just enough room for two or three cars to pull in off the road.

No popular country call-in, this, he noted as he walked past. Now the cliff on his left hand was becoming a little less steep. Here it only just cleared the roofs of the next six houses, the end one of which was obviously the village post office. After these came a six-foot wall. Peering over it, Robert could see a pleasant garden. The house to which it belonged was a good deal larger than the others and there was a brass plate on the iron gate guarding steps leading to a porched front door.

As Robert walked slowly by, he noticed the house was joined by a stone archway to another building, which must once have served as a coach-house. Under the archway a cream-coloured Mini was parked, its bonnet pointing towards the road. The only other buildings were the village shop with a wooden storehouse behind it. Emporium would be a better word, Robert decided. Judging by the hotchpotch in the window, they sold everything from ice-cream to firelighters. Further along there were only the boats, some drawn up almost to the edge of the road where it began to peter out into a dirt track alongside the river.

Robert stopped and rubbed a hand wearily across his eyes. Nothing for it but to go back to the pub and ask if there was anywhere to put up for the night. He was almost opposite the house with the brass plate when the dizziness hit him. Through a swirling black mist he managed to find the gateway and almost fell into a sitting position on the second step.

As he did so the door behind him opened and a girl's

clear voice said, "Surgery is over. Can you come back tomorrow?"

Quite conscious but beyond replying, he became aware that a car had roared to a standstill outside the gate and a moment later a hand pressed his head further between his legs. A voice above him said, "Okay, Rosie. I'll handle this."

From nearer at hand Robert heard the girl remark "Drunk, is he?" and then the hand was removed from the back of his head and felt in the pocket of his jacket where he had been trying to extricate the box of pills. One was slipped between his lips and a man's voice said, "Take it easy. As soon as you feel better we'll go into the surgery."

A couple of minutes later Robert stirred and began to heave himself slowly to his feet. Immediately a hand came under his arm and helped him into an upright position. He looked into the face of the tall man standing beside him and smiled ruefully.

"Sorry about that. Thank you for your help. I'm perfectly all right again now."

The hand urged him up the steps. "I think a few minutes on the couch in my surgery wouldn't come amiss. I'd like to have a look at you before you go on your way. Incidentally, I'm the doctor hereabouts. Name's Fairbairn."

At that moment the cream Mini sped out from under the archway and stopped in front of the gate.

"Sure you can manage, Peter?" The girl's eyes were on the figure propped by her brother's arm. The attire was shabby. The hair, though not long by some standards, had obviously not seen a barber's scissors for six to eight weeks, and the man had certainly not shaved today.

At the sound of her voice, both men had turned their heads. Robert noted a neat uniform coat and a blue cap framing a vivid face lit by dark eyes. His companion answered, "Quite sure. Don't waste any more time, Rose. You're going to Mrs. Wylie's, I take it?"

The girl grinned through the window as she put the car in gear. "Yes, and you're right. I'd better be off. Like time, Mrs. Wylie waits for no man," and the little car shot off in a cloud of dust and gravel.

As the sound of the engine faded into the distance, the two men went up the steps and into the house. When Peter Fairbairn had seen his unusual patient on to the surgery couch he excused himself and went down the hall into the large living-room at the back of the house. A handsome grey-haired woman was sitting knitting on the settee. There was a girl of some ten summers sprawling on the floor reading a book and another, a little older, sitting at the table apparently wrestling with a mathematical problem judging by the way she was screwing up her face and counting on the fingers of one hand. Looking up, she spotted her father at the door. "Oh, goody, Dad! You're back. What's eight sevens? Gran says she can't remember."

Peter grinned. "You ought to know by now, Jen. Fifty-six. Isa, can you rustle up a pot of tea? I've a customer in the surgery who looks as if he could do with one."

Isabel McCulloch laid her knitting aside and got up at once. She had given up her own home and come here to keep house when her daughter June had died eight years ago. As Peter stood aside to let her pass she inquired, "Could he manage a sandwich as well?" He nodded, fingering his earlobe as he frequently did when trying to work out a perplexing problem. After he had closed the door he went into the hall and opened a tall cupboard. In the bottom untidy piles of magazines and medical journals stood in rows. He opened several before a grunt of satisfaction indicated he had come across the one he was lookiong for. Tucking it under his arm, Peter closed the cupboard and went back to the surgery.

As he opened the door, the man on the couch sat up and swung his legs to the ground. "There's a cup of tea on the way. I daresay you could do with it," Peter said as he sat down behind his desk.

The man ran a hand across his eyes and, getting up, walked over and sat down on the patient's chair across the desk from Peter Fairbairn. "It's very good of you. I feel I've been rather a lot of bother already," he began. "Sorry to pick your front doorstep to have a blackout."

"Perhaps it's as well you did," Peter replied, and pushed the opened journal across the desk so that it lay before his patient. The man glanced down for a moment and then up again quickly to meet Peter's eyes.

"You must have an infernally good memory," the man said, "because I don't think we've ever met."

"No, but quite apart from that," Peter pointed a long finger at the photograph and paragraph on the open page, "I have heard quite a lot about you from Chuff Whittaker from time to time."

The man smiled. "Oh yes, Chuff. He's married to a cousin of mine. Great chap. Where is he now? I haven't heard from him for ages."

Peter grinned and taking the journal up again, pushed it into a drawer. "That surprises me because he's out in the Far East at the moment isolating rare bugs," he said. "He decided to do tropical medicine after his last stint as a hospital registrar." As Robert made no comment Peter continued, "Talking about rare bugs, where are you making for at the moment? I shouldn't have thought if you're headed north that strenuous hikes over our Scottish mountains would be quite the thing."

The man smiled. He fiddled for a moment with a paper-weight on the desk before replying. "Nowhere in particular really. I did originally think I'd look up an old aunt in Ayr. It seemed as good a place to make for as any. But she doesn't know I'm on the road, and if I never arrive it wouldn't matter. I got my general directions a bit mixed, I'm afraid."

Peter rubbed a hand over his hair. "Yes, you are a bit

off course in this little backwater, but it would be just the place to stay if you've time to kill."

"Another three months or so before I have to see Sir William again."

"In that case I've a suggestion to make. Why don't you stay here? It's ideal for gentle, rambling walks, fresh sea air, and if you don't mind a lack of luxury you're welcome to use the room over our garage until August. My sister Rosabel had it made shipshape for herself and my two daughters to sleep in when the relatives descend on us during the summer holidays. It's fairly comfortable. We put in water and electricity, although as I say, it's not the Ritz by any means."

The man was looking wearier than ever. "I couldn't possibly impose..." he began.

"Nonsense. Stay tonight anyway," Peter replied swiftly. "You're in no fit state to go any further today and I don't know where else you could put up in Bannford. I happen to know our one and only hotel is full with a big party of business men from Lancaster and they don't let rooms at the pub."

"In that case, thank you, I'd be..." and he broke off as the door opened and Isabel McCulloch came in carrying a tray.

Both men rose as she entered the room. She smiled as she put the tray down, her eyes on the stranger still standing beside the desk. "This is Robert Car..." Peter hesitated, then went on smoothly. "Robert Carr, Isa. He'll be staying in the 'flat' for a while." Then, "This is my mother-in-law, Mrs. McCulloch. She keeps the house, me and the family in order."

Isa McCulloch smiled and held out her hand. After a second's pause, the man shook it, murmuring a greeting. Isa said over her shoulder, "The mattresses are all aired. I'll look out some bedding when you are ready, Peter."

There was silence for a few moments after the door had closed behind her. Peter filled a cup and pushed it and the plate of sandwiches across the desk.

"Thanks for not giving my proper name. I'd prefer to keep out of the public eye for a moment if possible. The press seem to take a ghoulish interest in me."

The two men kept up a close conversation until the teapot had been emptied. Peter's keen eyes noticed that the colour had returned to the cheeks of the man sitting opposite to him, though he still looked very fatigued.

He got up. "I'll show you your quarters now if you like." He picked up Robert Carver's knapsack as he went to the door. "I suppose you're not allowed to drive?"

The man smiled ruefully. "No, that was one of the first things they did. Take my driving licence away," he replied. "One of the main reasons for the walking tour."

When they had climbed the outside staircase to the "flat" over the coach-house and Peter opened the door, Robert realized it was a good deal bigger than he had imagined from his brief glance as he had passed it earlier. The coach-house beneath must be big enough to house two if not three cars with ease. And when his host had told him that it had been altered to allow his sister and daughters to sleep in, he had understated the situation considerably.

In the light flooding in from two large windows in the south and west walls, Robert Carver found himself to be in a large pleasant room. Behind the door and to his right was a shower cabinet and beside it a sink with cupboards beneath. A water heater on the wall served them both. Beside the sink stood a small cooker, and a fanlight window high in the wall had obviously been adapted to take away both steam and cooking smells. Three beds, without mattresses, stood against the windowless wall with well-filled bookshelves on either side. Under the two windows, curtained in bright scarlet and gold brocaded material, were two comfortable-looking armchairs, a table and several upright chairs. It was the sort of spacious airy room a good many city dwellers would have been glad to occupy permanently, even without the magnificent views over the river and the estuary which greeted the two men as they sauntered over to the nearest window.

Peter Fairbairn dumped the knapsack down and looked around. "I think you'll be okay here. I'll bring a mattress and some bedding over. Oh yes, and some milk. I think Isa keeps tea, coffee and sugar permanently over here. Is there anything else you need?"

Robert Carver rubbed a hand over the stubble of his chin. "The only thing I can think of is a razor. Could you lend me one until I can get to a shop? I discovered this morning I must have left mine behind at my last port of call."

"Yes, of course. I've a spare one in the bathroom cupboard. I'll bring it over with the other things for you."

CHAPTER TWO

It was five to eight the following morning when Rosabel Fairbairn drove wearily into the yard and parked her car. When she entered the cosy room at the back of the house, the family had just started breakfast.

She took off her hat and ran fingers through her hair. "Gosh, I'm tired! That coffee smells lovely, Isa. I've had so many cups of tea I feel as if I'm full of red ink. I don't know where Mrs. Wylie gets it, but that's what her tea tastes like."

"Not such an easy night as you expected?" Peter asked, lowering the newspaper.

"No, for the first time she had a difficult confinement." Rosabel stirred her cup of coffee and raising it to her lips, sipped with satisfaction. "What with that and the other children playing up. Mr. Wylie's quite useless. He can manage to bring the coal in and boil a kettle and that's about all. I had to get the two smallest to bed as soon as I had made Mrs. Wylie more comfortable, and then get breakfast for all of them this morning and clear away before I left. Fortunately Junior arrived at five a.m., so he just gave me time to get finished. I'll have to go in later, of course, but they're all right for the moment. I dumped the children on one of the neighbours before I came away."

"A boy, is it, then?" Isa asked. At Rosabel's nod, her mouth too full of porridge to speak, Isabel went on, "I'll go down there and take them some dinner, so you go and have a few hours' sleep, Rosie. Don't forget you've got Jean Soutar due any minute now. When I saw her in Dalbeattie yesterday I wondered she had managed to get on the bus."

At Rosabel's groan Peter laughed. "Don't put the wind up her, Isa. I'm keeping my eye on Jean. She won't have her baby this week."

"Thank goodness," Rosabel laughed with relief. "One thing about you, Peter, if you make a prediction you're usually nearly always right. Incidentally, how did you get on with that odd character I left sitting on the front steps? Where'd he come from? I shouldn't have thought Bannford the place to attract hobos. He looked really down—clothes past their best, needing a haircut, and I shouldn't think he'd shaved for days. What was the matter with him?"

"For someone who only saw him for a couple of minutes, you didn't miss much," Peter remarked.

"Well, whatever else I got on my periodic reports in hospital, 'observation nil' wasn't one of them," Rosabel remarked complacently as she reached for the marmalade.

"I can tell you where he is," piped in Jennie, not to be kept out of the conversation any longer. "He's in our 'flat.' Katya and I helped Daddy take over the bedding and mattress last night. And he's nice, whiskers or not, isn't he, Kat?"

Katya Fairbairn, Peter's younger daughter, merely nodded solemnly in agreement.

Rosabel looked across at her brother, a question in her eyes. "He hadn't a bed for the night and I thought he oughtn't to go any farther. He's subject to occasional blackouts apparently. I offered him the use of the 'flat' for a few days."

"Couldn't he have gone to the Cottage Hospital?"

Peter rubbed a hand over his hair. "He could, I suppose, but it seemed more sensible for us to put him up. Why, you don't object do you Rose? He seems quite a decent chap."

Rosabel took a last gulp of coffee and stood up. "Good heavens, it makes no difference to me." She turned to Isa. "Thanks for the breakfast, Isa. I'll help clear away and then I'll go and try and get in a couple of hours' sleep. There's no need for you to go out to the Wylies', though. I must be up by noon again and you've quite enough to do.''

As she went upstairs, Rosabel wondered why she felt so uneasy about the man being given a bed for the night. She had hardly set eyes on him, as Peter had pointed out, for more than two minutes, and yet some instinct or premonition, call it what you will, had stirred to life deep inside her. Something said this stranger was going to disrupt all their lives.

She tried to shake off the feeling as she had a quick bath and climbed into clean pyjamas. As she pulled her curtains, she glanced across at the coach-house. One thing he didn't seem to believe in was early rising. There was no sign of life from the building across the yard.

But when she went downstairs three hours later, a clean uniform under her coat, and walked across the yard to her car, she stopped short. The cream paintwork was spotless and gleamed with polish. Rosabel fitted the key into the car door slowly. As she got into the car, her eyes widened still further. Someone had certainly been thorough. The inside was as spotless as the outside. Not a speck of dirt marred the footmats and the ashtray had been emptied, she noticed. To do this, Isabel must have produced the spare key kept hanging in the kitchen.

Before she turned into the road, Rosabel looked round quickly, but the yard appeared empty and she studiously refrained from lifting her face to the "flat" door. She couldn't explain why, even to herself, but she didn't want to know who had done her this good turn. It might have meant a reluctant "thank you." She was astonished at her own attitude as she drove down the village street and then turned in the direction of the Wylies' cottage. She firmly concentrated on her driving and on what sort of chaos she could expect to find when she reached her patient.

But Mrs. Wylie's neighbours had rallied round with a

will. Rosabel entered the cottage to find two clean and shiny children being fed at the kitchen table by a very pretty girl whom she recognized as the eldest daughter from the cottage next door. She smiled as Rosabel shut the door.

"Ah, there you are, nurse. I've taken Mrs. Wylie a tray. Mum's looking after the other two. Says she'll keep them for the rest of the day if that's all right with you."

"More than all right," Rosabel said. "Will you thank your mother, Susan? It's very good of you to help out. I was thinking in terms of scrambled eggs as I drove up here."

"There's more than enough if you'd like some too, Miss Fairbairn," the girl urged, indicating the big brown stewpot which stood on the sideboard.

"No, I've eaten, thanks." Rosabel hung her coat on the back of the door. "I'll go straight up and see to Mrs. Wylie and the baby if you can manage here."

She found Mrs. Wylie lying looking supremely pleased with herself and a "I've done a grand job" sort of look spread all over her face. "Nurse, what do you think Doctor said when he called in this morning?"

Rosabel smiled as she went across and shook down her thermometer.

"No idea, Mrs. Wylie. Tell me. What did Doctor say?" She knew her brother. He'd have been sure to think of something which would tickle this annual maternity patient of his.

"He wants to know if I'm going to stop at a team of eleven or whether I'm going on for a rugby football side," Mrs. Wylie chuckled. "He says they'll all be eligible to play for Scotland and he'll expect a free seat to see the match!" Mrs. Wylie almost literally held her sides. Forgotten was the night which had gone before and Rosabel's anxiety for her, but then she had probably not realized how very near Rosabel had been to sending Bill Wylie on his bike to get Peter out of bed.

While she was seeing to her patient and washing and

changing the baby, Rosabel found her mind wandering off. Who had cleaned her car? And why, if it had been done by the man Peter had taken in last night, should she feel this unreasonable resentment? She knew the car had been long overdue for a thorough wash and polish. She had just been so busy she had not got around to it. But perhaps she was barking up the wrong tree. Maybe Bill Johnston had called in when she had been asleep and had done her the good turn. If so, an unconscious thought popped into her mind, it would have been the first time he'd ever done so. In any case, you're going to the hotel to have dinner with Bill tonight, there'd be no reason for his calling in. She looked up suddenly from pinning the baby's nappy to answer Mrs. Wylie. From the look on that lady's face, it wasn't the first time she had spoken to Rosabel and received no answer. Determinedly dragging her mind back from thoughts of Bill Johnston, Rosabel got up, the baby in her arms, and walked across to the bed. It would never do for her to keep daydreaming on duty.

By the time that Rosabel had finished at the Wylies' the afternoon was well advanced, and she still had several calls to make before she could call it a day and go home. She was not feeling at all in the mood to go out, and as she drove home she could think of nothing she would have liked more than to be having a light supper and going to bed early.

It did not improve her temper or odd feeling of depression to notice, as she drove into the yard of the house, that a faint light showed through the door of the flat above the coach-house. As she got out, she slammed the door of her little car rather abruptly before walking over to the back door into the house. She was puzzled at her added feeling of ill-temper as she had noticed the light and realized that the stranger who had arrived last night was still on the premises. Peter should have sent him on his way by this time and it was a mystery to her why he had not done so. Her brother, though generous by nature, was not in the habit of offering a bed to casual strangers, and she couldn't explain, even to herself, his unexpected behaviour. However, it was really none of her business. After all, it *was* her brother's house, and although she had been the instigator of the conversion of the empty room over the coach-house as added accommodation, if Peter wished to lend it to anybody he fancied, surely he had a perfect right to do so.

Rosabel hastily put a more cheerful expression on her face as she turned the handle of the back door. Both her young nieces were sitting at the kitchen table eating their supper, and Isa was watching them eat and sipping a cup of tea. Jennie was the first to look up as the door opened. "Hello, Aunt Rosie. Had a hard day? You're looking tired."

"That's no way to greet me," Rosabel said as she put down her bag and removed her close-fitting uniform hat. "You should tell me I'm looking like all the flowers of May. You ought to know by this time, Jennie, that when people get over twenty-one they don't want to be told how tired they look because it's another way of saying how old and haggard they look." Both the little girls giggled. They were used to Rosabel telling them what an old lady she was getting, and it had become a standing joke between them. They both knew that though she worked hard, she was a great sport, never too tired to join in their games, tell them stories or take them on expeditions farther afield whenever she had free time. But she did look tired, Isa McCulloch thought as she looked carefully across at her son-in-law's young sister, and she got up quietly and walked across to the sideboard to fetch another cup and saucer.

"I expect you've been offered endless cups of tea all afternoon," she remarked, "but I daresay another one won't come amiss?" she suggested.

Rosabel sat down, still in her outdoor coat. "As a matter of fact, I haven't had a cup of tea since I was at Mrs. Wylie's. The neighbours have rallied round so well that I'm afraid I left them to get on. I saw Mrs. Wylie herself had some tea of course before I left, but those people next door seem to be seeing to the children all right and I honestly didn't see why I should stay and look after Wylie himself. I'm sure he's quite capable of cooking himself some bacon and eggs if he's hungry when he gets home from work."

"But my guess is he'll be wetting the baby's head this evening and food will be the last thing he thinks of," Isa remarked shrewdly. "Incidentally, Bill rang up this afternoon. He asked me to remind you that he's expecting you up there for dinner tonight. You hadn't forgotten, had you?"

Rosabel sighed as she stirred her tea and then looked up to catch Mrs. McCulloch's eye. "No, I hadn't forgotten, but to be quite honest if I could choose, it would be a hot bath, an early supper and to bed with that book you got me from the library. Still, I did promise Bill, so I'd better go upstairs and get changed. Is surgery over yet?" she asked as she got up and carried her cup over to the drainer.

"No," Mrs. McCulloch answered. "The waiting-room was still half full when I looked in a moment or two ago. We needed you to weed out the malingerers and get things moving. Still, Maggie promised she'd be in for the morning's surgery, so if you haven't a lot of morning calls there's no reason why you shouldn't have an extra hour in bed tomorrow morning."

"Some hope," Rosabel answered as she thrust her fingers through her hair. "I'll have to be up at the Wylies' first thing, otherwise Mrs. Wylie will be getting up, and she had such a tough time I want her to have at least a couple of days' complete rest. And she'll only do that if I keep a very firm eye on her for the rest of the week. You know what she's like, Isa."

Isa McCulloch nodded. "Yes. I went up there after the last baby was born to try and give her a bit of a hand because the younger children were being so trouble-some, but she would insist on getting up and doing for herself. I must say she's got courage, if nothing else.'"

"She's got that all right," Rosabel agreed. "I don't know anyone else who'd put up with Wylie. He's hopeless, you know."

Isa laughed. "Well, quite a lot of men are hopeless in a house, Rosie, as you'll find out as you get older. Some just can't do it and some won't."

"I think Wylie's one of the 'won'ts,'" said Rosabel as she went out of the door.

Upstairs she went through her wardrobe. She felt strangely uninterested in the prospect of an evening out and eventually chose a dress which she'd had for some time but which she knew Bill liked. It was a plain black with a pattern in oyster-coloured leaves scattered here and there. When she had washed and changed, she put on a pair of slim black patent pumps, also not in their first youth but which she knew would be kind to her aching feet. They were light and comfortable and favourites when she had had a hard day.

After she had done her face and hair, she regarded her reflection for a moment in the mirror. She certainly looked a bit weary this evening and perhaps it had been a mistake to wear black, but it was too late to change now into something more colourful. As she went downstairs again she decided that rather than walk up to the hotel by the steep path through the fir wood she would take her little car and drive down to the village and round to the other entrance to the hotel. It was lazy of her, she knew, but it would also save Bill having to walk her home later.

As she stepped out of the house by the rear door she stopped abruptly. Jennie and Katya were sitting on the bottom step of the wooden staircase leading to the "flat," and on an upturned box before one of the girls' bicycles sat the man who had arrived yesterday. He was tinkering with the front brake and as Rosabel hesitated for a momet she heard him say, "This brake block is worn out. If I get you a new one tomorrow will you promise to ride carefully until I can fit it for you?"

Rosabel began to walk slowly towards the group. She felt she ought to say something about the immaculate state in which she had found her car. At the sound of her footsteps, the three sitting outside the coach-house stopped talking and looked up. As she stopped in front of them and glanced at the man adjusting the nut on the bicycle, Rosabel received a slight shock. She had really only had a brief glimpse of him the night before. Now as he glanced up at her she realized he was quite different from what she had imagined. True, in her opinion, the hair still needed a trim, but the brown face, now clean and newly shaven, came as a surprise to her, as also did the lazy, smiling eyes. Halting, with a rather abrupt word of thanks on the tip of her tongue, she found herself gazing down into eyes of a clear grey framed by thick dark lashes. Beneath the lazy glance she detected a shrewdness which was examining her carefully as she stood there. A very faint flush tinted the warm cream of her cheeks. "I'm Rosabel Fairbairn," she began—and then, as the man offered no word to help her out, stumbled on, "I think it must have been you who cleaned my Mini this morning, and I wanted to say 'thank you.'"

There was silence for a few moments while the lazy eyes still scrutinized her carefully. The flush deepened in her cheeks. She was not to know that he was wondering why the extraordinarily beautiful girl standing in front of him should have such a weary, and perhaps sad, droop to her lips. Suddenly he got to his feet. "That's perfectly all right." He held out his hand. "And I'm Robert Carr...usually called Rob." He smiled down at her as he took her hand. "I think I did meet you just briefly last night before I passed out. I'm sorry I didn't say hello then," and his mouth tilted up whimsically. Rosabel found herself studying him as carefully as he had done her only a few moments before. As she met his steady regard she wondered why yesterday she had instinctively felt so opposed to him staying there. She just couldn't explain to herself why she had formed such a prejudice and on so slight an encounter. He certainly looked innocuous enough this evening. Just another softly spoken, chance-met stranger no different, as far as she could tell, from any other casually met tripper to this coast, and goodness knows she saw enough of these, especially during the summer months. Suddenly, she became aware that her hand still lay in a firm warm clasp, and that the encounter was being watched with grave curiosity by two pairs of bright young female eyes.

Rosabel snatched her hand out of his and pushed it into the side pocket of her coat saying, abruptly, "I must be going," then could have kicked herself. She wasn't usually so brusque and her usual calm had deserted her yet again. Perhaps after all this man wasn't the same as dozens of people she had met over recent years. Certainly something about him seemed to throw her off balance. To chase these unwelcome thoughts out of her mind Rosabel resolutely tried to pull herself together. She smiled at the two girls. "I think it's time you two were getting ready for bed, don't you?" she asked. "In any case I must be off. Good night, pets," and with a wave meant to include all three persons in the group she turned and walked over to the Mini.

As she slid into the driving seat and slammed the door she murmured, "Snap out of it. What's got into you?" And then immediately smiled as she realized that she was talking to herself, traditionally the first signs of lunacy. She grimaced to herself as she started the engine. Fancy behaving like a schoolgirl at her age!

But as she drove out of the gateway she couldn't resist a glance into the rear mirror. The man was standing between her two nieces, and all three were gazing after her. As she nosed the car on to the village street she was amazed at her urge to turn back and ring Bill to call the whole evening off. It was extremely odd, and she shook her head as if by doing so she could shake off these curious thoughts popping in and out of her mind as she drove in the direction of the hotel.

By the time she turned into the front driveway, rounded the first tee of the small golf course, and drove on to the apron in front of the hotel, she had resolutely dismissed all irritating thoughts completely from her mind. She sat a moment after she had switched off the ignition and gazed at the hotel. It certainly occupied a wonderful position here on top of the cliff. It wasn't a very large place. Originally it had been just a big family house, built of the local grey granite. But the man who had built it for his own convenience had either found it a little too large, or decided after all it was too out of the way for his purpose, because he had sold it. The purchaser had been a widow, and she and her three daughters had at once turned the place into a small family hotel, later buying more of the adjacent land and having it turned into a nine-hole golf course for the use of their guests. In course of time, they had added to the hotel itself, building two long wings on either side of the main building, and in a small pine copse which grew almost up to the windows of the southern wing, they had provided additional sleeping accommodation by building wooden chalets amongst the pine trees.

But when Bill Johnston had bought it five years ago, it had begun to look rather run down. The three daughters who had originally helped their mother to run it had all married and moved to different parts of the country. Left alone she had found difficulty in getting suitable staff. Business was beginning to drop off quite considerably when Bill had got wind that it might be for sale. Finding him interested, Mrs. Moore had been only too glad to come to terms and retire. He and his two sisters Kate and Jean took over, and a lot of alterations had been done. Although electricity had been run out to the chalets, there was no running water. Bill's first consideration had been to modernize these by piping water to them and he also built a bathroom and shower block for the use of the chalet occupants. There had been less to do in the main building itself, but over the years he had made improvements here and there and inside it now bore little resemblance to its general appearance when he had purchased it.

The money spent had certainly been a good investment. By means of advertisements in local and national newspapers, he now attracted people to the hotel from quite far afield, and had extended his season until it was rare for them to have fewer than about twenty guests staying. Parties of business men who wanted a quiet week-end with golf thrown in often came, driving from Glasgow or Edinburgh even in the winter months. It was hard work, especially during the busy summer months, but Bill seemed to thrive on it. Rosabel wondered how she would fit in here if she did marry him as Bill seemed to take for granted. It wouldn't be easy for her, she knew. Living with Bill meant also living with Jean and Kate Johnston. She and Jean had never really hit it off, perhaps because their dispositions were as different as chalk from cheese.

To start with Jean was an excellent cook, almost in the Cordon Bleu class, a first class housekeeper, and had an eye like a hawk for anything left undone by the staff. Rosabel, although she was a very good nurse and in her own way as meticulous over details, knew that she could never hope to fill Jean's place. She just couldn't see herself following people round to see if a speck of dust had been left lying on a table or a spoon had not been cleaned as thoroughly as usual. And as for cooking—well, she could do invalid diets and ordinary plain cooking, but anything more complicated such as the Continental dishes which Jean produced with the greatest ease were quite beyond her.

And Rosabel had to admit that these days a really good kitchen was an essential in a reputable hotel, even one in such a backwater as Bannford. People these days were not prepared to make do with ordinary fare. They wanted something out of the ordinary and were prepared to pay well if they could have them on the menu.

As Rosabel got out of the car she could see, through the lighted windows of the dining-room, that dinner was in progress. She went into the hotel and, making her way through to the staff quarters, knocked tentatively on the kitchen door. No one answered her knock and from the clatter going on inside she realized that it had probably gone unheard. She opened the door and peeped inside. Jean Johnston looked up from where she was decorating a large glass bowl of some delectable-looking dessert with whipped cream. "Ah, there you are, Rosabel. Bill was asking if you'd arrived. Go on through to the dining-room. Don't come in here, you'll only get in the way."

Rosabel withdrew her head and closed the door. She wasn't really surprised at the reception she had received. Jean often behaved as if she were more the owner of the hotel than Bill, though all the money which had gone into buying and modernizing the hotel had been Bill's alone, left to him by a wealthy godfather.

She was stirred out of her feeling of irritation at Jean's manner by the sight of Bill himself coming through the dining-room door. His face lit up at the sight of her. "My dear! I am glad to see you. I thought you must have forgotten that you had said you'd come up here this evening, though I did ring and remind Isa. Did she tell you?"

Rosabel nodded. "Yes, she told me, and of course I'd not forgotten," and she squeezed the hand holding her arm.

"Come on then," he said, "let's go into the office and have a quiet sherry. Just the two of us on our own. Everything seems to be going smoothly and I think we can leave Kate to see to the dining-room."

It was only a small room but one of Rosabel's favourite spots in the hotel. A thick double door which Bill had had fitted when he had modernized the place shut out all sounds of guests or staff. Rosabel slid her arms out of her coat, and throwing it over the back of a chair, wandered over to the window. It faced across the river, giving a beautiful view of the hills opposite since it opened on to the small fenced-in lookout garden on the cliff side of the building. Of course at this time in the evening, with the dusk coming down, Rosabel wasn't able to see the full beauty of the surrounding landscape, but the rosy clouds to the west and the sprinkling of lights beginning to appear in the windows of the houses scattered up and down the opposite side of the river gave her a warm feeling of pleasure.

Behind her she could hear the clink of glasses as Bill poured out the sherry. She turned as he came across the room and put a glass into her hand.

Seeing the look in his eye, Rosabel asked hastily, "How's the week-end golfing party going?"

Bill laughed as he took a gulp of his sherry. "Well, they all seem to be enjoying themselves. Most of them seem to have had two rounds of golf this morning and one at least this afternoon and they're now tucking into a gargantuan dinner. Jean has been most of the day preparing it. Not to mention Kate in the dining-room."

"Yes, I know," said Rosabel. "I put my head round the kitchen door on my way in and was instantly dismissed in case I should get in the way."

Bill chuckled rather ruefully. "Well, you know Jean. She likes to be monarch of all she surveys, and I must admit that she certainly does us proud as far as catering is concerned. You just wait until you see what she's put on for us tonight. I've asked Kate to come and tell us as soon as the dining-room starts to empty."

He stopped speaking for moment, eyeing her with obvious admiration an affection. "By Jove, Rosie, it's good to see you. It seems ages since you were last up."

"It's not all that long," Rosabel said, "and I did see you last Saturday, after all. With me hard at it most of the day and you at your busiest in the evening, it doesn't give us much chance to drop in on each other just when the spirit moves."

"I know," said Bill, and he rubbed his fingers

through his hair as he contemplated this unpleasant truth. He looked so comical with his fair hair ruffled up at the back that Rosabel laughed and reaching out a hand, smoothed his hair down again. Before she could withdraw her hand, Bill had taken it into a hard clasp, then lifted it to his cheek. He held it there for a moment before pressing a kiss into the palm. He smiled down into her eyes as he said quietly, "You know it would solve matters all round if you were to move in here. How about it?"

More to postpone giving an answer than to appear coy Rosabel asked, "Now how am I to take that suggestion? Do you want a hot and cold running chambermaid, a receptionist, another cook, or are you thinking of opening a first aid post up here?"

Bill squeezed her fingers before he allowed her to remove her hand from his clasp.

"You know very well what I mean, Rosie, so come off it," and strolling over to the desk he topped up his sherry glass. As he put down the bottle he turned to face her. "Don't you think it's about time we settled things definitely? The season starts to get quiet here at the end of September, as you know. What about an autumn honeymoon? It will be lovely abroad in October and there won't be half so many people holidaying."

This was coming to grips with a vengeance. Rosabel felt too tired after her long day to argue. On the other hand, she didn't want an acceptance to be taken for granted by this man for whom she felt only a very warm affection. Somehow she didn't feel as if she were ready to marry and settle down, though why she felt this way she couldn't explain even to herself.

But if she did agree now it would be so final. Bill would without doubt insist on slipping a ring on to her engagement finger and making it official. Already a great many of their friends took it for granted that it was only a matter of time before they named the day. She and Bill had been seeing each other on and off ever since she returned to live with Peter to take over the district and now, more often than not, they were asked out to parties as a couple.

However, until a proper announcement of their engagement was made, Rosabel still felt she had a way of escape. Why couldn't she make up her mind? Bill was still waiting for her answer. "Must I decide definitely tonight?" she asked. There was a moment's silence as he looked into her eyes.

"Still doubtful, are you, Rosie? Or just afraid of committing yourself?" She put her glass down carefully and fumbled for words.

"No, it's not that, Bill. Oh, don't let's talk about it any more tonight, I just don't feel like it. Let me think it over at home, alone, and then next time we meet I honestly will give you a straight answer, I promise."

Bill came over and slipped his arms round her. "Don't take too long making up your mind, Rosie. Something tells me to pin you down while I can and I'd like to face the busy part of the season with it all fixed. It would be nice to know that at the end of the summer I could relax, get married quietly and then both of us go off on an extended honeymoon. I've always known you weren't deliriously in love with me, but I thought you liked me well enough to say 'yes.' I'll be good to you, I promise, and I won't let Jean interfere if that's bothering you."

Rosabel put her hands on to his shoulders and looked up into his face. "No, it's not that. I wasn't thinking about either of your sisters. I really like them both very much indeed. It's just that I'm not sure of myself, and I would like a few days to think it over if you don't mind."

Bill kissed her gently on the lips. "All right, honey. I understand. I..." What he was about to say she didn't discover because at that moment there was a gentle knock on the door and his younger sister, Kate, put her head into the room.

"Hello, Rosie," she said, "glad to see you. I just

came to say it's all clear now and you two can have dinner any time you like.''

Bill turned and picking up his glass, drained it. As he set it down again he said, "Come on then. We might as well see what Jean's got left for us," and he ushered Rosabel out of the room and along to the dining-room.

As Kate had said, the dining-room had nearly emptied. There only remainend one couple, just finishing their main course, and at the long table which had obviously been laid for the golfing party, two men were still conversing quietly.

As Rosabel sat down at the table in the window which Kate had prepared for them, the pungent aroma of a good cigar floated across to her. She smiled to herself as she glanced across at the two men sitting having a second pot of coffee and with two brandy glasses by their right hands. They had obviously done themselves very well.

Rosabel suddenly noticed that the table she and Bill were occupying was only laid for two people. "Aren't Kate and Jean coming to join us then?" she was asking just as Kate arrived bringing their soup. She obviously heard the remark because as she put the plates down she said, "I hope you won't think us very rude, Rosie, but Jean and I like to see that everyone has finished before we sit down, then we load the dishwasher before we come in here for our own meal. You'd be surprised how much time it saves."

Bill had been correct in his assessment of Jean's prowess this evening in the kitchen. She seemed to have excelled herself on behalf of the special week-end guests because the meal commenced with game soup, served with tiny croutons. It was tasty and served very hot, just as Rosabel liked it. It was followed by sole poached in white wine and accompanied by its own sauce. The main dish consisted of fillet steaks liberally decorated with button mushrooms, winter broccoli, asparagus tips, creamed spinach and tiny alumette potatoes. By the time Kate had wheeled the big dessert trolly towards them, Rosabel thought that, delicious though the sweets looked, it was almost sacrilege to spoil the savoury meal which had gone before with anything other than at most, a small cup of coffee, and she smiled as she shook her head and declined the wide variety of desserts offered to her. Bill too refused anything more and taking out his cigarette case, offered it across the table.

When the coffee arrived, Kate had brought a small glass of liqueur for each of them and winked mischievously at Rosabel as she put them on the table and walked away to clear the remaining tables.

Bill picked up his glass and holding it to his nose, sniffed at the contents. He smiled across the table. "I hope you'll like this. It's some of a special brand a friend brought us back from France. I expect Kate thought we'd like to finish up in style."

Rosabel picked up her own glass and sipped appreciatively. It tasted very good and burned as it went down her throat. The delicious meal had done much to mellow her mood and she smiled across at Bill, all her affection for him in her eyes, wishing for the thousandth time since he had first suggested marriage that she could make up her mind whether she did wish theirs to be a permanent association or not. If she hadn't such a happy home with Peter and his daughters and Isa to look after them all—or maybe if she hadn't such an interesting and absorbing job, she might have been tempted to accept his proposal immediately. But in her heart of hearts she knew she was in no hurry to exchange her present existence unless she was completely sure of her ability to love Bill as much as he obviously loved her.

Marrying him would mean such a change in her life. She couldn't expect to continue district nursing. Bill would want her to take an interest in the hotel business, and as soon as she was proficient enough, an active part. She didn't know about Jean, but Kate certainly would not be there to help out for ever. She was much too attractive a girl. Rosabel didn't doubt that one of these days some man would sweep her off her feet and whisk her away from Bannford.

Soon after ten-thirty, Rosabel told Bill she would have to be getting home. He glanced at his watch and grimaced. "I hadn't realized the time had gone so quickly. It seems only minutes to me since you arrived. But I suppose you must get your beauty sleep and I've several things to attend to before the hotel settles down for the night, so perhaps we'd better say good night, Rosie," and they strolled back to his small office to collect her coat.

Before he'd let her get into the car, Bill pulled her into the shadows away from the glare cast by the lighted windows and kissed her long and lingeringly. All Rosabel's restlessness of mind returned as Bill's lips pressed hers and she gazed over his shoulder, realizing almost with a sense of disappointment in herself that her pulse had not hastened by as much as a second. Despite his obvious love for her and his expert caresses, Bill never seemed to make her temperature rise. Perhaps the fault lay in herself. Could she be one of those frigid females she had read about? No, that didn't seem likely. She had not spent her training years in one of Glasgow's biggest teaching hospitals without experiencing one or two occasions when a kiss had meant a weak feeling in her knees and the blood singing in her ears. Pretty student nurses are fair game, or so some of the medical students seemed to think, and when she had been eighteen Rosabel had quickly discovered that some of Matron's apparently over-strict rules had not been made without good reason.

As she drove the short distance home, Rosabel's mind was in a complete whirl. All she could concentrate on was reaching the refuge of her bedroom so that she could sit quietly and try and sort herself out. This was her usual custom if something bothered her.

But it wasn't at all in character for her to feel so indecisive about anything. When something big came up she was normally able to reach a decision without feeling anything more than that she must weigh the pros and cons carefully. Especially if it was something which might have a vital effect on her future—like when she had decided to take up district nursing instead of any of the other avenues open to her after she became state registered at the end of her nursing training. Admittedly, sometimes she had sought Peter's advice and on occasion she had gone to Isa for help, but never before had she had to determine her own mind in such a confused emotional state.

Driving through the gates and into the yard in her abstracted state of mind, Rosabel was startled nearly out of her wits to see the huge sliding doors of the coach-house suddenly begin to move as if by magic. She had been so deep in thought she hadn't noticed the shadowy figure standing to one side in the gloom, who at the approach of her headlights must have set the doors in motion. Rosabel had been subconsciously preparing to brake and get out to open the doors herself and the sight of the doors moving, as if without human aid, made her heart almost jump into her mouth with sheer fright.

Thrusting away the feeling of panic, she clung to her equilibrium as she realized that the figure must belong to the odd fellow at present occupying the room over the coach-house. Seeing the car drive in, he must have decided to help by opening the doors. Instead of which it had nearly frightened her out of her wits. As she drove into the coach-house and parked the Mini her feeling of fright was followed by a sudden spurt of anger, probably the result of realizing that her fear had been groundless.

She switched off lights and ignition and getting out slammed the door. As she walked towards the figure waiting, apparently, to close the doors again she burst into speech. "How dare you give me such a fright!" she demanded. "I suppose it never occurred to you how startled I would be to see the doors suddenly start to open when I wasn't expecting it. If you're intending to stay here for very much longer, I'd be obliged if you'd leave me to open and close the garage doors myself. I'm quite capable of it, I assure you!''

The hot, angry words dropped into a pool of silence. It gave Rosabel time to realize how abrupt they had sounded and she felt appalled at her gratuitous rudeness to someone who had, after all, only been trying to do her a good turn. In the darkness she could feel her face beginning to burn as she realized how her words must have sounded to the man to whom they had been directed. What made her feel even worse was that he made no attempt to speak and help her out.

She pulled herself together and standing very straight, looked in the direction of his face. In the darkness it was just a blur and she had no means of knowing what he was thinking, but even to a man like this she must make some apology for her illogical outburst. ''I shouldn't have said that,'' the words almost burst out of her. ''I do beg your pardon,'' and without waiting to hear if he accepted her apology or not, she walked off quickly in the direction of the house.

As she neared the house her pace slackened. There was a light in the kitchen and she didn't want to enter the house with her face still flushed with a mixture of anger and embarrassment. She knew neither her brother nor Isabel McCulloch would be curious enough to ask any awkward questions, but they might be surprised to see her coming in so obviously ruffled.

By the time she opened the kitchen door, Rosabel's colour had subsided somewhat. Isa was at the cooker making herself a hot drink before going to bed. She was wearing a night-dress covered by a pretty quilted dressing gown, and from curling tendrils of still half-damp hair, had obviously just been having a hot bath.

She glanced over her shoulder. ''Would you like some hot milk, dear? I'm just heating some.''

Rosabel put her handbag down on the kitchen table and pulling out a chair sat down. ''Don't think I'll bother, thanks, Isa. I had an enormous meal up at the hotel. I'd better not have anything else before I go to bed."

Mrs. McCulloch turned off the burner and poured the hot liquid into a mug. She glanced shrewdly at Rosabel.

"You're looking awfully tired, my dear, and not at all as if you'd just spent a pleasant evening. I suppose Jean wasn't in one of her awkward moods?"

Rosabel looked up and laughed rather ruefully.

"No. I only saw her for a short time—she was on the whole rather gracious tonight. I think everything in her little kingdom had gone so well she was feeling in a particularly good mood. No, she certainly didn't upset me. I think I must have a spot of late spring fever or something. Perhaps what I need is a good old-fashioned remedy like sulphur and treacle!"

"What you need is a good holiday," Isa remarked as she washed out the little saucepan. "Don't forget you've not really had one for over twelve months. I think we can discount your fortnight away last August."

Rosabel laughed again, even more ruefully than before. "Yes, wasn't it awful? Those poor children! They'd been so looking forward to their beach holiday too. I don't think I ever saw two such thorough doses of measles in all my experience Katya, when she finally came out in spots, had even more than poor Jennie, and that's saying something. Still, poor kids, they didn't do it on purpose and it was as bad for Peter as for me. It was just as much a busman's holiday for him too."

"Yes, I suppose it was, but it's you who looks in need of a good holiday now, my dear. What you need is something to take your mind off sick people. A fortnight nursing our two little monkeys when you should have been relaxing in the sunshine is catching up with you now. If I'd known what was going to happen I'd never have gone away and left you to it."

"Don't be silly," said Rosabel. "We had no way of guessing. Both the girls looked in perfect condition when we set off, remember—no signs of even a sniffle. They showed none of the usual pre-spot symptoms that normally occur. Even Peter was quite baffled to start with when Jennie started complaining of not feeling well. At least we were prepared for Kat, poor wee mite. She got it far worse than Jennie. Still, let's forget all about that. I'll have a really good holiday this year and make up for it."

But as she said good night at the top of the stairs, her remark about a good holiday brought back to mind Bill's suggestion of an autumn honeymoon. It seemed a long time to wait for a break from routine and maybe Isa was right. That was what she did need—just a break. But there was a big difference between a relaxing holiday of one's choice to relieve pressure of work and getting married and having a honeymoon as one's annual holiday.

Rosabel went into her bedroom and without putting on the light, went and stood at the window. Bill was a dear. She liked him more than any other man she had ever met. She'd probably be very content as his wife, but somehow she couldn't associate an ecstasy of feeling, a heart-stopping emotion when she let her thoughts dwell on Bill Johnston. She sighed as she began to get ready for bed. She had wanted to get here in the quiet to think things out, but honestly she felt too tired and bewildered at her own jumbled emotions to bother. When she finally fell asleep it was to dream endlessly, or so it seemed to her the next morning, of being dragged up the aisle by two nebulous beings to where a stern Bill stood waiting for her, his expression forbidding and his arms folded in scarcely concealed impatience.

She was quite glad when the hands of her clock pointed to eight-thirty and she could get up. Sunday morning was Rosabel's turn to get the early tea, and she had a quick wash and then padded downstairs in

dressing gown and slippers to get a tray ready and lay
the breakfast table while she waited for the kettle to
boil. Unless Peter had been called out, it was the one
morning when he and Isa could have a short lie in.

They both smiled sleepy greetings when Rosabel
took tea into their respective bedrooms. The girls were
already awake, sitting up reading and looking bright-
eyed and full of mischief. Katya gave Rosabel a quick
hug and kiss as she put the cups and saucers on the
bedside table between the twin beds.

"Half an hour, mind," Rosabel admonished them as
she went out with the empty tray. "No longer, or the
grapefruit will have gone cold." To the accompaniment
of merriment from her nieces in response to her
"sick" joke, Rosabel went along and got into her uniform. Sunday morning she usually gave an injection to
a diabetic patient whose companion went home for the
week-ends. It wouldn't hurt either to look in on Baby
Wylie, Rosabel thought as she quickly did her hair and
put a minimum of make-up on her face. Downstairs,
she put on the coffee, opened two tins of grapefruit and
sliced bread ready for toast. The others would be down
soon and Sunday's breakfast was always an uncooked
one.

When she eventually went out to get her car, she was
reminded afresh of her illogical outburst of temper the
night before. There was no sound from above, so the
man must still be sleeping.

Why was Peter letting him remain so long? It really
was mysterious. Though kind-hearted in the extreme,
her brother wasn't usually given to unaccountable
bursts of seemingly quixotic generosity such as he had
indulged on this occasion. And what had been the matter with the man, for that had never been explained.
Peter hadn't discussed Robert Carr's condition as he
frequently did when he had strange or untoward cases.
It had looked, in the brief glimpse she had had, either
to be a fit of drunkenness or merely a faint, and there
was nothing mysterious about either. Anyone could get

drunk and people fainted for all sorts of reasons, most of them simple. Odd that out of the variety of people who came to their door for help Peter should have chosen this one to do his good Samaritan act on.

She decided to call in on the Wylies before going to Miss Reekie's to give her the injection she required daily. She glanced at her watch. She mustn't be too long or there would be little time to change out of her uniform before joining the rest of her family for morning church. Peter liked them all to go together if he wasn't called out.

One glance round the door of the Wylies' cottage was enough to set Rosabel's mind at rest. Mrs. Wylie was waiting on her family just as if no addition had been made to it only a few days previously. The baby, already apparently acclimatized to a noisy environment, was sleeping peacefully in a corner of the kitchen, looking contented and the picture of health. Rosabel only stopped long enough to refuse Mrs. Wylie's repeated offers of a cup of tea before making her escape and driving on to her next call.

Miss Reekie was ready and waiting for her. She was a charming, elderly lady who eked out a modest annuity by doing illustrations for children's books. Rosabel had once voiced her liking for a drawing of a group of rabbits playing in a field. It now graced her bedroom wall, since Miss Reekie had insisted she keep it. Miss Mayhew, Miss Reekie's companion, had elderly parents living some twenty miles away and went home each week-end to see them. Rosabel had taught her how to give the injection so that Sunday was the only day she or her stand-in had to call. It also served the double purpose of making sure that Miss Reekie hadn't had an accident. She wasn't too steady on her feet, and was prone to lose her balance. One weekend, after Miss Mayhew's departure, she had fallen and lain for several hours unable to get up. A neighbour calling in with some eggs had fortunately found her and rung Peter Fairbairn.

The injection was soon given and Rosabel stopped only for a few more minutes. "Tell Isa I am expecting her this afternoon," Miss Reekie said as she was leaving. "She promised Winnie and me a new knitting pattern, so we're looking forward to trying it out."

Rosabel smiled to herself as she got into her car again and headed for home. Dear Isa, what would they all do without her? And not only the Fairbairn family but the whole village of Bannford itself.

When she got back she hurried into the house and upstairs to change for church. Mrs. McCulloch came out of her bedroom as Rosabel reached the upper landing. "Gosh, am I that late?" she asked.

"Well, it's almost twenty-five to, Rosie. Better hurry. And if you can get the girls to make haste too I'd be grateful," and with a twinkle in her eye she went downstairs, apparently to see that the roast went in before they left.

Rosabel put her head round the door of her nieces' room and told them the time. "Race you, Rosie," Katya said as she disappeared. But when she entered her own bedroom and looked through the window, Rosabel was a moment or two before she began getting out of her uniform. Her room looked over the garden and in the middle of the lawn she could see the wheelbarrow, half full of grass clippings. Strolling slowly behind the motor mower was the man her brother had taken in. He was walking slowly behind the mower, almost indolently, merely guiding it up and down the long lawn. He had an ancient felt hat on the back of his head, and the sleeves of his checked shirt were rolled above the elbows. Even from this distance, Rosabel could see his arms were brown and firmly muscled.

As she watched, her brother strolled into the garden. He was smoking a pipe and when he came up to the new "gardener" he took it out of his mouth and said something, apparently emphasizing the remarks because he pointed with the stem.

The man stood, a slight smile on his face and listened attentively. Rosabel would have given a great deal to be able to hear what was being said. She saw the man reply to whatever her brother had been saying and lean back on the handle of the mower, but further attention to the two in the garden was put at an end as Katya burst in.

"Beaten you—" she began, then stopped short as she realized that Rosabel was stll in her print dress. "Heavens, Rosie, you've hardly started. Come on! Daddy's ready, I know, I saw him getting the car out. What are you going to wear? I'll get it for you. Come on, hurry up!" While Katya took a blue linen suit and some shoes out of the wardrobe, Rosabel stripped off her frock and put on a pretty nylon blouse in a flowered pattern of blues, greens and soft yellows. Katya held the skirt ready for her to step into, zipped up the side and while Rosabel quickly combed her hair through again and retouched her make-up, she stood holding the jacket. "There's Dad blowing the horn. Got your gloves?" and without waiting for a reply, the little girl dashed out of the room and Rosabel could hear her jumping down the stairs two at a time.

She collected a clean handkerchief, put some coins for the collection into her side pocket, and picking up her gloves she ran out to catch up with her niece. Peter had the car at the gate, the others already in their places, and they all looked up as Rosabel let herself out of the front door and dashed down the front steps and got in. "Sorry to keep you," she gasped.

"I suppose the Wylies delayed you," Peter remarked as he set the car in motion. "Is the newest arrival doing all right?"

Rosabel laughed. "I think he's going to fit in famously. When I arrived this morning he was sleeping soundly in the kitchen while the others shouted and quarrelled over the breakfast table. Mrs. Wylie was making her usual clatter with the frying pan, and Mr. Wylie kept telling them all to 'shut up.' It was like bedlam!"

The little church which served their own village and the adjoining one of Rockspit was three-quarters full when they arrived. As they slipped into their pew, Rosabel noticed that the vicar's two sisters were already seated and she gave them a quick sideways smile before opening her prayer-book and finding the place. John McGill had only been with them for two years. He was a serious young man, a very good servant to his little flock, and much addicted to golfing when parish matters gave him an opportunity to get away, which wasn't often. As he came into the church to start the service, Rosabel gazed admiringly at his tall, well-made figure. He certainly was very handsome. Rosabel had seen quite a few of his female congregation gazing adoringly at him when they thought they were unobserved, not the least of them Kate Johnston. However, since he seemed to have no interest in women as a sex and treated them young and old with the same serious, old-fashioned courtesy, and as he had two sisters to look after his creature comforts and keep at bay any of the lady parishioners who might have contemplated making a nuisance of themselves, it seemed unlikely that there would ever be a Mrs. McGill.

Fiona and Penny McGill were standing talking to some of the congregation when the Fairbairn family came out into the warm sunshine. Penny was two years younger than Rosabel and worked for several of the surrounding farmers as secretary. She gave them each so many hours of her time per week keeping their accounts in apple pie order and the official forms they all had to fill in from time to time under control.

"How's everything?" Rosabel asked as she walked up to her. Penny smiled. She was a tall girl, fair like Rosabel, but her hair was ash-blonde where Rosie's was golden.

Her voice had an attractive husky note in it. "Fine. I've been meaning to come over. I want a spot of advice with some dressmaking I'm doing. Did I tell you I've suddenly become a sewing bee? Fiona wants me to try and make her one if this dress of mine is a success, but I thought Mrs. McCulloch might give me some tips. I've come to grief trying to fit the sleeves. They look awful.''

"Come tomorrow, then," Rosie told her, "after surgery. Isa doesn't like sewing on a Sunday or I'd ask you over this afternoon. Why not come in time for supper tomorrow? About seven-thirty if that suits.''

"Love to," Penny agreed. "Incidentally, who is the mystery man staying with you? The whole village is buzzing. I'd no idea you had a visitor until Fiona told me, and she only had it from one of the parish pussies. Is he nice?''

Rosabel's face lost its smile. "You'd better ask Peter," she replied abruptly, "not me. Anyway, he's only sleeping over the garage, you know, not actually staying with us as a visitor.''

Penny opened her mouth as if she was about to make another comment, then after a quick look at her friend's grim expression changed the subject. At that moment Kate Johnston strolled up to them.

"Hello, you two. What's going on? You look as if you're having a very serious discussion.''

Penny laughed, her tone rather obviously higher than usual as if not quite at her ease. "Only the difficulties of sewing, Kate. At least for beginners like me. I'm trying my hand at a bit of home dressmaking and not doing too brilliantly at the moment.''

"Jean used to do a lot of that before we got the hotel. Made all my things when I was in my teens. They were always perfect, but I'm afraid we rowed over styles. What I thought was mod and just me, Jean considered far too old.''

Rosabel smiled to herself. She could just imagine a younger Kate rebelling against elder sister's edicts on fashion especially when that person was one so sure of her own rightness as Jean Johnston always was.

The three girls began walking towards the gate. Rosabel could see her brother in conversation with Colonel

Brewer. He was an elderly widower who lived about three miles from Bannford and an old friend.

As Rosabel, Penny and Kate walked up, he raised his hat and smiled with old world gallantry. "Our three Graces, eh, Peter? This part of Scotland must have more than its fair share of beauty, judging by you girls. The young men hereabouts are lucky."

Lucky they might be, mused Rosabel, but there weren't so many eligible bachelors for them to be forming a queue for the favours of her friends and herself. In fact, in her opinion, there were far too many spinsters of marriageable age going begging in the district. Fiona McGill and Jean Johnston were not too old by any means yet to be considered on the shelf, and any man who got either of them would be sure of a household run on oiled wheels. Fiona, though a gentler character than Jean Johnston, ran the vicarage like a clock. No detail of parish life was ever ignored or neglected and though of course she wasn't able to do everything herself, she saw to it that when delegation was needed, only the most industrious and willing parishioners were pressed into service. The result since she and her brother had taken up residence in the Manse was an enormous increase in the congregations and not a whisper of disapproval or dissent ever to be heard in the district about the minister and his family.

CHAPTER THREE

By the time the Fairbairns arrived back at the house and Peter ran the car into the yard all sounds from the garden had ceased. When Rosabel went up to change into a cotton frock she noticed that the wheelbarrow was now full to overflowing with grass clippings. Pausing beside the window as she slid out of her skirt, she saw that two deck chairs had been put under the trees. The man was lying back in one, his old felt hat tipped over his eyes. In front of him stood the mower, together with a brush, oil can and a bundle of rags. Apparently he had been contemplating cleaning the machine when lassitude overcame him. Rosabel's lip curled as she turned away and took a cotton frock out of the wardrobe.

As she ran downstairs five minutes later, she took herself to task for her uncharitable attitude. After all, the man *had* cut the lawn, and as far as she knew without anyone asking him to do so. And it was an unusually hot day for this time of the year. He was entitled to rest after his labours if he wanted.

When she entered the kitchen it was to find Isa McCulloch basting a lovely, tasty-looking sirloin which she had just taken out of the oven. Potatoes were browning around it and pans on top of the stove were bubbling, showing that the vegetables were cooking nicely.

"Anything I can do, Isa?"

"Yes, I'd be awfully grateful if you'd lay the table, Rosabel. I hadn't time to do it before church. Colonel Brewer's coming along about one o'clock as well, so we'll be six for lunch. It's his housekeeper's week-end off, so I thought we'd better ask him over."

Rosabel put the cloth and mats on the dining table and returned to lay a tray with knives, forks and spoons. She had just gone to the cupboard to fetch side plates and glasses when her brother's head appeared round the kitchen door.

"Isa, do you think we've enough for one more to lunch?"

Mrs. McCulloch nodded. "Yes, of course." She looked a question.

"Then I'll ask Rob Carr to come in and join us," and before either Rosabel or his mother-in-law could make any comment he had withdrawn his head and disappeared again.

Rosabel raised her eyebrows as she looked across the kitchen. "My goodness! Peter has taken a shine to the fellow, hasn't he, Isa? I've never known him behave like this with anyone before. And it's not as if we know anything about him. He just appeared out of the blue and Peter's treating him like a bosom pal."

Isa turned away and began to count out dinner plates and put vegetable dishes to warm. For a moment Rosabel thought she wasn't going to comment and then Mrs. McCulloch said, "Well, he's really quite a nice man, you know, Rosabel."

"Yes, but…" Rosabel was beginning to put forward further objections to their additional guest when the door burst open and Peter's young daughters rushed in.

"Gran, is lunch ready yet? We're absolutely famished," Katya announced.

Mrs. McCulloch looked down and smiled. "You're always famished, Katya. You know very well it's not ready. You'll get your lunch on the dot of one o'clock, I promise you. In the meantime, if you can't hold out, what about a slice of bread and butter?"

"Gosh, yes—even an old crust would do," said Jennie, and Mrs. McCulloch laughed as she opened the pantry door and took out a loaf and the butter dish.

"Here you are. Cut yourselves a good thick slice and let's hear no more about being hungry."

The two children soon had the bread board on the table, and while Katya scrabbled in a drawer for the bread knife, Rosabel handed over a butter knife to Jennie.

"I expect you want to spread the butter an inch thick as usual. Don't get it all over yourself for heaven's sake. You're both so thin—where do you put it all? Got hollow legs?"

When Rosabel went to finish setting the dinner table, she could not resist a glance through the window. She could see a corner of the lawn sufficient to give her a glimpse of Peter and their visitor again deep in conversation. Peter was emphasizing his points with a wagging finger and the man was looking down as he listened, half smiling and nodding from time to time. As Rosabel watched she saw his lips move as he made some remark to her brother, and then turning away he picked up the brush and bundle of rags and began to clean the mower. Peter too turned away and began to walk in the direction of the kitchen door.

At five to one Colonel Brewer's car drove into the yard. He walked informally into the kitchen where Rosabel was dishing up vegetables, and Mrs. McCulloch was standing at the cooker, watching the gravy and putting last minute touches to her well-cooked lunch.

"Hum, smells nice in here. I wish my Mrs. Watson had your touch, Isa. I suppose I shouldn't complain, but somehow when she puts on a meal something always seems to be not quite right. Expect you've noticed it though when you've been over," he finished glumly.

"Well, I love cooking, Eric, and it has always come easy to me. Mrs. Watson leans more to the cleaning and polishing side of housekeeping, perhaps. Anyway I can't say I've noticed anything wrong when I've been over to have a meal with you, and the house is perfection. You must admit she keeps those antique pieces you're so proud of beautifully polished."

"Yes, I must say that for her," Eric Brewer admitted rather grudgingly, "but a man likes something rather special on his table occasionally, Isa, as I expect you well know. It smells like beef to me you're cooking. One of my favourites.''

Isa McCulloch smiled as she took off her apron. She and the Colonel had known each other for a great number of years and treated one another with little ceremony, though the Colonel, a stickler for good manners, never addressed her without his old-fashioned brand of courtesy.

He, Mrs. McCulloch, Peter and Rosabel were enjoying a pre-lunch sherry in the sunny living-room when the door burst open and Katya and Jenny propelled Robert Carver into the room. He had obviously done his best to tidy himself up for the family meal. His brown hair had been meticulously brushed, but was already beginning to curl again over his ears. His shirt-sleeves had been rolled down and buttoned and he had put on a tie, though Rosabel noticed that this did not hide apparent signs of wear on the collar. Still, she had to admit that at least the shirt was clean, and his voice as he acknowledged his introduction to Colonel Brewer was low and pleasant.

It gave her no clue to where he might have been born, though Rosabel suspected that he was not Scottish. He turned and smiled half quizzically as Peter said, "And of course you know my sister, Rosabel."

She half smiled in return, suddenly remembering their last meeting and her rudeness and subsequent apology. If he too was remembering, neither his expression nor his quiet words of greeting gave her any clue to what he must be thinking. She was glad when he turned away to accept the glass Peter was holding out to him. Rather to her surprise, she noticed that he was drinking not sherry, like the others, but a tomato juice.

The meal which followed was eaten without the feeling of unease around the table which she had anticipated. She had thought perhaps that the mixed company might have caused awkward silences while they all searched for a topic of conversation of general interest, but nothing deterred the little girls from chattering, not even a loaded plate set in front of them, and the three men soon discovered shared interests.

It wasn't until something was said about doctoring that the first embarrassing moment occurred. Peter looked across the table.

"You should talk to my sister about healing the sick. She has a pet theory about it."

Rosabel looked down, a blush beginning in her cheeks. She wished she had never voiced this particular notion of hers to her brother. Trust him to bring it up just at this moment! To try and change the subject she offered her nieces more vegetables, and her hand shook slightly as she spooned more potato on to Katya's plate.

But Peter wasn't to be put off, and she longed to hurl something hard at him as he continued, a twinkle in his eyes, "Look at her blushing! I know she doesn't want me to talk about it."

"What's this, Rosabel?" Eric Brewer cut in. "Come on now, tell us. Peter has whetted our curiosity."

"She'll not tell you," Peter answered for her. "I can see her looking daggers at me for mentioning it. But Rosie has always said that a bit of love does far more than all the treatments and medicines put together."

"Ah, a love cure," said Eric Brewer, nodding his head. "That's what you advocate, is it? What do you do, Rosabel? Cuddle them to death, or should I say 'to life'?"

At Rosabel's indignant flushed expression, the group around the table burst out laughing, with the exception of Robert Carver. Though he was smiling and obviously amused by the turn the conversation had taken, he certainly was not laughing outright at her unusual views.

As she glanced up, Rosabel subconsciously noticed that he hadn't joined in the general laughter at her discomfiture.

Peter wiped his eyes and said, "Sorry, old thing, but

your face is a picture. Don't get on your high horse now. I know when you do your rounds you're the soul of efficiency, but I've noticed you've cut out a lot of the starchiness, and people are pleased when I tell them I'm going to get you to call instead of being dismayed at having a nurse in their homes. I know some of the local people were quite frightened of the previous nurse because she used to lecture them on hygiene and ticked them off in no uncertain manner if they didn't carry out her directions to the letter. In a country practice, I must say I've found that if you let the little things slide that don't matter all that much, people do seem to get better much quicker. And those with no proper bathrooms do bless one for understanding their difficulties. There's usually some alternative one can suggest in case of sickness that they can understand and carry out. That's where Rosabel's idea comes into its own. She's got them all eating out of her hand around here. And she spread the happy notion that things should be done a certain way not because she's a nurse and I'm a doctor and we say so, but because little Johnny and old Grandpa are going to get better quicker, and by her methods they do frequently recover more rapidly. It's fantastic!''

"Not really," Mrs. McCulloch supported him. "What about that idea of Hitler's, to raise an Aryan race? When he bred his perfect children, took them away from their mothers at birth and raised them in special homes, half of them were backward mentally, and I'm sure it was just because they weren't loved or cuddled as they would have been, left in natural surroundings. Why, even animals know. Some people can't keep a cat for instance. Each new kitten they get wanders off and finds himself a new home where he'll get the attention he expects."

"Our cats never wander off, Gran," Katya piped up. "Why, when Cinders turned up, you shooshed and shooshed him away, saying one cat was quite enough, but he just wouldn't go."

"Yes, and I know why," Mrs. McCulloch said sadly, "because every time I put him out at the back door, you and Jennie nipped round and took him in at the front. And look at him now! As fat as butter and the laziest thing on four legs."

As if he knew his name, the enormous black and white cat lying in a patch of sunshine across the dining-room yawned and stretched. Thank goodness for a change of subject, Rosabel thought as she looked in his direction. Thanks to her brother's expansiveness, she had been the centre of attention for the last five minutes, and as she rose to clear and bring on the dessert she was glad to notice that more ordinary topics were once more being discussed round the table.

Bless Katya! She should have an ice-cream or an extra bar of chocolate this week for coming, however unwittingly, to her aunt's rescue.

As soon as coffee had been served, Rosabel vanished into the kitchen on the pretext that it was her turn to do the washing up. After a keenly shrewd glance in her direction, Isa McCulloch raised no objection, but settled herself more comfortably into an armchair, and poured herself a second cup of coffee.

Alone in the kitchen, Rosabel quite happily set about fitting all the used crockery into the big dishwasher. A glance out of the window assured her that the lawn now stood empty apart from the two deck chairs standing in solitary splendour at one end of the neatly shaven turf. When she had finished here it would be nice to go out and have a snooze in the sunshine, but she certainly wasn't going to risk meeting their rather odd guest. No, she'd collect the girls, if she could find them, and persuade them to go for a walk. They often went up the hill which stood behind the house. It was a nice walk over the top dropping down into the next village, and they could come back along the little coast track which wound along the side of the river.

Half an hour later the kitchen was back to normal, everything spick and span and in its place. Rosabel gave a last lingering wipe to the Formica top of the kitchen table and hung up the dishcloth.

Upstairs she discovered Jennie and Katya playing a game on the floor of their bedroom, but when she put her head round the door they both looked up.

"Do either of you feel like a walk?"

"Yes, I'd love to come," said Jennie, jumping up, and scattering the pieces of the Scrabble board.

Katya gave a yell of protest. "Oh, you mean thing! And I was winning too."

"Never mind!" Rosabel consoled her. "I'll have a game with you when we get back and you can beat me hollow. In the meantime, come on. Let's not waste this lovely afternoon."

Jennie was already putting on her shoes which she had discarded earlier, as Katya got slowly to her feet. "All right then, Rosie. I don't want to stay here on my own and it's quite obvious Jen's coming with you. How long before you go?"

Rosabel glanced at her watch. "Well, I just want to have a quick wash. Say in five minutes."

The three girls were soon climbing the hill which rose behind the house, and was known in the village as "Ben Bannford" since it really hadn't got a proper name of its own. When they reached the summit, a grassy plateau, dotted here and there with huge clumps of heather, they sat down on the one craggy stone sticking up in the middle.

From it they had a marvellous view. In front of them stretched the river winding down on its way to the Solway. To the right lay the village, and to the left Ben Bannford ran down in gentle slopes towards the next village.

Rockspit was much more a seaside and tourist place than Bannford would ever be. It had a caravan site, its big flourishing tourist hotel, not to mention a row of brightly coloured cabins which were let out to summer visitors. Rosabel, as she followed the girls down the track, could see that half of these had already been painted for the summer season. The blues, yellows and pinks stood out against the silvery sands.

By the time she reached the beach, both Katya and Jennie had their shoes and socks off and were dipping their feet in the sea, shrieking as the cold water crept over their toes.

"You're quite mad," Rosie said as she joined them. "It's always icy in May, and I don't think we've got so much as a handkerchief big enough to dry your feet when you come out."

"Never mind, Rosie, don't fuss," soothed Katya. "We can always run up and down until we're dry and then brush the sand off with our socks."

"Yes, and what's Gran going to say about that?" Rosie asked. "I'm sure she'll be pleased to have sandy socks in the washing machine tomorrow! Quite apart from anything else, I don't suppose it does the works any good."

But for all the notice the girls took she might not have spoken, and in any case, the damage was already done. Their feet and legs were well and truly wet.

She sat down on the sands and waited until they had finished their paddle. Ten minutes running up and down and playing with a small ball which Jennie produced from her pocket soon had them dry enough to put on their socks and shoes and start home. A glance at Rosie's watch had warned her that it was getting near to tea-time, and they wouldn't be at all popular if they weren't back in time to partake of Mrs. McCulloch's lavish Sunday afternoon tea.

They returned home by the river path. This was a small grassy track, just about wide enough to take a car. It wound from Rockspit along the river bank and back to Bannford itself. Although it would take car, it was an intrepid driver who attempted it, because the track itself was grassy and strewn with rocks and huge potholes. However, it made an excellent walk and saved the toil up Ben Bannford.

They were about half-way home when a solitary figure came into view. Katya at once let out a "Hullo" of welcome when she recognized the man. She rushed forward and got hold of his arm, gazing up into his face. Rosabel and Jennie were still too far away to hear what she was saying, but by the excited jumping up and down, they presumed that Katya was telling about the paddle they'd enjoyed half an hour before. Robert Carver was smiling down at her in an affectionate way, and Rosabel was surprised to see how it altered his face. In repose it had almost a monkish expression, but now, lit up by a brilliant smile, his eyes sparkling as he laughed at some particularly provocative remark of Katya's, it quite altered his appearance, and Rosabel was astonished to realize that some people might have considered him to be quite good-looking.

By the time she and Jennie had reached the other two, she had schooled her expression, and she smiled gently in a rather diffident manner as he said "Hullo" again.

"Aren't you coming back to have tea?" Katya demanded.

Robert had stopped as Rosabel and Jennie approached. "No, I think your gran did me very well giving me lunch today." He patted his abdomen. "I've rather overeaten, I'm afraid, so I'm walking it off. One of the boatmen said that this was a nice easy stroll to the next village, so I thought I'd walk round there. Might even have a paddle like you've had." And the corners of his eyes crinkled up as he made this last remark.

"I don't advise it unless you've got a towel," said Rosabel. "It's bitterly cold. Even the girls noticed it when they first went in. Solway has always been reputed to be one of the coldest stretches of water, and in May anyhow we don't expect it to be very warm anywhere round the British Isles."

"I agree," Robert nodded. "My days of swimming in British waters were over years ago. The Mediterranean for me every time."

Rosabel opened her eyes. He spoke so casually of swimming in the Mediterranean, it sounded as if he went there often. What would a tramp like him, and judging by the state of his garments, one with very little money, be doing in the Mediterranean? Still, he was one big mystery as far as she was concerned, and anyway, it was really none of her business.

Rosabel glanced at her watch. "Well, we shall be in trouble if we don't get back in time for tea, so I think we'll have to..." She stopped abruptly. She had just been going to say "We'll have to love you and leave you," when she realized how it would sound. She finished rather lamely, "Well, we'd better be going."

The man glanced at her across Katya's head. She was sure she saw a twinkle lurking deep in his eyes as if he had guessed the words on the tip of her tongue. As the girls also said "good-bye" and then raced ahead down the track, Rosabel was assailed again by a feeling of acute annoyance. Why did she always put her foot in it? Why did she always do or say something which ruffled her usual calmness when she was in proximity with this man? It wasn't that she really disliked him. She didn't know enough about him to dislike him. But ever since he had come so abruptly into their lives, she had seemed to jump from one awkward situation to another. It wasn't like her to be quite so gauche.

When they got back to the house, Mrs. McCulloch was in the kitchen buttering oatcakes and pancakes and getting out from the tins the various cakes which she always baked ready for each week-end. Peter was fast asleep on a deckchair in the garden, looking very peaceful indeed.

"Not often he gets a sleep like that," Rosabel remarked as she warmed the pot.

"No, it isn't," Mrs. McCulloch agreed. "I was glad to see him settle down there after Eric left. He was called out last night, as I suppose you know?"

"Yes," said Rosie. "What was it? Anything frightfully urgent? I forgot to ask him this morning."

"No! It was a false alarm. I don't mind when he has to get up for a baby, or someone who's had a serious attack, but I do think people ought to just wait for a while before they panic and ring for the doctor. It was old Mrs. Seddon again. She thought her husband had had a stroke."

"That's the third time she's done that," Rosie said. "How many shall I put in, Isa?"

Mrs. McCulloch glanced over, the subject of Mrs. Seddon obviously already forgotten.

"Oh, four spoonsful, I think. No, put in five, Peter likes it strong, and take in an extra jug of water, will you, Rosabel? Then I can water down the girls'."

Rosabel poured boiling water over the tea-leaves and put the teapot on the tray. As she carried it through to the living-room, she heard the girls chattering in the big cloakroom in the hall.

"Well, I don't care what you say, Jennie. I think he's absolutely *super*, and I'm awfully glad he came here."

"I didn't say I didn't like him," the second voice replied, "I just said that you're making yourself a fool over him, hanging on his arm and rushing across to speak to him every time he appears."

"Well, I can't help it if I've got a crush on him," said Katya. "He's the first really beautiful decent man who's ever taken any notice of me, and there's one thing about him, he doesn't talk down to me like everybody else seems to do. Even Rosie at times forgets and talks to us as if we were about three years old and stupid as well."

Rosabel smiled to herself as she put the tray down. She wasn't too grown up to remember how she had thought just the same thing herself about some of her older relations and particularly hated those who treated her as a little girl. There had been one aunt in particular who had persisted, even when she was in her late teens, in sending her presents much more suitable for a child of eight or nine. She must try in future never to talk down to Katya again, not even when she was feeling tired and a little exasperated at her sometimes importunate niece.

The next morning started badly. Peter had been called out at five a.m. to a confinement, and Rosabel, who had heard the telephone, and who had got up to make him a cup of tea, had accidentally turned off the alarm, and with the result that they were half an hour late getting up. Then Katya, who had a sewing lesson in the afternoon, found that she had mislaid the linen tablecloth that she was laboriously embroidering and a feverish search was made all over the house, before it was discovered under a pile of toys in the corner of her bedroom cupboard.

By the time the girls had left for school, and Isa and Rosabel had started to clear the breakfast table, they were both feeling rather exhausted. It didn't help when five minutes later the telephone went and it was the husband of Peter's receptionist to say that his wife had a heavy cold and wouldn't be able to come in and do the morning surgery.

Rosabel groaned when Isa came in and told her what had been said over the telephone. "Talk about troubles never coming singly, Isa! Never mind, I don't have to go out until ten o'clock, so if Peter's back in time to start surgery promptly, I'll be able to help him through it, I think."

But it was nearly ten-thirty before the crowded waiting room had emptied and Rosabel was able to get her own list and get out on her rounds. When she finally got back it was twenty past one. As she drove down the village street she suddenly remembered old Ben Munro at the village inn. He was the father of the licensee and a real character, being noted in the village for his temper. This was actually a reputation he no longer merited. Unable to move about very much, he now seemed to Rosabel no more than a rather pathetic old man unable to come to terms with his infirmities.

When she walked through the bar to get to the living

quarters, she noticed that Robert Carver was standing, a glass of amber liquid at his elbow, talking to two or three of the local fishermen. He nodded as she passed him to go behind the bar counter and up the stairs in the rear.

As she disappeared, Rosabel heard his voice behind her saying, "What about another round? My call, I think," and the licensee Tom Munro answered, "Right you are, sir. Coming up."

Rosabel's thoughts were mixed as she continued up the stairs to the sitting-room of the inn. So she had been right after all that first time. He *had* been drunk. It was quite evident from the casual ease with which he leaned on a bar and made friends with the regulars that he wasn't unfamiliar with the inside of a public house.

However, she dismissed thoughts of the man below as she knocked gently on the sitting-room door and went in. Old Mr. Munro greeted her as if he'd been waiting for a week for her to put in an appearance, instead of an hour.

"So you're here at last, nurse, are you? Think my old leg not good enough for your attention, I suppose?"

Rosabel half listened to his complaints as she undid her bag and got out the things she would need to do his dressing. The old man had been troubled for years with a varicose ulcer and he was often unable to walk. However, he flatly refused to go into hospital for treatment and possible surgery, so Peter and Rosabel between them had to do the best they could with more conservative methods.

When she got downstairs again, Robert Carver had gone. There was no sign of him as she drove along the village street and she wondered idly where he had got to. Driving into the yard she came upon him diligently washing her brother's car, and as she parked her small Mini beside the larger vehicle he glanced up and smiled in her direction.

"Did you want to put your car in the garage?" he

asked in his quiet way as Rosabel got out. "I can easily move if I'm in your way."

"No, it's all right," Rosabel answered. "As soon as I've had a spot of lunch I've got to go out again. I've only done half my list, I'm afraid."

He nodded, as he turned away to reach for the sponge in the bucket of water standing beside him. And then to Rosabel's surprise he put a hand on the wing of the car nearest to him and slid very gently to his knees and then full length on the ground.

She dropped her hat which she had taken off the moment before and was beside him in a flash. She loosened another button on the collar so that he had plenty of air, and then sitting him upright, she bent his head down between his splayed out legs.

He came to almost immediately, and opening his eyes, blinked at her. He put a hand up to the handle of the car door, and pulled himself to his feet.

"Sorry about that," he said abruptly.

Rosabel stood for a moment wondering what to do. She couldn't tell really whether he had lost his colour or not, because his skin was tanned an even brown. He seemed perfectly all right after that brief faint and she could only assume that he had over-indulged at lunchtime. Perhaps he hadn't bothered to have anything to eat.

She stood for a moment longer and then said, "Perhaps my brother ought to have a look at you."

"There's absolutely no need. I'm perfectly all right, thank you," and he turned away so definitely that she had no alternative but to walk slowly towards the house.

But Rosabel was too good a nurse to be put off so easily. When she reached the house she went into the surgery and stood for a moment in the middle of the room, deep in thought. Then she went towards the cabinet where her brother kept a supply of medicines and taking out the Alka-Seltzer, mixed a dose in a medicine glass.

When she got back to the yard, Robert Carver was apparently getting on with the cleaning of Peter's well used saloon, but as she walked towards him, she noticed that he was working just that little bit slower than before.

As soon as she was standing beside him, she held the glass under his nose. "I know you said you were perfectly all right," she began, "but I think you ought to have this."

He looked at her for a moment and then leaving the sponge on the roof of the car he reached out and took the glass, and glanced down into the contents which were still fizzing gently. When he looked back up at her, Rosabel could have sworn that she caught a glint of amusement deep in the grey eyes, but without a word he put the glass to his lips and tossed off the dose.

While he did this, she stood considering him. She couldn't possibly regard anyone who needed her professional attention in the light of an enemy. The fact that a few minutes earlier she had suddenly found herself giving him first aid had brought about a complete change in her attitude, almost like the turning of a switch. If her diagnosis were correct, and he was too weak to resist the impulse to drink more than was good for him, perhaps she might be able to teach him to avoid temptation and give up the habit. Even as the thought crossed her mind she recalled that generations of women had tried to woo countless men away from the bottle and had not succeeded.

When Rob held out the empty glass he smiled into her eyes, and though she was used to admiring glances, Rosabel felt her heart beat a little quicker. He could be a charmer, she thought, if he set his mind to it.

His mouth was still tilted in a half smile as he asked, "That isn't a crusading light I see in your eyes, is it?" And then as she didn't immediately reply continued, "Or is it just pity for the poor spineless derelict?"

Rosabel was quite taken aback. She had not realized that her thoughts had been so obviously mirrored in her eyes. She didn't believe in fibbing, but here a white lie would have to be told.

She shook her head and said, as if considering the matter, "I don't think it was either." She smiled ruefully. "But I did think perhaps I could help you in some way."

Robert Carver picked up the sponge again. "You're all helping me in your different ways. I was very fortunate to come to Bannford and meet your family." He set to on the car in a vigorous manner as he finished speaking and there was no doubting his dismissal this time. Rosabel stood in silence for perhaps half a minute and then, turning, walked quickly back to the house.

She was later than usual arriving home from her afternoon calls and she found that Penny McGill had already arrived. Peter had finished his surgery in good time, so as soon as Rosabel had washed her hands they were all able to sit down together to have supper. The babble round the table seemed deafening since the girls, with whom Penny was a firm favourite, took the opportunity to pelt her with questions about her job. They were both just at the age when they were beginning to dream of what they'd like to be when they were grown up. Kayta, the irresponsible tomboy, was still hooked on the apparently glamorous idea of becoming an air hostess, but Jennie, with her head not so far in the clouds, had more down-to-earth ideas. She was intrigued with Penny's unusual occupation, especially since Penny always had a fund of amusing stories about the farms she served. The farming community around Bannford always seemed to be able to produce some incident with which Penny would regale her young listeners.

Tonight's anecdote was about the prize sow getting out at one farm where she worked. It had taken the combined efforts of the entire farm staff, plus herself, to capture the recalcitrant animal. Penny's tale of how the sow had rushed her from behind, knocking her flat on her face in the muddy yard, raised shrieks of merriment from Rosabel's nieces.

"It's all very well for you to laugh," Penny said, trying hard to sound as if she didn't think it as funny as they did, "but you should have seen me when I finally got up. Having knocked me down, that wretched sow added insult to injury by running over my recumbent body and of course it pressed my face further into the mud and slush. I didn't think I'd ever get my face really clean again."

"I hope you sent them a bill for cleaning your things, Penny," Mrs. McCulloch said as the laughter died down.

Penny grinned. "Well, as a matter of fact, they're very good to me there, and in a way it was my own fault going out without putting on an old mac or something like that. I might have known that on a wet day I'd probably slip. Anyway, in a way it's been worth it. I've laughed about it so much since it happened that even the horror of my first glimpse of myself in a mirror afterwards didn't seem to matter."

As soon as supper was over, the youngsters were sent off to do their prep and Penny got out her material and laid it on the dining-room table.

"Oh, that *is* lovely!" Rosabel exclaimed involuntarily.

Certainly Penny had chosen wisely. It was a heavy synthetic material with a huge pattern of exotic flowers and leaves on a white ground. The colours themselves, burnt orange, lime green, black and several shades of mauve from Parma violet to purple, complimented Penny's particular brand of fairness and when she held the half-finished garment up to her face, Mrs. McCulloch, coming into the room at that moment, echoed Rosabel's remarks.

"My dear, it's just you. And I like that plain long style. Now what's going wrong you can't manage yourself?"

Rosabel sat down on the other side of the table and

watched as Isabel McCulloch's skillful fingers soon had the sleeves pinned in place and the neckline adjusted.

"Slip it on, my dear, then I can check to see if it hangs nicely."

It didn't take a minute for Penny to step out of her dress and into the evening dress, and only five more for Mrs. McCulloch to fit it to her satisfaction. She also complimented Penny on her dressmaking talents. "I wish Rosabel were as good. She and Katya make a pair when it comes to sewing."

Rosabel made a laughing grimace as she got up to help Penny off with the dress.

"We can't all be good at everything like you, Isa dear. Some of us have to be onlookers, you know," and as Penny offered grateful thanks for her help, Isa smiled at the two girls and hurried off to answer the telephone which could be heard ringing shrilly in the hall.

As she put her day dress on again and tidied her hair, Penny asked Rosabel who was taking her to the golf club dance this year.

"I suppose you'll be partnering Bill Johnston, will you?" she asked. "When's the wedding to be, Rosie, or shouldn't I inquire?"

Rosabel was silent for a moment or two before she answered. Then she looked up and asked a question herself. "Is everyone wondering the same thing, Penny?"

Her friend gazed frankly back at her. "Well, I have heard one or two people talk as if it's a foregone conclusion, but knowing you, I didn't agree with them. You haven't got that look of champagne bubbles and apple blossom about you, if you get my meaning. If you were really a hundred per cent in love that's how I think you'd look. No one would be in any doubt."

Rosabel blushed. "Transparent, am I? Well, Bill does want to marry me, and if I don't smell precisely of apple blossom, I am very, very fond of him, Penny. As a matter of fact," she went on with a sudden impulsive desire to confide in someone, "Bill has given me until tomorrow to make up my mind finally. He wants us to get married as soon as the season finishes in September."

"And you can't quite decide?" Penny asked. Rosabel shook her head. Penny turned away and began to fold up her pattern and material. "Well, my advice always is, if in doubt don't."

There was silence for a moment or two except for the rustle of paper as Penny wrapped up her things.

"I'm afraid it will hurt him so if I say no," Rosabel remarked, "I believe he thinks it as much a foregone conclusion as those other people you mentioned. The trouble is, perhaps that's my fault. I have gone out with him fairly regularly for some time now."

"What's that got to do with it?" Penny asked. "You never pretended to Bill that you were in love with him, I'll be bound, and if he likes to kid himself, I can't see you can blame yourself for that. No, I think you'll hurt him, and for that matter, yourself if you don't tell him now you don't want to marry him. For you don't, do you, Rosie? Honestly now?"

"Honestly, no," Rosabel admitted. "But I do feel very guilty about it all. I like Bill. He makes an attractive escort and I suppose some people would say I've just used him. I guess I was just thinking about myself and not even trying to look at it from his point of view. It was unspeakably selfish of me."

"Oh, stop blaming yourself," scolded Penny, throwing herself into an easy chair. "Bill's a big boy. He's been out with girls before. It probably suited him just as much as it did you to have an uncomplicated relationship all these months. He didn't suggest marriage earlier, I take it?"

"No," Rosabel answered. "It came up for the first time properly on Saturday night, though he has hinted once or twice that he'd like to settle down. I think the hotel and the responsibility of Jean and Kate has stopped him before."

"Yes, I'm not surprised," Penny commented frankly. "I quite like Kate, but Jean—ugh! Could you really contemplate having her as a sister-in-law? I couldn't."

"She's not bad, really she isn't, Penny. Not when you get to know her. And while we're playing truth and consequence like this, what about you and Ian Murray? *I've* been hearing rumours too."

Penny blushed and then laughed. "I deserved that! Yes, it's all true. Whatever you've heard, that is. He's taking me to the dance next week."

"Hence all the dressmaking?" Rosabel asked.

"Yes, somehow Ian's rather special, I want to do him proud at the dance. Do you like him, Rosabel?"

Rosabel nodded. "Yes, I've always liked him. I thought he was a bit spoiled when he was younger, but after that spell away from home at Agricultural College he seemed to have changed, and he certainly is no Momma's boy now."

They sauntered out to Penny's little car. It was just beginning to get dark and Rosabel glanced up at the light in the flat over the garage. As she put her key in the car door Penny nodded towards the flat. "Your mystery man still staying with you?"

Rosabel said, "There's nothing frightfully mysterious about him. He's somebody that Peter has been treating and he's stopping here for a little while. Apparently he's on a touring holiday and when Peter suggested that he might like to stop here for a bit, he accepted." Even as she said the words Rosabel wondered why she had dreamed up this rather distorted version of the truth. She didn't really know for sure that he was on a holiday, and certainly her brother was not formally treating him, although he had rendered first aid on the first day, and if, as she guessed, he really was an alcoholic, there wasn't a great deal that Peter could do, unless the man voluntarily agreed to go into hospital for treatment.

She turned the direction of Penny's thoughts from this particular subject by asking how Fiona was, and as her friend got into the car and closed the door Robert Carver was forgotten as they bade each other "Good night."

But when Rosabel finally got to bed it was to dream that she was getting married to Bill Johnston. Though she tried to run away from the top of the church, lead weights seemed fastened to her feet and she felt as if she were tied to the ground. She woke up still trying to struggle away from him, and sat upright in bed. It was very dark so she switched on the bedside light. Her small clock said three a.m.

Rosabel rubbed her hand over her hair and lay back again, gazing thoughtfully at the opposite wall. It wasn't like her to dream, and certainly not so vividly that she remembered every detail when she awoke. Perhaps it was an omen, or maybe just a subconscious reaction to the conversation she had had with Penny earlier. In any case it didn't look as if she really wanted to marry Bill.

She lay for ten minutes or more trying to sort out her ideas, and then realizing that sleep was far away, she got out of bed and putting on a dressing-gown padded quietly downstairs. A cup of tea and a biscuit would probably send her off to sleep again.

She had just made the tea and was waiting for it to brew when the telephone began to ring in the hall. Quickly she sped through and lifted the receiver. As Rosabel had feared it was a call for her brother, so taking down the name and address she went back to the kitchen and pouring out a cup of tea she went quietly upstairs.

Peter sighed as he sat up. "I was expecting this," he said when Rosabel gave him the message. "What are you doing up at this time, Rosie?"

"Couldn't sleep, so I decided to make myself a cup of tea," she said briefly as she left the room.

Downstairs again, she had just poured herself a cup of tea and was going to the pantry to get out the biscuit box when glancing through the window she realized that there was a light in the room over the garage. Someone else couldn't sleep either.

When her brother came down, she went to the back door with him and watched as he got the car out and drove away. The light was still on and after looking at it thoughtfully for a few minutes, she went back into the kitchen and took a mug from the cupboard. Filling it with tea and taking a couple of biscuits in her hand, Rosabel went out of the back door and across the yard.

As she mounted the wooden staircase to the flat door she wondered at herself. What on earth was she doing? However, having come this far, it was silly to turn back, and she knocked gently on the door.

Immediately a deep voice said "Come in" and turning the handle she pushed the door open and stood on the threshold. Robert Carver was sitting propped up in bed, his hair ruffled.

"I saw your light on and as I was making a cup of tea for Peter I thought you might like one," she told him.

A look of surprise appeared in his eyes for a second, then vanished. "Thanks very much, it would be most welcome."

Conversation died for a second as she crossed the room and put the mug and the biscuits down on the table beside the bed. His eyes followed her every movement and she was beginning to feel conscious of her long night-dress and the thin dressing-gown covering it.

She started to speak rather rapidly. "Well, I'd better get back to bed myself, otherwise I shall be fit for nothing in the morning. I'm afraid broken nights don't agree with me. Never was much good on night duty."

He didn't answer until she was back at the door, and then at his brief, "Well, many thanks for the tea. Good night!" she turned to look at him.

A suspicion of amusement in his voice had brought her head round in a flash. But when she looked at his face it appeared quite devoid of merriment. His mouth was serious and if his eyes held a gleam of mischief she couldn't see it from this distance. But there'd been no denying the amusement in his voice during that last short sentence; she hadn't imagined that. Was he making fun of her? Did he think her ridiculous running after him with drinks? Yesterday an Alka-Seltzer and tonight a cup of tea! She'd have to control her impulsive gestures or he would be getting the wrong ideas.

When she got back to bed it was still some time before she dropped off. She kept turning over in her mind tactful ways of telling Bill of her decision. But although she thought of several different ways of approaching the subject, none of them seemed satisfactory, and she finally decided she would have to wait for the next evening and play it off the cuff.

It turned out even worse than she'd anticipated. Bill picked her up about half past seven and they drove into Dumfries for dinner. For the first half of the evening everything was as usual. Although Rosabel was feeling tense and nervous she managed to put on a façade of gay amusement and chatted on as if it was just like every other meal they had shared in the past months. If Bill was a little quieter than usual it wasn't very apparent. He laughed just as gaily at some of her nonsensical stories about patients.

It wasn't until coffee had been served and he had ordered a liqueur for Rosabel that he turned to the subject that had probably been uppermost in both their minds for the entire evening. He looked at her across the table and said quietly, "Have you come to a decision, Roz, for I would like to know?"

Everything that Rosabel had thought of to say flew out of her mind. She looked across at him. Bill was such a nice man and she was really so very fond of him, but an inner voice told her not to be stupid, not to let her soft heart run away with her common sense. It was no good just being fond of someone when one had to decide whether one was going to spend the next fifty years with them, looking over the toast and marmalade at them every morning and sharing all the ups and downs of married life.

She cleared her throat. "Bill, I'm sorry." She didn't get any further.

He leaned across and patted her hand.

"Don't say any more. Only why, Rosabel, why? I thought everything was settled, it was just a case of getting you to name the day."

Rosabel could feel the colour coming up her neck and cheeks. She gazed down into the coffee cup and stirred it absently. "I can't explain Bill. But oh, I'm sorry! I feel I've not been fair to you."

"Oh, nonsense, I'm not going to have that sort of remark. Of course you've been fair to me. It was just that I thought you were as fond of me as I was of you."

"Yes, I thought so myself," Rosabel faltered. "But I'm not fond enough of you, Bill, to want to get married to you. Do you understand the difference?"

Bill looked silently at her and his soft brown eyes held the sort of look which made Rosabel's heart almost stop with compunction. The sort of look one sees sometimes in the eyes of a faithful dog who doesn't understand why he's being punished for something.

Poor Bill! If only she'd had the sense to see where things were leading some weeks ago instead of just going on as she had done. Taking his company for granted and not realizing that both he and everybody else for that matter were taking it as a foregone conclusion that she and Bill were serious about one another. She knew what would happen when the news got out. She would be dubbed as "heartless" or "frivolous" or "flirtatious" by every old tabby in the district, and the worst part about it was that in a way she realized that she deserved it. Whatever Bill might say to the contrary she hadn't been fair to him.

Next day was her half-day, but owing to a muddled address, it was nearly four o'clock before Rosabel arrived home. Peter was out on his rounds, the girls were still at school and Isa had gone out to have tea with an old friend. The house was quiet apart from the sounds from behind the surgery door where the receptionist was getting on with her work.

Rosabel went wearily upstairs to change out of her uniform. A bit of fresh air might do her good. She seemed to have been cooped up in houses all morning and the ring of complaining voices, even if they were genuine complaints, would ring less loudly in her ears, she felt, if she were to go for a brisk tramp up the hill behind the house.

She got into a shirt and a pair of old jeans, found a thick sweater, put on a pair of comfortable old walking shoes and set out. When she was on top of the small hill which overlooked the estuary, she sat down and leaned her back against a convenient rock.

How peaceful it was up here! As far as she could see, she was the only person for miles around. The little fishing boats tied up below bobbed on the ebbing tide and when she turned her head she could see a line of rollers where the river Bann met the Solway.

The sun was shining a little fitfully as if rain was on the way, but at the moment all was quiet. The wind had dropped and the air was mild and balmy. Rosabel sat there hoping that her throbbing head would ease. Perhaps she should have had a cup of tea before she came out, but she hadn't felt like going to the trouble of making it. All she could think of was coming up here and having a little peace and quiet with time to think.

Not that thinking was going to do any good, she'd made her decision and intended to stick by it. She'd have to put up with any recriminations which were likely to come her way. She hadn't yet told Peter and Isa what had happened, but she didn't doubt that they would hear the news from other sources before many days had passed. She wondered vaguely what their reactions would be. Though neither had actually mentioned it to her, it was probable that they too expected her and Bill to make a match of it.

She was just beginning to think that perhaps she had

better get up and go back to the house when something made her turn her head. Coming up the path from the direction of the village was the man she knew as Robert Carr. He was strolling easily along, a pipe between his lips, and as he saw her he raised one hand in a brief greeting.

"Hello there! I saw you set out about three-quarters of an hour ago and I wondered if you were coming this way."

So he'd been following her, Rosabel thought. How odd!

"You looked a bit white as you passed the window, and I wondered if you were all right, but I see your colour's come back now. Having come to my rescue a couple of times, I thought it only right that I should help you in similar circumstances."

Rosabel's eyebrows shot up. "Good gracious me," she said, "we're beginning to be a mutual benefit society." Then she saw the funny side of it and burst out laughing.

"That's better," said Robert. "When I came up the path just now you were looking very solemn indeed. Got a headache?"

Rosabel was surprised again. "I have, as a matter of fact," she said. "It's supposed to be my half-day, but it was more like three-quarters before I was free to knock off. It's not like me to get a headache like this. I don't know what I can have been doing."

What a fibber I am, she thought, as she finished speaking. Of course I know what's given it to me.

He had strolled up to her by this time and crouched down in the heather at her side. "I could get rid of it for you if you like," he offered.

Rosabel tilted her head back and looked at him, surprised to see how near his face was to her own. "What do you mean?"

"Well, I'm quite handy at soothing headaches away if you're willing to try, especially one caused by over-work and tension."

If Rosabel was surprised before she was doubly surprised now. Without showing it, however, she asked, "What do you want me to do?"

"Well, if you just take this wool thing off."

She slipped it over her head. Robert crouched behind her and she felt his thumbs beginning to knead into the muscles at the base of her neck. She bent her head forward. Immediately a feeling of relief began to surge through her. Whatever the technique he was using it was certainly being successful. She could feel his thumbs moving up and down her neck and then up into the hairline. It was as if someone was taking a brush and sweeping the headache away.

A few minutes later he removed his hands. "That better?" he asked.

As she pulled the sweater back over her head Rosabel nodded. "I don't know how you managed it, but you seem to have magic in your fingers. I feel a lot better now."

"Good," he said as he sat down behind her, and then putting the pipe almost under her nose, "Mind if I smoke?"

"Not at all," Rosabel said. "Help yourself."

"Would you like a cigarette?" he asked.

"I don't," said Rosabel. "Thanks very much."

"Good," he remarked. "I don't like to see women smoking."

Rosabel's head jerked round. "You've got very decided ideas on what women should and shouldn't do?"

"Oh, very decided," he agreed, and then laughed as he saw the affronted expression on her face. "I hope you're not a feminist."

"Well, not a complete one," she admitted. "On the other hand I don't believe that men should rule the world. I think they should permit women to help more. It would be a better place if women had more say."

Robert Carver burst out laughing. "I can see that if you'd been born fifty years ago Mrs. Pankhurst would have had an ardent follower!"

Rosabel laughed in her turn. "Oh no, I don't think I'm the sort to chain myself to railings, however deeply I felt about a subject. I think I'd try and get my way by different methods from those. I'm not a militant."

"I don't suppose you are," he said, considering her. Rosabel could feel herself beginning to flush. He made no secret about the fact that he was looking her over and assessing her every feature and as the colour deepened still more in her face he laughed again and apologized.

"Sorry," he said. "It's one of my worst faults. I forget that people don't understand. I'm not meaning to embarrass you or anything, but I do like to scrutinize people and satisfy myself about what makes them tick."

"And are you ever disappointed in what you find?" Rosabel asked.

"Oh, frequently," he said, "but that's what human nature is all about, isn't it? Nobody's perfect. On the whole I find that most people's virtues greatly outnumber their vices. And it's such an absorbing subject. Look at you. You went out last night with your young man and you've got a nervous headache today, so either you're blaming yourself for having treated him badly or he's done something to upset you, and now you're sitting thrashing it all out."

Rosabel gasped with astonishment. "What are you talking about?"

"Oh, I know a lot about what goes on in Bannford," he interrupted her. "After a few days propped up in the bar of the Fisherman's Arms there's very little of any interest in Bannford and district I haven't heard discussed."

"Well," Rosabel said, standing up, "and they say it's only women who gossip!"

Robert Carver laughed again as he swung himself to his feet and stood in front of her. He put his hands on his hips and glanced down, then he took his pipe out of his mouth and said, "That's one of the biggest fallacies."

"What is?" asked Rosabel.

"That fact that only women gossip. Of course men gossip as well."

"You're the first man I ever heard admit it," she said as she turned to walk back. "I shall treasure the memory of the first man who actually had the honesty to stand up and say that they chit-chat just as much as most women do over the coffee cups. Of course, what you men drink when you get together tends to loosen the tongue more!"

"The claws are showing," he said as he caught her up. "That's one of your feminine failings. Sarcasm is never nice on a lady's lips."

Rosabel glanced round, determined to put him in his place, but the look of whimsical delight in his eyes mollified her and against her will she burst out laughing again. As she led the way down the narrow path she couldn't help thinking that she was certainly going home in a very different frame of mind from the one in which she had left it. Not only was her headache a memory of the past, but she was feeling much more cheerful altogether, and for the last fifteen minutes she had completely forgotten the problem of Bill.

CHAPTER FOUR

FOR ONCE the village grapevine must have been a bit slow catching up with her news, Rosabel discovered. A few days later when they were having supper, her brother suddenly exclaimed, "By Jove, I'd forgotten! It's the golf club dance in a few days, isn't it? I'd better get some tickets or I shall discover that they've run out. You'll be going with Bill as usual, I take it, Rosabel? Don't need to pick up tickets for you."

At the sudden silence he looked across at her. "Well, as a matter of fact," Rosabel answered, "no, I shan't be going with Bill. I thought I'd come as your partner this year, Peter, if you don't mind."

Peter opened his mouth, and then encountering a speaking look from his mother-in-law at the other end of the table, closed his lips. He went on with his meal in silence for a few minutes and then he said, "Well, you can come with us by all means, Rosabel, you know you'd be very welcome, but I'm afraid you'll be the odd man out. John and Fiona McGill are coming with us and I understand young Ian Murray is squiring Penny."

"What about Colonel Brewer?" Rosabel asked, glancing at Mrs. McCulloch.

"Not coming this year," Isa answered. "He's gone off on a fishing holiday and won't be back until after the dance."

"Oh, I see," Rosabel said slowly. "Well, in that case, perhaps I'll give it a miss. I wouldn't want somebody to be sitting out on my account. Odd numbers are so uncomfortable."

"I'll tell you what we can do," Peter said suddenly.

"We'll ask Robert Carr to make up the party. I'm sure he'd be only too pleased."

Rosabel looked down the table, completely astounded. "Robert Carr at a dance?"

"Why not?" Peter asked.

There seemed no answer to that. At least no answer that one could make without sounding completely impolite, but somehow Rosabel couldn't connect the informally dressed Robert Carr with an occasion when the men would have to turn up in dinner jackets at least. The golf club had always prided itself on maintaining a strict degree of formality and although ladies were permitted to come in short dresses, gentlemen were not admitted in a lounge suit. There had been many attempts to get this rule changed, but the diehards had stuck fast, and Rosabel had to admit to herself that it did look rather nice with all the men dressed in either black and white or highland evening dress. It seemed to set off the ladies' dresses better.

Rosabel didn't know whether her brother was deliberately keeping her on tenterhooks or not, but for two days he never once mentioned the dance. The following morning, however, as she was crossing the yard to get her car, she came upon Robert Carver sitting on the bottom two steps of the wooden staircase overhauling the motor mower. He glanced up as she passed him and said "Good morning," and as she attempted to open the garage door he got up and walked across to help her slide open the heavy door.

"I hear we're going to the village hop together on Saturday," he remarked.

Rosabel looked up in astonishment. If that was his attitude, he certainly wasn't going to fit in!

"I wouldn't exactly call it a village hop," she said, and was annoyed at the tone of her voice. She sounded very prim, almost governessy. The light was dancing in his eyes again, she noticed, as she glanced upwards, and she flushed with annoyance. Why was it that he always seemed to catch her out like this? She wasn't usually stiff, formal and "square"—one could only describe it as that, and yet he always seemed to put her on the defensive, take away her poise and make her behave foolishly.

Usually she had no difficulty in making conversation. She had always found it perfectly easy to talk to the medical students and even the young housemen, although they were often on their dignity as soon as they were able to put "Dr." before their names. They seemed to change almost overnight from irresponsible schoolboys to responsible men of the world and Rosabel had early discovered that one had to tread rather carefully once the final exams had been passed and that first celebration was over. Some of them became unspeakably touchy if they weren't addressed by their correct title.

But she had never before felt that she had to watch every word she spoke, as she did with this man. Why, oh, why couldn't she be natural and at her ease with him? Perhaps it was because deep in his eyes she saw an imp of mockery and felt he was listening to her every word and weighing her every reaction. Her brother, she knew, would have called it conceit. She felt sure that it wasn't imagination on her part. Robert took an inordinate pleasure in teasing her, perhaps because he sensed that she longed to reform him and get him back on to the straight and narrow.

Rosabel was suddenly astounded to realize that she had no idea what this man did. As far as she could see, he just lived an aimless life, but he must have some occupation. He didn't seem to be completely without means, so either he must work at something or he must have a private income.

She looked back at him, new thoughts chasing themselves through her mind, and as if he sensed exactly where her thoughts were leading, he laughed suddenly.

"I suppose you imagine that I couldn't possibly turn up at a formal dance—well, not suitably attired, that is." As it had been precisely what Rosabel had been thinking she blushed and was more annoyed with herself than ever.

Robert watched the delicate rose run up her cheeks. "Guilty, as charged?" he asked. Rosabel turned away, more embarrassed than she had ever been in her life, and opening the door of her Mini, slung her bag down on to the passenger seat. She wondered whether she should deny the accusation, but she had never been a good liar and would sound quite unconvincing.

She turned back bravely to face him. "I'm sorry," she said. "Do I sound astoundingly rude to you? If I do, I must apologize."

Robert looked quite taken aback. Whatever he had expected her to say it was obviously not that.

"It's I who should apologize to you for teasing. Quite honestly you rise to the bait so beautifully every time that I can't resist it. I do beg your pardon. I shall be delighted if you will honour me by coming to the dance on Saturday. Will you?"

There was nothing else to do but to accept gracefully and Rosabel found herself saying, "Thank you, I'd like to go very much."

As she drove off down the road to her first case, she was trying to go over the conversation word by word. It suddenly dawned on her that this man, during the short time in which he had been in Bannford, had made a bigger impression on her than had Bill in all the months she had been going out with him. Although she knew nothing about Robert she couldn't help feeling a curious fascination whenever he came near her. It wasn't that he was outstandingly handsome, he didn't try and impress her with brilliant conversation, the only thing that she could think of was that she had never in her life met anyone quite like him before.

When she got to her first case she was very silent as she re-did the dressing on old Granny McWither's hand. The old lady had burned it last week trying to make a cup of tea while her daughter-in-law was out of the house, a thing which she was long past capable of doing. She wasn't a bit pleased to find that Nurse was quieter than usual and only replied to her curiosity by simple "Yeses" or "Noes." Usually she was good for a gossip and the old lady's bright eyes watched her as she replaced the bandage with a new one.

"You're very quiet this morning, me dear," she said finally, and Rosabel woke up to the fact that she was letting her private thoughts come between her and the business of the day. She took herself sharply to task and by the time that she left had talked the old lady back to her usual good humour.

When she reached home that evening she got out the only two evening dresses she possessed. One was a full-length dress which she had bought for a hospital dance at her old training hospital two years ago. The other was a short dress which she had only acquired last year.

She held them up in front of her and wondered which she ought to wear. The long dress was very pretty. It was a striped black and white nylon organdie, perfectly plain, with a shirtwaister top, the neckline exaggerated with a huge white collar. It was sleeveless and the skirt, which was fairly full, flowered down softly about her feet. The other dress was much more eye-catching. It finished three or four inches above Rosabel's knee and exposed her slim legs.

She couldn't make up her mind which she ought to wear. She had hung them up on the back of the wardrobe door just as her two nieces came into the room.

"Oh, are you deciding what you're going to wear on Saturday?" Katya cried immediately, and pranced up to the wardrobe. "Well, I like you in both, Rosie. Which are you going to have, the short or the long?"

Rosabel went over to the dressing-table and started to re-do her face ready for supper. "I can't make up my mind," she said. "Most people go in long dresses these days. Penny's going to. I expect you saw the one she was making?"

"Yes, it's absolutely super, I love that material," said

Jennie. "I wish Gran would make me a dress in it, but she said it's too old for me yet."

"The pattern's a bit big for somebody your age," Rosabel admitted. "But it is pretty just the same, I do agree. Which do *you* think I should wear, Jennie?"

Her older niece stood with her head on one side and looked at the two dresses. "Well, the short one's lovely, absolutely gorgeous," she said. "I thought you looked very nice when you wore that last time, Rosabel, but really for a dance this skirt is the one," and she fingered the black and white material lovingly. "I can just imagine it floating out when you waltz," she added.

"You and your romantic dreams of waltzes! Ever since you saw that film on television about two months ago you've thought of nothing else," Katya said scornfully.

"Well," protested Jennie, "you must admit you liked it too."

"I might have done, but I'm not going all gooey over it like you are. Just because that Grand Duchess married him in the end and the picture finished with them waltzing together gazing dreamily at each other, you've thought of nothing else except having a long dress yourself."

"Oh, I never thought of anything of the sort!" shouted Jennie, turning on her sister in anger.

"Now, now, girls, I quite agree with you. It's very romantic wearing a long dress. I think I'll probably wear that one in the end, but I haven't quite made up my mind yet. I'll probably leave it until Saturday to do that."

When Saturday came, however, Rosabel still hadn't made up her mind, and as far as she could see her partner hadn't made up his mind either about his clothes. He still lounged about the garden whenever she was home, although she had seen him cleaning Peter's car when she popped in for lunch on Friday morning, and her own Mini had appeared this morning immaculate and quite obviously polished, so he must have been up early. But she noticed no sign whatever of preparation for the dance. His hair was still rather overlong and unkempt, and when glancing through the bedroom window on Saturday morning she noticed him crossing the garden with a barrow-load of grass clippings, she wondered if he really intended to turn up for the dance at all.

But when she came in from the hairdressers later that afternoon, it was to find a florist's box with her name on it awaiting her on the table in the hall.

She undid the ribbons and opened the box. Inside on a bed of wet tissue paper lay a shoulder spray, intricately fashioned of white hyacinths and lilies of the valley. It was quite exquisite and would not be too heavy to pin on the shoulder of her dress. There was a card inside and when she picked it up she read in unfamiliar handwriting the words "I hope this will go with whichever dress you choose!"

Rosabel smiled. It was quite obvious that Jennie and Katya had been confiding in him. She took the spray upstairs with her and when she was ready she pinned it on to the dress—the shoulder of the black and white dress. Although she wouldn't admit it to herself, there had never really been any question in her own mind about which dress she was going to wear.

Jennie was quite right. The other dress was very pretty, very modern, very "with it," but it hadn't got the dreamy romance of this long flowing skirt. Somehow a long skirt did things for one, Rosabel thought, as she smoothed the soft folds. And her hair had come out just right this time, she thought, as she patted one wayward tendril back into place.

She put her powder compact, lipstick and a comb into her small evening bag, and picking up a stole, went downstairs. As she walked into the living-room she stopped almost in her tracks. Fiona and John McGill had already arrived and were sitting side by side on the settee. Isa was pouring out drinks, and her brother was leaning up against the mantelpiece talking to another man.

She knew who it must be, but she could hardly recognize him. The unruly hair had been diligently disciplined into place, the stark black and white of his suit showed up the deep tan of his face, and as he turned to the door laughter leapt into his eyes at the astounded expression which Rosabel was too late to hide.

Quickly she smiled as the others turned to greet her and by the time Robert had made his way to her side she was ready with a warm smile and a word of thanks for his flowers.

"I didn't know what colour you'd be wearing, so I played safe," he remarked, and Rosabel noted to herself that this couldn't have been the first time by a long way that he had bought a corsage for an evening guest. His manner was too assured by far, though the custom was not generally practised.

Certain men, of course, liked to give flowers. During her training one of her regular dates had bought her a nosegay every time they went out, however modest the entertainment. It had sometimes proved quite an embarrassment to sit through a film clutching not only her handbag and gloves but a bunch of damp violets, or whatever other flowers might be in season. She had been too soft-hearted to pretend to lose them in the dark, knowing how hurt he would have been.

Rosabel frowned as she realized that already Robert was drinking. His usual glass of amber liquid was bubbling on the mantelpiece, close to where he'd been standing when she came into the room. As Peter handed her a glass of sherry, Robert picked up his own glass and raised it in mock salute.

He guessed then that she considered he drank too much, and was being deliberately teasing. It wouldn't be very pleasant if his tiresomely tantalizing mood were to continue. And in additon she was going to have to face Bill for the first time since she had given him her refusal. He would certainly have to be present tonight if only in his capacity as owner of the hotel.

However, when they reached the hotel Rosabel

found her fears were without foundation. Bill was certainly there, but she could see that he was firmly ensconced behind the bar. A word with Kate, whom she met in the foyer, had ascertained that the barman had let them down at the last minute and that Bill was substituting and would do so, she presumed, for the whole evening.

Peter took his party straight in and to her relief Bill nodded casually across the top of the bar as if nothing had happened. Well, at least he wasn't going to sulk, she thought, not that she had ever seriously supposed he would. Bill wasn't the sulky sort, but she was relieved that he seemed to be taking her refusal in such good part. It showed what a nice person he was at heart.

Some of the youngsters were already dancing and Rosabel noticed Penny and Ian Murray talking animatedly together as they circled the floor. A very good quintet had been brought in for the evening, local boys whom Rosabel had danced to before. She knew that they were just as good at playing an old-time waltz or one of the old Scottish favourites as they were at the "twist" or the latest modern dance, and she looked forward to a thoroughly enjoyable evening.

John McGill, Isa, Fiona and Peter were already wending their way to the table at the other end of the room when Rosabel was startled as an arm encircled her waist and a voice said in her ear, "It's a pity to waste this jolly tune, I suggest we dance down to the table instead of walking." Before she could reply Rosabel was on the floor with the other couples.

She raised her head to glance at him and found that Rob's eyes were twinkling. "I don't suppose you expected that I *could* dance," he said.

"Now," Rosabel retorted, "suppose we call a truce for the night? I don't propose to spar with you all the evening."

"I'm very glad to hear it. You look too pretty to be so governessy."

Rosabel gasped with mingled astonishment and anger. "Oh, I'm not!"

"Oh yes, you are. Very often. And particularly where I'm concerned. I have a feeling that you thoroughly disapprove of me."

Rosabel felt hot with embarrassment; this was certainly coming to grips with a vengeance! She blushed as she looked up. "I'm sorry if I seem like that. I have no right to sit in judgment."

He looked taken aback at her sudden apology and then laughed. "Don't be silly," he said, and gave her a quick hug. He released her almost immediately so that for a second she wondered if she had imagined the quick pull towards him. He was holding her almost at arm's length again as they reached their table, so she could do no more than murmur a brief "Thank you. That was nice" as he pulled out a chair for her.

It was several partners later before he got up and asked her to dance again. The band was playing a lively tune and by the time they had danced not only the original number but two encores, Rosabel was feeling very warm. She was laughing as Robert twirled her to a standstill by the French windows. Someone had stood them wide open and the cool air coming in was very soothing after the heat of the room.

She gave a deep breath of pure exhilaration at the enjoyable exercise and then said impulsively, "Come on, let's go out and fill our lungs with fresh air," and grabbing Robert by the hand she pulled him over the threshold and out on to the grassy plateau which fronted the hotel of this, the river side.

They walked slowly over towards the parapet and leaning their elbows on it looked down. All they could see were the tops of the firs which crowded the hillside above the road. The zigzag path which led down from the hotel was quite concealed by the brave new shoots which had appeared on the Douglas pines during the past few weeks.

Across the river lights were twinkling in the houses

and Rosabel wondered dreamily what the people over there were doing. Some of them of course would be getting ready for bed. Country people didn't keep late hours, but she knew one or two, patients of hers, who would certainly be sitting up to see some special programme on TV. The next time she visited them they'd be telling her about it and asking her if she'd watched it too.

Away to her left, the moon was rising. It wasn't high enough yet to bathe the landscape in a silvery glow, but in another hour or less it would be well risen and by the time they left to drive home from the dance, she guessed that it would be in full moonlight.

Rosabel gave a sigh of pure gladness and then suddenly realized that since they came out, neither she nor Robert had spoken. They had leaned side by side, her bare arm brushing against his black one, and hadn't exchanged a single word. When she was with Bill she had always felt the need to talk. She had always had to tell him some story or ask his opinion about something. There had rarely, if ever, been companionable silences, and yet with this man, almost a complete stranger to her, she had spent at least five to ten minutes without feeling the slightest need to make conversation.

She glanced sideways sharply to find that he was watching her. Even in this dim light she could see the whimsical smile curling up one corner of his mouth.

"Do you know at times you have the most interesting face?"

"That wasn't what you were going to say," Rosabel interrupted him. "Funny face, more likely."

"Let me continue," he reprimanded mildly. "Interesting face, I said. During the last few minutes all sorts of expressions have flitted across it as your thoughts changed. You looked across the river at the lights. I could imagine what you were thinking then. Next you looked to the left. I don't quite know what you were thinking then because I couldn't see your face for a minute, but when you turned back again you had a sort of inward bewilderment on it. Now what could have caused that, I wonder?''

Rosabel had no intention of telling him, so she quickly said, "You really are the most analytical person I've ever met! Do you have to try and find out what everybody's thinking and how everybody ticks?''

"Oh, always," Robert said. "People interest me, don't they interest you?''

"Well, of course they do," Rosabel answered. "People are my business, but they aren't yours.'' As the words left her lips she wondered why she had said them. She didn't really know whether they were his business or not because she knew so little about him. Why had she made such an unsubstantiated comment when she didn't really know what Robert did for a living?

She waited to see if he would proffer this information voluntarily, but he did no such thing. He didn't even challenge her statement that people were not his business. He continued to look at her, the whimsical smile still curling his lips as if she were under a microscope.

Now why had she thought that? But he did look at her sometimes as if she was pinned to a board like a specimen. Perhaps that was why he made her feel so gauche and why she lost her temper so often and flared up when she was in his vicinity. And who was she to grumble if he appeared to be studying her? Hadn't she been watching him, criticizing his drinking habits? Didn't she think that he ought not to visit the Fisherman's Arms quite as often as he did?

"*Now* what are you worrying about?" he asked. "Since I said I watched you because people interested me you've gone all prickly again. The truce seems to be over.''

Rosabel made herself relax. She laughed. "I'm sorry," she said, "and I'm sorry I have to keep apologizing to you. I don't know why it is, but you make me feel in the wrong all the time.''

Robert threw up his hands and pretended to get into a position of mock defence. "Now don't try and put all the blame on me, because that's what you're doing in a subtle womanish sort of way. You're apologizing in a backhanded manner."

Rosabel stood silently for a few minutes. "What do you want me to say, then? Just how do you want me to act."

"Oh, naturally, of course," he said, standing upright, "just be yourself. Don't be prickly. Don't be on the defensive and don't worry if I seem to be studying you. I can't help it, it's second nature, I suppose. As I said, people have always interested me and I've just got into a habit of watching their reactions. If it annoys you, you will have to forgive me. Now it's my turn to say I'm sorry."

Rosabel couldn't do anything else but laugh at this mollifying speech. Certainly if he had rubbed her up the wrong way a few minutes ago, he was doing his best to put her at her ease once more. She suddenly realized that they had been out here for quite some time. Oddly enough no one else had wandered out too in search of a breath of fresh air, and Rosabel suddenly realized that the reason why they had not done so was because supper was being served.

Through the open windows she could clearly hear the clatter of crockery. It would make their entry into the room very noticeable and she flushed in the darkness as she realized that unwittingly she had brought on herself a situation that wasn't going to be easy to carry off.

In a small place like Bannford, everybody was interested in everybody else to a certain extent. The mere fact that she'd come to the dance, not with Bill, but with a man who was more or less a stranger to the district, would cause enough comment. But the fact that she had spent between twenty minutes and half an hour outside with him in the darkness would certainly cause even more. Nothing would be said directly to her, of course, but she imagined what poor Isa would have to put up with for the next two or three days every time she met one of her patients.

Oh well, she thought, better get it over with, the sooner we go in the better, and she turned to Robert. "I think supper's under way. Peter will be wondering where we've got to."

He must have realized the implications of what she left unsaid and he chuckled. "Giving the tongues something to wag about tomorrow, are we?" he said.

Rosabel wondered whether to deny it or not and then realized that it would be quite useless. He wouldn't believe her anyway, so she nodded, "Yes, I'm afraid so. You know what it's like in a small place."

"Don't I just!" he agreed as he took her elbow and walked her over to the open door. "In my little world, nothing, absolutely nothing is sacred."

Rosabel longed to ask him where his little world was, but by this time they were inside the crowded room and as they joined the table where Penny McGill and Ian Murray were now sitting as well as the others, she realized that her opportunity was lost. Though she hated asking personal questions. Even if she'd had the opportunity she wouldn't have taken it. If Robert wanted her to know what he did, where he lived and who his relations were, no doubt he would tell her in due course.

She enjoyed the second half of the dance as much as she had enjoyed the first, though after a particularly energetic session of the Gay Gordons she had looked up to find Bill watching her from the doorway, an extremely sombre expression in his eyes, and the laughter had died out of her face as she turned away to walk back to the table. If Robert noticed the sudden quenching of her enjoyment he made no comment and merely offered her his cigarette case. When she shook her head he had lit one for himself and she felt sure he was watching her thoughtfully through the smoke.

CHAPTER FIVE

THE NEXT MORNING Rosabel was up at a quarter to eight. She had promised Nurse McClaren, who did the district next to her own and whose Sunday off it was, that she would go and see her two diabetics.

She was just getting into uniform when a muffled giggle from below the window made her glance outside. Katya and Jennie, dressed in jeans and thick sweaters, were standing astride their bicycles while Robert, an old cycle of Peter's propped up against the outside stair-case, was trying to pump air into the tires. The baskets on the front of the girls' bicycles contained their swimming things. This was obviously an early morning bathing party, and a pre-arranged one at that. Both girls knew they couldn't go swimming in the river without an adult in attendance and they must have had to ask permission from either Isa or their father.

As Rosabel let the curtain fall back into place she saw Robert lay down the pump, get on to the saddle and bounce up and down experimentally. The girls giggled more than ever, hands covering their mouths so as not to disturb the sleeping members of the household. Rosabel couldn't help a small smile touching the edge of her own lips. It really was very good of Robert to get up so early after a late night. Despite her prejudices she couldn't help feeling he must be a kind man at heart, and as she went down to make herself breakfast she realized that in the last twenty-four hours she had thought far more about the guest in their flat than she had about Bill, with whom she had been friendly for months.

Well, she certainly needed something else to think

about, but this would never do. She knew what the district would say. "Off with the old love and on with the new." Kind as most of the people were, they dearly loved a bit of gossip. And gossip was one thing that doctors and nurses had to try and avoid whenever possible.

Next morning the post arrived just as the girls were leaving for school. Isa collected her letters and with a word of apology got up from the table leaving Peter and Rosabel to go through their own mail.

Rosabel had a thick letter from an old friend who had trained with her and when she laid it down she was very thoughtful. Peter glanced up and caught the expression on her face.

"You're looking very serious this morning. Not bad news, is it?" he inquired as he gathered his own letters together preparatory to going in and starting surgery.

"Not really," Rosabel replied. "It's a letter from that old friend of mine. You remember, I trained with her—Joan Rivers. She's working in London now and she said that they're absolutely crying out for people to do intensive care nursing. She wonders if I'd be interested."

"But you're not, are you?" asked Peter.

"I don't know. I've been here some time now and perhaps it's time for me to be making a change. It might be the very thing."

Peter got to his feet. "Well, in my opinion you're just not the type."

Rosabel looked up. "What do you mean 'not the type?'"

"You know what this intensive care training means, don't you?" asked Peter.

"Well, of...."

"Just a minute and let me finish. It's very interesting work, agreed, and very necessary, but most of the patients *are* very seriously ill, the mortality rate is extremely high amongst them. Do you really think you're temperamentally suited to nursing people who have very little chance of survival? Your chief object in life is to make people well and feel cheerful, isn't it?"

Rosabel was silent for a second. "I suppose you're poking fun at my 'love cure' theory?"

"No, I'm not, you know that I heartily concur. But to instil into a patient the will to live is the biggest thing, the greatest thing, in getting people well. It's stronger than any drug man ever invented. Patients who are admitted to intensive care units, very, very ill, as they usually are, are mostly beyond the point of no return. I don't feel you've got the temperament for it, Rosabel. You'd find that it would depress you, that sort of nursing, day after day."

"Well," Rosabel said, "you may be right, but I've come to the point when I feel I must make a move."

"Because of Bill, you mean?" Peter asked.

Rosabel looked up, startled; her brother certainly saw rather more than he let on.

"Not exactly," she said, "although that does come into it, but I think I'll have to consider Joan's suggestion very seriously. I can't stay here for ever, Peter, lovely though it's been to live with you and Isa and the girls. I think that I have to move on now to the next stage of nursing, even if it's not this but some other branch. Don't you agree?"

Peter walked towards the door. "I see your point, Rosabel," he agreed, "though I will say this. We shall just hate you to go, and it seems to me silly to fix anything up yet with the summer before you. Why not wait until the autumn before you make a change?"

"It might come to that," said Rosabel, "Joan says in her letter that the course starts every six months, so it will probably be towards winter time when the next one starts. I would have to find out about that, though, if I do decide to go in with her."

She thought about it on and off all the morning as she went her rounds and her brother's words were brought back to her during the afternoon. When she went back to lunch she received a message that the ma-

tron of the local cottage hospital was trying to get hold
of her, and when she rang back and spoke to the matron it was to discover that she wanted to discharge two
patients into Rosabel's care.

"They're not really fit to go out of hospital, Nurse Fairbairn, but we're so desperately short of beds. I'm sorry,
my dear, to give you all this extra work. They'll both
need a careful eye keeping on them for a week or so."

Rosabel found that Matron's words were only too
true when later that afternoon she called on the first
of the patients in question. It had been raining during
the afternoon and Rosabel wiped her feet carefully as
she went into the immaculate house. When she got
into the room immediately at the top of the stairs, she
was very worried when she saw the state of the old
man lying in the bed. He looked very poorly and the
room itself, though immaculately clean and tidy, was
most unwelcoming.

Rosabel judged that it faced north and would receive
very little sunshine. It was quite a large room, but all it
contained was a narrow single bed, a dressing-table
without so much as a comb or a pin tray on it and two
straight-backed chairs on either side of the bed. There
wasn't a flower or a magazine to be seen and the curtains on either side of the small window looked as if
they had been drilled into place.

To Rosabel's astonishment, when she turned from
taking her patient's pulse and temperature, it was to
find that Mrs. Brown had vanished. As she wanted to
ask her one or two questions she went out of the room,
only to find her on her knees on the staircase removing
a small piece of mud which must have dropped from
her shoe as she came in.

As she got half-way down the staircase Mrs. Brown
raised her eyes and looked at her almost belligerently
before turning and leading the way downstairs into the
kitchen.

"Your husband isn't at all well. I suppose you realize
that, Mrs. Brown?" Rosabel began.

"Well, of course I do," the woman retorted as she briskly put away her dustpan and brush. "He should never have come home, in my opinion."

"No, I daresay he could have done with a few more days in hospital, but I expect they told you, they're very short of beds up there and they only sent your husband home because there was no alternative. Don't worry, between us we'll look after him all right. Now, can you tell me if he's had anything to eat since he came home?"

"I took him up a tray," Mrs. Brown said, "but he wouldn't touch it, not any of it, not even the tea."

"Perhaps he didn't feel like it," Rosabel began. "I wonder if I might ask you for a cup of warm milk. I'll take that up to him now and see if I can get him to drink it. I suppose you haven't a feeding cup?"

"I'm afraid I haven't. We've never had the need for one before and I wasn't told that he'd require one."

"Never mind. An ordinary cup will do."

When the milk was ready Rosabel carried it upstairs. Mr. Brown was still lying with his eyes closed and his face was deathly white. Rosabel sat down beside the bed and touched his shoulder gently. His eyelids fluttered for a moment before he opened them and looked at her.

"Your wife tells me that you haven't had anything to eat. I wonder whether you could just sit up if I helped you and have this cup of milk? I've a tablet for you to take at the same time."

He nodded, an almost infinitesimal movement of the head which Rosabel took to mean agreement, and with practised ease she raised him gently and flicked his pillows into a more comfortable position. She had the tablet ready and gave it to him before holding the cup to his lips.

Slowly he managed to get down half the milk and then shook his head when she tried to get him to drink a little more.

"Never mind," smiled Rosabel, "you've done quite

well for the moment." It was quite obviously no good pressing him. She'd make a point of getting in to see him first thing in the morning.

But when she arrived shortly after nine o'clock the next morning, it was to find Mr. Brown looking as if he hadn't moved since the night before. His bed hadn't a crease and was tucked in even more correctly than it would have been in hospital.

Rosabel took his temperature and was glad to find that it was only very slightly above normal. She went downstairs wishing that he were a patient of her brother, but Mr. Brown's doctor lived on the other side of Rockspit. Although Rosabel knew him well, she certainly couldn't be as blunt in her comments as she would have been if this had been one of Peter's patients.

She knocked on the kitchen door and Mrs. Brown's voice answered her. She was sitting at the kitchen table drinking a cup of coffee.

"I wonder if I might ask you—has your husband had any breakfast?"

"No, he refused to have anything," Mrs. Brown said shortly.

"Has he...."

"He's been washed, if that's what you were going to ask, and I've made his bed, you can see I have. I've done everything that would have been done if he'd been in hospital, but I can't make him eat if he doesn't want to."

"No, I quite understand," said Rosabel. "Don't worry, we shall just have to get him to take things slowly. Perhaps if he had a little cereal mixed in warm milk I could persuade him to take it."

Mrs. Brown got up and walked over to a large cupboard. She took out a packet of cereal and some sugar and put them down on the kitchen table.

"Here you are. You can take whatever you want yourself, I'm going to do the shopping now," and without waiting to see whether Rosabel looked surprised, angry or bewildered at this peculiar attitude, she picked up her coat, put it on and went out of the back door saying as she did so, "I shall be back in twenty minutes. I don't suppose you'll be gone by then."

Rosabel was quite used to odd households, so she wasn't particularly surprised at this. She warmed up some milk in a pan and mixed a small amount of cereal. By delving into the drawers in the kitchen she found a small traycloth and set the tray as attractively as she could.

When she went upstairs she found the old man still lying just as she had left him. She put the tray down and going over to the window eased it open a little. The air was warm and balmy. He could enjoy that even if the sun didn't reach here.

She was determined, if Mrs. Brown was not back by the time her patient had finished his breakfast, that she'd go and have a look at the other bedrooms. There was no reason as far as she could see why the old man should have to stay in this dismal, rather cold-looking little room. Surely one of the other bedrooms faced south and must be full of sunshine this lovely morning.

While she was giving him his cereal she tried to get him to talk. "You know, Mr. Brown, you're not helping yourself behaving like this. Why won't you eat when I'm not here? Your wife tells me that you wouldn't have anything last night and again this morning."

The old man sighed. He looked at Rosabel's face for a few minutes. "Mary's a good lass. I must admit she keeps the place beautifully," and he glanced round the small bleak room. "But you know, my dear, she should have married the house and not me, she's really much more interested in it than she is in a. . . ."

"Never mind," soothed Rosabel as she spooned a bit more cereal into his mouth. "Some women are like that, you know."

"Aye," he agreed, "but I would have preferred one

who thought more about human beings than places. Aye...." He stopped, feeling that he'd said too much.

By the time he had finished breakfast he looked quite exhausted and seemed glad to lie down again. When Rosabel had put her things back into her bag she let herself softly out of the room. There was no sound from down below, so she went and had a look into the other bedrooms.

One was quite obviously occupied by Mrs. Brown herself. Rosabel walked into the third bedroom. This would have done admirably, she thought as she glanced around. The sun was pouring in through the window and when she walked over and looked out it was to find that it gave a view of a really beautiful garden. It was quite obvious that the old man was a keen gardener.

She glanced around. Here too the furniture was rather spartan, but it would need only five minutes and a couple of strong arms to wheel the bed over until it was against the window where Mr. Brown could lie and look out into the garden.

Rosabel nodded to herself as she went out of the room. When she went downstairs again Mrs. Brown was just letting herself in. Rosabel walked determinedly into the kitchen.

"I've got your husband to take some breakfast and I think he'll have a little sleep now. I'm coming in again this afternoon to see how he is, and if he's feeling up to it I shall probably change his dressing and give him a blanket bath."

"It's quite unnecessary, you know," Mrs. Brown said shortly. "I think I know how to keep my own husband clean."

"I'm sure you do," Rosabel said soothingly, "but he's had a very serious operation and I think for a few days it would be advisable if you didn't try to wash more than just his hands and face."

"Just as you say, Nurse," shrugged Mrs. Brown. "I don't want to do anything Dr. Birdwood wouldn't like."

Rosabel had to lower her eyes in case Mrs. Brown should see a sudden gleam of amusement appear there. Quite obviously she was doing her best to put "Nurse" in her place, and if Dr. Birdwood called that morning she felt sure that Mrs. Brown would have quite a tale to tell him.

Well, she might just as well give Mrs. Brown a good tale to tell.

"There's another thing, Mrs. Brown. I think your husband would be better if he was moved to another bedroom."

"What do you mean?"

"Well, the bedroom he's in is rather dark, I think he'd be better if he was moved to a sunnier room. I hope you'll forgive me, but I glanced into your other rooms and found one looked over the garden. I think he'd be far better in there. He'd feel more cheerful and when he's getting better and can sit up he'll be able to look at his garden. It's very beautiful. I'm sure you must be proud of it."

For a minute Mrs. Brown looked quite taken aback, but she was obviously pleased by the compliment about the garden and a half reluctant smile tilted her mouth as she glanced out of the kitchen window. "It is nice, I must admit. Archie isn't bad in the garden, although he's quite, quite stupid about having any flowers picked. He never lets me bring any into the house."

"I'm sure now that he's so ill and can't get down into the garden he wouldn't object if you put one or two into a little vase on his windowsill."

"Well, I don't know," Mrs. Brown said. "I think it would be better to ask him."

"I'll tell you what," said Rosabel. "Instead of picking the flowers out of your garden, would he have any objection if I brought a few out of ours? We've got hundreds and my brother's always giving them away."

Mrs. Brown seemed quite taken aback. Whether she had never had any flowers brought to her or whether the offer from the district nurse seemed strange, Rosabel couldn't tell, but before she left she had wrung a reluctant agreement from Mrs. Brown. Not only could her husband be moved this afternoon, but Rosabel could fill the whole house with flowers if she wished so long as they were not picked out of the Browns' garden.

Rosabel drove away feeling quite satisfied with herself. She'd another scheme in the back of her mind. She wasn't going to be able to move even a frail old man like Mr. Brown from one bedroom to another on her own. She could hardly ask Peter, the Browns were not his patients, after all, but there was absolutely no reason why she couldn't ask Robert Carr. He was a big, strong man and it would do him good to give her a hand.

He had said that he liked to observe people. Well, he could come and observe the Browns. It would be interesting to hear what he made of Mrs. Brown.

When Rosabel got home, she went up to the flat to look for him, but there was no sign of Robert. When she had had a sandwich and a quick cup of coffee, she walked down to the Fisherman's Arms where, as she had guessed, Robert was in the bar chatting to two of the local fishermen. Seeing her on the other side of the room he raised his brows questioningly, and as Rosabel just stood there and gazed at him he murmured something to the two men he was with and then strolled over to her.

"You wouldn't be looking for me, by any chance?" he asked. "From the way you were gazing steadfastly across the room I could only suppose that you'd come in search of me. Nothing wrong up at the house, is there?"

"No, it isn't that. I was wondering if you were busy this afternoon."

He pushed his hands through his hair and looked down at her. "Well, I had planned to run the mower over the lawn. It's beginning to get long again with that rain yesterday. There's something you want me to do, is there?"

"Well, there is as a matter of fact," Rosabel told him. "I was wondering whether you could possibly come and help me move a patient."

Whatever he had been expecting her to say it was certainly not this, because Rosabel saw a look of complete surprise come into his eyes for an instant, before it vanished and he burst out laughing.

"Full of surprises, aren't you? Certainly I'll come and help. What's the matter? Is he too heavy for you?"

"It's not that he's a heavy man, but I want to move him from one bedroom to another, and as he's just home from hospital, I feel that two people ought to do it. I don't think his wife's frightfully co-operative, so...."

"It's all right, you don't have to say any more. Certainly I'll come and help. We'll manage it without him even being woken up if he happens to be asleep when we arrive."

Rosabel laughed. "Well, I've certainly never managed to move a patient without waking him or her up, but I'm quite sure if you say you can do so..."

"All right," said Robert, holding his hands up. "We had a truce the other night. Let's try and continue it, shall we?"

Rosabel turned away, saying over her shoulder, "If you could be ready about a quarter past two?"

"Yes, I'll be somewhere around," he said, and turned back towards the bar.

He was certainly around all right. Long before Rosabel was ready herself she could hear the rattle of the mower as he pushed it up and down the lawn. As he carried the freshly mown grass cuttings over to the compost heap, his rough baritone was raised in song.

He was singing, much to her surprise, the Beatles' latest number. Somehow she didn't associate him with "pop," but then what did she associate him with? He was a man of many mysteries, and thinking it over, she realized that she didn't, as yet, know any of his tastes.

When she walked out to gather the flowers which she had promised Mrs. Brown, he stopped mowing and shouted over the noise of the engine, "Are you ready for me now?"

Rosabel shook her head as she walked across the lawn. "No, I want to pick a few flowers to take with me."

"My goodness, this patient must be special," he commented. "He's certainly getting the royal treatment."

"It's just that he's rather garden-proud and isn't keen on his wife picking the flowers out of the garden. I promised I'd take her some of ours."

"Oh, one like that, is he?" said Rob as he pushed the grass clippings more tightly into the box on the mower. "Your patient is one of those wedded to his garden."

Rosabel was silent in sheer surprise. This aspect of the situation had never even occurred to her, not even when Mrs. Brown had said that her husband didn't like the flowers to be cut. She didn't usually side against her own sex. Perhaps Mrs. Brown's unco-operative attitude towards her had something to do with making her feel prejudiced. While Rob continued to push the mower up and down, she remained silent and thoughtful as she bent down and cut an armful of primulas, pansies, tulips, and forget-me-nots to take with her.

Rosabel put the old collapsible stretcher which her brother kept for emergencies into the boot of the car before she shouted to Robert that she was ready to leave. Immediately he abandoned the mower on the edge of the lawn and coming towards her said, "Just wait a second, will you, while I wash my hands?" and disappeared before she could reply. When he came down from the flat he helped her into the driving seat before going round and getting into the passenger seat himself.

As they turned into the main road Rosabel couldn't help saying rather tartly, "You don't drive, then?"

Robert turned and looked at her, an impish smile curving his lips. "Well, what do you expect? They took my licence away. Of course you will have realized that."

Rosabel's lips curled with scorn. So she hadn't been very far out after all. If he'd had his licence taken away from him it could only be for one reason that she could think of.

When they got to their destination, she was surprised to be greeted with a smile as the door opened. It was a rather strange smile, but it was a smile none the less, and it reached Mrs. Brown's eyes as she took in the armful of flowers in Rosabel's arms. Going upstairs, Rosabel also discovered that not only had Mrs. Brown made up the bed in the sunny room overlooking the garden, but it had been pulled nearer the window, and by the time that Robert and Rosabel had got her patient on to the stretcher and into the new bedroom, Mrs. Brown had put a tastefully arranged bowl of flowers on the windowsill.

To Rosabel it made all the difference, but she certainly hadn't bargained for her patient's reaction. As they settled him into his new abode the first thing he saw was the bowl of flowers on the windowsill. Immediately a roar of protest emerged from him. "Didn't I tell you...."

Rosabel was quite surprised at the strength of the voice. She knew what he was going to say before the words were half out and she laid a hand quietly on his arm. "No need to shout, Mr. Brown. I know you think your wife cut those flowers, but I can assure you that she didn't. She explained to me that you didn't like flowers taken out of your garden, so I brought some from ours. We thought they'd brighten up your room. And they do, don't they? They look perfect there on the windowsill."

The roar of protest died on Mr. Brown's lips. He looked again at his floral decoration and then turned his eyes to Rosabel's face as if half disbelieving her.

"It's quite true," Mrs. Brown said, "Nurse brought them with her when she came with this gentleman."

Apparently realizing that he'd been rather ungracious, the sick man looked in Rosabel's direction and mumbled something that sounded like "I'm sorry."

"I know what gardeners are like, although I must say my brother doesn't mind what we cut so long as we leave just a few blooms waving in the breeze."

And if Mr. Brown, by the expression on his face, quite obviously felt sorry for Peter Fairbairn's efforts at gardening, he didn't say any more.

When Rosabel got down again to the car it was to find Robert sitting in the passenger seat quietly smoking a cigarette. She looked at him for a moment or two and then said, "Perhaps I'd better run you home now."

"No, I'd like to come with you on the rest of your rounds." He glanced at his watch. "It's almost three o'clock now, so you can't have very many more to do."

Rosabel took out her list and ticked off the Browns. "I've got five more calls I must make and possibly a sixth, but I may be able to leave that until the morning," she said.

"Fine! I'm quite happy to come along with you. I can finish the lawn this evening."

Rosabel's eyes twinkled as she leaned forward and switched on the ignition. "I must say one of the treats which you've provided in the last couple of weeks is freedom from grass cutting. I just hate when my turn comes round to do the mowing. Peter's so busy I can't leave it all to him, and I must admit it's pretty difficult to get a gardener, even an odd job man, around here. Most of the men prefer to go fishing if they've got any spare time."

Rather to Rosabel's surprise she enjoyed his company. Conversation started immediately she came out of each house and got back into the car. If she was curious about Robert Carver's tastes, it was quite obvious that he was equally interested in hers, because he questioned her closely on a number of subjects from her taste in music to her opinions on "spare part" surgery.

In the middle of a heated discussion on whether or not they ought to import fruit from apartheid countries she suddenly started laughing and said to him, "How on earth did we get on to this topic?"

Robert stopped in the middle of a sentence and rubbed his hands through his hair so that it looked rougher than it usually did. "I can't think," he said. "I believe it started with us discussing whether everybody who came to Britain ought to get free health service, though how that got on to fruit I can't remember now," and he chuckled infectiously.

Rosabel, as they drew up outside her last call, found herself laughing with him and she was quite astonished as she glanced at her watch to notice that it was nearly twenty-five past five. Never could she remember an afternoon going quite so quickly. Even if it meant that she would have to spend at least a couple of hours this evening writing up her notes, she couldn't help feeling it was well worth it. She'd thoroughly enjoyed the three hours she'd spent in this man's company, though even to herself she was a little ashamed to admit it.

The following Sunday was her day off call as well as her brother's, and on the Saturday evening Peter announced that if the weather was fine, he proposed that they should all take a picnic and go and spend the day at a cove on the other side of the river.

"Willy will take us over, I spoke to him this afternoon and he said that the tide would be right if we were all ready by a quarter to ten. It will mean missing morning church and I don't suppose John McGill will be very pleased with us, but never mind, it's only once in a while. Do you think we can all be ready by that time, Isa?"

Isabel McCulloch looked up. "I'm certain we can. If we're going on a picnic the girls could be ready by six, couldn't you?"

Jennie and Katya giggled. "Oh, Gran, you are silly,"

they said. "Well, we suppose we *could* be ready by six, but I don't think we'd remember everything we'd like to take with us. You know what we're like at forgetting things."

"Don't I just," agreed their grandmother. "But if we start getting things out tonight, and Rosabel and I get the food ready tomorrow morning first thing, I see no reason why we shouldn't be down on the quay by half past nine at the latest. We wouldn't want to miss the tide, now would we?"

As usual there seemed a mountain of things to be taken, quite apart from enough food to last the family for the day. There were all the swimming togs, balls, bats, extra shoes and socks for the children, mackintoshes in case it rained, ground sheets and rugs to sit on, and extra woollies in case they got wet. There was quite a mound waiting in the hall when Rosabel went upstairs to fetch her anorak.

To her surprise this morning she had discovered that Robert was joining the party. Her brother had said nothing about it the evening before, but maybe he thought that she might protest, though why he should she couldn't imagine. Since the night of the dance she and Robert had maintained perfectly amicable relations, so her brother must have noticed this. He was an acutely observant man and very little which occurred in his own household passed unnoticed, though very often he didn't mention his observations. Perhaps the fact that he had to be mother and father to his two girls made him more perceptive than most men.

By the time Rosabel came down again, her anorak tucked under her arm, the party was ready. Robert had sauntered through from the back of the house, his hair looking as if it hadn't seen a comb this morning. He was wearing a most disreputable pair of trousers and a thick woolly.

He grinned when he caught her glance and said mockingly, "Good morning. I've got my best Sunday suit on, as you can see, for the expedition."

Rosabel flushed slightly; it was uncanny the way that he could read her thoughts, but perhaps she had given herself away by the expressive side glance when she had seen him coming. It wasn't that she specially liked men to be dressed up and certainly not for an outing of this kind, but even for a seashore picnic and a boat journey first she had to admit that Robert looked rougher than usual. Peter in his thick fisherman's jersey and old corduroys looked neatness itself in comparison, but then of course he wore his hair much shorter, and that, in her opinion, made a difference. Even when the wind was at its wildest, as it could be on this coast, she had never seen her brother's hair in very much of a disarray. He had a slight curl to it and it fell naturally into place.

By the time they had collected all their things, everyone carrying their share, and had walked down the road to the little jetty, the boat was ready and waiting for them. The old motor at the back of the launch was chugging spasmodically as if it had got an acute attack of asthma and as they all climbed aboard, Rosabel wondered, as she had wondered very often in the past, whether the boat would actually get them there.

Willy, however, seemed to have a sort of magic touch with the old coughing, spluttering engine. By the time they were all comfortably seated he had already cast off and they were on their way across the wide estuary. The beach to which they were going was an old favourite and they always got Willy to take them over since it was quite inaccessible by road. He usually took them over first thing in the morning if the tides were right and collected them again in the late evening, unless it came on to rain, when he would appear like a genie out of a bottle to take them back and save them from too severe a soaking.

There was a long swell rolling in and after two or three attempts to get into the cove Willy shook his head. "I'm afraid you people will have to get out and wade in," he said. "I daren't risk the boat any nearer inshore.'' So with one accord Peter and Robert rolled up their trousers and slipped over the side.

Peter reached up and lifted his mother-in-law out and Robert turned to Rosabel. She was already rolling up her own slacks and quickly told him that she was perfectly capable of getting ashore by herself.

"Nonsense," he said, "we can't expect the ladies to wade," and before she could say any more he had reached over the gunwale, lifted her firmly in his arms and was striding towards the beach.

Rosabel knew that it would have been very foolhardy to struggle, so she clasped him firmly round the neck and contented herself by glaring into the distance.

A low chuckle sounded in her ear. "I suppose I shall have to pay for this for the rest of the day!"

"I may be annoyed, but I'm not a sulker," Rosabel replied briskly.

Robert chuckled again. "Well, I'm very glad to hear it. There's nothing worse than a moody woman," and before she could retort he had set her on her feet on the sand and had turned back to go and fetch one of the girls.

By the time they had got all their goods ashore and taken them up the beach to a sheltered corner where the wind couldn't get at them and they could enjoy as much of the sun as they desired, Willy had started up the boat again and was almost half-way across the estuary.

The girls had got into their bathing costumes as soon as they were set ashore and were already dashing towards the waves to have a paddle.

Katya screamed as the cold water went over her toes. "Ooh, it's colder than usual, I'm sure it is!"

Rosabel sat down beside Isa on one of the rugs. "Well, if Katya thinks it's cold, it must be cold, and I certainly shan't be going in for a bathe." She settled herself back comfortably. "The Sunday papers for me for the next hour!"

But if she expected to be able to enjoy them by herself she was very much mistaken. Mrs. McCulloch was content to lean back and just watch the children, enjoy the scenery and doze, but Peter possessed himself immediately of one of the Sunday papers and when Rosabel reached for the second she had the middle part twitched out of her grasp almost before she could glance at the front page.

"Greedy," said a voice beside her, and she turned to see that Robert had thrown himself on his stomach and was already scanning the pages he had just removed from her grasp.

"You might have asked me."

"I knew that if I did you'd refuse immediately," he said, and then grinned up at her, "isn't that so?"

Rosabel couldn't help an answering grin appearing on her own face. "Well, you know me—just a bundle of contrariness."

"Yes, I'd gathered that," he said. "That's why I didn't give you a chance to refuse me," and without waiting to see if she intended to reply to him or not, he turned firmly back to read the pages he had purloined.

All was silent, the only sound being the screams of the gulls overhead and the murmuring voices of the girls coming from the water's edge. Rosabel had finished with the front page and had just turned to glance at the gossip columns on page two, when her brother suddenly remarked, "There's a very interesting article in this paper about the advances made in recent years in tropical medicine, you ought to read it."

Rosabel looked up, vaguely astonished. She wondered why her brother could think that she was interested in tropical medicine. It wasn't a subject which was very likely to come her way unless she decided to nurse overseas. Then she suddenly realized that his remark had not been addressed to her but to the man lying by her side. He had turned his head towards Peter and had said, "Who's it written by?"

Her brother mentioned some name quite unknown to Rosabel. In any case, her mind was firmly fixed on the curious situation of her brother imagining that Robert would be interested in an article on tropical medicine, except in a general way, and she was just beginning to wonder if she could ask some pertinent questions and have her curiosity set at rest when Isa interrupted them by saying, "I knew it! Trust Katya!" and getting to her feet began to run in the direction of the little girl.

Rosabel immediately put the paper down and got up too. She knew Katya of old. If anyone was accident-prone, she was.

She soon saw what had happened and began to laugh. Katya, in an effort to tease Jennie, had over-reached herself. She had stepped on an unexpected piece of stone or rock just below the surface of the water and fallen flat on her face, and as she was about to get up out of the shallow water one of the big rollers had come in and knocked her flat again.

By the time Rosabel and Isa had got to the water's edge, Jennie had pulled her sister to her feet, but the child was full of sea-water and she was coughing and spluttering as she tried to get her breath. Isa took her granddaughter firmly by the arm and patted her briskly on the back. Tears were starting from the child's eyes as she drew air at last into her lungs.

"Oh, Gran, stop it, I'm okay. And look at my hair! It's absolutely wringing wet!"

Katya shook the heavy hair out of her eyes. Rosabel reached for a dry towel and began to pat the sea-water off her face.

"It was her own fault," Jennie said, "she was teasing me with the biggest, horridest dead jellyfish you've ever seen. You know how I hate the beastly things. And I think she must have slipped and fallen on something. Anyway, over she went and the sea knocked her down again. I told her the breakers catch you unawares and one did, it just served her right!"

"Now, Jennie," Mrs. McCulloch put in, "Kat's had her lesson. You don't need to rub it in. Come and sit down for a minute and get your breath," she said to the younger girl, and taking the towel out of Rosabel's hands she put it round Katya's shoulders and led her firmly away.

"That's a good beginning," Rosabel remarked to Jennie as the other two walked away. "I hope this isn't going to set the pattern for the rest of the day. I don't feel like spending my time mopping up people. It's my day off from that sort of thing."

Jennie laughed. "I don't suppose it will, and Kat isn't hurt after all. She only got a tummyful of sea-water. I bet it will make her feel sick, though," she said in a typical sisterly fashion and with a great deal of satisfaction in her voice.

It didn't appear though, when lunch time came round, to have impaired Katya's appetite in the smallest degree. She even joined her father and sister for a swim before lunch. Rosabel had stuck to her decision not to bathe, and it didn't altogether surprise her that Robert made no effort to get into a pair of swimming trunks either.

When she gazed at him questioningly he said, "I don't go in waters quite as cold as these—the hot Med for me every time." Rosabel remembered him saying this to her before. Somehow he looked the sort to go in more for fishing trips or even birdwatching. Certainly not the type to go sitting on sunny shores enjoying a blazing sun.

Maybe she wasn't a particularly good judge of character, though she felt he was proving true to her first opinion when he produced a clinking bag and placed it beside the hamper. As Isa lifted out the bottles Robert said with a wicked grin, "My contribution towards the picnic."

Peter, coming up the beach with the girls, was just in time to hear this last remark. "Good! I realized when I was well on the way that we'd forgotten the beer. It's good of you to have brought some."

"Oh, I've not only brought beer," Robert said,

"I've brought something for everybody," and to the girls' delight he produced small bottles of cider for them, half a bottle of sparkling white wine for Rosabel and Isa, and two large bottles of beer for himself and Peter.

Isabel, as usual, had provided very ample fare. There were home-made sausage rolls, sandwiches, small individual salads in polythene bowls, a leg of chicken apiece, and she followed all this by producing tinned fruit salad as dessert.

By the time they had finished and the used things repacked, Rosabel felt as if she couldn't have moved an inch, and she lay back on the rug with a sigh of satisfaction. "I feel I shall sleep for a week after this."

"You won't, you know," said a voice in her right ear, "because in half an hour's time you and I are going for a brisk walk over that hillock over there. I want to know what's on the other side."

Rosabel turned a lazy head and opened one eye. "Nothing very exciting, I'm afraid. This place is practically inaccessible. You can get a little way, but not far. I'll show you later, but I've just got to have a snooze after all that food."

"Now who could resist that?" Robert answered. "You have your beauty sleep but I'm going to have my walk, so prepare yourself to be nudged sharply in the near future." Rosabel smiled faintly and turned her face away. It really was heavenly lying here on the soft sand just comfortably warm without being too hot, and she settled down to drift blissfully off to sleep.

It seemed only two minutes later when a hand took hold of her arm and shook it gently. She didn't take any notice for a minute and then as the fingers grasped a little tighter, she opened her eyes and found she was staring straight into Robert's face. He was looking at her quite seriously, scrutinizing her with care.

Rosabel was a little taken aback. It was quite alarming enough to be woken up out of such a deep sleep, but to find his face so close to her own was most disturbing. It had crossed her mind once or twice that he might be very attractive to a certain sort of girl, but she had never thought that the certain sort of girl might be herself.

The expression in his eyes was quite unreadable. He gave absolutely nothing away. The deep crows' feet at either side of his eyes and the tilt of his mouth spoke however of a warm genial character. No one would have called his face weak by any means. He had a strong determined chin and sometimes when he set his mouth very firmly, Rosabel felt sure that he was the sort of man who made a decision and stuck to it. He could also, she thought, be a little intimidating. She hadn't realized it before, but in a quiet sort of way there was an authority about him. He might wear rough clothes, he might have an unkempt appearance, but despite this he had a dignity which showed through his careless attitude to life and his unconventional method of dressing.

"Time to go for that little walk we were talking about earlier," he said. "The others went ten or fifteen minutes ago. I told them we'd follow as soon as you woke up, but it's taken me ages to get you round. Do you always go off into a dead sleep like this?"

"Not always," Rosabel said, "but I'm not usually full of wine at lunch-time. It always makes me sleepy."

"Oh, is that it?" he said with a grin. "I saw you knocking it back."

"Ooh, what a dreadful thing to say! I only had a glass and a half."

"Two glasses," he said firmly.

"Okay, two glasses if you say so, but it *was* delicious."

He rolled over and sat up. "I'm glad you enjoyed it. I brought it for that purpose, although I thought you might disapprove."

"Me? Disapprove? Father insisted we didn't grow up intolerant teetotalers."

"Yes, I remember now. You had some sherry the

other night, didn't you? Still, in these days when most girls of your age are on vodkas and tonics, it's unusual to find one who only has the odd glass of sherry or a very occasional glass of wine."

Rosabel felt that the conversation was getting beyond her. She got to her feet and began to brush some of the sand off her slacks. "Much better for the complexion," she said lighty, "you know what the hard stuff can do. Bring me out in spots, and that would never do."

He had also risen and was standing looking down at her. "Well, I shouldn't think there's much danger of that. You've got a very clear skin."

Rosabel looked at him in a rather surprised manner, Robert had made the remark not as if he were paying her a compliment, but more as if he had her under a microscope. She realized that he actually was looking at the skin of her face in a most analytical manner. What an astonishing creature he was.

By the time they had gone through the thick bracken and reached the top of the low mound which overlooked the beach they could see the others down below, then heads and shoulders sticking out of a sea of greenery. Rosabel put her hands to her mouth and gave a loud "Hulloo!" and Peter looked up and waved and shouted. They had obviously been quite a way along the track which wound its way up and over the hill behind and were on their way back to the beach.

"Is it worth going down there?" Rosabel asked, "or shall we wait here for them?"

"Certainly not," said Robert. "We came out for a walk and a walk we're going to have."

Rosabel shrugged. "Very well, come on, but on your own head be it. It's very uneven and swampy in parts."

When the two parties met, Katya bounced up to Robert and Rosabel with an, "I told Daddy you hadn't heard. It's no good going any further. Just look at our feet!"

They looked. The two girls had removed their shoes

and four bare feet were generously adorned with mud and green slime. Isa pulled a face at her own filthy beach shoes. "At lest we've saved you. It's like a bog further on. We were in it before we noticed."

"There goes your walk," Rosabel said to Robert.

"If it's exercise you're after," her brother offered, "we're having a game of beach cricket as soon as we've cleaned ourselves up."

Over an hour later Rosabel wasn't sorry to see the boat returning to pick them up. The tide had gone right out by this time. What wind there had been had dropped and there was hardly a ripple on the water, so Willy had no difficulty in getting the boat near in to shore. As the girls waded out to throw their share of the burdens over the gunwale of the boat, he leaned down and hoisted Katya in. "Had a good day, girlie?"

"Super," Katya beamed. "It's been absolutely marvellous, I wish we could do it *every* Sunday!"

"Sure and you'd soon be tired of that if it was every week-end," the old man said. "I know you girls."

Katya giggled, "Jennie and I don't get tired of things. Besides, nobody could get bored in Bannford."

"Humph," the old boatman grunted, "that's not what I hear from some of the other village lassies."

"They don't know when they're lucky," Katya said scornfully. "I expect you're talking about Milly and Jeannie down at the cottages, I've heard them talking. That's just because there isn't a dance every night of the week. But we don't want to go dancing."

"Well, not now you don't," Willy said, "but I expect when you're a wee bit older."

"No, not even then," said Katya. "Oh, we might go once in a while."

Rosabel, who had just got into the boat, laughed at the patronizing tones in her voice. "And what will you be doing with your time, young lady, if you're not wasting it on frivolities like dancing?"

"Oh, I shall be studying for my degree," Katya declared.

Jennie laughed, "You know that's probably what she *will* be doing, Rosabel."

"Yes, I shouldn't be surprised." It was a family joke that young Katya already had a brain like a computer. Rosabel could visualize her going through university with the greatest of ease, emerging with a first-class degree when she left.

Jennie now was another matter. Although she too had inherited Peter's brains, nursing and not university was her goal.

By this time Isa and the two men had arrived. Willy started the engine again and they were soon chugging across the estuary towards home. There was silence except for the noise of the engine. The girls were tired, sated with the day's fresh air and activity. There would be no trouble getting them to bed tonight, Rosabel thought.

She sat, enjoying the soft breezes blowing through her hair. It had really been a very nice day. But as she sailed back her eyes wandered to the little village ahead with the hotel on the hill above it. She suddenly felt absolutely conscience-stricken. She hadn't given Bill a thought all day.

CHAPTER SIX

SHE FELT EVEN MORE SO the following morning when she accidentally bumped into Kate Johnston in the village street. Rosabel pulled up and leaned through the window to shout "Hallo" to her, and Kate got off her bicycle and walked over.

When they had exchanged one or two remarks Kate suddenly said accusingly, "I don't know what's going on between you and Bill, but we've not seen you all week, Rosabel. He seems utterly miserable. What's gone wrong between you two?"

Rosabel felt very uncomfortable. It really wasn't her job to tell Bill's sisters that she had refused to marry him and she hated to be accused in this manner. She had always liked Kate and was rather surprised at the way in which Bill's younger sister had taken up the cudgels on her brother's behalf.

As she hesitated, searching for words, Kate said, "Why don't you come up and see him this evening? I know he'd be delighted and Jean and I are going into Dumfries, so you'd have him to yourself."

Rosabel didn't quite know how to get out of this invitation. "I'll come if I can," she half promised.

"Yes, do that," Kate said as she turned the bicycle round. "I'll tell Bill to expect you."

"No, please don't," Rosabel shouted after her, but whether Kate heard or not she didn't know because with a wave of her hand she got on her bicycle and rode away.

Rosabel put the car into gear and set off again. She was very thoughtful as she went on to her next case. She wished that she had never run into Kate. She cer-

tainly didn't want to make the first move where Bill
was concerned. It would give other people, not to mention Bill himself, the wrong ideas. Any overtures on
her part might make him think that she was beginning
to change her mind about her decision and she certainly hadn't done that. If he wanted to remain friendly
with her and she hoped he did, then it was up to him to
make the first move.

That evening when she had had supper and written
up her notes, Rosabel set off up the path behind the
house. Instead of turning towards the hotel, however,
she walked up the hill until she got to the little summit
and sat in her favourite position, leaning back against
one of the convenient stumps of granite.

She had been there about fifteen minutes when she
suddenly realized that she was not alone. She had
heard no sound of approaching feet, not so much as a
twig breaking, when Robert dropped into the heather
beside her. He sat close to her but a little way behind
so that she couldn't see his face without turning
round. He didn't say anything, but putting a hand on
the nape of her neck, he began to rub it with his
fingers.

Rosabel was thinking what a comforting gesture this
was and how much she enjoyed the feeling of his hand
moving to and fro across her neck when he suddenly
said, "Come up here to think things out, have you?"

She gave a jump of surprise, wondering if he was
quite so curiously perceptive with everyone he met. He
certainly divined her thoughts without the slightest difficulty and she didn't quite know how to answer him.

Honesty seemed the best so she said, "It's Bill Johnston up at the hotel, as you probably guessed."

The hand continued to move backwards and forwards soothingly across her neck, so she went on, "I
don't quite know what to do about him. I've rather
drifted into a situation, I'm afraid."

"Yes, that's very easily done," said the voice from
just behind her. "You can start going around with

someone quite casually and all of a sudden everyone seems to take it for granted that you're heading up the aisle.''

"Yes," Rosabel said, "that's what happened in our case. It was thoughtless of me perhaps, but I never took Bill seriously and I was quite taken aback when he seemed to take it for granted that we would be getting married at the end of this year. The only people who don't seem to expect me to marry him are my brother and Mrs. McCulloch.''

"Well, perhaps they're the sensible sort of people who think you're quite old enough and sensible enough to run your own life," Robert said. "I must admit that I agree with them, though you don't want to let your soft heart draw you into any more trouble. I take it that you've now given him a direct and honest answer. If you have, then stick by it. A clean break is the best break, you know.''

Rosabel swivelled round to look up at him. "It's a bit difficult in a small place like this," she said almost pleadingly.

"It doesn't make any difference what the size of the place is," Robert maintained, "human nature's the same whether it's in the country or a big city. In the country everybody knows everybody else's business, so it seems different, that's all.''

Rosabel gave a half-hearted laugh. "You may be right. It's the fact that people who know you well are watching what you're going to do next that's unnerving. That and the fact that..." and she stopped abruptly. She hesitated to tell Robert that Bill's sisters were trying to talk her into making things up. But for some reason she couldn't explain to herself she wanted to set the score right with this man. She didn't want him to think she was the sort of girl who liked to play men on a string, just to have another scalp dangling off their belt. While she hesitated he suddenly asked, "What about a walk down to Rockspit?''

Rosabel got to her feet. "A good idea," she said,

looking down at him. "I'm a bit tired of myself this evening. Let's talk about something else."

He laughed as he got up. "What are we to talk about? Any suggestions?"

"Oh, anything," shrugged Rosabel as she set off down the path ahead of him, "shoes and ships and sealing wax if you like."

Robert laughed again as he caught up with her. "Well, ships by all means," he said. "Tell me more about Willy who took us out yesterday. He's a very interesting old chap, I must say."

WHEN SHE WAS GETTING READY for bed that night Rosabel's fingers were slow as she picked up her comb to do her hair before she got into bed. She stared at her reflection in the mirror. What am I coming to? she thought. I set out tonight to have a quiet think. And what happened? I went down to Rockspit with Robert Carr and held his hand all the way home—yes, all the way home. I just can't think how that happened. She looked down at the hand in question almost as if it were to blame.

As she got into bed an extraordinary feeling came over her. She couldn't, she couldn't possibly be falling in love with this odd man who had landed himself on their doorstep. She couldn't possibly be so stupid. But as she snapped out the bedside lamp it occurred to her that she not only could, but had already been stupid enough to fall at least half-way in love with him. There was something about him that appealed to her, despite the fact that she disapproved of his drinking habits and a lot of other things which she wasn't prepared to enumerate to herself at this time of night. As she went off to sleep, she found she was wondering what it would feel like to be kissed by him, and a happy smile curled her lips as she drifted off into unconsciousness.

But the next morning as she headed off for work her thoughts were a good deal more sober. Perhaps it would be a good idea after all to think seriously about taking this course in intensive care therapy. She must settle down and write a long letter to Joan and get an interview arranged. She could see trouble ahead if she went on the way she was going. The whole village would call her "flighty." Not that she cared all that much for public opinion, but it did matter where her brother was the local doctor. It didn't do to have any gossip attached to one's name.

She wasn't made to feel any cheerier either when she arrived to give Mr. Brown his blanket bath to find that her patient was sitting up in bed gazing with a long face at his garden. She tried various avenues of conversation as she was attending to him, but received only monosyllables in reply, so she waited until she had nearly finished and then asked, "What's the matter, Mr. Brown? You don't seem at all yourself this morning."

He didn't answer for a second and then his gaze returned to the window. Before he could answer her Rosabel said again, "I thought you'd be happier here in this nice sunny room looking out on your garden. It really is a picture."

Immediately Mr. Brown said, "It may be a picture to you, Nurse, but it's certainly not a picture to me. My neighbour said he'd come in and look after it while I was ill, but just look at those weeds down there! They've grown since I came in here the other day."

Rosabel strolled over to the window and looked down. As far as she could see the flower beds were all weeded, neat and tidy.

"And look at the lawn too," Mr. Brown went on. "It's been needing a trim for a week, judging by the length of it. It would only take half an hour to run a mower over it. Be a hayfield before you can say Jack Robinson," he finished glumly.

Rosabel turned with her back to the window and looked at him. "Do you mean to say that you're going to make yourself worse worrying over a garden?"

"Well, it's important to me," Mr. Brown explained.

"I spend all my spare time out there when I'm well and I just hate to see it getting untidy," and then he looked up and caught Rosabel's eye. "I expect you think I'm a funny kind of a fellow, Nurse, but I can't help it, any more than my wife can help making a fuss over the house. I expect in a way we're two of a kind."

Rosabel straightened up. "Well, if it's really worrying you I'll see what I can do to help," she said. "I'm not promising anything, mind you," as he looked eagerly at her, "but I've got a friend who just might come and do a bit for you. You remember, he came and helped carry you in here."

Mr. Brown grunted. He didn't look as if he placed any great faith in Rosabel's intention to ask Robert to come and give a hand in the garden, but he seemed a little more cheerful as Rosabel packed her things and said "Good morning" to him.

It occurred to her as she returned home at lunchtime what an awkward situation she had put herself in by half-promising Robert's help as a gardener. It really was rather impertinent of her to presume that he would be prepared to go and do something for one of her patients. But he was an easy-going man, so when she drew up into the yard outside the garden she saw him strolling from the direction of the garden, she went over before her courage could desert her and said to him, "I've a favour to ask you."

He looked at her and laughed. "You know I'm yours to command," he said, and laughed again as her eyes widened.

"It's Mr. Brown—you remember, the man I got you to help me with the other day. I've discovered it was a big mistake to move him. Now he can see his beloved garden he's worrying himself silly about two or three weeds and the length of the grass!"

At the chagrin in her voice Robert threw back his head and burst out laughing. "So much for your notion that he'd like a sunny room," he said. "I think his wife had the right idea in the first place. She's probably had experience of him. I suppose you want me to go and spend the afternoon acting as jobbing gardener?"

Rosabel looked up anxiously. "Would you?" she asked. "I know it's a bit of a cheek."

"Never mind," said Robert, and he patted her on the shoulder as he walked off towards the stairs leading towards the flat. "What time do you think I'd better go up there?"

"Oh, any time after lunch," Rosabel called after him. "Would you like me to run you up there?"

Robert halted half-way up the staircase and swung round. "No, that's all right," he said. "I've fixed up your brother's bicycle, I'll go up on that," and he disappeared from view.

As Rosabel strolled up to the back door of the house she suddenly realized how easy it had all been. But if she expected her request to have no repercussions of any sort, she was quite misled. That evening she was stacking the dishwasher for Isa when Robert's head appeared round the kitchen door. "One good turn deserves another," he said. "Put your coat on and we'll walk over to Rockspit for a drink."

Rosabel looked up. "I don't think I..."

"No excuses," Robert said, and held up his hand in mock solemnity. "I did what you wanted this afternoon and tidied up the old boy's garden. It looks like Kew Gardens now. You must go and inspect it."

"Oh, I shall," said Rosabel. "I have to see him every day, you know. He's still a very sick old man."

"I'd gathered as much," said Robert, "or you wouldn't be in such a tizzy about him."

"I'm not," protested Rosabel, "but I do like to..."

"I know. You think your patients will get well quicker with a bit of help and affection."

She found herself blushing scarlet. Put like that it sounded rather childish—a "do-gooder" run mad—but she never intended it that way. She supposed she really ought to be more ethical in her methods, but she had been putting her theories into practice ever since she had taken up district nursing and so far the results had been good. But there were some who might not agree.

As she joined him at the door Rosabel eyed Robert thoughtfully. His astringent remarks gave her food for thought. Bill would never have pointed out to her what her actions might look like to other people.

She had to admit next day when she called on the Browns that Robert had not spoken without justification. The garden did look very different from yesterday. The lawn was like the top of a billiard table, the edges neatly clipped, and not a weed raised its head in the flower beds. It must have taken several hours' work. When she had thoughtlessly and carelessly offered his services she hadn't really realized what she was letting him in for. It was no wonder that he'd made those remarks last night before they set out for Rockspit.

When she got home that evening she must sit down and write her letter to Joan. Not only the situation over Bill, but the arrival of Robert Carr and her interest in him were flashing red danger signals in her mind.

But she didn't get the letter written that evening. They had only just finished clearing up after supper when Penny McGill burst in on them.

"I couldn't wait another instant," she said as she put her head round the sitting-room door and, seeing Isa and Rosabel comfortably seated in two chairs came in and closed the door. She held out her left hand. "Ian and I have got engaged. We went to Dumfries this morning and got the ring. Don't you think it's lovely?"

Both Rosabel and Mrs. McCulloch made the usual remarks and wished Penny lots of luck. The ring, a beautiful solitaire diamond, suited Penny's small capable hand.

"When's the wedding to be?"

"Oh, very soon," Penny told them. "There's nothing for us to wait for, you know. There's a cottage empty quite near to Ian's father, so we're going to move in there for a start. It will be quite big enough for two. I shall keep on with my work and of course we'll be married here and John will officiate, so we thought the beginning of August.''

"As soon as that?'' commented Rosabel.

Penny blushed. "Does it sound as if we're rushing things? But as I said we've nothing to wait for, and Ian's father has agreed to a short honeymoon so long as we're back for the harvest.'' She laughed—a happy bubbling sound of sheer joy. "What I really came to ask was could I have Katya and Jennie as bridesmaids?''

Isa smiled. "I don't think it's a case of asking. Once they know you're getting married it would be impossible to refuse them. They'll both be delighted. What about Ian's sister? Won't she want to be bridesmaid as well?''

"Apparently not,'' said Penny. "I did ask her first, of course, but she's a very shy girl, as you probably know.''

Rosabel nodded. "Yes, I did meet her once and thought how quiet she seemed.''

"She asked me if I'd excuse her and I immediately thought of the youngsters here. I've known them and you as long as we've been up here, and I'd really love them to be my bridesmaids.''

Just at that moment the door behind her opened and the girls themselves came in. Isa laughed. "Speaking of angels!'' she said.

Jennie looked enquiringly. "What is it, Gran?''

"Good news for you,'' her grandmother said. "Penny's engaged to be married and...'' but she hadn't time to say more before the girls fell upon Penny, snatching her left hand from behind her back and gazing with admiration at the ring.

"Oh, it's beautiful!'' exclaimed Katya. "I suppose you wouldn't let me try it on, would you, Penny?''

Penny laughed and obligingly slipped the ring off her finger. Both the girls had to try it on, though it slipped round their small fingers.

"Come on, you two,'' ordered Rosabel, "hand it

back before it gets lost or damaged," and Katya reluctantly slipped it off her finger and gave it back to its owner.

"You didn't hear the most exciting news," Mrs. McCulloch told them. "Penny wants you to be her bridesmaids."

At this there was a concerted shriek and Peter's head came round the door. "I've got very long-suffering patients," he said, "but this is my night for evening surgery. Do you two girls think you could control your excitement just for half an hour?" and he withdrew before they could tell him the reason for the shouts and exclamations.

Penny didn't need much persuading to stay for the rest of the evening and tell them all the plans. She and Ian were proposing to get married in the morning so they could catch the train and spend the first night in London before flying off for their honeymoon. Ian fancied Italy. He had had a very good holiday there two years ago and wanted to take Penny back to revisit the place. Then the conversation turned to wedding outfits. Both the girls had entirely different ideas on what they ought to wear until in the end Mrs. McCulloch turned and said, "Now be quiet, you two. This is Penny's wedding and she decides what you wear. We'll have a day in Dumfries all together, you two, Penny and I—now isn't that the best idea?"

Penny nodded. "I think it is, Mrs. McCulloch. I'd sooner buy ready-made dresses, but if we can't find anything that suits both the girls I'm sure between us we could make something, don't you?"

While all this was being decided, Rosabel sat listening thoughtfully. She wished she could have met someone like Ian Murray, rich enough to get married immediately without waiting to save up and eligible in every other way. She wasn't a dedicated career girl by any means. A loving husband, two nice healthy kids— now that would be something for a woman to feel really proud of.

She had to go into the county town early the next morning to see her supervisor. As she came out of the nurses' home she bumped into Bill Johnston. "Good heavens, Bill, what are you doing here?" she asked.

"I had to come in on business," Bill answered her, and glanced at his watch. "It's just on lunchtime, Roz. How about coming and having a bite with me?"

Rosabel could hardly refuse and they walked down the street together. As they waited for a table he suddenly said, "I've not seen you since the golf club dance."

"Well, that's not long ago," Rosabel said, immediately on the defensive. She wondered if Kate had told him to expect her the other evening, but if Kate had done so Bill didn't say.

"I wondered if I should come down and see you," he went on, "but I hear you've been busy."

Rosabel flushed. She might have known that somebody would tell him that she had been seen out walking with Robert Carr! It annoyed her that the information should be taken back to Bill so very promptly. It seemed to put her in a bad light. There was absolutely no reason for her to feel on the defensive, yet oddly she did so. She realized that her feelings for Robert Carr must be deeper than she had thought if she couldn't laugh it off.

However, Bill was going on, "I suppose you've heard about Ian Murray's engagement?" he asked. "Kate's very cut up about it."

Rosabel looked surprised. Kate cut up about Ian and Penny getting engaged—why should she?

"You know she went out with him two or three times," Bill went on.

"But that's ages ago, over a year at least."

"We don't seem very lucky, we Johnstons, in our love life," Bill commented as he twisted his glass from side to side.

Rosabel bit her lip. It wasn't very sportsmanlike of him to have made a remark like that to her. She wished she hadn't bumped into him, for the meal that was to follow was going to be a very uncomfortable one she could see.

As if he sensed her anger, Bill changed the subject. He started to tell her about some American guests they had had, and the peculiar demands they had made. Before the meal was half over he had talked Rosabel into her usual sunny frame of mind again and she was laughing at Jean's acid comments from behind the closed kitchen door.

"It's a good thing we had it soundproofed," Bill said, "because I should think they'd have asked for their bills and left at once if they'd heard what she was saying. Waffles for breakfast was just too much. And when one of them complained that the tea wasn't like he usually had it in America, I really thought she'd hit the roof! You know what a marvellous cup of tea she always makes, you've remarked about it several times."

Rosabel nodded as she ate her cheese and biscuits. "Yes, but some people do have funny tastes."

"So I've found out, to my cost," Bill answered her. "Still, they were very generous with their praises when they departed and one even asked Kate to go and visit him if she were ever in America."

"No reason why you shouldn't both go," said Rosabel. "You can get to America in six hours now."

"Maybe," Bill said, "but it wouldn't be Kate I'd be wanting to go with, you know."

Rosabel could see they were steering back into deep waters and she hastily changed the subject, keeping on light and trivial matters until it was time for them to part. She had several calls to make before she could return home, so with what she hoped was tactful diplomacy she thanked him for the lunch, bade him a hasty "Good-bye" and set off for the car park where she had left her car.

She sighed with relief as she got into the Mini and slammed the door. Somehow she couldn't believe Robert would behave like this under similar circumstances. If a girl refused to marry him he would take his dismissal in a much more sensible manner, she felt sure. Yes, that was it, she thought as she put the key into the ignition. Bill wasn't taking it all sensibly, he really was behaving rather like a spoiled boy who couldn't have the big rubber ball he'd set his heart on.

Maybe that was why Ian had broken off with Kate. It wasn't because he liked having a good time and no strings attached but because he too had found unattractive characteristics in Kate.

On the surface Bill's younger sister seemed very nice, but Rosabel realized that she didn't know her well enough to prophesy how she would react to an unfortunate love affair.

As she went up to her room that evening to change before supper, Rosabel wondered how she was going to excuse herself from going over to Rockspit. She felt sure that Robert would come in and suggest a walk. She was therefore surprised when nine o'clock arrived and he still hadn't put his head round the door.

And when she finally went up to bed there was no light shining from the room over the garage. She couldn't help wondering where he was and what he was doing. "Time you started thinking about *really* important things," she told herself severely, and getting out a pad she sat on the edge of the bed and wrote the long-delayed letter to Joan Rivers.

She asked her for more information about the training, where she would have to come for an interview, how long the course was and a dozen other questions, and she addressed the envelope and sealed it before she finally got between the sheets and put the light out.

At least this was a step in the right direction. Things couldn't go on as they were or she would be getting herself more and more muddled and more involved with the attractive stranger staying over the garage.

Wherever Robert had been the night before he hadn't lingered in bed this morning. When Rosabel went down to the garage to collect her car he was walking up and down the lawn pushing the mower and whistling cheerily.

He shouted a "Hallo, good morning" as she backed the car out of the garage, and then as she wound the window down he came over, "Sorry I didn't wash the car last night."

Rosabel looked at the mud splashes on the bonnet. "That's all right," she said. "It doesn't have to be cleaned every shower. I only used to do it once a week before you came here."

"Well, since I am here," Robert said, "there's no need for you to dirty your hands. Leave it out when you come back this evening and I'll give it a going-over."

Rosabel nodded her thanks as she put the car in gear and drove out through the gate. If he was going to clean the car there'd be no walk this evening either. She was ashamed of her feeling of disappointment and she looked reassuringly towards the letter which she had brought out to post. The sooner it was on its way to London the better.

When she went into the dining-room that evening it was to find that the table was only set for four. She went into the kitchen. "Isn't Peter going to be in for supper tonight, Isa?" she asked.

"Didn't you know?" Isa said. "Eric's come back with an enormous salmon which he says he can't eat all by himself and he's asked Peter and Robert to go over for supper this evening."

"Aren't you going as well, Isa?"

Isa looked up from the pan she was stirring and laughed. "Oh, I've not been invited this evening," she said, "it's a strictly men only affair. Eric's asked Gordon Murray as well and I think the four of them are going to have a jolly evening together over a good meal with a game of cards to follow."

"If that's the case," said Rosabel as she turned towards the door, "I'll be able to have the surgery all to myself. I'd like to get on top of my paper work. I did a lot the other evening, but I haven't got through half. If you don't mind being left to watch the television on your own, Isa, I'll go and get on with it after supper.''

"You can start now if you like," Isa said. "Supper won't be ready for about twenty minutes. I'll give you a call.''

Rosabel nodded and walked through into the surgery. It was very quiet in there. She moved some of Peter's things to one side so she wouldn't get them muddled with her own and opening her bag took out all her paper work and laid it out.

As she surveyed it she gave a sigh. There was even more than she had realized, and the sooner she set to and got on with it the better. When she had been to see her supervisor the other day she had been told when she could take her holiday. She wondered where to go. She hadn't made any arrangements and although she would very much have liked to go abroad and make sure of some hot sunshine, she didn't want to go on her own.

As soon as the Murray/McGill wedding was over Peter was going up to Glasgow to do a refresher course and he had arranged for the girls to go and spend a month with some old friends of his who lived in Ireland. There Jennie and Katya could enjoy three or four glorious weeks of swimming, riding and other outdoor sports with friends of their own age. Isa herself had arranged to spend a fortnight with her sister in Aberdeen, so for part of August Rosabel realized that she'd be in the house alone.

She wondered what it would be like to have the big old place to herself and it crossed her mind to wonder whether Robert would be there still. Nothing had been said about how long he was going to stay, but he seemed to be turning into a permanent guest in the village.

The following evening when she drove into the garage he was sitting at the bottom of the outside staircase oiling the girls' bicycles. He had turned them upside-down on the concrete in front of him and was going over them carefully. He looked if anything more disreputable than ever and his hands were dirty with grease and oil off the chains of the bicycles.

As Rosabel came out of the garage he looked up and smiled. "I suppose you wouldn't like to take pity on me and take me out to dinner? Oh, I'll pay for the meal, of course, but you provide the transport. I imagine there must be some nice little pubs around here."

Rosabel stopped in front of him. "You're not serious, are you?"

"Never more so. I thought it would make a change for you too."

"To go out to dinner?" she asked, "or to be asked to provide the car?"

Robert grinned. "I suppose it is a bit unusual," he said, "but you know how I'm fixed," and he spread his hands.

Rosabel nodded grimly. "Yes, you told me the other day, remember."

He looked at her again, his face quite solemn, but she could see that his eyes were dancing with amusement. "So I did," he said, "and if I remember rightly, you looked very disapproving."

Rosabel didn't quite know how to answer this comment. If she told him how disapproving she was she might not know when to stop, and after all, she had been brought up to be polite and not to moralize over other people. Perhaps an evening in her company with just a sherry to start with and maybe half a bottle of wine with the meal would make him see there were better things to do than spend every lunch and evening time leaning on a bar. He was persuadable after all. When they went to Rockspit and called in for a drink he had needed no inducement to leave early. He hadn't wanted to stay on and have drink after drink, and he could control himself if he wanted. Perhaps all he needed was a prod in the right direction.

"Give me twenty minutes to have a quick bath and

change and I'll be with you. There's a very nice little place about ten miles away where they do an absolutely super steak."

"That's the place," he said immediately. "I'm a steak addict. Twenty minutes now. Not a minute longer," and he gave the wheel of Katya's bicycle a spin.

To Rosabel's astonishment when she came downstairs dressed in a yellow silk frock patterned with big white daisies, it was to find Robert sitting chatting to Isa and looking incredibly immaculate. He wore a lounge suit in a deep shade of grey with a spotless white shirt, and although the hair was shaggy it had been smoothed down into some sort of order.

He got up as soon as he saw Rosabel at the door and his eyes ran admiringly down her. "Hm, you look good enough to eat," he said.

Rosabel flushed slightly and her glance flew from his face to Isa's. If Isabel was surprised at this compliment she didn't show it. Her head was bent over a darn in one of Katya's socks and she looked quite unconcerned.

"I'm glad you think so," Rosabel said lightly. "We girls aim to please, you know."

She wondered why she had made such a flippant remark as she turned hurriedly and headed for the back door. Better get into the car quickly before she said anything else so banal. What could Robert, not to mention Isabel, be thinking of her? But if she thought that this bad beginning was going to cause a feeling of uneasiness between herself and her supper partner she was quite wrong. Within two minutes Robert had restored her feeling of complete relaxation. He talked quietly all the way over the moorland to their destination, and as she drove into the car park, Rosabel knew that she had been subtly put at her ease.

When they went into the inn their table was ready and Rosabel found she didn't have much trouble in persuading Robert that a pre-dinner drink was quite unnecessary. The fillet steak when it arrived was all that she had promised. It was bursting with mushrooms and flanked by grilled tomatoes and tiny button onions. They had preceded it with soup and fresh salmon poached in wine so that by the time the last morsel of steak had gone Rosabel felt she couldn't face another mouthful.

Robert grinned at her across the table. "Eyes bigger than your tummy?" he asked.

Rosabel nodded. "But it was delicious, wasn't it?"

"All that you said it would be. I must say I enjoy a good steak. We'll have to come here again," and he looked appreciatively around the little dining-room.

Since his attention was elsewhere Rosabel was free to study him. She was getting curiouser and curiouser about this man and wished she were bold enough to ask him personal questions. She hadn't even known for instance that he possessed a lounge suit, and she doubted that it would have fitted into the knapsack.

As he turned back and met her eyes it was almost as if he read her thoughts. "You should have been called Eve, not Rosabel," he said.

Rosabel flushed; the inference was obvious. "I know I'm inquisitive, but you're a puzzle to me."

"Well, at least you're an honest Eve," Robert said, and he smoothed his thumb gently across her hand as it lay on the table.

Rosabel jerked her hand back quickly as if she had been stung and put it on to her lap. If Robert was offended by this gesture he made no sign of it, but Rosabel wished he wouldn't make these casual unmeaning gestures. She was beginning to like his touch far too much, and since it could lead nowhere, it would do neither herself nor himself any good to encourage it. Better to try and keep things on a strictly friendly footing between them if that were possible.

To turn his mind away from her gesture of withdrawal she said quickly, "You haven't told me if you enjoyed yourself over at Colonel Brewer's last night. Did you have a thoroughly cosy stag evening?"

Robert laughed. "I must say we had a very stimulating evening, but then I was with three very interesting men. The old boy's a cracking good story-teller."

"Yes, I know he is," Rosabel agreed, "even at drawing-room tales. I imagine, uninhibited by the ladies, he's really something."

When they got home a little after half past ten and walked into the house it was to find Isa McCulloch standing in her dressing gown answering the telephone. Seeing Rosabel, she said into the receiver, "Oh, here she is. Just a moment, please, I'll get her to come and speak to you."

Isabel covered the mouthpiece with her hand. "It's Mrs. Gregg from Wallace's farm, Rosabel. She insists on speaking to you. Better hurry up, because she's in a call box."

Rosabel came forward to take the phone. Mrs. Gregg was another of her "hardy annuals" who had a baby with great regularity every year. She had already had four and was well on the way to producing the fifth. As Rosabel took the phone from Mrs. McCulloch and put it to her ear, she was confused by the excited jabbering of Mrs. Gregg's voice.

She was a Devon girl whom Gregg had met and married while on a holiday down in the south of England, and used as she was to the soft Scottish burr, it took Rosabel a moment or two to adjust her ear to the Devonshire accent. "It's Mrs. Wallace," Mrs. Gregg said. "Did you hear what I was saying, Nurse? I want you to come at once, you must come at once—I think he's gone mad!"

"What on earth are you talking about? What's wrong with Mrs. Wallace? She's not my patient, nor my brother's. If she's ill you must get her own doctor."

Mrs. Gregg's husband was Farmer Wallace's head cowman and lived in a cottage quite near to the old stone farmhouse. Rosabel knew Wallace. He was a man of about fifty, dour, uncommunicative and who rarely stopped to exchange a "good morning" if you passed him on the road. His wife had died about five years ago and then last year, to everyone's astonishment, he had gone away for a short holiday and appeared with a timid whey-faced girl of about twenty on his arm. Nobody had seen very much of the new Mrs. Wallace, and it was reputed that her husband didn't permit her to go out very often. Certainly she had never joined the women's organizations in the district, and even Isa, usually a mine of information, knew little about her.

"I can hear her screaming dreadful up there, Nurse. She must be having the baby now."

"Baby? What baby?" Rosabel asked.

"Her's having a baby. Farmer Wallace wouldn't even let her go to the doctor."

"Do you mean to say she's never seen anybody?"

"Well, not as far as I know," Mrs. Gregg replied. "I went up when I heard all the screaming and tried to get in, but Farmer Wallace wouldn't answer, so I thought I'd better come and ring you."

"But I'm not doing the confinements this week," said Rosabel. "It's Nurse McClaren's turn." She and the jolly girl in charge of the adjoining district took it in turns, week and week about. They found this fitted in very well and only once during the time the system had been in operation had two women gone into labour simultaneously.

"I've been on to her already," Mrs. Gregg shouted into the receiver, "but she's already out on a case, so I got on to you straight away. You will come, won't you, Nurse, right away? I hate to think what's happening in there, and her's only a bit of a girl."

Rosabel realized that she would have to do something. "Yes, I'll come right away, now don't you worry."

As she turned from the phone, she looked at Peter's mother-in-law. "Did you get all that, Isa?"

"Well, part of it," said Isabel. "Farmer Wallace's wife is having a baby and nobody knows anything about it."

"They do now," said Rosabel. "Apparently she's

screaming fit to beat the band and he won't let anyone into the house to help. I'd better go and change," she said, glancing down at her silk frock. "I can't go like this."

Robert, who had been quietly standing by listening to the telephone conversation, said, "I think I'd better come with you."

Rosabel looked up astonished. "There's no need."

"I think there is," Robert contradicted.

"And I agree," said Mrs. McCulloch. "Farmer Wallace is a peculiar man and at this time of night I don't think you ought to go on your own. Yes, go with her, Robert. In the meantime I'll try and contact Peter."

By the time they reached Wallace's rather isolated farmhouse it was to find quite a few people gathered in the yard. The screams were not as violent as Mrs. Gregg had made out over the telephone, but they were quite alarming enough to make Rosabel hurry as she got out of the car and walk quickly across to where Mrs. Gregg was standing with her husband and two or three other farm labourers and their wives. "Have you tried to get in again?"

Mrs. Gregg shook her head. "I haven't, but my Bill went up and knocked on the door and asked Himself if he should fetch the doctor, and he told him to go away and mind his own business."

"Why is he so against doctors?" Rosabel asked.

"Well, first Mrs. Wallace died having a baby and Wallace said 'twas the doctor's fault. I think myself 'twas because she was well over forty and worked right up to the end. Did too much, poor soul."

Rosabel could see a glimmering of the reason this obstinate man had not called in medical advice. People could be very obdurate in these parts, and she walked forward to the farm door with some trepidation. To her surprise she found Robert standing beside her shoulder to shoulder, and as the door was pulled abruptly open from within he propelled her inside the house and the door was shut before she had time to catch her breath.

She had no time to stop and argue with the red-faced, angry man who tried to bar her progress. Ducking under his arm, she went towards the pathetic little figure crouching in the armchair beside the fire, moaning like a small kitten. It didn't take Rosabel more than three minutes to realize that here was a case more of hysteria and fear than of actual pain, and she had soon persuaded the trembling girl to get to her feet and be assisted up the staircase. Engaged in soothing the bewildered girl, Rosabel had been vaguely aware of shouts and muffled threats behind her, but the shouting had died down long before she was half-way up the stairs. Whatever Robert had said to the infuriated father-to-be, he had certainly managed to quell his protestations at their uninvited entry into his house.

But a brief examination of Mrs. Wallace brought a frown to Rosabel's brow. The baby was certainly not lying in the correct position and she would need a doctor's help.

With a promise of bringing up a cup of tea, she went off downstairs to have a word with Robert. To her amazement she found the two men sitting on either side of the kitchen table, a large earthenware teapot between them, drinking tea and discussing the price of beef stock, as if they had known each other for years.

"Mrs. Wallace would like a cup of tea," and fetching another cup and saucer from the dresser she proceeded to pour one out, added sugar liberally and took it upstairs.

The little patient's eyes brightened as she saw Rosabel come back into the room. "I thought you'd gone," she said.

"I may have to pop out for few minutes to get some things," Rosabel answered, "but I shall be back again. Just lie quietly and if you get another pain try and relax. Your baby's not coming yet, I can assure you."

When she went down the stairs again she caught Robert's eye and he quietly got up and sauntered over to where she was standing in front of the fire. Quickly

Rosabel told him how the land lay. "There's no phone here," she said, glancing round her. "I never thought of telling Isa that."

"Never mind," said Robert. "You can leave me here to keep an eye on things. I'll pop upstairs and look at the patient in a moment."

"You won't frighten her?" Rosabel asked.

"No," Robert said, and gave his quiet smile, "just leave it to me. If you can bring Peter back with you, all to the good."

Rosabel drove fast, blessing the fact that as it was late there was little traffic on the roads and fervently hoping that the village constable was safely tucked into his bed. As she rushed into the house she found Peter having a cup of tea. "Oh, you're home—good!" she said. "Another crisis! Come into the surgery. I'll tell you all about it while I'm assembling what we'll need."

Peter rose wearily to his feet. "I've only just got in."

"We haven't a second to lose. I've had to leave Robert Carr dealing with a pregnant woman and a very irate husband," and Rosabel proceeded to put her brother in possession of all the facts.

If anything, Peter drove even faster on the return journey to the Wallaces' than Rosabel had done on her way to fetch him. She clung to the door as they rounded corners on two wheels and prayed they would both arrive in one piece. She knew Robert was quite capable of calming two agitated people, but a confinement case, especially one like this, would be quite beyond him. Of course the ideal solution would have been to send him to collect Peter, but with no licence she could hardly risk letting him drive her car. However extenuating the circumstances, there would have been serious trouble had he been stopped.

When they reached the farm the bystanders had departed, and all seemed quiet. But as Rosabel pushed open the farmhouse door there came a cry. Peter immediately snatched the bag out of Rosabel's hand and started forward just as Mr. Wallace got out of a chair and lunged towards them. There was no sign of Robert and as Peter made for the stairs, Farmer Wallace grabbed Rosabel's arm in so strong a grasp she was unable to free herself.

He looked as if he were about to have an apoplexy and Rosabel knew she would be better employed for the next five minutes in preventing him from following her brother upstairs and causing a scene. She walked into the kitchen, and since he was still holding her arm, her captor had to come too.

She looked up into his angry face. "You'd better let go of me now and calm down, Mr. Wallace."

He seemed as if he were struggling for speech as she went on. "My brother was at home and as I needed his advice I've taken the liberty of bringing him with me. I know he's not your wife's doctor, but I was worried about her condition. Your wife is very young, she's inexperienced, and she should have had medical advice long ago. It was very wrong of you not to permit it."

By this time Mr. Wallace had found his voice. "And what's it got to do with you, young lady? My Milly was perfectly all right until today."

"Do you think so?" Rosabel asked. "I haven't seen your wife before, but she seems to me to be very run down."

"You quacks think you know everything. I tell you Milly was all right until today. I've seen to it that she's had plenty to eat, lots of milk, just as it says in the books. I wasn't having what happened five years ago."

Rosabel felt sudden remorse. In his own way this man had done what he thought was best, and probably had complications not occurred, everything would have gone quite smoothly. He'd probably have had to fetch one of the women in at the end, but they were all experienced in having babies, and certainly Mrs. Gregg would have known exactly what to do.

By this time he seemed more calm, so Rosabel looked around the kitchen and her eyes alighted on the kettle. "I wonder if you would make some tea. I really think I ought to go up and see how my brother's getting on."

Rather reluctantly he released her, walked over to the big iron kettle lifting it as if it only weighed a feather. As he took it to the tap over the big stone sink Rosabel said, "Now you won't come up, will you, Mr. Wallace, until I call you?"

He gave her a grudging "All right" as she turned towards the kitchen door and without waiting to see whether he followed or not, hurried along the hall and up the stairs.

As she quietly pushed open the bedroom door, it was in time to see the backs of the two men urgently bending over the bed. Her brother had not had time to take off his jacket, but Robert was in his shirt sleeves, the cuffs turned back and rolled high above the elbows. Hearing her footsteps, he turned his head and said, "Come on, Rosabel, you're just in time. Have you got something to wrap the little lad in?"

Rosabel hurried forward and took the squirming creature out of her brother's hands. She was amazed that everything had happened so quickly. When she left to go for help she could have sworn that it would be several hours before Mrs. Wallace had her baby. Rosabel set competently about seeing to him. "Do you want me to help with Mrs. Wallace?" she asked as she turned towards the wooden cradle standing in the corner of the room.

"Yes, we're almost done," her brother said, and Rosabel went towards the bed to wash and tidy the rather tearful young mother who lay there. She was too busy for the next fifteen minutes to notice that the two men had quietly gone downstairs, and when she finally turned towards the door, it was to see that Peter was bringing in the new father, his face bright with anticipation.

"I haven't had time to give him a real bath," Rosabel began. "I've been seeing to your wife."

As if she anticipated this remark would annoy her husband, young Mrs. Wallace burst into tears again and it took Rosabel another five minutes to calm her down. By this time Mr. Wallace had duly admired the baby and he now sat down and took one of her listless hands in his.

"It's all right, Milly love. You've done very well. He's a bit small at the moment, but he'll grow, so Doctor says. We'll soon fatten him up."

In his way he was doing his best to be kind and Milly looked apprehensively up into his face before she realized that he wasn't angry. "I'm so glad it's a boy," she hiccoughed. "That's what you wanted, isn't it?"

"Of course I did. Now Doctor says you ought to have a sleep, so off you go. Nurse is going to come again first thing in the morning. You'll be all right now, won't you?"

Milly nodded. For once it seemed she had pleased her elderly husband. When she had agreed to marry him she hadn't banked on being kept practically a prisoner in this out-of-the-way place. She was a "townee" and used to a busy urban existence.

When they finally got into the car Rosabel eased herself on to the back seat. "I'm glad that's over," she said as the car started forward out of the farmyard. "I wasn't counting on dragging you out tonight, Peter. I'm sorry, but really it was a bolt from the blue."

Her brother laughed. "It must have been a bit of a facer. I hear you and Robert went out for dinner and came back to find this little lot awaiting you."

Rosabel chuckled tiredly. "At least it came to a satisfactory conclusion. When I examined her I thought she'd left it too late."

"Well, it wasn't a breech presentation as you thought," her brother said. "The poor little chap had turned into the umbilical cord."

"Bad as that, was it?" said Rosabel. "Well, I'm glad you were able to see to it and not me. I couldn't have managed alone."

"I'm sure you couldn't," her brother agreed. "As it was it took the two of us."

Tired though she was, Rosabel's eyes opened wide. So her brother must have co-opted Robert's help. No doubt when Peter had explained he'd been able to help him deliver the baby. She felt too tired to work it all out now, and as the car sped homewards she closed her eyes in relief.

CHAPTER SEVEN

THE NEXT MORNING'S POST brought an invitation. The Murrays were giving a buffet supper and dance the following Saturday to celebrate Ian's engagement, and Rosabel, Peter and Isabel McCulloch were all invited.

The girls were loud in their protestations that they, too, were not to be allowed to come, but as it didn't start until eight o'clock, Peter pointed out that it was too late even for Jennifer.

"You'll have to wait until you're a bit older," Peter said as he quietened his two daughters' exclamations of disappointment. "Content yourselves with having the prime role of bridesmaids. You'll be able to shine at the wedding and get all the compliments you desire."

Both the girls chuckled. "Well, we're certainly going to see that we get the nicest frocks. Gran and Penny are going to take us into Dumfries soon so that we can choose. If we can't find something really gorgeous Gran is going to make them for us."

Mrs. McCulloch looked resignedly towards her two granddaughters. "I suppose I shall have to if we can't find anything suitable, but I'd much prefer to buy something ready made," she said. "I don't get time for a lot of sewing these days."

"But you wouldn't mind, I know, for a special occasion like this," Katya said persuasively.

"You're not to let them pester you, Isa," ordered Peter. "I'm quite sure if they can't get something in Dumfries one of the big shops in Glasgow would send you some dresses on approval." Their protestations that Gran liked to do things for them were soon stopped by their father ordering them to go and brush their teeth and get off to school.

"Rather nice to have a night up at the Murrays'," he remarked as the girls went out of the door. "They've made that old farmhouse absolutely beautiful. Have you seen it recently, Isa?"

"Yes," Isa McCulloch replied. "I was up there having tea about a month ago. They've certainly spent a lot of money on it, but it's well worth it. They've had central heating put in and improved the old living-room no end. I always thought it rather dark before, but now they've put in those two extra windows, it makes an enormous difference."

On Saturday evening Rosabel inspected her wardrobe. Of all her dresses she liked the yellow silk the best. It was one that Isabel had helped her to make. The heavy silk clung lovingly to her figure and the golden-yellow certainly suited her.

She slipped the frock over her head and surveyed herself in the mirror. Her hair looked just right tonight and she dabbed some perfume behind her ears before collecting a coat and going downstairs.

To her surprise she found Robert waiting with her brother in the sitting-room and her astonishment must have shown because he said, "Oh yes, I'm coming too. Didn't you know I'd been invited?"

Rosabel had the grace to blush slightly. "To be quite honest I never gave it a thought. But then of course you did meet Ian's father at Colonel Brewer's the other night, didn't you?"

"That's it," Robert nodded, "and he was immediately taken with my scintillating personality and couldn't resist asking me to his son's engagement party."

Rosabel giggled. "There's no need to be facetious," she said. "I'm delighted you're coming."

"Now you've made my day. Come on, I think I hear Isa in the hall and we don't want to be late. We might miss all the fun."

Peter's receptionist had come in to look after the

girls, so there would be no reason to leave before the party was over. They arrived to find about fifty other guests assembled in the Murrays' big farmhouse. At the end of the room an attractive buffet had been laid out with fresh salmon patties, vol-au-vent of various sorts, hot sausage rolls, cold meats and enormous bowls of salad. Mr. Murray had hired a waiter for the occasion to see to the drinks, so as the trays went round Rosabel got more and more anxious as to how much Robert was drinking.

As soon as they arrived she had got separated from him and now could only see the back of his head across the room.

She found she couldn't concentrate on what the people around her were saying and excusing herself started to make her way across the room. An expression of anxiety must still have been on her face as she reached Robert, because he stood there, eyebrows lifted and a look of enquiry in his eyes.

Rosabel couldn't help glancing down at the glass in his hand and wondering how many of these he had emptied. As if he guessed her thoughts he said, "Come to check up on me, have you?"

The blood flamed in her face, but the look of severity, which Rosabel realized had been put on for her benefit, vanished from Robert's face as quickly as it had come and he burst out laughing.

They were standing alone, shut in by the groups of gossiping people. "It's nice to know my girl likes to see that I'm all right and has my welfare at heart," and he put an arm round her waist and squeezed Rosabel against him for a second.

Rosabel's face flamed even brighter. "Stop, shhh, don't!" she said quickly. "Someone will see you," and she glanced round quickly to see if any of the near neighbours had seen what was going on, but was relieved to notice they all seemed to be preoccupied with their own conversations.

"What if someone does see us?" asked Robert. "It

doesn't matter all that much. After all, I'm a very demonstrative fellow and you'll have to get used to this sort of thing when we're married."

Rosabel gave a gasp, but before she could open her lips he went on, "You must know by now that I've put the Indian sign on you. You'd be a complete fool if you didn't. As soon as I knew there was nothing serious between you and that fellow up at the hotel I made my mind up. You were the girl for me."

This was too much for Rosabel and her eyes sparkled with anger, but before a word could pass her indignant lips Robert said, "Shh, someone will hear you," and gave her yet another squeeze.

Despite his admonitions, Rosabel fully intended to give him a piece of her mind when she suddenly realized that her brother and Fiona McGill were making their way across the room. Fiona was looking especially nice tonight. She was wearing a turquoise dress in a tunic style with little silver buttons along the shoulders and a very beautiful silver filigree necklace round her throat.

She was a quiet girl, apt to be self-effacing, and Rosabel was surprised to see how outstanding she looked tonight.

"The Murrays have certainly done us proud," Peter remarked. "Isn't it a wonderful party? Have you tried the buffet yet, you two? They've brought in a huge dish of fried chicken and I just couldn't resist it. I've been making an absolute pig of myself, haven't I?" and he glanced down at Fiona for corroboration.

She looked up and smiled into his eyes and Rosabel got a jolt of surprise. She didn't think she was an imaginative sort of person, but she was sure that a moment or two ago she had detected a great spark of affection in Fiona's glance as she had looked up at Peter.

Poor Fiona, there wasn't much chance for her there. Peter had been besottedly in love with June and he'd never really got over her death. Still, it must be a lonely life for him despite having the company of his daughters as well as Isa and herself in the house. Perhaps in time he would turn to Fiona. She personally would be very happy to see Fiona installed in the house by the river at Bannford, but it would mean changes all round.

The conversation had changed while her thoughts had been wandering. "It's warm enough to dance outside, they think," Peter said, "so we're going to have moonlight dancing on the lawn. I hope they've cut the grass nice and short. I'm not too hot on a ballroom floor. On uneven turf I'll be jumping all over everybody's feet."

Rosabel laughed. "Never mind, I don't suppose we girls will be any cleverer on grass in high heels, so watch your shins, Peter!"

After the dancing, champagne had been opened and everyone had drunk the health of Penny and Ian, looking impossibly happy standing hand in hand at one end of the long room. Then as the older members of the party started to collect their coats some of the younger ones had the bright idea of getting Gordon Murray's boat and going for a sail.

Rosabel and Peter immediately excused themselves on the pretext of having to get up early the next morning, but after Rosabel had collected her coat and said "Good-bye" to Mr. and Mrs. Murray she found Robert waiting for her. Isa and Peter had left and they were going on the sailing trip with the others after all, he informed her. As she was hustled into one of the waiting cars she whispered fiercely, "You know I've got to get up early in the morning. I shall be like a limp rag."

"Nonsense. You're a strong, healthy girl. A bit of moonlight will do you far more good. You don't get half enough fun, in my opinion. In London most girls of your age are out every night of the week dancing or going to theatres."

His comments about the habits of girls in London set Rosabel off on a new train of thought and she relapsed into silence. He must live in London, then, if he knew so much about what went on. She glanced at him as the car started and wished she knew more about his background.

When they got on the water Rosabel was glad she had brought a big coat with her. It was a good deal cooler than it had been in the sheltered garden at the Murrays'. But she needn't have worried about feeling cold, because when she settled herself on a seat facing the bows it was to find a strong arm firmly encircling her waist.

She glanced down at the hand, wondering whether it would be policy to try and remove it or whether it would be less trouble to leave it where it was. To her relief on glancing round she saw everybody seemed to be more interested in their own concerns than in watching what she and Robert were doing.

What a good thing the Johnstons hadn't come to the party. She supposed they must have been invited. Perhaps they had thought it better policy to refuse. It might have proved embarrassing to Kate if what Bill had told her were true. On the other hand they might just be very busy up at the hotel. It was a waste of time worrying about the Johnstons' reactions in any case. Much better, she thought, to relax and savour the enjoyment of sailing slowly through this wonderful summer night.

The moon shone down on the river as they headed towards the harbour mouth. It was so still Rosabel was sure she could hear the lapping of the waves across the bay. Hardly anybody spoke. Like herself, they must have been enthralled with the enchantment of the night. She leaned back against the broad shoulder and felt Robert's arm tighten.

He was having it all his own way tonight, she thought, but things would be different tomorrow. His cool reference to a marriage, for instance. It took two to make a bargain and she was far from sure that she wanted to make a bargain with the semi-stranger behind her.

But when she went out of the house the next morning at a quarter to nine her heart melted slightly. He had run the Mini out of the garage ready for her to get in and drive straight out on her calls. Unlike herself, there had been no need for him to get up early. He certainly was a thoughtful man, unpredictable too. She'd fully expected him to insist on kissing her good-night before they'd parted last night, but all he had done was press a light kiss on the back of her hand before walking away.

But if she had been feeling mollified this morning he annoyed her again when she returned for lunch. He and Peter were sitting in deck chairs on the lawn, a glass of beer by their sides and looking thoroughly comfortable and at home with one another.

They both waved and then continued with their conversation, virtually ignoring her. Rosabel turned her back on them and marched into the house. She was still feeling piqued by the time she had changed and gone downstairs to give Isa a hand with the lunch. She knew she was being unreasonable, but she couldn't control her feeling of let-down at Robert's apparently indifferent greeting.

I wonder what I really expected him to do, she thought. He couldn't jump up and embrace me in front of Peter. On the other hand he didn't need to wave quite so half-heartedly, as if last night didn't even happen.

When lunch had been eaten and cleared away she told Isa that she was going for a walk. "I shall probably go in the direction of the golf hotel. I haven't seen the Johnstons for ages," she said offhandedly.

Isa turned as if to make a comment and then changed her mind. "Just as you like, my dear," she said. "Will you be back for tea?"

Rosabel hesitated for a minute in the doorway. Isa's unspoken words hung in the air. I suppose I'm being supremely foolish, she told herself as she went to change her shoes. But in any case I'm going for a walk whether I go up to the hotel or not, and she set out resolutely refusing Jennie's and Katya's offer to come with her.

She was only half-way down the road, however, when she met Bill coming in the opposite direction. His eyes searched her face. "How are you? I haven't been down to the house because I thought I wouldn't get a very warm welcome."

Rosabel laughed rather shakily. Bill's eyes looked like a spaniel's that had been beaten and didn't quite know why. Kate was right. His face did look thinner than it had a fortnight ago. Rosabel's warm impulsive heart softened. He was waiting for her to make the next move and she gave his arm a squeeze.

"Don't be silly, Bill. I don't know why you should feel you'd be unwelcome just because..." She stopped.

"Just because you decided that after all I wasn't the love of your life?" Bill finished.

Rosabel flushed. It wasn't a very pretty way of putting it and she felt angry with him, but he was going on.

"You're seeing quite a lot of somebody else now, so I'm told."

Rosabel ground her teeth with rage. Not that she hadn't expected the local gossips to have carried the news of her occasional outings with Robert back to the golf hotel. It might even have been Kate herself. Perhaps she'd been a little taken in by Kate's seemingly happy-go-lucky character. She hadn't been happy or carefree the last time they had met and had discussed Penny and Ian's engagement. In fact Kate had seemed quite sour about it. Being heartbroken was one thing, being a sore loser was another, Rosabel thought. Despite her anger she hadn't forgotten her intention of trying to cheer Bill up, to take the beaten look out of his eyes.

"I've come out for some fresh air. Why don't we go up to the top and over the hill into Rockspit? It'll only take us about an hour if we step out," and she turned without waiting for his reply and led the way.

She knew that if anybody looked up from the doctor's garden they would be easily identifiable against the skyline as they passed the back of the house. Was she small-minded to hope that the lazy man whom she had left still lying in a deck-chair would raise his eyes and notice as they passed by? That would teach him to make casual and pretentious proposals of marriage!

But when she got home Rosabel realized that her intention to teach Robert a lesson had proved more a punishment for herself than to him. She had no way of knowing whether he had been in the garden when she passed or not, and Bill had proved such a dull companion that she had longed to be back home doing something useful. It was one thing having a tramp on one's own, thinking one's own thoughts. It was quite another to go along with a man who alternatively sulked and berated one. To start with Rosabel had answered his reproaches, but as they still continued she had lapsed into silence and this had seemed to annoy Bill more than her defence of herself.

There wasn't a pin to choose between him and Kate, Rosabel decided as she marched up to her room to have a wash and brush her hair before tea, and when she went down into the sitting-room Isa gave one quick glance at her face.

As Rosabel sat down she just inquired mildly, "Did you meet anybody while you were out, Rosabel?"

Rosabel was a minute or two before she replied and then she looked up and met Isa's glance. She couldn't help a reluctant twinkle coming into her own.

"Yes, I ran into Bill Johnston," she said, "and he came for a walk with me."

Isabel didn't say anything but looked down at the knitting in her hands. "It's none of my business," she said, "but I always think a clean break's the best thing, Rosabel. Now I'll say no more about it."

Rosabel chuckled. "Oh, sensible Isa," she said. "What would we do without you? Thanks for not wanting to hold a post-mortem. Shall I get the tea?"

"There's just the tea to be brewed. Everything else is ready on the trolley. The girls are upstairs finishing prep which should have been done yesterday, and Peter's been called out. Perhaps you'd go over and see if Robert would like to join us. I think he's been having an afternoon snooze."

"What, at this time?" said Rosabel, glancing at her watch.

"Well, after you went out he gardened until after four, so I should think he was ready for a rest," Isabel said. "He's been hard at it most of the day. He did the lawn this morning too."

"Most industrious of him," Rosabel commented rather scathingly as she got up and went towards the door.

If Isabel glanced at her retreating back in an amused way she didn't notice and stalked off to the kitchen to put the kettle on.

She was spared the chore of going over to see if Robert would like to join them for tea. Isabel had been unduly sanguine when she had thought that both the girls were doing prep. Katya must have slipped out, because as Rosabel glanced through the kitchen window she was in time to see the door of the flat open and Katya emerge pulling a protesting Robert behind her.

The window was open and she could clearly hear her niece's voice. "Come on! Tea will be ready by now and I'm absolutely bursting for some of Gran's meringues. She made them specially this morning and they're absolutely oozing cream!"

He followed her down the stairs looking as if he had just woken up from a deep sleep, his hair was rumpled and he was blinking in the sunlight. "I'll have to visit your cloakroom," he said. "I daren't present myself looking like this."

Rosabel gave a snort of derision as she switched off the electric kettle and poured the boiling water over the tea-leaves. He wasn't usually so particular about his appearance, she thought, and then pulled herself up short. She had to admit that on occasion he could be very fastidious. Last night he had looked as neat and tidy as any of the other men present at the party—and yes, his hair had been cut! Perhaps her disapproval hadn't fallen on such deaf ears after all, she thought, as she put the tea-pot and hot water jug on the trolly and began to wheel it towards the kitchen door.

If she went into the sitting-room in anticipation of another brisk passage of arms with Robert Carr, she was doomed to disappointment. He greeted her as casually as ever, and sitting himself down in an easy chair, permitted the two girls to wait on him. Peter strolled in just as they started tea and the two men began an earnest conversation about an article which had appeared that morning in the paper. Rosabel, as she handed round sandwiches, bread and butter and cakes felt left out of it. Men, she thought, could make you feel most isolated, as if you lived in another sphere and talked on a different wavelength. If they liked each other and had things in common, as her brother Peter and this man obviously had, you just couldn't get a word in edgeways once they had started a conversation.

When he had finished tea, Robert excused himself and departed. Rosabel felt let down. After an uncomfortable afternoon in Bill's company she had to admit to herself that she had returned home subconsciously looking forward to a verbal skirmish with Robert, only to find herself ignored. She sat and watched television until bedtime, feeling disgruntled with herself and life in general, but it wasn't until next morning when she called on Mr. Brown to give him his bed bath that she realized where Robert had spent the previous evening.

The old man was sitting chuckling with glee and rubbing his hands.

"What's pleased you so much this morning?" Rosabel asked as she shed her hat and coat.

"Just you go and look through the window, Nurse, and you'll see. Not that I approve of working on the

Sabbath, mind, I don't. But that Mr. Carr of yours came round last night and went over my garden again. Looks a treat, it does."

Rosabel strolled over to the window as she rolled up her sleeves. It certainly did look beautiful. Robert must have put in several hours' hard work again last night and the general improvement outside was working wonders with her patient. Mr. Brown looked better already. At the first opportunity Rosabel knew she was going to have to eat a large piece of humble pie. Wiser than herself, Robert realized that the treatment once begun would have to continue until the old man was out and about again.

The next morning brought a reply from Joan Rivers. She told Rosabel her name was down for the next course and that she would have to come to London to be interviewed. "I've put my name down too," she enthused in her letter. "I'm thrilled that you think you would like to try it. If we could get on the same course it would be absolutey wonderful. It's years since we saw very much of each other, and it would give us an opportunity to go around together. There are bags of parties here and every so often we can get free tickets for one of the shows. I think you'd love London. I certainly do."

During her lunchtime, Rosabel had five spare minutes, so as it was another lovely day she wandered out into the garden and sat on the big garden swing to re-read the letter. She still hadn't really made up her mind that giving up district nursing and going to London was the right thing. But on the other hand it would solve a lot of the difficulties which were crowding in on her more and more.

Lost in thought, she became suddenly aware that Robert was walking across the lawn towards her. He flung himself down on the grass beside the garden swing. "You look as beautiful as a spring day," he commented.

Rosabel felt the colour creeping up her face. She looked down at him and laughed. He really was an amazingly difficult man to quarrel with.

"I suppose the only answer to that is 'Thank you, kind sir'!"

"Well, it's as good as any," he said as he scraped out his pipe with an old penknife and knocked the ash on to the grass beside him. He closed the knife and put it away in his pocket. "I don't know whether it's an effort to prove your independence," he said, "or whether you feel genuinely sorry for the chap, but you're wasting your sympathy, you know."

Rosabel's faint flush deepened into a real blush, this time more of anger than embarrassment. So her jaunt with Bill had not gone unnoticed! She glanced down at Robert's face. He was looking blandly innocent, but she guessed it covered a deliberate attempt to take a rise out of her. Yes, the faint mockery deep in his eyes was plain to see.

She didn't take her glance away from his as she began slowly, "I could say that it was none of your business."

"Ah, but you'd be quite wrong, as I told you the other evening at the Murrays'. From now on it is my business."

"You're surely not expecting me to take all that nonsense you were talking the other evening seriously? To start with I don't know anything about you. I don't even know what you do."

He rubbed the back of his head. "At the moment, nothing. I'm living in a sort of vacuum."

"There you are, you see," she said, "you don't really intend to tell me anything sensible."

He looked at her and burst out laughing. "It's no good asking questions and then answering them yourself. I've done all sorts of things."

"I'm sure you have," Rosabel snapped. "I can just imagine! Advertising. Public relations. Import and Export," she said, scorn in her tone.

For a moment she saw surprise in his eyes and then he laughed again. "My goodness, I never really knew a girl like you for jumping to conclusions! But why all the scorn poured on Public Relations and Advertising? Products and people have to be advertised, otherwise you'd never sell either, and as for Importing and Exporting, well, it's got to be done, otherwise the country's economy would go absolutely to pot. You obviously regard the people who do this as being quite beyond the pale."

"No, no, I don't," Rosabel said hastily. "I don't know about any of those businesses to really arbitrate or give an opinion, it's just that.... It's just that advertising people portrayed in TV programmes seem rather brash."

He was looking quite stern and Rosabel received a shock as she looked down and saw the glimmer of anger in the grey eyes looking up at her. "Never condemn a profession or a trade of any sort unless you really know what goes on."

"I know," she said, suddenly docile. "I'm like a little girl who uses big words and doesn't really know what they mean."

He burst out laughing suddenly. "So many people condemn out of ignorance, you know. But we're straying from the point."

"That reminds me," Rosabel said swiftly. "I must thank you for going again and working in Mr. Brown's garden. He was cock-a-hoop this morning when I went in to see him. The garden looks absolutely beautiful, Rob. It is good of you."

Robert's eyebrows slowly went up. "Well, you didn't think we could just leave things as they are with the old man lying up there fretting himself to flinders over the weeds, did you?" he said. "If we've got to put your love cure really into operation we have to see it out to the bitter end. But I suppose, young lady, you didn't think about that when you asked me to come that first time?"

Rosabel looked down at her hands. "I must admit it was very thoughtless of me, but I didn't. Of course, if I'd stopped to think."

"Ah," Robert said, "if we stopped to think. My goodness! I wonder how many mistakes, big and little, have been followed by somebody saying that. But never mind, my dear child," and he patted her benignly on the knee, "all is forgiven. Your ever loving Robert will continue to go up there and do the odd hour or two until the patient is on his feet again, so don't worry."

Rosabel laughed. "I'm very sorry I involved you without thinking about it properly," she apologized again.

Robert got to his feet and sat down beside her on the hammock. His sudden drop to the broad seat made the hammock swing wildly, and she reached out half blindly for support.

Immediately he turned sideways and drew her into his arms. She glanced hurriedly towards the house, but the windows winked back blindly at her and she remembered that apart from the receptionist busy at the front of the house, it would be empty. Peter would have gone on his calls and Isa, she knew, was arranging a garden fête and wouldn't be back until tea-time.

She looked back at the man beside her to find him studying her face quite seriously, feature by feature. "You're very, very pleasing to look at."

"Well, thanks," she said, "for those few kind words."

"Lots of beautiful women aren't a bit pleasing to look at, at least, not to me. They have such cold expressions, as if they're afraid that smiling will make them seem too human."

Rosabel tried to push him away. "You and your theories about this and that! You're full of odd clichés."

"Am I?" he sounded surprised. "I hope I don't keep trotting them out one after the other. People who do are such unutterable bores."

He turned her face towards him and gently stroked the cheekbone. Rosabel wondered whether he was going to kiss her and half hoped that he would. Here in the secluded garden no one would see them, and she had wondered several times what it would be like to feel his lips on hers.

But he obviously had no such intention. He still studied her face and then he suddenly rubbed his thumb gently across her upper lip. "Yes, they curl up nicely at the corners," he said.

This was too much for Rosabel's sense of humour and she let out a shout of laughter.

"You must do that often after we're married. It's the finest medicine in the world," Robert remarked.

Rosabel drew back so that his hands slipped away. "You're really taking far too much for granted," she protested.

"No, I'm not. And if you're worrying about that chap up at the hotel, don't. I think that's most of the trouble. If he were completely out of your mind, you'd be able to turn your full attention to me. If I know anything about human nature, all he wants is to settle down and get married—any nice, respectable, well brought up, amenable girl would do. No reflection, mind, on you, Rosabel. It's just that he thinks he's reached the settling down age."

Rosabel flushed again with annoyance. It was probably true, she realized. Bill *had* got to the settling down age and if she hadn't been available his attention might have alighted on somebody else in the district. But she had been available, she had lived nearby and she'd been friendly with his younger sister. It was rather squashing to her self-confidence to be told, though. So much nicer to believe that someone had fallen desperately in love with you for yourself alone and that nobody else would do.

She looked at Robert and wondered if she should put this point of view to him, but meeting his eye, she thought this a waste of time. With his uncanny perspicacity he had probably read her recent thoughts and worked this out for himself. Had he too got to the settling down stage? She was even more on his doorstep than she was on Bill Johnston's.

She suddenly saw he was shaking his head. "I can see what's going through your mind, young lady, and you're quite wrong. I haven't got to the age when I think I ought to settle down. In fact, my meeting you has been damned inconvenient. I didn't want to fall in love at this particular time, and it's very worrying, I can tell you."

Rosabel's forehead crinkled in a frown. It was a rather peculiar statement to make and she sat waiting for him to go on and explain further. But he didn't do so. In fact he almost seemed to have forgotten she was there, because he was gazing down at the ground between his feet and frowning. She hadn't his facile ability for reading other people's thoughts and she wondered what dismal conjectures could be going through his mind to make him look so miserably stern.

Suddenly she glanced at her watch. "Good heavens! Look at the time! I ought to have been on my way ten minutes ago. All my patients will be grumbling. If I'm late with the first one, I shall be late all afternoon."

Robert got up, the harsh expression disappearing. He pulled her to her feet and stood with her hands in his. "Knowing you, I'm sure you'll get through very competently," he said. "I'll turn the car for you, if you like."

"No, it's all right. Don't do that," she said. "I've only to get my bag, powder my nose and I shall be ready. It won't take me a minute to drive round the yard and out again."

He laughed. "Afraid I shall drive it into the wall?" he called after her as she ran towards the house.

As she left it came to her that she still didn't know any more about Rob Carr. Either because of her own interruptions or by clever manipulation she still hadn't discovered what his business interests were. And why should it be inconvenient at this moment for him to have fallen in love? It seemed a unique way of describing the situation, particularly if he hoped to persuade her to spend the rest of her life with him.

It was usually when pressure was being put on a man to propose that he said it was inconvenient. Not when the girl was running as hard as she could in the opposite direction. Or was she? If she was honest with herself hadn't she been giving Robert a great deal of encouragement? She suddenly realized that she hadn't any wish to discourage him. He intrigued her both mentally and physically. Even his generally untidy appearance was not unendurable. In fact she felt that she liked him as well dressed in a sweater and corduroys as in a suit, shirt and tie.

She wondered if Robert had conveyed his intentions to her brother. If so, Peter had said nothing about them. He rarely mentioned Robert and when he did, seemed faintly amused about something, although what it was Rosabel couldn't imagine.

The following morning brought a bombshell in the shape of a letter from their Aunt Muriel. She often came and spent a fortnight or so with them during the summer months, during which time she did her best, as she described it, to tidy up the household. How Isabel McCulloch put up with her interference Rosabel didn't know. She rarely commented, but just put everything back to where it had been before Aunt Muriel's arrival.

This year, as Peter opened the letter addressed in their aunt's spidery writing he gave a groan. "You'll never guess," he said, "Aunt Muriel's coming in ten days' time and what's more she's bringing Cousin Hubert and his wife with her. What have we done to deserve them?"

There was a general groan round the table, loudest from Katya. "Oh no," she exclaimed, "not Cousin Hubert!"

Her father looked up. "It's two years since he was here. Can you remember that far back?"

"Remember?" Katya burst out, "when the whole time I couldn't do one thing right! Jennie was the blue-eyed girl, but it was 'Don't do this, Katya' and 'Stop doing that, Katya' and 'It's bad manners to do such and such a thing!' I was fed up!"

Peter Fairbairn laughed, "Perhaps it will be the other way round this time. She's given to favourites, Aunt Muriel. She can't help it. Come on, girls. Off you go or you'll be late for school."

"I'm sorry about this," he said to Isabel as his two daughters dashed out of the room still arguing about Aunt Muriel's arrival. "I'm afraid it's going to make a lot of work. Still, with a bit of luck they'll not stay longer than ten days, although she does say here," he glanced down at the letter again, "that they'd like to stay a fortnight *at least*!"

Isa got up and started to stack the dirty breakfast dishes. "I daresay we shall all survive it. If you just agree with her all the time it rather takes the wind out of her sails," and picking up the tray she walked out of the room.

When she had gone, Peter folded the letter slowly and put it back in its envelope. "It means I'll have to tell Rob to find other quarters, but I daresay they'll put him up at the Fisherman's Arms. He seems to have made himself well-liked along there."

"Oh, no, not the Fisherman's Arms!" Rosabel exclaimed before she could stop herself.

Her brother raised his brows. "Why ever not?" he began and then a gleam of amusement appeared deep within his eyes. "Were you thinking perhaps you could find him some other digs in the village? But you know they'll be getting pretty busy."

"I'll find him somewhere," Rosabel said hastily. "Don't do anything for a moment, Peter."

Peter got to his feet, the smile now having reached his lips. He picked up all his correspondence and walked over to the door. "If you'd like some brotherly advice," he said, "you'll ask Rob where he'd like to stay before you fix things up. I get the impression he doesn't like to be organized."

As Rosabel got rid of the debris from breakfast she thought over what Peter had said. Robert would certainly *not* like to be organized, and in any case she really had no right whatsoever to go and look for somewhere for him to stay. Better to tell him first that he would have to vacate the room over the garage for a short time. But there was no reason why she shouldn't find out if there was anywhere in the village where he could have bed and breakfast. If she had somewhere up her sleeve ready to produce he would perhaps be persuaded not to go and stay at the Fisherman's Arms where temptation would be always under his nose. She would pop along at lunchtime and call at one or two of the cottages along the road here where summer visitors were accommodated.

It was a blustery day, unlike the mild weather they had been enjoying recently, and when Rosabel went out to get the car she noticed there was quite a nip in the wind. By the end of the day she was feeling thoroughly tired. In some of the hillier parts the wind had been distinctly vicious and twice she had to chase after her cap.

She was holding it in her hand that evening as she called at the first cottage down the road from the doctor's house. To her relief she discovered at this, her first call, that they could put Robert up for the duration of her aunt's visit.

"'Tis only a wee room, Nurse, you understand, but I'm sure it would do for Mr. Carr. He's a very obliging gentleman."

Rosabel's eyes opened wide. In the short time he had been in Bannford Robert had certainly made his mark. As she walked the short distance home she reflected that she had never heard Bill described in such intimate terms. He was referred to usually as "Yon Mr. Johnston up at the hotel."

She was wondering how she was going to broach the

subject to Robert when he came clattering down the steps into the yard. "Ah, there you are," he said. "I wondered when you'd be home. Are you coming for a walk after supper?"

Rosabel nodded, relieved to have her problem so neatly solved. There'd be plenty of opportunity this evening to bring up the subject of where he was to stay when he had to vacate the flat.

But when she joined him an hour later, clad in slacks and a thick chunky sweater, she found him in a distinctly intractable frame of mind. He was at his most teasing, and Rosabel, looking at him, wondered what had precipitated this mood. It was going to make it very difficult when the time came to suggest an alternative sleeping place for him. She was well aware that he knew she did everything in her power to curtail his drinking and she also knew that for some reason it amused him.

Perhaps other girls had tried to reform him and failed, or maybe a crusade on his behalf amused and flattered his male ego.

By the time they had arrived at Rockspit Rosabel had persuaded him to go down on to the beach instead of into the little inn where they usually ended up for a drink before setting out to walk home. He set up a cairn and then collecting a pile of smaller stones to use as missiles, he came and sat down beside her.

"It strikes me that you've got something on your mind. What is it?"

Rosabel looked at him in surprise. She never failed to be astonished that he saw so much, and here he was taking the wind out of her sails once again.

She watched as he knocked the top stone off the cairn with unerring aim before she answered. "Has Peter told you that we're having visitors the week after next?"

"Yes, as a matter of fact he did mention it earlier this evening."

"Then you know that we shall have to...."

"Yes, I know that I shall have to give up my occupancy of the flat. Well, I can always move into the Fisherman's Arms," and he slanted a glance down at her.

Rosabel flushed. "I wanted to speak to you about that. There is a room for you at one of the cottages, if you like."

At this Robert laughed outright. He turned and hugged her briefly before straightening up again and continuing his assault on the large pile of stones. "If it will make you rest any easier I'll stay wherever you like, but I have to go back to London fairly soon, so perhaps this will be as good a time as any since you need the flat."

Rosabel was silent, gazing out to sea. She had got used to his presence and the sudden suggestion that he was leaving struck her dumb. It had never occurred to her that he might choose this opportunity to return to wherever he had come from, though it was quite obvious that he must have a family somewhere and a business or profession awaiting him. He didn't give the impression of being a truly indolent man, though for some reason he was not prepared to tell her why he had taken this protracted holiday.

Maybe he had been warned for health's sake that he must take a break. Whatever the reason he was looking considerably healthier than when he had first turned up in Bannford.

The Sunday before Aunt Muriel was due to descend on them Peter arranged a small dinner party. He and Fiona McGill, Penny and her fiancé and Rosabel and Robert all went over and had dinner at a hotel on the other side of Castle Douglas, and on the return home they called to have a liqueur at a small inn noted for this particular beverage.

To their surprise they found Kate and Bill Johnston sitting rather glumly in the bar having a glass of shandy each.

Peter strolled over to them. "Hallo, you two. What

are you doing here? It's not often we see you out during the season."

Bill looked up as the others joined them and rose to his feet. As they sat down he said, "Well, it's a fairly quiet evening and Jean said she could cope on her own, so Kate and I came out for a breather and we dropped in here for a noggin before going back. We've been pretty busy recently and we were glad when the numbers dropped this week."

Rosabel found herself studying the brother and sister rather more closely than usual. If she wasn't mistaken Bill seemed ill at ease, and Kate's manner towards her did not hold the warmth which once it had. Rosabel noticed that she had managed to take the seat next to Robert and as drinks were brought for all of them it became obvious to her that Kate was making every effort to attract his attention. She was gazing up into Robert's face and carrying on a very animated conversation, once or twice laying her fingrs on his arm as she emphasized a point.

Rosabel wondered if the others noticed what was going on. Perhaps she was being unnecessarily jealous, but it did seem as if Kate, perhaps out of mistaken loyalty for her brother, was doing her best to make her mark with Robert. He was gazing down with an expression on his face which Rosabel found very difficult to define, then suddenly turned his head to surprise an expression in her own eyes Rosabel had not meant to reveal.

As he continued to gaze she found herself quite unable to turn away. With his usual acuteness Rosabel knew he was reading in her eyes "I love you, please don't look at any other girl" and he was answering, she discovered, his grey eyes for once perfectly serious, "Don't worry, I don't intend to," and then she realized that both Bill and Kate had caught the long exchange of looks.

Rosabel blushed deeply. She didn't like such a precious moment being observed by anyone, and certainly not by the Johnstons of all people. She scarcely knew how she got through the next half hour, though she was supremely conscious of Robert sitting on the other side of the small bar table. Good manners, however, kept her seated, answering when spoken to, mouthing platitudes, but wishing she and Robert were a dozen miles away and free from even the congenial company of the two McGill sisters and her brother.

When Peter finally got up and said that it was time they were going Rosabel heaved a small inward sigh of relief. Walking to the car, she immediately restored to her usual good humour and "all's well with the world" feeling by Robert's hand closing over her own. He didn't let go until they were seated in the back of Peter's car and then it was only to take it again in an even closer clasp between his own two warm palms.

When they reached home he came into the house with them, though he made no attempt to get her alone. Indeed he seemed to want her to say "good night" and go up to bed, and when Peter said to him, "Do you want a few words with me, Rob?" he nodded.

Rosabel wondered for a moment if Robert were old-fashioned enough to be going to ask Peter for permission to marry her, but it was so out of date these days and somehow out of character. He was the sort of man who would certainly take it for granted that if a girl said "yes" to him, then her family must be agreeable. Somehow he didn't fit in to the picture of a Victorian suitor asking for permission to pay his addresses.

Certainly the conversation which she could hear taking place in the study below was far longer than would have been necessary had Robert been asking Peter if he had any objection to their marriage. Long after she had undressed, washed and gone back to her bedroom again and climbed into bed, she could hear the murmur of voices coming up from the room below, and though she lay for a long time waiting for the square of light which shone out on to the garden to disappear, it was almost one o'clock when she heard her brother lock up and come to bed.

It was really no surprise, therefore, when Robert told her the following afternoon that he was going to London instead of taking up his residence at the small cottage down the road. "I think I told you I'd got business in London," he said, "and I've decided this is as good a time as any to go up there and get it over with."

She wished she could have asked Robert exactly what his business was. But he obviously wasn't going to say, and she was too shy to ask him outright.

The following morning another letter arrived on Rosabel's breakfast plate from her friend Joan. "I've put your name down for interview," Joan wrote, "but I'm wondering if you could combine it with a few days' holiday. I don't know how you're fixed for a summer holiday this year, but as you know my father is stationed in Gibraltar and I shall be going out there in July for two weeks. Mother says there's stacks of room in the quarters, so if you'd like to stay you'd be more than welcome. I've made the date for your interview to coincide with the beginning of my holiday in case you can manage it."

Rosabel was thoughtful as she put the letter back into the envelope. She had tentatively put her name down for September, but felt sure her supervisor would be willing to let her alter the dates if she let her know immediately. It was worth a try, anyway. For all Robert's talk about intending to marry her, and for all her feelings towards him, his unwillingness to tell her any of his private business made it seem to her as if it might be better to go ahead and make plans of her own. Though it would almost tear her heart out to think of anything which didn't include him, the chances were that after his visit to London he would not return to Bannford.

In fact, he had never said that he would. He had only announced that when Aunt Muriel arrived he would be leaving.

She wondered if she should ask her brother's opinion. It seemed likely that the discussion the night before had touched on this subject. But he and Robert were being so secretive it was almost as if there were something shameful in the explanation. Trust men to stick together and not reveal what it was!

CHAPTER EIGHT

THE NIGHT BEFORE Aunt Muriel was due to arrive and Robert to depart from Bannford, he and Rosabel went out to have dinner together.

Rosabel had found time to ask her supervisor about holiday dates and had got the go-ahead. She intended to tell Robert of her plans, but it wasn't until they were sitting in the lounge of the small inn after they had dined that she found the courage to break the news to him.

As she poured coffee she said, "Oh, incidentally, Rob, when you get back from London I may have gone off on holiday."

"Why, what do you mean? I thought you planned to go in September. Wasn't that the idea?"

"It was, but I've changed my mind. Remember Joan Rivers—I told you I did my training with her, she's now in one of the big London hospitals. She wants me to go to Gibraltar and stay with her family for a fortnight. Peter's going to spend August taking a refresher course and the girls are going to Ireland to stay with friends, so it means I'm rather at a loose end this year. Now this has come up it seems too good an opportunity to miss, especially as I have to go to London for an interview in July."

"What sort of an interview?"

"I'm thinking of giving up district nursing and going in for intensive care."

"No good at all, my dear girl. You are quite temperamentally unsuited to it."

Rosabel looked up. Though not exactly in her brother's words, they were certainly the same in their meaning. What made these two men immediately veto her plans to do this sort of training? To hear them talk anyone would think that she died a little death every time she lost a patient. Nurses were trained from the first to keep emotion apart from their work, and she thought she was fairly successful at doing this, but her brother who knew her intimately and this man who seemed to sense her every mood both considered her to be quite unfit for it.

But if she thought Robert was going to argue she was quite mistaken, because he went off on another tack.

"What date do you intend going to Gibraltar? Are you staying in a hotel?"

"No," said Rosabel. "Joan's father is in the Army so I shall be staying with the family. We should have a grand time."

Robert looked at her sideways and his eyes twinkled. "Oh, I'm sure you will. All those lovely subalterns!"

Rosabel burst out laughing. "You know that wasn't the reason I accepted. I was thinking of all that sunshine and sea bathing, as a matter of fact. Although we get plenty of bathing here the water's beastly cold. Think of that lovely warm blue sea. Mm, it'll be gorgeous!"

Robert grinned. "You sound like one of the advertisements on commercial television," he said. "All you need now is the packet of chocolates which won't fatten you or the detergent which will make all your holiday clothes whiter than white, then you're all set."

"At least the pay would be better," she said after a moment. "We're not overpaid in the medical profession."

"No, and you want to make your work twice as difficult and twice as gruelling by going on an intensive care unit. I wish I had the right to absolutely forbid you to do so."

His expression as he finished speaking was harsh and Rosabel gazed at him as if she was suddenly meeting a stranger. Almost as if he sensed her bewilderment

Robert's face relaxed into its usual whimsical smile. "I'm sorry, my dear girl—talking through the top of my hat again, you'll be thinking. Forgive me." And without waiting for her to make another comment or ask him what he had meant when he said he would like to forbid her to go into the new training he started to tell her a ridiculous story which Rosabel, her mind on other things, scarcely heard.

After a few minutes he said accusingly, "You're not listening, dear girl."

Rosabel glanced up at him through her lashes. "As a matter of fact I wasn't—sorry," she said. In her turn she wasn't prepared to go into any explanations of where her thoughts had been wandering. Instead she asked if she might have more coffee and he hailed a passing waiter.

When it arrived Rosabel poured Robert another cup and then one for herself before looking across at him. "How are you getting back to London? Would you like me to run you to the local station?"

"Now that's a good idea," he said. "I'm hoping to set off in the morning and then I ought to be in London by early evening, but won't it interfere with your schedule?"

"I do have a busy morning planned," she answered, "but if you tell me the time of your train I'm sure I could fit it in. I wouldn't like you to have to carry that huge rucksack."

Robert grinned. "I don't intend to take it with me. I'm leaving it as a guarantee that I'll be back shortly," and he glanced up as if waiting for her to contradict his statement.

Rosabel smiled inwardly. At least he did intend to come back. He wasn't going away to London intending to write later on some slim pretext and tell her he wouldn't be coming back. Robert Carr made all sorts of peculiar statements, but he was never untruthful. But was he sincere in his feelings for her? She'd give a year's pay to know the answer to that question.

Though Rosabel felt a hollow emptiness when she knew Robert's train had departed, by evening time she was heartily glad he was out of the way. Aunt Muriel had written to say they would be arriving in time for supper, and Isabel had taken this to mean around seven o'clock, which was the time the family usually had their evening meal. But seven came and even eight o'clock with no sign of Aunt Muriel, Hubert or Ann, so that Mrs. McCulloch had finally given the girls their supper and packed them off upstairs to get ready for bed and finish off any remaining homework which still hadn't been done.

Downstairs she had hastily sliced up the rest of the chicken, put it in a good rich gravy with the sausages and small forcemeat balls and had placed the big casserole in the oven to keep warm. The roast potatoes, by this time overdone and virtually uneatable, were disposed of and Isa began preparing fresh vegetables.

The car finally arrived just after nine, and Aunt Muriel expressed surprise that her letter had been misconstrued.

"Naturally I just meant supper before going to bed," she said. "I never thought about coming here for our evening meal. We wanted to show Ann the castle at Carlisle, didn't we, Ann?"

Hubert's meek, demure-looking little wife nodded in agreement. Rosabel could never decide whether Ann had always been rather shy before she had married Hubert or whether the years with him and Aunt Muriel had produced the rather peculiar disposition which she now showed to the world. One scarcely knew whether to like or dislike her, and since she was very heavy going when it came to conversation, she soon tired anyone who tried to draw her out.

When the luggage had been carried in Isabel said, "I'll clear your places off the table, then, if you've had dinner."

"No, no. We can manage to nibble a bit, I expect, if you'll just wait while we wash our hands," Aunt Muriel said hastily, and she pushed Ann ahead of her up the stairs.

Back in the living-room, Rosabel and Peter exchanged speaking looks. It wasn't wise to comment out loud because Aunt Muriel, who maintained that she was getting very deaf, nevertheless seemed to hear extraordinarily well on occasion. By the time the visitors had washed and come downstairs again another fifteen minutes had ticked by, and Rosabel was feeling uncomfortably hungry. She had kept going, but this was her one big meal of the day and she was usually ready for it soon after seven.

The first course, iced melon with a slice of orange stuck on like a sail, passed without comment, but when the huge casserole was brought in with the freshly boiled potatoes and peas, Aunt Muriel could contain herself no longer. As she picked up her knife and fork she remarked to the table at large, "I always think this dish is much better with creamed potatoes, and I never have any frozen vegetables in the house. Ann always sees to it that we have fresh vegetables," and she glanced up the table towards Isabel McCulloch.

If she hoped she was going to get any retort she was disappointed, because Isabel placidly went on eating as if nothing had been said. Foiled by this lack of interest in her unkind comments on the appetizing meal before her, Aunt Muriel waited until dessert was placed on the table.

When she noticed that two pieces had been cut out of the big lemon meringue pie she looked at it as if she was being offered yesterday's sweet.

"And when was this made, Isabel?" she began.

Isabel looked up from serving Ann and Rosabel. "When was this made? Why, this afternoon, Muriel. When did you think it was made? You know you can't keep a lemon pie, and it has to be eaten the day it's baked."

Muriel glanced at Isa for a moment or two, realizing that both her broadsides had been turned aside, so she transferred her gaze to Rosabel, sitting across the table and looking with rapt attention at her own slice of pie.

As a matter of fact Rosabel was miles and miles away, wishing she had a crystal ball to see precisely what Rob Carr was doing at this moment. She was quite startled when her aunt's abrupt voice said, "No sign of you getting married yet, Rosabel, I suppose?"

Rosabel glanced up, still deep in thought, to meet the hard gaze from across the table.

She smiled apologetically. "I'm afraid not, Aunt. No one will have me, you see."

Peter's chuckle was not echoed by the visitors sitting round the table. Hubert went on eating solidly, Ann glanced from face to face drinking in every word and Aunt Muriel turned her gaze from Rosabel to her nephew sitting at the head of the table.

"It's nothing to laugh at, Peter. At her age I was married and had two children. It's about time she was thinking about settling down. Now who is there around here who would be suitable?"

"Really, Aunt!" exclaimed Peter. "One leaves girls to decide for themselves these days. Rosabel's perfectly happy in her work, so there's no reason for her to start shopping around for a husband, now is there?"

"Shopping around? What a disgusting expression! Really, you young people!"

Peter laughed again and glancing down towards his angry aunt, bowed courteously. "Many thanks for those few kind words, Aunt Muriel. It's a long time since anyone described me as 'young,' and if Katya and Jennie were here they'd shriek their heads off."

"Yes, that reminds me. Where are the girls? I haven't seen them yet."

Isabel answered from the other side of the table, "They're in bed and asleep, I hope, but you'll see them tomorrow, Muriel, don't worry."

"And just as spoilt as ever, I expect," said Aunt Muriel. "Really, Isabel, the way you run after those girls!"

Isabel looked across at her. "Well, they're the only

granddaughters I have, you know," she said mildly. "And grandmothers are reputed to be the worst spoilers in the world. You haven't any grandchildren, have you, Muriel?"

As Peter said about half an hour later in the kitchen, "I think honours were about even, don't you, Rosabel? Really, she gets worse year by year! I'm not surprised Dad used to say he was frightened of her when he was a little boy."

Aunt Muriel had been their father's eldest sister. They often wondered why she insisted year after year on coming to see them, because during their father's lifetime she had never been near the place. Peter always said that it was partly curiosity and partly because it gave them a cheap holiday. Neither Hubert nor his mother were over-generous with money, and the thought of having to pay hotel prices would have sent a shudder through their careful souls.

Rosabel was away next morning early, but she arrived back at lunchtime to find that instead of the usual family meal around the kitchen table Isabel had laid it in the dining-room and that the entire family were assembled. The two children were looking very gloomy and Katya's eyes were red.

Coming into the room after washing her hands, Rosabel felt as if she could have slapped Aunt Muriel for spoiling the happy atmosphere. She wondered what she had been saying to the children to reduce them to this state, because as a rule no happier girls could be found anywhere and the house normally rang to the sound of their laughter. There was certainly no laughter today and Aunt Muriel was sitting waiting to be served looking like and avenging angel.

It was rather a silent meal, and Peter, after a long look at his daughters' faces, said, "I forgot to tell you, Isabel, I'm going into Dumfries this afternoon and I shall be there until about six. Would you like to bring the girls in today so that they could choose their bridesmaids' dresses?"

Isabel gave him a grateful look. "I think I could manage that all right, Peter. I can leave a cold supper."

The three guests looked anything but pleased at this pronouncement, but Peter went on as if he noticed nothing. "You won't mind, I know. It's difficult for Isabel to get into Dumfries on the bus, and the girls are going to be bridesmaids next month. I expect you've heard."

"Actually I haven't," Aunt Muriel snapped, "but now that I know perhaps you'd be good enough to give me the details. Who is getting married? When is it? And why have your girls been chosen? I presume it's no relation."

"Oh, no relation at all," Rosabel chipped in. "As a matter of fact it's the vicar's sister."

"I didn't know you were even friendly with the vicar."

"But we introduced you when you were here last year."

"Oh, *that* young man. I recall him now," Aunt Muriel said rather grandly. "I remember remarking to you that he seemed rather out of place."

Rosabel laughed. "What made you think that? John McGill's one of the nicest of men."

She was sorry immediately the words were said. She could almost see the wheels turning in Aunt Muriel's head. "Now don't get any ideas, Aunt Muriel," she said. "I have no intention of becoming the vicar's wife, you know."

"Really," sniffed Aunt Muriel, "young people these days have no modesty or decorum!"

It was evident that Peter thought this conversation had gone far enough. "Well, that's settled, then," he said. "If you girls have finished your meal, pop up and get ready." Without needing further bidding Katya and Jennie excused themselves and getting up raced out of the room.

"I do wish you'd make them walk a little more quietly and in a more ladylike manner, Isabel," Aunt Muriel said after they had gone.

"What for?" Isabel retorted. "They're only children, after all, and you must expect them to rush everywhere. I'd be worried if they didn't. Forget about the children for a moment. You'll be all right this afternoon, won't you, if I take the opportunity to go in with Peter? You did say you were thinking of motoring along the coast this afternoon, didn't you, Muriel? I heard you discussing it with Hubert and Ann this morning."

Aunt Muriel had the grace to go a little pink in the face as she said, "We did think we might go out for a little run when I've had my rest, but you will be back by seven, won't you, Isabel?"

"Oh, long before then," Isabel said. "The shops shut at half past five. Don't worry, everything will be ready for your meal this evening, even if it is cold," she finished as a last retort.

As Rosabel went out on her afternoon rounds she was feeling particularly depressed. As if it weren't enough to have this terrible void with Robert gone, in addition there was the irritation of Aunt Muriel. The only feeling of comfort she had these days was the sight of Robert's grubby old haversack standing just inside the door of the flat. She had got into the stupid habit of patting it each time she went up to the flat. She was even using the bed which he had used, leaving the two others for her nieces.

So far there had been no word from him either by post or telephone. Would he be back before she left for her holiday? She was due to go in ten days' time and had made arrangements with Joan to have her interview the afternoon before they left for Gibraltar.

With things so much in the air between herself and Robert, Rosabel felt she would have enjoyed the prospect of a holiday much more if her mind had been settled instead of seeming to go round in circles. It was all very well to fall deeper and deeper in love with Robert, but when it all boiled down, she knew so very little about him. Perhaps a period right away from here would make her able to get everything into proper perspective.

During the next week she didn't really have a great deal of time to dwell on her personal problems. She felt she had to give Isabel a hand when possible and at night she had to creep quietly into bed so as not to disturb the two girls.

She was usually too tired to stay awake for long. At times like these Robert seemed very far away and before she drifted off to sleep her eyes would seek that corner of the room where she knew his knapsack lay as if to assure herself once more that he would be coming back.

When his postcard finally arrived it told her little, and two days later when he telephoned she was over at the Manse talking wedding clothes with Penny and Fiona and so missed a word with him.

Peter gave her the message when she returned. "How did he seem?" she asked.

"Very well. He hopes to be back in a day or two," Peter said. "He sent you his love," and his eyebrows went up to meet his hair.

Rosabel was glad they were alone in the surgery together, though she knew that her brother was much too tactful to have given her this message even in front of Isabel.

The night before Aunt Muriel's departure, Rosabel managed to creep out of the house for a walk. It wasn't really inviting weather. The sunny morning had not lasted and by two-thirty it had been raining steadily. Now it was beginning to clear up again and everything smelled fresh and clean.

She didn't have time to do more than go up the hill and look at her favourite view. She stood there almost knee-deep in heather, its flowers as yet unopened, and looked out at the estuary. She must be every kind of a fool, she thought, to contemplate leaving this lovely place. She hadn't enjoyed leaving it even to do her training. She had been born not twenty miles away from here, and the gentle Lowland hills were a part of her. Nevertheless it was time she was moving on. The unsatisfactory end to her friendship with Bill and the even more unsatisfactory relationship which she and Robert were sharing provided two good reasons.

She stopped and plucked a small sprig of heather and poked it with a finger. The buds were still tightly closed and she wondered whether she would still be here when they opened. This particular spot held so many happy memories for her. Robert's warm hand on the nape of her neck. His habit of standing behind her and leaning his chin on the top of her head and his habit of running a thumb contemplatively up and down the back of her hand. Yet he had never kissed her properly. She wondered why.

She sighed as she turned to retrace her steps. It was beginning to get dark and time she was back.

There was a light in the kitchen and she popped her head round the door. Isabel was standing in her dressing-gown, heating some milk and she said softly, "Come on in, the others have gone to bed."

"Rather early, isn't it?" said Rosabel.

"I suppose it is, but after you went there was a frightful row and now they've gone to bed hardly speaking to one another." Rosabel giggled as Isabel continued. "Oh, Rosie, I wish you'd been here! It was like a pantomime. Hubert and Muriel had poor Ann running up and downstairs with the baggage, and apparently this afternoon when they were in Dumfries, Hubert secretly bought himself a bottle of Drambuie. He must have put it under some sacking in the boot and in the process of packing the bags in, Ann broke it. Now the whole car smells of liqueur whisky. Muriel vows she won't travel in the car tomorrow. Hubert says if she weren't so intolerant about drink he'd have been able to buy the bottle openly, and Ann has just sat there and cried great big crocodile tears and not spoken a word. It was as much as I could do to keep my face straight!"

Rosabel wiped her eyes. "Well, I must say I'm not

sorry to have missed that little contretemps," she said. "How glad I'll be when they drive away tomorrow. Poor Isa! You've had the worst of it by far. Don't you feel as if there'll be a huge weight lifted off your shoulders?"

"Oh, they're not as bad as all that," said Isabel. "They're really three very unhappy people. If they'd only stop and take stock of themselves I'm sure they wouldn't be quite so obnoxious. I never thought I'd feel sorry for Ann, but I must say I did tonight. Muriel turned on her, and I don't think she knew any more about the Drambuie than Muriel did herself. In fact, I'm sure she didn't, or she wouldn't have put a heavy suitcase down on top of it. And talking about getting ready, have you got anything packed for your own holiday?"

Rosabel ran her fingers through her hair. "Not a thing, but I don't really care as Gibraltar is in the sterling area and if I've forgotten anything I can always buy, can't I? So I'm just not worrying. I've fixed with Michael to run me to the station on Friday morning and I think that's all I need do except go to the bank. I'll do that when I go in to report to the Supervisor on Wednesday afternoon. It would be my week for home confinements, though. McClaren's due off in ten days' time herself, and she wanted to do it next week, so I could hardly ask her to change, now could I? I only hope nothing comes up at the very last minute, but I'm quite sure it will. It always does."

"Poor you," Isabel sympathized as she lifted the milk off the stove. "You wouldn't care for a hot drink, would you, Rosabel?"

Rosabel shook her head. "Thanks, I think I'll have something cold," and she went to the refrigerator and took out a jug of milk, "but I wouldn't say no to a biscuit if your going to have one."

Isabel nodded her head towards the tin on the table. "Help yourself. I suppose you're going to take it over to the flat to drink?"

Rosabel nodded and kissing Isabel a quick "good night" she departed. She chanced putting on the light, dimming it quickly so that it wouldn't waken the girls. Neither of them stirred and Rosabel remembered that it was their night for swimming. Both of them must be far too tired to be roused by the electric light being put on.

When she was comfortably in bed, Rosabel sat and sipped her drink and let her thoughts wander to the subject which interested her the most—Robert's return to Bannford. In three more days she wouldn't be here to welcome him. She had a definite appointment for her interview, and in any case Joan would be horrified if she missed their plane to Gibraltar. So she prayed Robert would come soon.

The next morning Rosabel said good-bye to her aunt and her two cousins. They appeared to have settled their differences and Aunt Muriel seemed determined to make a gracious exit. Rosabel suspected that already she was planning her next year's visit, and she certainly wasn't going to jeopardize her chances of returning for a free holiday.

She was sorry, though, to be vacating the flat. Sleeping over there, his old knapsack lying across the room, Rosabel had felt nearer to Rob Carr than she did in her own comfortable little room in the house. If only she'd had a letter, but probably like most men he was a poor correspondent.

Two evenings later Rosabel was helping Peter file case cards in the surgery when there was the sound of a car skidding to a halt in front of the house. A door slammed, voices were heard and Rosabel stood frozen at the filing cabinet.

Peter raised his brows. "Methinks I hear a familiar voice," he remarked, but he spoke to thin air, because Rosabel had dropped the pile of cards and was flying out of the room.

She and Robert met in the passageway. He stood, his back to the door, his hand behind him still on the knob, and looked at her, and Rosabel herself came to a full stop about a foot away, her eyes on his.

Something about him was different, and for a moment she couldn't think what it was. And then she realized that deep within the grey eyes a flame danced, a combination of merriment, tenderness, triumph and excitement, a look she thought never to see in Robert's face. He didn't say a single word, just held his arms wide and she walked straight into them as his lips met hers.

She'd thought about the kiss often, she'd dreamed about it, wondered how it would feel. But none of her daydreams came up to the reality. When his voice mockingly said above her head, "You can open your eyes now," she came back to earth slowly and looked up at him, a faint smile in her own eyes.

"I don't want to come back to earth," she said, "can't I go on another orbit, please?" and she held up her lips invitingly.

Robert laughed and spanked her lightly. "You're a minx, that's what you are, Rosabel. I always suspected it and now I'm sure. Come along, I think I'd better say 'Hallo' to the others because there's lots I want to say to you, and the sooner I get my greetings over the sooner we'll be alone to have a long heart-to-heart talk."

Rosabel turned him in the direction of the surgery. "Peter's in here. I don't know where Isabel is, but I suspect in the kitchen."

"I'll see your brother first then Isa afterwards. I expect she'll have enough supper to spare for one more."

Rosabel laughed happily as she followed him into the surgery, "I expect so, she usually has."

But if they were hoping for a cosy evening together, their hopes were soon shattered. Robert and Peter had hardly finished saying "Hallo" to one another when the telephone shrilled, and when Peter answered, it was only to hand the receiver to Rosabel. She listened for a moment or two and then said, "It's quite obvious I'm needed immediately. I'll come at once," and put the receiver back in the cradle.

"I might have known!" she sighed as the two men looked at her in silence. "Two weeks before it's due. Wouldn't you know on the last night before my holidays!" and she turned, shoulders sagging, towards the door. But she had only just reached the corridor when a warm arm came round her shoulder and she was twisted round to face the way she had come.

She could see the laughter in his eyes. "No heart-to-heart after all tonight—never mind, love. I've booked to fly out with you and your friend, so there's lots of time for explanations. Now get off and deliver that baby."

Why this sudden decision? What had happened while he had been in London? He looked somehow as if someone had left him a fortune, and Rosabel was eaten up with curiosity as she dashed out to get the Mini.

It was a very weary girl who returned to the house in the early hours of the morning. As she let herself in the tall clock in the hall was chiming half past five. She put down her bag and took off her hat. Really not much point in going to bed now.

She went into the kitchen and quietly made herself a pot of tea, carrying the small tray into the surgery. She would spend the next three-quarters of an hour making up her notes.

When she finally sat back and poured herself a second cup of the now almost cold tea she gave a sigh of relief. At least all her paper work was done. She wouldn't have to do it at the last minute and everything was ready to hand over to the standby nurse who would arrive first thing in the morning.

She rose and stretched. There would be just time to have a leisurely bath before she went downstairs again to start the breakfast. She would be able to save Isabel a job this morning.

When she was bathed and dressed she looked at herself in the mirror. She knew when she got to London it would be a bit of a rush to get across for her interview. She would probably only have time to freshen up so she had prepared for this eventuality. The uncrushable fabric of her suit should stand the journey pretty well, and as she glanced at herself in the mirror she thought it was modern and yet not too modern to alienate the strict disciplinarian who would no doubt be interviewing her.

The plain navy blue was decorated with bands of deep turquoise and suited her fair colouring very well indeed. She wore a pair of comfortable slingback court shoes and a well polished handbag and suede gloves in a matching turquoise lay on the bed.

When she had done her face and hair Rosabel went downstairs. She put on an apron and quietly began the family breakfast. She had only just got rashers of bacon arranged in the grilling pan when her nieces dashed into the kitchen.

"Hallo, Roz, you're up early," Katya said, bouncing over to the stove, "and looking absolutely great too," she added as she stood back to regard her aunt.

"What, even with an apron on?" Rosabel asked.

"Yes, even then, and you smell absolutely gorgeous—mmm!" Katya said. "It's nicer than bacon and eggs, and that's something!"

Rosabel laughed. Katya was just at the age when smells meant a lot to her, and to be told that she smelled nicer than bacon and eggs was a compliment far greater than an outsider would have thought. "Come on, you two. Sit down and start your cereals."

The girls sat down at the big kitchen table and started in, one on a large bowl of puffed rice and the other on cornflakes. It wasn't long before Isabel arrived, followed by Peter. There were exclamations at seeing Rosabel already down and when she explained that she hadn't been to bed at all, expressions of regret for the loss of her night's sleep.

Peter sighed and shook his head as he sat down and

spread out the morning paper. "My goodness, I don't envy you with a long journey ahead."

"Oh, I've had a bath, Peter, and piled on the make-up. I don't suppose if I took it off I would look quite so keyed up and ready for anything. Goodness knows what I shall look like by the time I get to London. I'm hoping Robert will let me snooze for an hour."

"Yes, he's going back with you," said Katya. "Now what about that? He's only just arrived and now he's going away again. I call that a swizzle!"

"Miss Moffat will mark us late if you don't hurry up and eat instead of talking all the time," Jennie reminded her. "Come on, we haven't got long."

When it was time for them to leave Rosabel took off her apron and walked out under the archway with the girls.

They both kissed her enthusiastically. "You will send us lots of photographs and postcards and letters with lovely stamps on, now won't you?" begged Jennie. "You know I haven't got any of the Gibraltarian stamps and I would like some."

"Don't worry," Rosabel laughed as she hugged them both, "I'll get a whole new mint collection for both of you."

"Not for me," said Katya. "I don't care all that much about stamps. It's the photographs I want and the postcards and the views. I'm collecting them for a scrapbook. Jennie can have the stamps off all my cards if she likes."

"That's settled, then," said Rosabel. "Now off you go," and she waved her hand as the two girls got on to their bicycles.

She was shading her eyes and watching them out of sight when a car appeared in the distance, driving far too fast, Rosabel thought, for the narrow village street. As it tore down towards her she saw that it was one of the very latest sports cars to come on the market, painted a clear green and driven by one of the most beautiful girls she had ever seen. It drew to a screech-

ing halt before the archway and the driver called across
to her.

Rosabel walked over and looked down into the huge
brown eyes. "Can you tell me where Dr. Fairbarn's
house is?"

"This is it," Rosabel answered. The driver of the car
pushed open the door, slung her long slim legs out of
the driving seat and stood up. As she walked round the
bonnet towards Rosabel she was able to see that the
figure matched the face. The girl was wearing a trouser
suit of some linen material in a beautiful tangerine
shade, and round her neck hung a long scarf figured
with bright flamboyant flowers. She wore very little
make-up except about the eyes, and even then Rosabel
noticed that the thick curling lashes were nature's own.
The dark shining hair hung in curls to her shoulders,
framing a face which in some way was oddly familiar to
Rosabel.

"Well, if this is Dr. Fairbairn's house," the girl said,
"I want to see Dr. Carver."

Rosabel's clear brow furrowed for a moment. "Who
did you say?" she asked. But just then the girl looked
over her shoulder.

"Oh, don't bother, there he is," and she sped past
Rosabel, through the archway and towards the steps
leading to the flat. Robert was coming down them
slowly, and the girl, hardly seeming to touch the
ground, sped across, ran up the steps to meet him and
flung both arms round his neck.

Rosabel could hear her greeting quite clearly. "Oh,
Rob! Rob darling! I thought I'd missed you. I've been
driving most of the night to get here before you left,"
and she drew the brown head down towards her with
one graceful hand. Even at that distance, as she raised
her arm, Rosabel could see the flash of a huge diamond
on the third finger of her left hand, and she turned
hurriedly away and walked into the house.

She was so blinded by tears as she went down the
corridor that she cannoned into her brother. "What-

ever's the matter?" he asked, putting his arms round her.

He drew her swiftly into the empty surgery. Rosabel couldn't answer him. "What happened?" Peter went on. "You're not hurt, are you?"

"No...it's..." Rosabel sat down in a chair for a minute and bowing her hands on the desk sobbed brokenheartedly. By and by she sat upright. No man was worth it, she decided to herself, and she put out a hand. "I haven't got a handkerchief, Peter," she said, and he put a clean one into her hand.

She blew her nose defiantly and looked up. "A girl has just arrived and she asked for Dr. Carver. Apparently she meant Robert. She seems to know him very well indeed. Why ever didn't he tell me his real name?"

Peter looked down at her for a moment in silence, obviously collecting his thoughts for a reply. "You knew!" Rosabel accused him.

He strode round his desk and sat down. "Perhaps if I give you this magazine it'll explain things to you," and he opened a drawer and took out the journal in which he had recognized Robert Carver's photograph a few weeks previously.

"I don't think I want to know," Rosabel said, pushing the magazine away. "It's quite obvious he's been pulling my leg all along the line. The quicker I get away from here this morning the better."

Peter regarded her for a moment in silence. "Don't do anything in a hurry. Stop and think first."

"I'm not deciding things in a hurry," Rosabel said in her own defence, "but I don't think I can stand any more." She got to her feet. "Don't come with me, Peter. I've got to decide this for myself," and she went quickly out of the room.

She didn't go back into the kitchen. She didn't want to answer the questions which she knew Isabel would be bound to ask when she saw her tear-stained face. Instead she went quickly to her bedroom and put the remaining things in her bag. Having done this and locked the suitcase she went into Peter's bedroom next door and lifting the extension, phoned the garage.

She got through to the man who drove the local taxi straight away. "Is that you, Mick? Do you think you could come round right away and collect me, because I'm ready now?"

If Mick was surprised at the change of plans he made no comment, just saying, "Yes, I can come any time you like, Miss Fairbairn."

Rosabel went back into her own room and collecting her gloves, handbag and suitcase she went downstairs. She had touched up her make-up and knew that most of the traces of her recent bout of tears would have disappeared.

"Is Robert ready? I didn't think you were off so soon," Isabel remarked as they met in the hallway.

"I don't think he'll be coming with me," said Rosabel. "He's got a visitor. Well, good-bye," and she gave Isabel McCulloch a quick hug before she could make any comment about this hasty departure.

She put a quick head round the surgery door and seeing that her brother was alone said, "I'm going now Peter."

"I think you're making a mistake," he said as he got up and walked towards the door. "Does Robert know you're leaving?"

"There's no sign of him. Now, please, please don't try to stop me."

Her brother spread his hands. "It's your decision. You're over twenty-one and if you can't see you're making a big mistake you're a muggins."

He gave her a kiss. "Look, love, have a nice holiday," and he let her go as the sound of a horn at the front door announced the arrival of the taxi.

She went swiftly down the front steps and got into the car. As she was closing the door she thought she heard Robert calling her name, but of course it must have been just a figment of her imagination—wishful thinking, in fact. The sports car still stood firmly in front of the archway and there had been no sign of him when she had given one brief last look through her bedroom window before coming downstairs.

CHAPTER NINE

IF SHE HAD HOPED that on the train she would be able to catch up on her sleep she was mistaken, because as the miles rolled by under the swiftly moving wheels she found herself getting more and more tense, and going over the same little scene in her mind. Perhaps it would have been wise to sit down and think calmly and even read the article in the medical journal. She racked her brain to try and recall any information she might have heard about a Dr. Carver. She had seen a brief glimpse of Robert's smiling face in the photograph at the top of the article which Peter had tried to get her to read and the headline "Health Researcher's World Tour Cancelled." Subconsciously she must have read the few words, and now they popped into the forefront of her mind.

But that surely couldn't be Robert. Or could it? There was no answer to the thoughts milling around in her brain, and when she finally arrived in London she felt anything but equal to the interview which faced her.

Joan met the train in and they had quickly grabbed a taxi. There was just time for Rosabel to have a good wash and to do her face in Joan's flat before walking round the corner to the big teaching hospital where her interview was to be held.

When she was ushered into the outer office it was to find that four or five other girls were sitting waiting and looking as nervous as she felt herself.

They had been sitting for some ten minutes when Rosabel received her first surprise. The door leading into the inner office opened and to her astonishment

Robert came out, saying over his shoulder, "I'll see you for dinner, then, when I get back," and a female voice from within replying, "I shall look forward to it," before the door closed.

He advanced across the room, glanced briefly at the waiting applicants, but if he noticed her he gave no sign.

Rosabel felt glued to her seat. How on earth had he managed to get down to London ahead of her, and what was he doing seeing Matron? From the fragment of conversation she had just overheard, he knew her well.

Her second unwelcome surprise of the day came when she was interviewed by the occupant of the inner office. Matron sat erectly, a tiny figure in the large desk chair, her calm eyes fixed intently upon Rosabel. It was a critical gaze no doubt produced by years of experience in summing up applicants at a glance.

The jolt came at the end of the interview when the soft voice said, "Well, Miss Fairbairn, your qualifications are very good, but somehow I don't think that you'd find you were suited to this particular kind of nursing."

In her bewilderment, Rosabel hardly heard the rest of the explanations for her failure to get a place on the course. It had never crossed her mind that she wouldn't pass. Sure of her nursing abilities, she had supposed her acceptance to be more or less automatic, and it hadn't occurred to her that she might be turned down.

As she got up and walked out of the office and back to Joan's flat she still couldn't quite believe it, and Joan, when she was told the outcome of the interview, looked quite flabbergasted.

"Well, of course I have heard of people not being accepted before," she said, "but never people with your record, Roz. I just can't understand it."

There was little time, however, to discuss the matter further. If they were to be on time for their flight they had to hurry and get to Heathrow airport.

Sitting in the plane a couple of hours later, Rosabel received her third surprise of the day. People had been going up and down the aisle ever since they took off, but in her confusion and fatigue of mind she had hardly registered their comings and goings. This time something made her look up. Coming from a seat higher up was Robert, but if she expected a friendly greeting, she was again to be disappointed. As he passed her he merely nodded as he might have done to any passing acquaintance, and he had gone long before Rosabel could even nod in return.

Joan was telling her a long story about something that had happened in the ward the week previously, so it was only necessary to nod now and again to show she was paying attention. But her thoughts were gyrating wildly. What was Robert doing popping up here and there all day? He certainly must have sprouted wings to get down from Bannford to London in the first place, but to have managed to keep the dinner date she had overheard him making and still have caught this plane was nothing short of miraculous.

And in any case, why had he wanted to? Surely he hadn't willingly left behind that gorgeous girl who had turned up so unexpectedly? No man in his right mind would want to swop her had he first call on her affections, and in view of what Rosabel had seen there could be no doubt about that point.

Men! she thought as she closed her eyes wearily. She would never understand them.

By the time they touched down in Gibraltar, Rosabel had been asleep for some time. She only aroused herself unwillingly when Joan shook her by the arm and told her to fasten her seat belt. Looking out of the window Rosabel gulped with sheer fright. Not only did the plane come in over the sea to land, but it carried along the concrete runway to where yet again water gleamed in the lights from the airport. It was not until later that Rosabel realized that the airport's main runway ran across the narrow neck of land where the borders of

Gibraltar and Spain met, and that each end finished in the sea, the Atlantic on one side and the Mediterranean on the other.

As soon as they were through Customs, Joan was enveloped in the long arms of a tall, jolly-looking man in a Major's uniform. When he finally released his daughter, Jack Rivers shook Rosabel by the hand and quickly shepherded the two girls out to the car. Still half asleep, Rosabel gained only a fleeting impression of a comfortable, modern house, a smiling woman in a pretty dressing-gown, before she was thankfully shedding her clothes and slipping between cool sheets in the tastefully furnished guest room she was to share with Joan.

Before she fell asleep, Rosabel felt a weary curiosity as to Robert's whereabouts. She had reluctantly quelled the impulse to look over her shoulder as she had left the plane to try and catch another glimpse of him. As far as she knew he didn't know her address here, though he could, she supposed, have discovered it easily enough by asking Peter.

Joan's mother let the girls sleep late the following morning and it was nearly eleven o'clock when Rosabel opened her eyes to a sun-dappled room. She smiled as she glanced at the other bed. Joan was still blissfully asleep, and Rosabel turned on her back and hitched the pillows into a more comfortable position.

She didn't know whether the Army were responsible or if the Rivers themselves had chosen the tasteful light golden furniture, but the effect was a delight to the eye. Long curtains in a heavy, woven linen in shades of flame, cream and lemon hung at the window. The walls were painted in cream, the carpet was yellow and the bedspreads were composed of crochet squares, intricate in design, spelling out hours of work by some loving fingers.

Rosabel was just thinking how much she would love a cool drink when there came a knock on the door. It opened as Joan's mother wheeled in a trolley.

"Good morning, my dear. I hope you slept well? No need to ask if Joan did. Look at her!" And Rosabel laughed as her friend opened her eyes then yawned unashamedly.

"Breakfast! How super! All my favourite things too. Look, Roz—orange juice—*with* ice. Lots of coffee, and croissants. Have you got black cherry jam for me too, Mum?" and without waiting for an answer she reached towards the trolley which had been pushed between the twin beds and lifted the top off the jam jar.

"Goody! Now I know I'm really home," and as Mrs. Rivers walked towards the door Joan raised her glass of orange juice and toasted her mother. "To you, Mum. You're the greatest!"

As soon as they had eaten, the two girls got up, showered and dressed, made their beds and pushing the trolley between them, went to find Joan's mother. Rosabel discovered that the house was built on a split-level plan. The bedrooms were all at road level, but to get to the living quarters of the house, they had to negotiate five wide steps. This floor contained the kitchen, dining-room and a huge living-room. Again several steps lower, a huge covered patio hung over the cliff below.

Rosabel gave a gasp as Joan led her to the balustrade. Below and to the right she could glimpse the harbour. Below and immediately in front the ground sloped down to a sparkling sea. Two small sailing boats and a larger vessel which Rosabel guessed to be in the minesweeper class were passing, making towards the harbour. The larger vessel gave a derisive toot on his siren as he easily overtook the yachts.

"Admiring our view, are you, Rosabel?" a voice said immediately behind her, and Rosabel turned to see that Joan's father had come out on to the balcony. At her nod, he began to point out landmarks of interest—the Spanish town of Algeciras across the bay and the outline of the coast of North Africa.

"When it's clearer you can see Tangier. You might

like to trip over there before you go back. I'll try and arrange it. But that's not why I dropped in. I wanted to warn you two that there's a dance up at the hospital tonight. We're all invited. And I'm going into town now and I wondered if you two would like a lift."

"Of course they'll come in with you," Joan's mother said as she joined them. "What girls don't want to look at shops? They can stop in for lunch too if they want to save rushing back. I shan't cook a proper meal until this evening anyway, so it will only be a salad if you do come home, Joan."

"In that case, Mummy, Roz and I will take our time. I might even get my hair done. I didn't have time before I came away. Too busy in the ward."

Rosabel was fascinated by the town. It seemed so strange to see Arab women, heavily garbed in thick materials and wearing the face veil, jostle dark Latin-type women and, alongside them, fresh-complexioned boys in British Army uniform, to see one shop filled with carpets, plush wall hangings and brassware and the very next stocked with British products in well-known tins and packets.

Two things struck the enchanted Rosabel. The first was the number of babies and toddlers shopping with their mothers, and the second, the gentle courtesy of these people.

In the narrow street there was no hurrying. Taxis idled and actually stopped to let mothers with prams and youngsters clinging to their skirts cross in safety, and in the shops the assistants seemed genuinely anxious to send them out thoroughly satisfied with their purchases. There was none of the thinly veiled incivility which one often encountered at home, nor any impatience if they lingered over their choice.

Leaving Joan at a beauty salon to have her hair washed and set, Rosabel made her way to the cable car which would take her up to see the famous apes. She was glad she did not suffer from vertigo as the fragile-looking red car climbed the grey rock to the level where the Barbary apes wandered the hillside.

Rosabel was just in time to see one of her fellow travellers lose her sunglasses as a particularly mischievous ape snatched them from her hand. Though several bystanders made a concerted effort to cut him off, the monkey was much too artful to be caught, and as the general laugh rang out, Rosabel saw the warning notices and guessed that this wasn't the first time he had played this little trick.

Tucking her own sunglasses safely into her handbag, she walked up to see where the baby monkeys were housed. They were indeed worth a visit, and after some fifteen minutes of watching their amusing antics, Rosabel wandered back along the road to await the next cable car. Joan would be ready to leave the hairdressers' by the time she got back.

After a quick lunch the two girls finished their shopping, wrote and mailed their picture postcards and then took a taxi back to the house. They found Mrs. Rivers drinking tea with a very handsome young man in khaki uniform, who got to his feet and whistled appreciatively when Joan and Rosabel came into view.

Joan's mother smiled wickedly. "Good news travels fast here! This is Lieutenant Anthony Smith. My daughter Joan and a friend, Rosabel Fairbairn. Tony has come to see if he can escort you to the dance tonight," she added as the two girls shook hands and sat down in the chairs Tony Smith hastily pulled round for them.

"I was wondering how long it would be before word got around," Mrs. Rivers added. "I quite thought Harry Ward would be here too." Tony Smith looked a trifle embarrassed, but before he could reply a ring was heard at the front door.

He got to his feet. "I expect that's him now," he stammered. A tall frowning figure was ushered in who glared angrily in his direction as he subsided once more into his chair.

"Hello, Harry, I was expecting you." Mrs. Rivers' smile was more than impish. "I expect you've come to ask if Joan will go to the dance with you."

Harry Ward hesitated for a moment. He was obviously torn between surprise at Mrs. Rivers' remark and anger at his friend.

"I suppose Tony invented some excuse to get you to the other end of the Rock this afternoon," Mrs. Rivers went on before he could reply.

The two young men could control themselves no longer. With a mock angry, "I'll deal with you back in barracks!" Harry Ward cuffed the side of his friend's head before greeting Joan and being introduced to Rosabel.

"I hope I'm not too late to ask you to the dance tonight," he said, as Joan handed him a cup of tea. "Tony may have got his bid in first, though."

"I don't think Daddy has made other arrangements. If he hasn't why don't the four of us go together? We'd like that, wouldn't we, Roz?"

Rosabel nodded her agreement. The two boys seemed very nice. They were obviously a great deal younger than their sophisticated manner was meant to reveal and should be pleasant, uncomplicated partners for the dance. She had quite enough to think about without getting entangled with an admirer here, and one moreover connected with her host and hostess. She wanted a holiday which would be free from problems and which would give her a breathing space to think about what she was going to do on her return to Scotland.

When she saw Joan's long summer evening dress in fine white floating lawn, printed with a trailing leaf design in deep blue and soft jade green, Rosabel was glad she had packed her long black and white dress. It had stood the journey well, but she played safe and borrowed an iron, gave the big white collar a press and ran the iron over the wide skirt.

They all looked very distinguished, Rosabel thought, when the family were assembled ready to leave. Joan's father was wearing dress uniform and her mother a gown in smoky grey-blue chiffon relieved by a trailing sash in cerise. Her handbag, Rosabel noticed, exactly matched the brightly coloured sash, and with her gentle air of refinement she looked every inch the "Colonel's lady" of the poem.

What a difference the right clothes made, Rosabel thought as they went out to the car, comparing the present elegance of her hostess with the motherly figure in cotton morning dress and apron who had brought their breakfast that very morning.

As they joined the receiving line, Rosabel caught a glimpse of Tony and Harry awaiting them anxiously. As soon as they reached the entrance to the ballroom both she and Joan were whisked on to the floor by their impatient swain. Rosabel, looking up, discovered that she had been annexed by Tony Smith. He was a nice young man, she decided, reminding her of the medical students of her training days. He seemed very juvenile after Robert. No problem here. She could give him the gentle brush-off any time she liked.

They had finished the dance and Tony had escorted her over to the big table where Joan's mother and father were talking to a number of friends when Rosabel suddenly stiffened. Standing on the other side of the table, talking to a tall man wearing the insignia of a medical officer, was Robert. Rosabel hastily looked away, but in the general confusion of finding seats she found herself beside him. As Robert's hand came out to hold her chair good manners obliged her to look up and say "thank you."

That was her undoing. Try as she would, Rosabel could not control the expression which flooded into her eyes, and though she hastily looked away she knew Robert had seen and interpreted it.

She felt sick with shame, but determined that at least no one else should discover her hopeless infatuation for this man. She half turned a shoulder and began to talk animatedly to Tony sitting at her other side, but when the orchestra again struck up one of the latest tunes, to her amazement somehow or other she found herself taking the floor with Robert.

Even in her indignation at being manipulated so deftly into doing something against her will she had to admire the dexterity with which he had got his way. Her mouth was still half open in protest as she felt herself being led into the swinging rhythm.

She forced herself to look away over his shoulder as they danced, maintaining a silence which oozed unspoken indignation. But if she thought this attitude was going to disconcert her partner she was soon to discover her mistake.

They danced in complete silence for about three minutes and then Robert chuckled. Involuntarily Rosabel's eyes flashed to his face. It was so surprisingly dear and familiar that she felt herself softening and had to steel her thoughts against him.

Here the two mocking devils deep within his eyes came to her aid. Had he shown a second's tenderness she knew she would have been lost, but he was quite obviously in anything but the attitude of a repentant lover.

"Ah, Miss Fairbairn, now I have your full attention. May I say how beautiful and exciting you're looking tonight. Good enough to eat, I'd say. You're going to have that poor, inoffensive young man hardly knowing whether he's coming or going by the end of the evening if you continue to give him as much of your undivided attention as you've done so far. He looks quite besotted already, so you can hold your fire and cast a few favours in other directions without fear of losing his attention."

Rosabel clenched her teeth. She had known Robert in many different moods, but never malicious like this. Had he come nearly two thousand miles just to quarrel? She lifted her chin and looked defiantly into his mocking eyes.

"If you're going to be unpleasant, I don't believe I

want to dance any more," and she attempted to withdraw her fingers from his and side-step on to the edge of the dance-floor.

Her efforts were instantly frustrated. The light clasp on her hand tightened and his right arm held her unyieldingly against him.

He laughed aloud. "Oh no, dear girl! I've not come all this way to have you refuse to speak to me, or to cause a scene either, for that matter," he continued, a grimmer note in his voice. "You're going to continue to accept me into the party with apparent approval and treat me with as much interest as you do the other eligible men in the party. More, in fact."

Rosabel asked dryly, "You did say 'eligible men?'"

"Touché," Rob replied, a note of real amusement breaking into his former grim tone. "Now relax and let what will be will be. You look as if someone has just told you you're down on the next theatre list."

Rosabel burst out laughing. She couldn't stay at daggers drawn with Robert for long. Whatever his failings she had very little pride where he was concerned, and she feared that in his usual clever way he had divined this. What was the use of using pride to fend off a man who knew without being told that you were quite literally crazy about him?

Rather to her surprise Robert behaved from then on with the greatest circumspection. True, he manoeuvred several more dances, which made Tony Smith begin to look rather sulky as the evening drew to a close. But he made no effort to get her alone, and long before the supper dance he had got on very good terms with Joan's parents.

When they were undressing later that night, Joan looked curiously across at her friend. "I didn't know you were acquainted with our famous Dr. Carver," she remarked as she eased herself out of her dress and hung it in the built-in wardrobe.

Rosabel, already in nightie and dressing-gown, was creaming her face. "Famous? I didn't know he was famous,'' she remarked, completely ignoring the rest of Joan's question.

"Well, of course he is. You must have read of him being appointed to the head of the World Research Expedition even if you missed all the furore when he was taken ill so mysteriously.''

Rosabel sat completely still, a face tissue suspended in her hand. "Ill?''

"So you don't know him that well after all? They'd only been gone a few weeks when Dr. Carver picked up some peculiarly rare bug in the East Indies. They shipped him home and for ages he was at death's door with our old Professor, Sir William Kellar-Littler, nearly doing his nut. When he did get him on his feet it was only to find he was subject to blackouts, severe headaches and temporary amnesia. They tried all kinds of treatments, I believe, and then he suddenly disappeared from the hospital. I heard from one of the girls who was specialling him that he more or less discharged himself and that he and the Prof had a row in which he washed his hands of him. Of course it was just a rumour. I've heard since that the Prof sent him off on holiday on condition he continued with the drugs he'd been having and that he reported every so often and let Sir William know how he was doing. But how do you come to know him, Roz?''

"He's a friend of Peter's.'' Rosabel told herself she was telling the strict truth.

As she climbed into bed Joan's eyes twinkled. "Oh, I see,'' she remarked lightly. "That's why he's turned up in Gibraltar, is it?'' and she turned off the bedside light.

"Honestly, Joan....''

Joan laughed in the darkness. "All right, sweetie, I didn't mean to tease or pry. Good night now,'' and Rosabel smiled to herself as she snuggled down. Trust Joan to come up trumps! She would wait patiently to be told the whole story in Rosabel's good time.

Rosabel wasn't too surprised when there was a ring

at the bell the following morning. She and Joan had joined Mrs. Rivers on the balcony for a late breakfast, and as Robert came out to greet them she knew this was just what she had expected.

She watched him curiously, trying to see him with an unbiased eye, as he talked to Mrs. Rivers and Joan. It was quite obvious that they liked him already despite the briefness of their acquaintance—and when he asked if he might take Rosabel out to lunch, they took it for granted that Rosabel was willing to go.

There was silence for a few moments after they had got into the hired car and Robert had set it in motion. "Where are we going?" Rosabel asked in a small voice.

Somehow Robert's profile was not very reassuring. "Round to the eastern side. I've rooms in a hotel there."

The drive took place in almost complete silence. Apart from a chance remark on the wonderful water catchments, the purported length of the tunnels inside the Rock itself and the general charm of the place, he said little. When he had driven through a small village, now athrong with holiday-makers, and parked the car in front of the hotel, he steered her through the foyer, down a corridor at right angles to the main entrance and then down a flight of stairs into what was obviously a new wing.

He turned into a corridor and opened a door about halfway along. The small entrance led into a sunny sitting-room with French doors leading on to a balcony hanging over the water. To her right Rosabel caught a glimpse of a bedroom and bathroom before Robert gently pushed her forward and she walked out through the sitting-room and on to the balcony itself, furnished with a table and two comfortable, well-upholstered chairs.

But Rosabel's glance at the sparkling greeny-blue waters, the magnificent sea-view was fleeting. She turned to face Robert feeling somehow it was she who was on the defensive.

Before she could utter a word he advanced purposefully towards her saying, "Before we settle our differences there's something I want to do," and he took her firmly in his arms and kissed her lips.

But Rosabel's head was so full of questions that she was unable to give the romantic moment her full attention. Instead of melting against his manly bosom as any proper heroine of fiction would have done she raised her head and demanded, "Who told you you could kiss me? Certainly not that girl who arrived in Bannford so inopportunely."

Robert's eyes danced. "No, as a matter of fact it was Professor Sir William Keller-Littler who gave me permission to kiss you now I'm pronounced A.1, and do you mean to tell me, my jealous little love, that you didn't recognize the world-famous model Gwennie Carver?"

Rosabel's figure, still encircled by his arms, remained completely immobile for one astounded moment as she took in this piece of information. She raised questioning eyes to his amused face. "Your sister?"

"None other. She'd just returned from six months in the States and of course, hearing that I'd been on the sick list, she couldn't wait to see her loving brother. An impulsive sort of girl, my sister, but then I'm used to impulsive girls," and the mocking devils in his eyes laughed at her once again. "Now can you keep quiet for one minute while I take the Prof's prescription properly and complete my cure," and his mouth met hers for the second time.

He could certainly find no fault on this occasion with Rosabel's concentration. Little did he know that now she was giving the moment her full attention it was even more heart-stopping than his first kiss. She felt as she had known she would feel one day with some man—warm, protected, completely right, and with her quickened heartbeats sounding like a drum.

As he released her Rosabel felt for a chair and sat

down quickly before her rubbery knees buckled under her. "No one would ever guess you'd been ill. And that reminds me—why all the secrecy? Why didn't you tell me the real trouble instead of letting me make a fool of myself imagining you were an alcoholic?"

Robert sat down on the other chair and reached for her hands. Holding them in a comforting clasp, he replied ruefully, "I'm sorry about that, my sweet. But it was so funny the way you immediately jumped to the conclusion that because I had dizzy spells and you saw me once or twice in the Fisherman's Arms with a glass of ginger ale in my hand, I must be a dipsomaniac. I'm afraid my perverted sense of humour came to the surface and I neglected to put you right."

"But your driving licence?" Rosabel asked him.

"Well, of course they had to suspend it. Not because of drunken driving, as you so promptly surmised, but because when I arrived in Bannford and for several months previously I'd been having blackouts. They couldn't risk me having one at the wheel of a car, so my licence was temporarily withdrawn. They weren't to know that I was going to be loved and coerced into good health again so soon by the sweetest girl in Scotland," and he lifted first one hand and then the other and kissed her fingers.

Rosabel sat looking down at the rough brown hair. "Nonsense," she replied softly. "Whatever your Prof was giving you must have already begun to take effect."

Robert sat back, releasing her. "Well, all I know is I'd been taking the same drugs for some time without any visible improvement. It seems too much of a coincidence that they should suddenly have started to act just when I met you. No, I believe you cured me, just as I cured you of your feeling of guilty responsibility for that Johnston chap. You'd have married him and been miserable ever after if I hadn't happened along."

Rosabel laughed shakily. "Both saved from a fate worse than death, then, in your opinion?"

Robert leaned back and surveyed her with satisfaction. "You might say so. In fact when you've apologized for running away so impulsively and unnecessarily without giving me a chance to explain we might have a drink to celebrate our engagement, don't you think?"

Rosabel gasped. "You haven't asked me yet," she managed to stammer out indignantly.

Robert got to his feet and pulled her out of her chair. "My dear girl, I've been doing nothing else one way and another for weeks. If you're expecting me to go down on one knee, think again. I'm not the sort. But I do love you dearly, and from the expression in your eyes last night, I think the feeling is reciprocated. So shall we skip all the verbal sparring and get down to brass tacks? Such as what sort of a ring you'd like, and whether a Christmas wedding would appeal? I know a rather jolly little inn way up in the Austrian Alps which would make an ideal honeymoon hotel. How about it?"

Rosabel looked up. What did it matter if he had misled her deliberately and her pride was a little bruised? She couldn't imagine going on with her life without him.

She stood on tiptoe, slid two loving arms round his neck and laid her cheek against his.

"Yes, please," she replied in a very small voice, and hugged him close.

THE AUTHOR

Ruth Clemence, after a distinguished service in the Royal Air Force and a succession of unsuitable jobs, met the man she would marry when she lived on the Isle of Man. Her writing career developed after he whisked her back to England, and when arthritis made her inactive, she says her romance writing saved her sanity.